The Editor

STEPHEN ARATA is Mayo Distinguished Teaching Professor and Associate Professor of English at the University of Virginia. His books include *Fictions of Loss in the Victorian Fin de Siècle* and editions of William Morris's *News from Nowhere* and George Gissing's *New Grub Street*.

W. W. NORTON & COMPANY, INC.
Also Publishes

THE NORTON ANTHOLOGY OF AFRICAN AMERICAN LITERATURE
edited by Henry Louis Gates Jr. and Nellie Y. McKay et al.

THE NORTON ANTHOLOGY OF AMERICAN LITERATURE
edited by Nina Baym et al.

THE NORTON ANTHOLOGY OF CHILDREN'S LITERATURE
edited by Jack Zipes et al.

THE NORTON ANTHOLOGY OF CONTEMPORARY FICTION
edited by R. V. Cassill and Joyce Carol Oates

THE NORTON ANTHOLOGY OF ENGLISH LITERATURE
edited by M. H. Abrams and Stephen Greenblatt et al.

THE NORTON ANTHOLOGY OF LITERATURE BY WOMEN
edited by Sandra M. Gilbert and Susan Gubar

THE NORTON ANTHOLOGY OF MODERN AND CONTEMPORARY POETRY
edited by Jahan Ramazani, Richard Ellmann, and Robert O'Clair

THE NORTON ANTHOLOGY OF POETRY
edited by Margaret Ferguson, Mary Jo Salter, and Jon Stallworthy

THE NORTON ANTHOLOGY OF SHORT FICTION
edited by R. V. Cassill and Richard Bausch

THE NORTON ANTHOLOGY OF THEORY AND CRITICISM
edited by Vincent B. Leitch et al.

THE NORTON ANTHOLOGY OF WORLD LITERATURE
edited by Sarah Lawall et al.

THE NORTON FACSIMILE OF THE FIRST FOLIO OF SHAKESPEARE
prepared by Charlton Hinman

THE NORTON INTRODUCTION TO LITERATURE
edited by Alison Booth, J. Paul Hunter, and Kelly J. Mays

THE NORTON INTRODUCTION TO THE SHORT NOVEL
edited by Jerome Beaty

THE NORTON READER
edited by Linda H. Peterson and John C. Brereton

THE NORTON SAMPLER
edited by Thomas Cooley

THE NORTON SHAKESPEARE, BASED ON THE OXFORD EDITION
edited by Stephen Greenblatt et al.

For a complete list of Norton Critical Editions, visit
www.wwnorton.com/college/English/nce_home.htm

A NORTON CRITICAL EDITION

H. G. Wells
THE TIME MACHINE
AN INVENTION

AUTHORITATIVE TEXT
BACKGROUNDS AND CONTEXTS
CRITICISM

Edited by

STEPHEN ARATA

UNIVERSITY OF VIRGINIA

W. W. NORTON & COMPANY
New York • London

W. W. Norton & Company has been independent since its founding in 1923, when William Warder Norton and Mary D. Herter Norton first published lectures delivered at the People's Institute, the adult education division of New York City's Cooper Union. The Nortons soon expanded their program beyond the Institute, publishing books by celebrated academics from America and abroad. By mid-century, the two major pillars of Norton's publishing program—trade books and college texts—were firmly established. In the 1950s, the Norton family transferred control of the company to its employees, and today—with a staff of four hundred and a comparable number of trade, college, and professional titles published each year—W. W. Norton & Company stands as the largest and oldest publishing house owned wholly by its employees.

The text of this book is composed in Fairfield Medium with the display set in Bernhard Modern.
Book design by Antonina Krass.
Composition by TexTech, Inc.
Manufacturing by Maple-Vail Book Manufacturing Group.
Production manager: Eric Pier-Hocking.

Library of Congress Cataloging-in-Publication Data

Wells, H. G. (Herbert George), 1866-1946.
The time machine : an invention authoritative text backgrounds and contexts criticism / H. G. Wells ; edited by Stephen Arata.—1st ed.
p.   cm.
Includes bibliographical references.

ISBN 978-0-393-92794-8 (pbk.)

1. Time travel—Fiction.   2. Wells, H. G. (Herbert George), 1866–1946.
Time machine.   I. Arata, Stephen.   II. Title.
PR5774.T5 2009
823'.912—dc22   2008034563

W. W. Norton & Company, Inc., 500 Fifth Avenue,
New York, N.Y. 10110-0017
wwnorton.com

W. W. Norton & Company Ltd.
15 Carlisle Street, London W1D 3BS

7 8 9 0

Contents

Criticism   177

Preface

The Time Machine: An Invention was H. G. Wells's first published novel, and it remains among his best-known and most influential works. Writing to a friend shortly before the story began its serial run in the *New Review*, Wells predicted that its fate would determine his professional future. "If it does not come off very much," he wrote, "I shall know my place for the rest of my career." In the event, *The Time Machine* came off more than well enough to secure him a prominent place in the London literary scene of the 1890s. In turn it inaugurated the series of popular and in some ways prescient "scientific romances"—*The Island of Dr. Moreau*, *The Invisible Man*, *The War of the Worlds*, and *When the Sleeper Wakes* all appeared between 1896 and 1899—that launched Wells into one of the twentieth century's most successful literary careers.

Wells was famously prolific as a writer and—especially as his output increased after the turn of the century—notoriously casual about the craft of writing. He took great pains with *The Time Machine*, however. The idea for a story concerned with time travel occupied Wells as early as 1888, while he was still a student at the Normal School of Science in Kensington, London. From then to the publication of *The Time Machine* by William Heinemann in 1895, he produced at least six distinct versions of his time-travel story. No fewer than four of these made their way into print.[1] In addition, Wells left copious unpublished materials in the form of manuscript drafts and corrected and annotated typescripts that help illuminate key stages in the long process of composition.

This Norton Critical Edition of *The Time Machine* includes in their entirety the two earliest printed incarnations of the tale: *The Chronic Argonauts* (1888) and the seven installments of an untitled (and, like *The Chronic Argonauts*, unfinished) time-travel narrative Wells contributed to the *National Observer* (1894). Also included are ample excerpts from the serial version of *The Time Machine* published in the *New Review* (1895), as well as selections from

---

1. See "A Note on the Text" (pp. ix–x) for an account of the novel's composition and publication history.

Wells's manuscripts of passages that do not appear in any printed version of the story. For interested readers, this wealth of documents provides a rare glimpse into the apprenticeship of a major author. More important, it allows us to measure with greater precision Wells's achievement in the final Heinemann version of the novel. With each revision, he saw more clearly how the conceit of time travel could be used to give vivid dramatic life to some of his culture's most significant fantasies and fears. The novel's continued hold on readers more than a century later suggests that those fantasies and fears—about, most notably, the possibilities for human progress in a world governed by biological evolution and increasingly shaped by scientific and technical innovation—have not entirely lost either their imaginative purchase or their ethical urgency.

While he worked on *The Time Machine* in the first half of the 1890s, Wells also pursued some of the novel's major themes in his journalistic writings. Like many other enterprising authors of his generation, Wells took full advantage of the late-Victorian boom in periodical publication to establish his credentials as a writer and to practice his craft. By the time his first novel was published, Wells was already the author of dozens of periodical pieces, many of which draw fruitfully on his scientific training. This Norton Critical Edition includes generous extracts from a range of Wells's scientific journalism, focusing on topics—evolution, degeneration, species extinction, the concept of time on a geologic scale, and the laws of biology as they apply to human history—that are central to *The Time Machine*. In these essays as in his scientific romances of the 1890s, Wells addressed a reading public that over several decades had become increasingly sensitive to, and savvy about, the possible practical consequences of advances in scientific knowledge. For this Norton Critical Edition I have assembled a handful of extracts from widely known texts by Victorian scientists and social critics which attempt, in tones ranging from triumph to studied neutrality to profound unease, to reconcile the findings of science with traditional ethical, religious, and political beliefs. Wells was familiar with all these texts, and in *The Time Machine* he engages in a complex dialog with each of them.

Finally, this edition gathers a selection of vibrant critical responses to Wells's novel, from contemporary reviews through important midcentury valuations to more recent work informed by the insights of historicist, psychoanalytic, and poststructuralist criticism. My goal in assembling this selection is to give a sense of the exciting range and depth of the critical responses that Wells's novel continues to provoke.

A Note on the Text

This Norton Critical Edition reprints the first London edition of *The Time Machine*, published by William Heinemann in May 1895. The novel was generally well received by readers and reviewers alike, and it helped establish Wells's reputation as an important literary figure in late-Victorian London.

The Heinemann edition was the end product of an unusually long gestation period stretching back to Wells's student days at the Normal School of Science. Intermittently over nearly a decade, Wells worked on versions of a story centered on time travel. The prehistory of *The Time Machine* includes tales published in three separate periodicals, each tale differing from—though clearly related to—the others. All three provided materials that eventually made their way into the Heinemann edition. This Norton Critical Edition includes substantial portions of these early efforts, allowing readers to trace the stages of the novel's development.

Wells's first attempt at a time-travel story was titled *The Chronic Argonauts*. It appeared in three installments (April–June 1888) in the *Science Schools Journal*, the periodical started by Wells and published by the Normal School of Science. In his 1934 *Experiment in Autobiography*, Wells dismisses *The Chronic Argonauts* as a "romance" begun "very much under the influence of Hawthorne" which primarily demonstrated that as a writer he "still had [his] business to learn." Wells left the story incomplete, breaking it off abruptly at the close of the third installment.

Between 1889 and 1892, Wells produced but did not publish at least two full revisions of the tale, the manuscripts of which have not survived. Then, in 1894, he was invited by its editor W. E. Henley to contribute material to the *National Observer*. Wells responded to the invitation by returning to "that old corpse of the Chronic Argo" (as he put it in a letter to a friend) and reviving it again, this time ostensibly as a series of free-standing articles on the topic of time travel. The seven unsigned pieces that eventually appeared in the *National Observer* between March and June 1894 are essayistic for long stretches, but they are also linked together by a narrative that in its general features anticipates the final *Time Machine*.

Once again Wells's story breaks off before its conclusion, this time presumably as a result of Henley's abrupt departure from the *National Observer*. Quickly resurfacing as the editor of the *New Review* (published by Heinemann), Henley invited Wells to revise and expand his time-travel pieces for the new publication. Wells agreed, and the story, at last completed and for the first time titled *The Time Machine*, appeared as a monthly serial between January and June 1895. Wells made further revisions for the first book edition. Most notably, he reworked the opening chapter and excised a portion of "The Further Vision" chapter. (The *New Review* versions of both sections are included in the current volume on pp. 120–27.)

Nearly thirty years after its initial book publication, Wells again undertook to revise his novel. The occasion this time was the publication in 1924 of the twenty-eight-volume Atlantic Edition of *The Works of H. G. Wells*, the first volume of which opens with *The Time Machine*. For this edition, Wells produced what he calls a "revised definitive version" of the novel, based in part on changes he had jotted down as early as 1898. The only significant alteration Wells made, however, was to reduce the number of chapters from sixteen to twelve. He also dispensed with the chapter titles and in a handful of places made minor changes in wording. The Atlantic Edition provided the copy text for subsequent editions and collections published during Wells's lifetime, though he continued to tinker with *The Time Machine* through the four more incarnations of the novel that appeared between 1927 and 1933.

Standing somewhat apart from the lineage described above is an edition published in New York by Henry Holt in 1895. While the 1895 Heinemann *Time Machine* is conventionally called the first edition, it actually appeared three weeks after the Holt. The extent of Wells's participation in preparing this edition—assuming he had any at all—remains unclear. The Holt text combines passages from the *National Observer, New Review*, and Heinemann versions of the story in ways that have led some scholars to speculate that it is based on an unrevised manuscript of Wells's. How it came into Holt's possession has never been established. The Holt edition itself has never been reprinted or used as the copy text for other editions of the novel.

In addition to generous selections from the pre-Heinemann versions of Wells's tale, this Norton Critical Edition includes two extended passages from Wells's manuscripts that do not appear in any of the published texts.

The Text of
THE TIME MACHINE
AN INVENTION

NOTE.—The substance of the first chapter of this story and of several paragraphs from the context appeared in the 'National Observer' in 1894. The "Time Traveller's Story" appeared, almost as it stands here, in the pages of the "New Review." The Author desires to make the customary acknowledgments [*Wells's note*].

To

WILLIAM ERNEST HENLEY[1]

---

1. As editor of the *National Observer*, Henley ran seven installments of Wells's tale between March and June 1894. When Henley became editor of the *New Review* in late 1894, he commissioned a revised version of the story, which ran from January to June 1895. Wells made further revisions for the first book edition, published in May 1895 by William Heinemann.

I. Introduction

The Time Traveller (for so it will be convenient to speak of him) was expounding a recondite matter to us. His grey eyes shone and twinkled, and his usually pale face was flushed and animated. The fire burnt brightly, and the soft radiance of the incandescent lights in the lilies of silver caught the bubbles that flashed and passed in our glasses.[1] Our chairs, being his patents, embraced and caressed us rather than submitted to be sat upon, and there was that luxurious after-dinner atmosphere, when thought runs gracefully free of the trammels of precision. And he put it to us in this way—marking the points with a lean forefinger—as we sat and lazily admired his earnestness over this new paradox (as we thought it) and his fecundity.

'You must follow me carefully. I shall have to controvert one or two ideas that are almost universally accepted. The geometry, for instance, they taught you at school is founded on a misconception.'

'Is not that rather a large thing to expect us to begin upon?' said Filby, an argumentative person with red hair.

'I do not mean to ask you to accept anything without reasonable ground for it. You will soon admit as much as I need from you. You know of course that a mathematical line, a line of thickness *nil*, has no real existence. They taught you that? Neither has a mathematical plane. These things are mere abstractions.'

'That is all right,' said the Psychologist.

'Nor, having only length, breadth, and thickness, can a cube have a real existence.'

'There I object,' said Filby. 'Of course a solid body may exist. All real things—'

'So most people think. But wait a moment. Can an *instantaneous* cube exist?'

'Don't follow you,' said Filby.

'Can a cube that does not last for any time at all, have a real existence?'

Filby became pensive. 'Clearly,' the Time Traveller proceeded, 'any real body must have extension in *four* directions: it must have Length, Breadth, Thickness, and—Duration. But through a natural infirmity of the flesh, which I will explain to you in a moment, we incline to overlook this fact. There are really four dimensions, three which we call the three planes of Space, and a fourth, Time. There is, however, a tendency to draw an unreal distinction between the former

---

1. "Lilies of silver" could refer either to silver fittings shaped like lilies attached to the electric light fixtures or to a lily pattern engraved on the Time Traveller's silverware. In either case the reflected light sparkles in the bubbles of his guests' after-dinner drinks.

three dimensions and the latter, because it happens that our consciousness moves intermittently in one direction along the latter from the beginning to the end of our lives.'

'That,' said a very young man, making spasmodic efforts to relight his cigar over the lamp; 'that . . . very clear indeed.'

'Now, it is very remarkable that this is so extensively overlooked,' continued the Time Traveller, with a slight accession of cheerfulness. 'Really this is what is meant by the Fourth Dimension, though some people who talk about the Fourth Dimension do not know they mean it. It is only another way of looking at Time. *There is no difference between Time and any of the three dimensions of Space except that our consciousness moves along it.* But some foolish people have got hold of the wrong side of that idea. You have all heard what they have to say about this Fourth Dimension?'

'*I* have not,' said the Provincial Mayor.

'It is simply this. That Space, as our mathematicians have it, is spoken of as having three dimensions, which one may call Length, Breadth, and Thickness, and is always definable by reference to three planes, each at right angles to the others. But some philosophical people have been asking why *three* dimensions particularly—why not another direction at right angles to the other three?—and have even tried to construct a Four-Dimensional geometry. Professor Simon Newcomb was expounding this to the New York Mathematical Society only a month or so ago.[2] You know how on a flat surface, which has only two dimensions, we can represent a figure of a three-dimensional solid, and similarly they think that by models of three dimensions they could represent one of four—if they could master the perspective of the thing. See?'

'I think so,' murmured the Provincial Mayor; and, knitting his brows, he lapsed into an introspective state, his lips moving as one who repeats mystic words. 'Yes, I think I see it now,' he said after some time, brightening in a quite transitory manner.

'Well, I do not mind telling you I have been at work upon this geometry of Four Dimensions for some time. Some of my results are curious. For instance, here is a portrait of a man at eight years old, another at fifteen, another at seventeen, another at twenty-three, and so on. All these are evidently sections, as it were, Three-Dimensional representations of his Four-Dimensional being, which is a fixed and unalterable thing.

---

2. Simon Newcomb (1835–1909), professor of mathematics and astronomy at Johns Hopkins University, raised (and rejected) the possibility of constructing a four-dimensional geometry during an address delivered at the annual meeting of the New York Mathematical Society in December 1893.

'Scientific people,' proceeded the Time Traveller, after the pause required for the proper assimilation of this, 'know very well that Time is only a kind of Space. Here is a popular scientific diagram, a weather record. This line I trace with my finger shows the movement of the barometer. Yesterday it was so high, yesterday night it fell, then this morning it rose again, and so gently upward to here. Surely the mercury did not trace this line in any of the dimensions of Space generally recognized? But certainly it traced such a line, and that line, therefore, we must conclude was along the Time-Dimension.'

'But,' said the Medical Man, staring hard at a coal in the fire, 'if Time is really only a fourth dimension of Space, why is it, and why has it always been, regarded as something different? And why cannot we move about in Time as we move about in the other dimensions of Space?'

The Time Traveller smiled. 'Are you so sure we can move freely in Space? Right and left we can go, backward and forward freely enough, and men always have done so. I admit we move freely in two dimensions. But how about up and down? Gravitation limits us there.'

'Not exactly,' said the Medical Man. 'There are balloons.'

'But before the balloons, save for spasmodic jumping and the inequalities of the surface, man had no freedom of vertical movement.'

'Still they could move a little up and down,' said the Medical Man.

'Easier, far easier down than up.'

'And you cannot move at all in Time, you cannot get away from the present moment.'

'My dear sir, that is just where you are wrong. That is just where the whole world has gone wrong. We are always getting away from the present moment. Our mental existences, which are immaterial and have no dimensions, are passing along the Time-Dimension with a uniform velocity from the cradle to the grave. Just as we should travel *down* if we began our existence fifty miles above the earth's surface.'

'But the great difficulty is this,' interrupted the Psychologist. 'You *can* move about in all directions of Space, but you cannot move about in Time.'

'That is the germ of my great discovery. But you are wrong to say that we cannot move about in Time. For instance, if I am recalling an incident very vividly I go back to the instant of its occurrence: I become absent-minded, as you say. I jump back for a moment. Of course we have no means of staying back for any length of Time, any more than a savage or an animal has of staying six feet above the ground. But a civilized man is better off than the savage in this respect. He can go up against gravitation in a balloon, and why

should he not hope that ultimately he may be able to stop or accelerate his drift along the Time-Dimension, or even turn about and
travel the other way?'

'Oh, *this*,' began Filby, 'is all—'

'Why not?' said the Time Traveller.

'It's against reason,' said Filby.

'What reason?' said the Time Traveller.

'You can show black is white by argument,' said Filby, 'but you will
never convince me.'

'Possibly not,' said the Time Traveller. 'But now you begin to see the
object of my investigations into the geometry of the Four Dimensions.
Long ago I had a vague inkling of a machine—'

'To travel through Time!' exclaimed the Very Young Man.

'That shall travel indifferently in any direction of Space and Time,
as the driver determines.'

Filby contented himself with laughter.

'But I have experimental verification,' said the Time Traveller.

'It would be remarkably convenient for the historian,' the Psychologist suggested. 'One might travel back and verify the accepted
account of the Battle of Hastings, for instance!'[3]

'Don't you think you would attract attention?' said the Medical
Man. 'Our ancestors had no great tolerance for anachronisms.'

'One might get one's Greek from the very lips of Homer and
Plato,' the Very Young Man thought.

'In which case they would certainly plough you for the Little-go.
The German scholars have improved Greek so much.'[4]

'Then there is the future,' said the Very Young Man. 'Just think!
One might invest all one's money, leave it to accumulate at interest,
and hurry on ahead!'

'To discover a society,' said I, 'erected on a strictly communistic
basis.'[5]

'Of all the wild extravagant theories!' began the Psychologist.

'Yes, so it seemed to me, and so I never talked of it until—'

'Experimental verification!' cried I. 'You are going to verify *that*?'

'The experiment!' cried Filby, who was getting brain-weary.

'Let's see your experiment anyhow,' said the Psychologist, 'though
it's all humbug, you know.'

---

3. The defeat of the Saxons under King Harold by Norman forces under William the Conqueror at Hastings in 1066, which led to the conquest of England, is arguably the most
   famous battle in British history.
4. "To plough" was slang for "to fail." The first examination toward the B.A. degree at Cambridge University was colloquially called "the Little-go." The correct pronunciation of
   ancient Greek was a lively topic of debate throughout the nineteenth century. By the
   1890s German scholars had long led the field of classical studies; the implied joke here is
   that they would have corrected the pronunciation of Homer and Plato themselves.
5. That is, a society in which money would be useless.

The Time Traveller smiled round at us. Then, still smiling faintly, and with his hands deep in his trousers pockets, he walked slowly out of the room, and we heard his slippers shuffling down the long passage to his laboratory.

The Psychologist looked at us. 'I wonder what he's got?'

'Some sleight-of-hand trick or other,' said the Medical Man, and Filby tried to tell us about a conjuror he had seen at Burslem,[6] but before he had finished his preface the Time Traveller came back, and Filby's anecdote collapsed.

II. *The Machine*

The thing the Time Traveller held in his hand was a glittering metallic framework, scarcely larger than a small clock, and very delicately made. There was ivory in it, and some transparent crystalline substance. And now I must be explicit, for this that follows—unless his explanation is to be accepted—is an absolutely unaccountable thing. He took one of the small octagonal tables that were scattered about the room, and set it in front of the fire, with two legs on the hearthrug. On this table he placed the mechanism. Then he drew up a chair, and sat down. The only other object on the table was a small shaded lamp, the bright light of which fell full upon the model. There were also perhaps a dozen candles about, two in brass candlesticks upon the mantel and several in sconces, so that the room was brilliantly illuminated. I sat in a low arm-chair nearest the fire, and I drew this forward so as to be almost between the Time Traveller and the fireplace. Filby sat behind him, looking over his shoulder. The Medical Man and the Provincial Mayor watched him in profile from the right, the Psychologist from the left. The Very Young Man stood behind the Psychologist. We were all on the alert. It appears incredible to me that any kind of trick, however subtly conceived and however adroitly done, could have been played upon us under these conditions.

The Time Traveller looked at us, and then at the mechanism. 'Well?' said the Psychologist.

'This little affair,' said the Time Traveller, resting his elbows upon the table and pressing his hands together above the apparatus, 'is only a model. It is my plan for a machine to travel through time. You will notice that it looks singularly askew, and that there is an odd twinkling appearance about this bar, as though it was in some way unreal.' He pointed to the part with his finger. 'Also, here is one little white lever, and here is another.'

6. A town in Staffordshire, England.

The Medical Man got up out of his chair and peered into the thing. 'It's beautifully made,' he said.

'It took two years to make,' retorted the Time Traveller. Then, when we had all imitated the action of the Medical Man, he said: 'Now I want you clearly to understand that this lever, being pressed over, sends the machine gliding into the future, and this other reverses the motion. This saddle represents the seat of a time traveller. Presently I am going to press the lever, and off the machine will go. It will vanish, pass into future time, and disappear. Have a good look at the thing. Look at the table too, and satisfy yourselves there is no trickery. I don't want to waste this model, and then be told I'm a quack.'

There was a minute's pause perhaps. The Psychologist seemed about to speak to me, but changed his mind. Then the Time Traveller put forth his finger towards the lever. 'No,' he said suddenly. 'Lend me your hand.' And turning to the Psychologist, he took that individual's hand in his own and told him to put out his forefinger. So that it was the Psychologist himself who sent forth the model Time Machine on its interminable voyage. We all saw the lever turn. I am absolutely certain there was no trickery. There was a breath of wind, and the lamp flame jumped. One of the candles on the mantel was blown out, and the little machine suddenly swung round, became indistinct, was seen as a ghost for a second perhaps, as an eddy of faintly glittering brass and ivory; and it was gone—vanished! Save for the lamp the table was bare.

Every one was silent for a minute. Then Filby said he was damned.

The Psychologist recovered from his stupor, and suddenly looked under the table. At that the Time Traveller laughed cheerfully. 'Well?' he said, with a reminiscence of the Psychologist. Then, getting up, he went to the tobacco jar on the mantel, and with his back to us began to fill his pipe.

We stared at each other. 'Look here,' said the Medical Man, 'are you in earnest about this? Do you seriously believe that that machine has travelled into time?'

'Certainly,' said the Time Traveller, stooping to light a spill at the fire.[1] Then he turned, lighting his pipe, to look at the Psychologist's face. (The Psychologist, to show that he was not unhinged, helped himself to a cigar and tried to light it uncut.) 'What is more, I have a big machine nearly finished in there'—he indicated the laboratory— 'and when that is put together I mean to have a journey on my own account.'

'You mean to say that that machine has travelled into the future?' said Filby.

1. A strip of wood or twisted paper used to light a candle or a lamp or, as here, a pipe.

'Into the future or the past—I don't, for certain, know which.'

After an interval the Psychologist had an inspiration. 'It must have gone into the past if it has gone anywhere,' he said.

'Why?' said the Time Traveller.

'Because I presume that it has not moved in space, and if it travelled into the future it would still be here all this time, since it must have travelled through this time.'

'But,' said I, 'if it travelled into the past it would have been visible when we came first into this room; and last Thursday when we were here; and the Thursday before that; and so forth!'

'Serious objections,' remarked the Provincial Mayor, with an air of impartiality, turning towards the Time Traveller.

'Not a bit,' said the Time Traveller, and, to the Psychologist: 'You think. *You* can explain that. It's presentation below the threshold,[2] you know, diluted presentation.'

'Of course,' said the Psychologist, and reassured us. 'That's a simple point in psychology. I should have thought of it. It's plain enough, and helps the paradox delightfully. We cannot see it, nor can we appreciate this machine, any more than we can the spoke of a wheel spinning, or a bullet flying through the air. If it is travelling through time fifty times or a hundred times faster than we are, if it gets through a minute while we get through a second, the impression it creates will of course be only one-fiftieth or one-hundredth of what it would make if it were not travelling in time. That's plain enough.' He passed his hand through the space in which the machine had been. 'You see?' he said, laughing.

We sat and stared at the vacant table for a minute or so. Then the Time Traveller asked us what we thought of it all.

'It sounds plausible enough to-night,' said the Medical Man; 'but wait until to-morrow. Wait for the common-sense of the morning.'

'Would you like to see the Time Machine itself?' asked the Time Traveller. And therewith, taking the lamp in his hand, he led the way down the long, draughty corridor to his laboratory. I remember vividly the flickering light, his queer, broad head in silhouette, the dance of the shadows, how we all followed him, puzzled but incredulous, and how there in the laboratory we beheld a larger edition of the little mechanism which we had seen vanish from before our eyes. Parts were of nickel, parts of ivory, parts had certainly been filed or sawn out of rock crystal. The thing was generally complete, but the twisted crystalline bars lay unfinished upon the bench beside some sheets of drawings, and I took one up for a better look at it. Quartz it seemed to be.

2. I.e., below the threshold of visual perception.

'Look here,' said the Medical Man, 'are you perfectly serious? Or is this a trick—like that ghost you showed us last Christmas?'

'Upon that machine,' said the Time Traveller, holding the lamp aloft, 'I intend to explore time. Is that plain? I was never more serious in my life.'

None of us quite knew how to take it.

I caught Filby's eye over the shoulder of the Medical Man, and he winked at me solemnly.

III. *The Time Traveller Returns*

I think that at that time none of us quite believed in the Time Machine. The fact is, the Time Traveller was one of those men who are too clever to be believed: you never felt that you saw all round him; you always suspected some subtle reserve, some ingenuity in ambush, behind his lucid frankness. Had Filby shown the model and explained the matter in the Time Traveller's words, we should have shown *him* far less scepticism. For we should have perceived his motives: a pork-butcher could understand Filby. But the Time Traveller had more than a touch of whim among his elements, and we distrusted him. Things that would have made the fame of a less clever man seemed tricks in his hands. It is a mistake to do things too easily. The serious people who took him seriously never felt quite sure of his deportment: they were somehow aware that trusting their reputations for judgment with him was like furnishing a nursery with eggshell china. So I don't think any of us said very much about time travelling in the interval between that Thursday and the next, though its odd potentialities ran, no doubt, in most of our minds: its plausibility, that is, its practical incredibleness, the curious possibilities of anachronism and of utter confusion it suggested. For my own part, I was particularly preoccupied with the trick of the model. That I remember discussing with the Medical Man, whom I met on Friday at the Linnæan.[1] He said he had seen a similar thing at Tübingen,[2] and laid considerable stress on the blowing-out of the candle. But how the trick was done he could not explain.

The next Thursday I went again to Richmond[3]—I suppose I was one of the Time Traveller's most constant guests—and, arriving late, found four or five men already assembled in his drawing-room. The Medical Man was standing before the fire with a sheet of paper in one hand and his watch in the other. I looked round for the Time

---

1. Founded in 1788 and named for the great Swedish naturalist Carl von Linné (1707–1778), the Linnaean Society was one of London's most distinguished scholarly societies. Relevant to Wells's tale is the fact that in July 1858 the Linnaean was the site of Charles Darwin's first public presentation of the theory of natural selection.
2. A German university city, near Stuttgart.
3. An attractive residential suburb on the river Thames a few miles southwest of London.

Traveller, and—'It's half-past seven now,' said the Medical Man. 'I suppose we'd better have dinner?'

'Where's ———?' said I, naming our host.

'You've just come? It's rather odd. He's unavoidably detained. He asks me in this note to lead off with dinner at seven if he's not back. Says he'll explain when he comes.'

'It seems a pity to let the dinner spoil,' said the Editor of a well-known daily paper; and thereupon the Doctor rang the bell.

The Psychologist was the only person besides the Doctor and myself who had attended the previous dinner. The other men were Blank, the Editor afore-mentioned, a certain journalist, and another—a quiet, shy man with a beard—whom I didn't know, and who, as far as my observation went, never opened his mouth all the evening. There was some speculation at the dinner-table about the Time Traveller's absence, and I suggested time travelling, in a half jocular spirit. The Editor wanted that explained to him, and the Psychologist volunteered a wooden account of the 'ingenious paradox and trick' we had witnessed that day week. He was in the midst of his exposition when the door from the corridor opened slowly and without noise. I was facing the door, and saw it first. 'Hallo!' I said. 'At last!' And the door opened wider, and the Time Traveller stood before us. I gave a cry of surprise. 'Good heavens! man, what's the matter?' cried the Medical Man, who saw him next. And the whole tableful turned towards the door.

He was in an amazing plight. His coat was dusty and dirty, and smeared with green down the sleeves; his hair disordered, and as it seemed to me greyer—either with dust and dirt or because its colour had actually faded. His face was ghastly pale; his chin had a brown cut on it—a cut half-healed; his expression was haggard and drawn, as by intense suffering. For a moment he hesitated in the doorway, as if he had been dazzled by the light. Then he came into the room. He walked with just such a limp as I had seen in footsore tramps. We stared at him in silence, expecting him to speak.

He said not a word, but came painfully to the table, and made a motion towards the wine. The Editor filled a glass of champagne, and pushed it towards him. He drained it, and it seemed to do him good: for he looked round the table, and the ghost of his old smile flickered across his face. 'What on earth have you been up to, man?' said the Doctor. The Time Traveller did not seem to hear. 'Don't let me disturb you,' he said, with a certain faltering articulation. 'I'm all right.' He stopped, held out his glass for more, and took it off at a draught. 'That's good,' he said. His eyes grew brighter, and a faint colour came into his cheeks. His glance flickered over our faces with a certain dull approval, and then went round the warm and comfortable room. Then he spoke again, still as it were feeling his way among his words. 'I'm going to wash and dress, and then I'll come

down and explain things. . . . Save me some of that mutton. I'm
starving for a bit of meat.'

He looked across at the Editor, who was a rare visitor, and hoped
he was all right. The Editor began a question. 'Tell you presently,'
said the Time Traveller. 'I'm—funny! Be all right in a minute.'

He put down his glass, and walked towards the staircase door.
Again I remarked his lameness and the soft padding sound of his
footfall, and standing up in my place, I saw his feet as he went out.
He had nothing on them but a pair of tattered, blood-stained socks.
Then the door closed upon him. I had half a mind to follow, till I
remembered how he detested any fuss about himself. For a minute,
perhaps, my mind was wool gathering. Then, 'Remarkable Behaviour of an Eminent Scientist,' I heard the Editor say, thinking (after
his wont) in headlines. And this brought my attention back to the
bright dinner-table.

'What's the game?' said the Journalist. 'Has he been doing the
Amateur Cadger?[4] I don't follow.' I met the eye of the Psychologist,
and read my own interpretation in his face. I thought of the Time
Traveller limping painfully up-stairs. I don't think anyone else had
noticed his lameness.

The first to recover completely from this surprise was the Medical
Man, who rang the bell—the Time Traveller hated to have servants
waiting at dinner—for a hot plate. At that the Editor turned to his
knife and fork with a grunt, and the Silent Man followed suit. The dinner was resumed. Conversation was exclamatory for a little while,
with gaps of wonderment; and then the Editor got fervent in his
curiosity. 'Does our friend eke out his modest income with a cross-
ing? or has he his Nebuchadnezzar phases?' he inquired.[5] 'I feel
assured it's this business of the Time Machine,' I said, and took up
the Psychologist's account of our previous meeting. The new guests
were frankly incredulous. The Editor raised objections. 'What *was*
this time travelling? A man couldn't cover himself with dust by
rolling in a paradox, could he?' And then, as the idea came home to
him, he resorted to caricature. Hadn't they any clothes-brushes in
the Future? The Journalist, too, would not believe at any price, and
joined the Editor in the easy work of heaping ridicule on the whole
thing. They were both the new kind of journalist—very joyous, irrev-
erent young men. 'Our Special Correspondent in the Day after
Tomorrow reports,' the Journalist was saying—or rather shouting—

---

4. I.e., someone posing as or playing at being a beggar.
5. "To cross" is slang for to swindle, though the Editor may instead be asking whether his
   host supplements his "modest income" with the meager sum of money he could earn by
   sweeping street crossings. In the Old Testament, King Nebuchadnezzar was punished by
   God and forced to live like a beast for seven years (see Daniel 4:28–33). In both cases the
   Editor is facetiously suggesting that the Time Traveller leads a double life.

when the Time Traveller came back. He was dressed in ordinary evening clothes, and nothing save his haggard look remained of the change that had startled me.

'I say,' said the Editor, hilariously, 'these chaps here say you have been travelling into the middle of next week! Tell us all about little Rosebery, will you?[6] What will you take for the lot?'

The Time Traveller came to the place reserved for him without a word. He smiled quietly, in his old way. 'Where's my mutton?' he said. 'What a treat it is to stick a fork into meat again!'

'Story!' cried the Editor.

'Story be damned!' said the Time Traveller. 'I want something to eat. I won't say a word until I get some peptone[7] into my arteries. Thanks. And the salt.'

'One word,' said I. 'Have you been time travelling?'

'Yes,' said the Time Traveller, with his mouth full, nodding his head.

'I'd give a shilling a line for a verbatim note,'[8] said the Editor. The Time Traveller pushed his glass towards the Silent Man and rang it with his finger-nail; at which the Silent Man, who had been staring at his face, started convulsively, and poured him wine. The rest of the dinner was uncomfortable. For my own part, sudden questions kept on rising to my lips, and I dare say it was the same with the others. The Journalist tried to relieve the tension by telling anecdotes of Hettie Potter.[9] The Time Traveller devoted his attention to his dinner, and displayed the appetite of a tramp. The Medical Man smoked a cigarette, and watched the Time Traveller through his eyelashes. The Silent Man seemed even more clumsy than usual, and drank champagne with regularity and determination out of sheer nervousness. At last the Time Traveller pushed his plate away, and looked round us. 'I suppose I must apologize,' he said. 'I was simply starving. I've had a most amazing time.' He reached out his hand for a cigar, and cut the end. 'But come into the smoking-room. It's too long a story to tell over greasy plates.' And ringing the bell in passing, he led the way into adjoining room.

'You have told Blank, and Dash, and Chose about the machine?' he said to me, leaning back in his easy-chair and naming the three new guests.

6. The Earl of Rosebery (1847–1929) became prime minister in March 1894—an event still in the future for the guests at this dinner party but in the past for the first readers of Wells's story in the *New Review*. (The allusion to Rosebery does not appear in the earlier *National Observer* version of the story.) Rosebery was also a noted breeder of racehorses, so perhaps the Editor is asking for some betting tips as well. In fact, Rosebery's horses won a number of high-stakes races in 1894 and 1895.
7. Protein.
8. The Editor is offering top rates for the Time Traveller's eyewitness story: a shilling per line would be well above the standard pay for freelance journalism.
9. Evidently fictitious. The context suggests a popular actress or music-hall entertainer.

'But the thing's a mere paradox,' said the Editor.

'I can't argue to-night. I don't mind telling you the story, but I can't argue. I will,' he went on, 'tell you the story of what has happened to me, if you like, but you must refrain from interruptions. I want to tell it. Badly. Most of it will sound like lying. So be it! It's true—every word of it, all the same. I was in my laboratory at four o'clock, and since then . . . I've lived eight days . . . such days as no human being ever lived before! I'm nearly worn out, but I sha'n't sleep till I've told this thing over to you. Then I shall go to bed. But no interruptions! Is it agreed?'

'Agreed,' said the Editor, and the rest of us echoed 'Agreed.' And with that the Time Traveller began his story as I have set it forth. He sat back in his chair at first, and spoke like a weary man. Afterwards he got more animated. In writing it down I feel with only too much keenness the inadequacy of pen and ink—and, above all, my own inadequacy—to express its quality. You read, I will suppose, attentively enough; but you cannot see the speaker's white, sincere face in the bright circle of the little lamp, nor hear the intonation of his voice. You cannot know how his expression followed the turns of his story! Most of us hearers were in shadow, for the candles in the smoking-room had not been lighted, and only the face of the Journalist and the legs of the Silent Man from the knees downward were illuminated. At first we glanced now and again at each other. After a time we ceased to do that, and looked only at the Time Traveller's face.

IV. Time Travelling

'I told some of you last Thursday of the principles of the Time Machine, and showed you the actual thing itself, incomplete in the workshop. There it is now, a little travel-worn, truly; and one of the ivory bars is cracked, and a brass rail bent; but the rest of it's sound enough. I expected to finish it on Friday; but on Friday, when the putting together was nearly done, I found that one of the nickel bars was exactly one inch too short, and this I had to get re-made; so that the thing was not complete until this morning. It was at ten o'clock to-day that the first of all Time Machines began its career. I gave it a last tap, tried all the screws again, put one more drop of oil on the quartz rod, and sat myself in the saddle. I suppose a suicide who holds a pistol to his skull feels much the same wonder at what will come next as I felt then. I took the starting lever in one hand and the stopping one in the other, pressed the first, and almost immediately the second. I seemed to reel; I felt a nightmare sensation of falling; and, looking round, I saw the laboratory exactly as before. Had anything happened? For a moment I suspected that my intellect had tricked me. Then I noted the clock. A moment before, as it seemed, it had stood at a minute or so past ten; now it was nearly half-past three!

'I drew a breath, set my teeth, gripped the starting lever with both hands, and went off with a thud. The laboratory got hazy and went dark. Mrs Watchett[1] came in, and walked, apparently without seeing me, towards the garden door. I suppose it took her a minute or so to traverse the place, but to me she seemed to shoot across the room like a rocket. I pressed the lever over to its extreme position. The night came like the turning out of a lamp, and in another moment came to-morrow. The laboratory grew faint and hazy, then fainter and ever fainter. To-morrow night came black, then day again, night again, day again, faster and faster still. An eddying murmur filled my ears, and a strange, dumb confusedness descended on my mind.

'I am afraid I cannot convey the peculiar sensations of time travelling. They are excessively unpleasant. There is a feeling exactly like that one has upon a switchback[2]—of a helpless headlong motion! I felt the same horrible anticipation, too, of an imminent smash. As I put on pace, night followed day like the flapping of a black wing. The dim suggestion of the laboratory seemed presently to fall away from me, and I saw the sun hopping swiftly across the sky, leaping it every minute, and every minute marking a day. I supposed the laboratory had been destroyed and I had come into the open air. I had a dim impression of scaffolding, but I was already going too fast to be conscious of any moving things. The slowest snail that ever crawled dashed by too fast for me. The twinkling succession of darkness and light was excessively painful to the eye. Then, in the intermittent darknesses, I saw the moon spinning swiftly through her quarters from new to full, and had a faint glimpse of the circling stars. Presently, as I went on, still gaining velocity, the palpitation of night and day merged into one continuous greyness; the sky took on a wonderful deepness of blue, a splendid luminous colour like that of early twilight; the jerking sun became a streak of fire, a brilliant arch, in space, the moon a fainter fluctuating band; and I could see nothing of the stars, save now and then a brighter circle flickering in the blue.

'The landscape was misty and vague. I was still on the hillside upon which this house now stands, and the shoulder rose above me grey and dim. I saw trees growing and changing like puffs of vapour, now brown, now green: they grew, spread, shivered, and passed away. I saw huge buildings rise up faint and fair, and pass like dreams. The whole surface of the earth seemed changed—melting

---

1. The Time Traveller's housekeeper.
2. A roller coaster.

and flowing under my eyes.[3] The little hands upon the dials that registered my speed raced round faster and faster. Presently I noted
that the sun-belt swayed up and down, from solstice to solstice, in a
minute or less, and that, consequently, my pace was over a year a
minute; and minute by minute the white snow flashed across the
world, and vanished, and was followed by the bright, brief green of
spring.

'The unpleasant sensations of the start were less poignant now.
They merged at last into a kind of hysterical exhilaration. I remarked,
indeed, a clumsy swaying of the machine, for which I was unable to
account. But my mind was too confused to attend to it, so with a
kind of madness growing upon me, I flung myself into futurity. At
first I scarce thought of stopping, scarce thought of anything but
these new sensations. But presently a fresh series of impressions
grew up in my mind—a certain curiosity and therewith a certain
dread—until at last they took complete possession of me. What
strange developments of humanity, what wonderful advances upon
our rudimentary civilization, I thought, might not appear when I
came to look nearly into the dim elusive world that raced and fluctu-
ated before my eyes! I saw great and splendid architecture rising
about me, more massive than any buildings of our own time, and
yet, as it seemed, built of glimmer and mist. I saw a richer green flow
up the hill-side, and remain there without any wintry intermission.
Even through the veil of my confusion the earth seemed very fair.
And so my mind came round to the business of stopping.

'The peculiar risk lay in the possibility of my finding some substance in the space which I, or the machine, occupied. So long as I
travelled at a high velocity through time, this scarcely mattered: I
was, so to speak, attenuated—was slipping like a vapour through the
interstices of intervening substances! But to come to a stop involved
the jamming of myself, molecule by molecule, into whatever lay in
my way: meant bringing my atoms into such intimate contact with
those of the obstacle that a profound chemical reaction—possibly a
far-reaching explosion—would result, and blow myself and my apparatus out of all possible dimensions—into the Unknown. This possibility had occurred to me again and again while I was making the
machine; but then I had cheerfully accepted it as an unavoidable
risk—one of the risks a man has got to take! Now the risk was

3. Inserted at this point in Wells's manuscript are the lines from section CXXIII of Alfred
   Tennyson's *In Memoriam* (1850), which this sentence obliquely invokes and whose sentiment it echoes:

   > The hills are shadows and they flow
   > From form to form, and nothing stands;
   > They melt like mist, the solid lands,
   > Like clouds they shape themselves and go.

inevitable, I no longer saw it in the same cheerful light. The fact is that, insensibly, the absolute strangeness of everything, the sickly jarring and swaying of the machine, above all, the feeling of prolonged falling, had absolutely upset my nerve. I told myself that I could never stop, and with a gust of petulance I resolved to stop forthwith. Like an impatient fool, I lugged over the lever, and incontinently the thing went reeling over, and I was flung headlong through the air.

'There was the sound of a clap of thunder in my ears. I may have been stunned for a moment. A pitiless hail was hissing round me, and I was sitting on soft turf in front of the overset machine. Everything still seemed grey, but presently I remarked that the confusion in my ears was gone. I looked round me. I was on what seemed to be a little lawn in a garden, surrounded by rhododendron bushes, and I noticed that their mauve and purple blossoms were dropping in a shower under the beating of the hailstones. The rebounding, dancing hail hung in a little cloud over the machine, and drove along the ground like smoke. In a moment I was wet to the skin. "Fine hospitality," said I, "to a man who has travelled innumerable years to see you."

'Presently I thought what a fool I was to get wet. I stood up and looked round me. A colossal figure, carved apparently in some white stone, loomed indistinctly beyond the rhododendrons through the hazy downpour. But all else in the world was invisible.

'My sensations would be hard to describe. As the columns of hail grew thinner, I saw the white figure more distinctly. It was very large, for a silver birch tree touched its shoulder. It was of white marble, in shape something like a winged sphinx,[4] but the wings, instead of being carried vertically at the sides, were spread so that it seemed to hover. The pedestal, it appeared to me, was of bronze, and was thick with verdigris.[5] It chanced that the face was towards me; the sightless eyes seemed to watch me; there was the faint shadow of a smile on the lips. It was greatly weather-worn, and that imparted an unpleasant suggestion of disease. I stood looking at it for a little space—half-a-minute, perhaps, or half-an-hour. It seemed to advance and to recede as the hail drove before it denser and thinner. At last I tore my eyes from it for a moment, and saw that the hail curtain had worn threadbare, and that the sky was lightening with the promise of the sun.

'I looked up again at the crouching white shape, and the full temerity of my voyage came suddenly upon me. What might appear when that hazy curtain was altogether withdrawn? What might not

4. A mythical creature with the body of a winged lion and the head of a woman.
5. The green rust that forms on brass, copper, or bronze, all three of which oxidize much more slowly than iron does—an indication that this statue is exceptionally old.

have happened to men? What if cruelty had grown into a common passion? What if in this interval the race had lost its manliness, and had developed into something inhuman, unsympathetic, and over-whelmingly powerful? I might seem some old-world savage animal, only the more dreadful and disgusting for our common likeness—a foul creature to be incontinently slain.

'Already I saw other vast shapes—huge buildings with intricate parapets and tall columns, with a wooded hill-side dimly creeping in upon me through the lessening storm. I was seized with a panic fear. I turned frantically to the Time Machine, and strove hard to readjust it. As I did so the shafts of the sun smote through the thunderstorm. The grey downpour was swept aside and vanished like the trailing garments of a ghost. Above me, in the intense blue of the summer sky, some faint brown shreds of cloud whirled into nothingness. The great buildings about me stood out clear and distinct, shining with the wet of the thunderstorm, and picked out in white by the unmelted hailstones piled along their courses. I felt naked in a strange world. I felt as perhaps a bird may feel in the clear air, know-ing the hawk wings above and will swoop. My fear grew to frenzy. I took a breathing space, set my teeth, and again grappled fiercely, wrist and knee, with the machine. It gave under my desperate onset and turned over. It struck my chin violently. One hand on the saddle, the other on the lever, I stood panting heavily in attitude to mount again.

'But with this recovery of a prompt retreat my courage recovered. I looked more curiously and less fearfully at this world of the remote future. In a circular opening, high up in the wall of the nearer house, I saw a group of figures clad in rich soft robes. They had seen me, and their faces were directed towards me.

'Then I heard voices approaching me. Coming through the bushes by the White Sphinx were the heads and shoulders of men running. One of these emerged in a pathway leading straight to the little lawn upon which I stood with my machine. He was a slight creature—perhaps four feet high—clad in a purple tunic, girdled at the waist with a leather belt. Sandals or buskins—I could not clearly distinguish which—were on his feet; his legs were bare to the knees, and his head was bare. Noticing that, I noticed for the first time how warm the air was.

'He struck me as being a very beautiful and graceful creature, but indescribably frail. His flushed face reminded me of the more beau-tiful kind of consumptive—that hectic[6] beauty of which we used to hear so much. At the sight of him I suddenly regained confidence. I took my hands from the machine.

6. Flushed or feverish.

V. In the Golden Age[1]

'In another moment we were standing face to face, I and this fragile thing out of futurity. He came straight up to me and laughed into my eyes. The absence from his bearing of any sign of fear struck me at once. Then he turned to the two others who were following him and spoke to them in a strange and very sweet and liquid tongue.

'There were others coming, and presently a little group of perhaps eight or ten of these exquisite creatures were about me. One of them addressed me. It came into my head, oddly enough, that my voice was too harsh and deep for them. So I shook my head, and pointing to my ears, shook it again. He came a step forward, hesitated, and then touched my hand. Then I felt other soft little tentacles upon my back and shoulders. They wanted to make sure I was real. There was nothing in this at all alarming. Indeed, there was something in these pretty little people that inspired confidence—a graceful gentleness, a certain childlike ease. And besides, they looked so frail that I could fancy myself flinging the whole dozen of them about like nine-pins. But I made a sudden motion to warn them when I saw their little pink hands feeling at the Time Machine. Happily then, when it was not too late, I thought of a danger I had hitherto forgotten, and reaching over the bars of the machine, I unscrewed the little levers that would set it in motion, and put these in my pocket. Then I turned again to see what I could do in the way of communication.

'And then, looking more nearly into their features, I saw some further peculiarities in their Dresden china type of prettiness. Their hair, which was uniformly curly, came to a sharp end at the neck and cheek; there was not the faintest suggestion of it on the face, and their ears were singularly minute. The mouths were small, with bright red, rather thin lips, and the little chins ran to a point. The eyes were large and mild; and—this may seem egotism on my part— I fancied even then that there was a certain lack of the interest I might have expected in them.

'As they made no effort to communicate with me, but simply stood round me smiling and speaking in soft cooing notes to each other, I began the conversation. I pointed to the Time Machine and to myself. Then, hesitating for a moment how to express Time, I pointed to the sun. At once a quaintly pretty little figure in chequered purple and white followed my gesture, and then astonished me by imitating the sound of thunder.

'For a moment I was staggered, though the import of his gesture was plain enough. The question had come into my mind abruptly: were

---

1. In classical mythology, the Golden Age was the earliest and happiest age of human society, when care and hardship were unknown.

these creatures fools? You may hardly understand how it took me. You see I had always anticipated that the people of the year Eight Hundred and Two Thousand odd would be incredibly in front of us in knowledge, art, everything. Then one of them suddenly asked me a question that showed him to be on the intellectual level of one of our five-year-old children—asked me, in fact, if I had come from the sun in a thunderstorm! It let loose the judgment I had suspended upon their clothes, their frail light limbs and fragile features. A flow of disappointment rushed across my mind. For a moment I felt that I had built the Time Machine in vain.

'I nodded, pointed to the sun, and gave them such a vivid rendering of a thunderclap as startled them. They all withdrew a pace or so and bowed. Then came one laughing towards me, carrying a chain of beautiful flowers altogether new to me, and put it about my neck. The idea was received with melodious applause; and presently they were all running to and fro for flowers and laughingly flinging them upon me until I was almost smothered with blossom. You who have never seen the like can scarcely imagine what delicate and wonderful flowers countless years of culture had created. Then some one suggested that their plaything should be exhibited in the nearest building, and so I was led past the sphinx of white marble, which had seemed to watch me all the while with a smile at my astonishment, towards a vast grey edifice of fretted stone. As I went with them the memory of my confident anticipations of a profoundly grave and intellectual posterity came, with irresistible merriment, to my mind.

'The building had a huge entry, and was altogether of colossal dimensions. I was naturally most occupied with the growing crowd of little people, and with the big open portals that yawned before me shadowy and mysterious. My general impression of the world I saw over their heads was of a tangled waste of beautiful bushes and flowers, a long-neglected and yet weedless garden. I saw a number of tall spikes of strange white flowers, measuring a foot perhaps across the spread of the waxen petals. They grew scattered, as if wild, among the variegated shrubs, but, as I say, I did not examine them closely at this time. The Time Machine was left deserted on the turf among the rhododendrons.

'The arch of the doorway was richly carved, but naturally I did not observe the carving very narrowly, though I fancied I saw suggestions of old Phœnician[2] decorations as I passed through, and it struck me that they were very badly broken and weather-worn. Several more brightly-clad people met me in the doorway, and so we entered, I, dressed in

---

2. The Phoenicians, whose culture flourished ca. eighth through sixth centuries BCE, are thought to have introduced the alphabet to the ancient Greeks. Their characteristic decorative motifs include highly stylized figures of human and animals, along with depictions of fabulous creatures, such as griffins and sphinxes.

dingy nineteenth-century garments, looking grotesque enough, gar-
landed with flowers, and surrounded by an eddying mass of bright,
soft-coloured robes and shining white limbs, in a melodious whirl of
laughter and laughing speech.

'The big doorway opened into a proportionately great hall hung
with brown. The roof was in shadow, and the windows, partially
glazed with coloured glass and partially unglazed, admitted a tem-
pered light. The floor was made up of huge blocks of some very hard
white metal, not plates nor slabs—blocks, and it was so much worn,
as I judged by the going to and fro of past generations, as to be deeply
channelled along the more frequented ways. Transverse to the length
were innumerable tables made of slabs of polished stone, raised, perhaps, a foot from the floor, and upon these were heaps of fruits.
Some I recognized as a kind of hypertrophied[3] raspberry and orange,
but for the most part they were strange.

'Between the tables was scattered a great number of cushions.
Upon these my conductors seated themselves, signing for me to do
likewise. With a pretty absence of ceremony they began to eat the
fruit with their hands, flinging peel and stalks, and so forth, into the
round openings in the sides of the tables. I was not loth to follow
their example, for I felt thirsty and hungry. As I did so I surveyed the
hall at my leisure.

'And perhaps the thing that struck me most was its dilapidated
look. The stained-glass windows, which displayed only a geometrical
pattern, were broken in many places, and the curtains that hung
across the lower end were thick with dust. And it caught my eye that
the corner of the marble table near me was fractured. Nevertheless,
the general effect was extremely rich and picturesque. There were,
perhaps, a couple of hundred people dining in the hall, and most of
them, seated as near to me as they could come, were watching me
with interest, their little eyes shining over the fruit they were eating.
All were clad in the same soft, and yet strong, silky material.

'Fruit, by the bye, was all their diet. These people of the remote
future were strict vegetarians, and while I was with them, in spite
of some carnal cravings, I had to be frugivorous also.[4] Indeed, I
found afterwards that horses, cattle, sheep, dogs, had followed the
Ichthyosaurus into extinction.[5] But the fruits were very delightful;
one, in particular, that seemed to be in season all the time I was
there—a floury thing in a three-sided husk—was especially good,
and I made it my staple. At first I was puzzled by all these strange
fruits, and by the strange flowers I saw, but later I began to perceive
their import.

3. Unusually large or overgrown.
4. Feeding on fruits.
5. A marine reptile that became extinct roughly 140 million years ago. It resembled a dolphin.

'However, I am telling you of my fruit dinner in the distant future now. So soon as my appetite was a little checked, I determined to make a resolute attempt to learn the speech of these new men of mine. Clearly that was the next thing to do. The fruits seemed a convenient thing to begin upon, and holding one of these up I began a series of interrogative sounds and gestures. I had some considerable difficulty in conveying my meaning. At first my efforts met with a stare of surprise or inextinguishable laughter, but presently a fair-haired little creature seemed to grasp my intention and repeated a name. They had to chatter and explain their business at great length to each other, and my first attempts to make their exquisite little sounds of the language caused an immense amount of genuine, if uncivil, amusement. However, I felt like a school-master amidst children, and persisted, and presently I had a score of noun substantives at least at my command; and then I got to demonstrative pronouns, and even the verb 'to eat'. But it was slow work, and the little people soon tired and wanted to get away from my interrogations, so I determined, rather of necessity, to let them give their lessons in little doses when they felt inclined. And very little doses I found they were before long, for I never met people more indolent or more easily fatigued.

VI. The Sunset of Mankind

'A queer thing I soon discovered about my little hosts, and that was their lack of interest. They would come to me with eager cries of astonishment, like children, but, like children, they would soon stop examining me, and wander away after some other toy. The dinner and my conversational beginnings ended, I noted for the first time that almost all those who had surrounded me at first were gone. It is odd, too, how speedily I came to disregard these little people. I went out through the portal into the sunlit world again so soon as my hunger was satisfied. I was continually meeting more of these men of the future, who would follow me a little distance, chatter and laugh about me, and, having smiled and gesticulated in a friendly way, leave me again to my own devices.

'The calm of evening was upon the world as I emerged from the great hall, and the scene was lit by the warm glow of the setting sun. At first things were very confusing. Everything was so entirely different from the world I had known—even the flowers. The big building I had left was situate on the slope of a broad river valley, but the Thames had shifted, perhaps, a mile from its present position. I resolved to mount to the summit of a crest, perhaps a mile and a half away, from which I could get a wider view of this our planet in the year Eight Hundred and Two Thousand Seven Hundred and One, A.D. For that, I should explain, was the date the little dials of my machine recorded.

'As I walked I was watchful for every impression that could possibly help to explain the condition of ruinous splendour in which I found the world—for ruinous it was. A little way up the hill, for instance, was a great heap of granite, bound together by masses of aluminium,[1] a vast labyrinth of precipitous walls and crumbled heaps, amidst which were thick heaps of very beautiful pagoda-like plants—nettles possibly—but wonderfully tinted with brown about the leaves, and incapable of stinging. It was evidently the derelict remains of some vast structure, to what end built I could not determine. It was here that I was destined, at a later date, to have a very strange experience—the first intimation of a still stranger discovery—but of that I will speak in its proper place.

'Looking round, with a sudden thought, from a terrace on which I rested for awhile, I realized that there were no small houses to be seen. Apparently, the single house, and possibly even the household, had vanished. Here and there among the greenery were palace-like buildings, but the house and the cottage, which form such characteristic features of our own English landscape, had disappeared.

'"Communism," said I to myself.[2]

'And on the heels of that came another thought. I looked at the half-dozen little figures that were following me. Then, in a flash, I perceived that all had the same form of costume, the same soft hairless visage, and the same girlish rotundity of limb. It may seem strange, perhaps, that I had not noticed this before. But everything was so strange. Now, I saw the fact plainly enough. In costume, and in all the differences of texture and bearing that now mark off the sexes from each other, these people of the future were alike. And the children seemed to my eyes to be but the miniatures of their parents. I judged then that the children of that time were extremely precocious, physically at least, and I found afterwards abundant verification of my opinion.

'Seeing the ease and security in which these people were living, I felt that this close resemblance of the sexes was after all what one would expect; for the strength of a man and the softness of a woman, the institution of the family, and the differentiation of occupations are mere militant necessities of an age of physical force. Where population is balanced and abundant, much child-bearing becomes an evil rather than a blessing to the State: where violence comes but rarely and offspring are secure, there is less necessity—indeed there is no necessity—of an efficient family, and the specialization of the sexes with reference to their children's needs disappears. We see some beginnings of this even in our own time, and in this future

---

1. The British spelling of *aluminum.*
2. The disappearance of the family as the basic unit of society (and with it the disappearance of the single-family house) in favor of more communal living arrangements was a feature of left-wing utopian writings throughout the nineteenth century.

age it was complete. This, I must remind you, was my speculation at the time. Later, I was to appreciate how far it fell short of the reality.

'While I was musing upon these things, my attention was attracted by a pretty little structure, like a well under a cupola. I thought in a transitory way of the oddness of wells still existing, and then resumed the thread of my speculations. There were no large buildings towards the top of the hill, and as my walking powers were evidently miraculous, I was presently left alone for the first time. With a strange sense of freedom and adventure I pushed on up to the crest.

'There I found a seat of some yellow metal that I did not recognize, corroded in places with a kind of pinkish rust and half-smothered in soft moss, the arm-rests cast and filed into the resemblance of griffins'[3] heads. I sat down on it, and I surveyed the broad view of our old world under the sunset of that long day. It was as sweet and fair a view as I have ever seen. The sun had already gone below the horizon and the west was flaming gold, touched with some horizontal bars of purple and crimson. Below was the valley of the Thames, in which the river lay like a band of burnished steel. I have already spoken of the great palaces dotted about among the variegated greenery, some in ruins and some still occupied. Here and there rose a white or silvery figure in the waste garden of the earth, here and there came the sharp vertical line of some cupola or obelisk. There were no hedges, no signs of proprietary rights, no evidences of agriculture; the whole earth had become a garden.

'So watching, I began to put my interpretation upon the things I had seen, and as it shaped itself to me that evening, my interpretation was something in this way. (Afterwards I found I had got only a half truth—or only a glimpse of one facet of the truth):

'It seemed to me that I had happened upon humanity upon the wane. The ruddy sunset set me thinking of the sunset of maninld. For the first time I began to realize an odd consequence of the social effort in which we are at present engaged. And yet, come to think, it is a logical consequence enough. Strength is the outcome of need: security sets a premium on feebleness. The work of ameliorating the conditions of life—the true civilizing process that makes life more and more secure—had gone steadily on to a climax. One triumph of a united humanity over Nature had followed another. Things that are now mere dreams had become projects deliberately put in hand and carried forward. And the harvest was what I saw!

'After all, the sanitation and the agriculture of to-day are still in the rudimentary stage. The science of our time has attacked but a little department of the field of human disease, but, even so, it spreads its operations very steadily and persistently. Our agriculture and

---

3. Mythical creatures with the bodies of lions and the heads and wings of eagles.

horticulture destroy a weed just here and there and cultivate perhaps a score or so of wholesome plants, leaving the greater number to fight out a balance as they can. We improve our favourite plants and animals—and how few they are—gradually by selective breeding; now a new and better peach, now a seedless grape, now a sweeter and larger flower, now a more convenient breed of cattle. We improve them gradually, because our ideals are vague and tentative, and our knowledge is very limited; because Nature, too, is shy and slow in our clumsy hands. Some day all this will be better organized, and still better. That is the drift of the current in spite of the eddies. The whole world will be intelligent, educated, and co-operating; things will move faster and faster towards the subjugation of Nature. In the end, wisely and carefully we shall readjust the balance of animal and vegetable life to suit our human needs.

'This adjustment, I say, must have been done, and done well: done indeed for all time, in the space of Time across which my machine had leapt. The air was free from gnats, the earth from weeds or fungi; everywhere were fruits and sweet and delightful flowers; brilliant butterflies flew hither and thither. The ideal of preventive medicine was attained. Diseases had been stamped out. I saw no evidence of any contagious diseases during all my stay. And I shall have to tell you later that even the processes of putrefaction and decay had been profoundly affected by these changes.

'Social triumphs, too, had been effected. I saw mankind housed in splendid shelters, gloriously clothed, and as yet I had found them engaged in no toil. There were no signs of struggle, neither social nor economical struggle. The shop, the advertisement, traffic, all that commerce which constitutes the body of our world, was gone. It was natural on that golden evening that I should jump at the idea of a social paradise. The difficulty of increasing population had been met, I guessed, and population had ceased to increase.

'But with this change in condition comes inevitably adaptations to the change. What, unless biological science is a mass of errors, is the cause of human intelligence and vigour? Hardship and freedom: conditions under which the active, strong, and subtle survive and the weaker go to the wall; conditions that put a premium upon the loyal alliance of capable men, upon self-restraint, patience, and decision. And the institution of the family, and the emotions that arise therein, the fierce jealousy, the tenderness for offspring, parental self-devotion, all found their justification and support in the imminent dangers of the young. *Now*, where are these imminent dangers? There is a sentiment arising, and it will grow, against connubial jealousy, against fierce maternity, against passion of all sorts; unnecessary things now, and things that make us uncomfortable, savage survivals, discords in a refined and pleasant life.

'I thought of the physical slightness of the people, their lack of intelligence, and those big abundant ruins, and it strengthened my belief in a perfect conquest of Nature. For after the battle comes Quiet. Humanity had been strong, energetic, and intelligent, and had used all its abundant vitality to alter the conditions under which it lived. And now came the reaction of the altered conditions.

'Under the new conditions of perfect comfort and security, that restless energy, that with us is strength, would become weakness. Even in our own time certain tendencies and desires, once necessary to survival, are a constant source of failure. Physical courage and the love of battle, for instance, are no great help—may even be hindrances—to a civilized man. And in a state of physical balance and security, power, intellectual as well as physical, would be out of place. For countless years I judged there had been no danger of war or solitary violence, no danger from wild beasts, no wasting disease to require strength of constitution, no need of toil. For such a life, what we should call the weak are as well equipped as the strong, are indeed no longer weak. Better equipped indeed they are, for the strong would be fretted by an energy for which there was no outlet. No doubt the exquisite beauty of the buildings I saw was the outcome of the last surgings of the now purposeless energy of mankind before it settled down into perfect harmony with the conditions under which it lived—the flourish of that triumph which began the last great peace. This has ever been the fate of energy in security; it takes to art and to eroticism, and then come languor and decay.

'Even this artistic impetus would at last die away—had almost died in the Time I saw. To adorn themselves with flowers, to dance, to sing in the sunlight; so much was left of the artistic spirit, and no more. Even that would fade in the end into a contented inactivity. We are kept keen on the grindstone of pain and necessity, and, it seemed to me, that here was that hateful grindstone broken at last!

'As I stood there in the gathering dark I thought that in this simple explanation I had mastered the problem of the world—mastered the whole secret of these delicious people. Possibly the checks they had devised for the increase of population had succeeded too well, and their numbers had rather diminished than kept stationary. That would account for the abandoned ruins. Very simple was my explanation, and plausible enough—as most wrong theories are!

VII. A Sudden Shock

'As I stood there musing over this too perfect triumph of man, the full moon, yellow and gibbous,[1] came up out of an overflow of silver

---

1. The moon in its gibbous phase is between half and full. The moon cannot be simultaneously gibbous and full, as the Time Traveller seems to say here, so perhaps he means that the moon is approaching full.

light in the north-east. The bright little figures ceased to move about below, a noiseless owl flitted by, and I shivered with the chill of the night. I determined to descend and find where I could sleep.

'I looked for the building I knew. Then my eye travelled along to the figure of the White Sphinx upon the pedestal of bronze, growing distinct as the light of the rising moon grew brighter. I could see the silver birch against it. There was the tangle of rhododendron bushes, black in the pale light, and there was the little lawn. I looked at the lawn again. A queer doubt chilled my complacency. "No," said I stoutly to myself, "that was not the lawn."

'But it *was* the lawn. For the white leprous face of the sphinx was towards it. Can you imagine what I felt as this conviction came home to me? But you cannot. The Time Machine was gone!

'At once, like a lash across the face, came the possibility of losing my own age, of being left helpless in this strange new world. The bare thought of it was an actual physical sensation. I could feel it grip me at the throat and stop my breathing. In another moment I was in a passion of fear, and running with great leaping strides down the slope. Once I fell headlong and cut my face; I lost no time in stanching the blood, but jumped up and ran on, with a warm trickle down my cheek and chin. All the time I ran I was saying to myself, "They have moved it a little, pushed it under the bushes out of the way." Nevertheless, I ran with all my might. All the time, with the certainty that sometimes comes with excessive dread, I knew that such assurance was folly, knew instinctively that the machine was removed out of my reach. My breath came with pain. I suppose I covered the whole distance from the hill crest to the little lawn, two miles, perhaps, in ten minutes. And I am not a young man. I cursed aloud, as I ran, at my confident folly in leaving the machine, wasting good breath thereby. I cried aloud, and none answered. Not a creature seemed to be stirring in that moonlit world.

'When I reached the lawn my worst fears were realized. Not a trace of the thing was to be seen. I felt faint and cold when I faced the empty space, among the black tangle of bushes. I ran round it furiously, as if the thing might be hidden in a corner, and then stopped abruptly, with my hands clutching my hair. Above me towered the sphinx, upon the bronze pedestal, white, shining, leprous, in the light of the rising moon. It seemed to smile in mockery of my dismay.

'I might have consoled myself by imagining the little people had put the mechanism in some shelter for me, had I not felt assured of their physical and intellectual inadequacy. That is what dismayed me: the sense of some hitherto unsuspected power, through whose intervention my invention had vanished. Yet, of one thing I felt assured: unless some other age had produced its exact duplicate, the machine could not have moved in time. The attachment of the levers—I will show you the method later—prevented anyone from tampering with it in that way when they were removed. It had moved, and was hid, only in space. But then, where could it be?

'I think I must have had a kind of frenzy. I remember running violently in and out among the moonlit bushes all round the sphinx, and startling some white animal that, in the dim light, I took for a small deer. I remember, too, late that night, beating the bushes with my clenched fists until my knuckles were gashed and bleeding from the broken twigs. Then, sobbing and raving in my anguish of mind, I went down to the great building of stone. The big hall was dark, silent, and deserted. I slipped on the uneven floor, and fell over one of the malachite[2] tables, almost breaking my shin. I lit a match and went on past the dusty curtains, of which I have told you.

'There I found a second great hall covered with cushions, upon which, perhaps, a score or so of the little people were sleeping. I have no doubt they found my second appearance strange enough, coming suddenly out of the quiet darkness with inarticulate noises and the splutter and flare of a match. For they had forgotten about matches. "Where is my Time Machine?" I began, bawling like an angry child, laying hands upon them and shaking them up together. It must have been very queer to them. Some laughed, most of them looked sorely frightened. When I saw them standing round me, it came into my head that I was doing as foolish a thing as it was possible for me to do under the circumstances, in trying to revive the sensation of fear. For, reasoning from their daylight behaviour, I thought that fear must be forgotten.

'Abruptly, I dashed down the match, and knocking one of the people over in my course, went blundering across the big dining-hall again, out under the moonlight. I heard cries of terror and their little feet running and stumbling this way and that. I do not remember all I did as the moon crept up the sky. I suppose it was the unexpected nature of my loss that maddened me. I felt hopelessly cut off from my own kind—a strange animal in an unknown world. I must have raved to and fro, screaming and crying upon God and Fate. I have a memory of horrible fatigue, as the long night of despair wore away; of looking in this impossible place and that; of groping among moonlit ruins and touching strange creatures in the black shadows; at last, of lying on the ground near the sphinx, and weeping with absolute wretchedness, even anger at the folly of leaving the machine having leaked away with my strength. I had nothing left but misery. Then I slept, and when I woke again it was full day, and a couple of sparrows were hopping round me on the turf within reach of my arm.

---

2. A greenish mineral of copper carbonate used to make decorative objects and, occasionally, furniture.

'I sat up in the freshness of the morning, trying to remember how I had got there, and why I had such a profound sense of desertion and despair. Then things came clear in my mind. With the plain, reasonable daylight, I could look my circumstances fairly in the face. I saw the wild folly of my frenzy overnight, and I could reason with myself. Suppose the worst? I said. Suppose the machine altogether lost—perhaps destroyed? It behoves me to be calm and patient, to learn the way of the people, to get a clear idea of the method of my loss, and the means of getting materials and tools; so that in the end, perhaps, I may make another. That would be my only hope, a poor hope, perhaps, but better than despair. And, after all, it was a beautiful and curious world.

'But probably the machine had only been taken away. Still, I must be calm and patient, find its hiding-place, and recover it by force or cunning. And with that I scrambled to my feet and looked about me, wondering where I could bathe. I felt weary, stiff, and travel-soiled. The freshness of the morning made me desire an equal freshness. I had exhausted my emotion. Indeed, as I went about my business, I found myself wondering at my intense excitement overnight. I made a careful examination of the ground about the little lawn. I wasted some time in futile questionings, conveyed, as well as I was able, to such of the little people as came by. They all failed to understand my gestures: some were simply stolid; some thought it was a jest, and laughed at me. I had the hardest task in the world to keep my hands off their pretty laughing faces. It was a foolish impulse, but the devil begotten of fear and blind anger was ill curbed, and still eager to take advantage of my perplexity. The turf gave better counsel. I found a groove ripped in it, about midway between the pedestal of the sphinx and the marks of my feet where, on arrival, I had struggled with the overturned machine. There were other signs of removal about, with queer narrow footprints like those I could imagine made by a sloth. This directed my closer attention to the pedestal. It was, as I think I have said, of bronze. It was not a mere block, but highly decorated with deep framed panels on either side. I went and rapped at these. The pedestal was hollow. Examining the panels with care I found them discontinuous with the frames. There were no handles or keyholes, but possibly the panels, if they were doors as I supposed, opened from within. One thing was clear enough to my mind. It took no very great mental effort to infer that my Time Machine was inside that pedestal. But how it got there was a different problem.

'I saw the heads of two orange-clad people coming through the bushes and under some blossom-covered apple-trees towards me. I turned smiling to them, and beckoned them to me. They came, and then, pointing to the bronze pedestal, I tried to intimate my wish to

open it. But at my first gesture towards this they behaved very oddly.
I don't know how to convey their expression to you. Suppose you
were to use a grossly improper gesture to a delicate-minded woman—
it is how she would look. They went off as if they had received the
last possible insult. I tried a sweet-looking little chap in white next,
with exactly the same result. Somehow, his manner made me feel
ashamed of myself. But, as you know, I wanted the Time Machine,
and I tried him once more. As he turned off, like the others, my tem-
per got the better of me. In three strides I was after him, had him by
the loose part of his robe round the neck, and began dragging him
towards the sphinx. Then I saw the horror and repugnance of his
face, and all of a sudden I let him go.

'But I was not beaten yet. I banged with my fist at the bronze panels. I thought I heard something stir inside—to be explicit, I thought
I heard a sound like a chuckle—but I must have been mistaken.
Then I got a big pebble from the river, and came and hammered till
I had flattened a coil in the decorations, and the verdigris came off
in powdery flakes. The delicate little people must have heard me
hammering in gusty outbreaks a mile away on either hand, but nothing came of it. I saw a crowd of them upon the slopes, looking
furtively at me. At last, hot and tired, I sat down to watch the place.
But I was too restless to watch long; I am too Occidental[3] for a long
vigil. I could work at a problem for years, but to wait inactive for
twenty-four hours—that is another matter.

'I got up after a time, and began walking aimlessly through the
bushes towards the hill again. "Patience," said I to myself. "If you
want your machine again you must leave that sphinx alone. If they
mean to take your machine away, it's little good your wrecking their
bronze panels, and if they don't, you will get it back as soon as you
can ask for it. To sit among all those unknown things before a puzzle
like that is hopeless. That way lies monomania.[4] Face this world.
Learn its ways, watch it, be careful of too hasty guesses at its meaning. In the end you will find clues to it all." Then suddenly the
humour of the situation came into my mind: the thought of the
years I had spent in study and toil to get into the future age, and
now my passion of anxiety to get out of it. I had made myself the
most complicated and the most hopeless trap that ever a man devised.
Although it was at my own expense, I could not help myself. I
laughed aloud.

---

3. I.e., European. The Time Traveller unself-consciously invokes stereotypes of Western
("Occidental") restlessness as opposed to Eastern or "Oriental" languor.
4. Obsession with a single idea, leading to insanity.

'Going through the big palace, it seemed to me that the little people avoided me. It may have been my fancy, or it may have had something to do with my hammering at the gates of bronze. Yet I felt tolerably sure of the avoidance. I was careful, however, to show no concern, and to abstain from any pursuit of them, and in the course of a day or two things got back to the old footing. I made what progress I could in the language, and, in addition, I pushed my explorations here and there. Either I missed some subtle point, or their language was excessively simple—almost exclusively composed of concrete substantives and verbs. There seemed to be few, if any, abstract terms, or little use of figurative language. Their sentences were usually simple and of two words, and I failed to convey or understand any but the simplest propositions. I determined to put the thought of my Time Machine, and the mystery of the bronze doors under the sphinx, as much as possible in a corner of memory, until my growing knowledge would lead me back to them in a natural way. Yet a certain feeling, you may understand, tethered me in a circle of a few miles round the point of my arrival.

VIII. Explanation

'So far as I could see, all the world displayed the same exuberant richness as the Thames valley. From every hill I climbed I saw the same abundance of splendid buildings, endlessly varied in material and style; the same clustering thickets of evergreens, the same blossom-laden trees and tree ferns. Here and there water shone like silver, and beyond, the land rose into blue undulating hills, and so faded into the serenity of the sky. A peculiar feature, which presently attracted my attention, was the presence of certain circular wells, several, as it seemed to me, of a very great depth. One lay by the path up the hill, which I had followed during my first walk. Like the others, it was rimmed with bronze, curiously wrought, and protected by a little cupola from the rain. Sitting by the side of these wells, and peering down into the shafted darkness, I could see no gleam of water, nor could I start any reflection with a lighted match. But in all of them I heard a certain sound: a thud—thud—thud, like the beating of some big engine; and I discovered, from the flaring of my matches, that a steady current of air set down the shafts. Further, I threw a scrap of paper into the throat of one; and, instead of fluttering slowly down, it was at once sucked swiftly out of sight.

'After a time, too, I came to connect these wells with tall towers standing here and there upon the slopes; for above them there was often just such a flicker in the air as one sees on a hot day above a sun-scorched beach. Putting things together, I reached a strong suggestion of an extensive system of subterranean ventilation, whose true import it was difficult to imagine. I was at first inclined to associate it with the sanitary apparatus[1] of these people. It was an obvious conclusion, but it was absolutely wrong.

'And here I must admit that I learned very little of drains and bells and modes of conveyance, and the like conveniences, during my time in this real future. In some of these visions of Utopias and coming times which I have read, there is a vast amount of detail about building, and social arrangements, and so forth. But while such details are easy enough to obtain when the whole world is contained in one's imagination, they are altogether inaccessible to a real traveller amid such realities as I found here. Conceive the tale of London which a negro, fresh from Central Africa, would take back to his tribe! What would he know of railway companies, of social movements, of telephone and telegraph wires, of the Parcels Delivery Company, and postal orders[2] and the like? Yet we, at least, should be willing enough to explain these things to him! And even of what he knew, how much could he make his untravelled friend either apprehend or believe? Then, think how narrow the gap between a negro and a white man of our own times, and how wide the interval between myself and these of the Golden Age! I was sensible of much which was unseen, and which contributed to my comfort; but, save for a general impression of automatic organization, I fear I can convey very little of the difference to your mind.

'In the matter of sepulture,[3] for instance, I could see no signs of crematoria nor anything suggestive of tombs. But it occurred to me that, possibly, there might be cemeteries (or crematoria) somewhere beyond the range of my explorings. This, again, was a question I deliberately put to myself, and my curiosity was at first entirely defeated upon the point. The thing puzzled me, and I was led to make a further remark, which puzzled me still more: that aged and infirm among this people there were none.

'I must confess that my satisfaction with my first theories of an automatic civilization and a decadent humanity did not long endure. Yet I could think of no other. Let me put my difficulties. The several big palaces I had explored were mere living places, great dining-halls and sleeping apartments. I could find no machinery, no appliances of any kind. Yet these people were clothed in pleasant fabrics that must at times need renewal, and their sandals, though undecorated, were fairly complex specimens of metal-work. Somehow such things must be made. And the little people displayed no vestige of a creative tendency. There were no shops, no workshops, no sign of importations

1. The sewage system.
2. Money orders.
3. Burial.

among them.[4] They spent all their time in playing gently, in bathing in the river, in making love in a half-playful fashion, in eating fruit and sleeping. I could not see how things were kept going.

'Then, again, about the Time Machine: something, I knew not what, had taken it into the hollow pedestal of the White Sphinx. Why? For the life of me I could not imagine. Those waterless wells, too, those flickering pillars. I felt I lacked a clue. I felt—how shall I put it? Suppose you found an inscription, with sentences here and there in excellent plain English, and, interpolated therewith, others made up of words, of letters even, absolutely unknown to you? Well, on the third day of my visit, that was how the world of Eight Hundred and Two Thousand Seven Hundred and One presented itself to me!

'That day, too, I made a friend—of a sort. It happened that, as I was watching some of the little people bathing in a shallow, one of them was seized with cramp, and began drifting downstream. The main current ran rather swiftly, but not too strongly for even a moderate swimmer. It will give you an idea, therefore, of the strange deficiency in these creatures, when I tell you that none made the slightest attempt to rescue the weakly-crying little thing which was drowning before their eyes. When I realized this, I hurriedly slipped off my clothes, and, wading in at a point lower down, I caught the poor mite, and drew her safe to land. A little rubbing of the limbs soon brought her round, and I had the satisfaction of seeing she was all right before I left her. I had got to such a low estimate of her kind that I did not expect any gratitude from her. In that, however, I was wrong.

'This happened in the morning. In the afternoon I met my little woman, as I believe it was, as I was returning towards my centre from an exploration: and she received me with cries of delight, and presented me with a big garland of flowers—evidently made for me and me alone. The thing took my imagination. Very possibly I had been feeling desolate. At any rate I did my best to display my appreciation of the gift. We were soon seated together in a little stone arbour, engaged in conversation, chiefly of smiles. The creature's friendliness affected me exactly as a child's might have done. We passed each other flowers, and she kissed my hands. I did the same to hers. Then I tried talk, and found that her name was Weena, which, though I don't know what it meant, somehow seemed appropriate enough. That was the beginning of a queer friendship which lasted a week, and ended—as I will tell you!

'She was exactly like a child. She wanted to be with me always. She tried to follow me everywhere, and on my next journey out and about it went to my heart to tire her down, and leave her at last, exhausted and calling after me rather plaintively. But the problems of the world

4. That is, there is no sign that goods are imported from other places.

had to be mastered. I had not, I said to myself, come into the future to carry on a miniature flirtation. Yet her distress when I left her was very great, her expostulations at the parting were sometimes frantic, and I think, altogether, I had as much trouble as comfort from her devotion. Nevertheless she was, somehow, a very great comfort. I thought it was mere childish affection that made her cling to me. Until it was too late, I did not clearly know what I had inflicted upon her when I left her. Nor until it was too late did I clearly understand what she was to me. For, by merely seeming fond of me, and showing in her weak futile way that she cared for me, the little doll of a creature presently gave my return to the neighbourhood of the White Sphinx almost the feeling of coming home; and I would watch for her tiny figure of white and gold so soon as I came over the hill.

'It was from her, too, that I learnt that fear had not yet left the world. She was fearless enough in the daylight, and she had the oddest confidence in me; for once, in a foolish moment, I made threatening grimaces at her, and she simply laughed at them. But she dreaded the dark, dreaded shadows, dreaded black things. Darkness to her was the one thing dreadful. It was a singularly passionate emotion, and it set me thinking and observing. I discovered then, among other things, that these little people gathered into the great houses after dark, and slept in droves. To enter upon them without a light was to put them into a tumult of apprehension. I never found one out of doors, or sleeping alone within doors, after dark. Yet I was still such a blockhead that I missed the lesson of that fear, and, in spite of Weena's distress, I insisted upon sleeping away from these slumbering multitudes.

'It troubled her greatly, but in the end her odd affection for me triumphed, and for five of the nights of our acquaintance, including the last night of all, she slept with her head pillowed on my arm. But my story slips away from me as I speak of her. It must have been the night before her rescue that I was awakened about dawn. I had been restless, dreaming most disagreeably that I was drowned, and that sea-anemones were feeling over my face with their soft palps.[5] I woke with a start, and with an odd fancy that some greyish animal had just rushed out of the chamber. I tried to get to sleep again, but I felt restless and uncomfortable. It was that dim grey hour when things are just creeping out of darkness, when everything is colourless and clear cut, and yet unreal. I got up, and went down into the great hall, and so out upon the flagstones in front of the palace. I thought I would make a virtue of necessity, and see the sunrise.

'The moon was setting, and the dying moonlight and the first pallor of dawn were mingled in a ghastly half-light. The bushes were inky

5. Tendrils or feelers.

black, the ground a sombre grey, the sky colourless and cheerless. And up the hill I thought I could see ghosts. Three several times, as I scanned the slope, I saw white figures. Twice I fancied I saw a solitary white, ape-like creature running rather quickly up the hill, and once near the ruins I saw a leash[6] of them carrying some dark body. They moved hastily. I did not see what became of them. It seemed that they vanished among the bushes. The dawn was still indistinct, you must understand. I was feeling that chill, uncertain, early-morning feeling you may have known. I doubted my eyes.

'As the eastern sky grew brighter, and the light of the day came on and its vivid colouring returned upon the world once more, I scanned the view keenly. But I saw no vestige of my white figures. They were mere creatures of the half-light. "They must have been ghosts," I said; "I wonder whence they dated." For a queer notion of Grant Allen's came into my head, and amused me. If each generation die and leave ghosts, he argued, the world at last will get overcrowded with them.[7] On that theory they would have grown innumerable some Eight Hundred Thousand Years hence, and it was no great wonder to see four at once. But the jest was unsatisfying, and I was thinking of these figures all the morning, until Weena's rescue drove them out of my head. I associated them in some indefinite way with the white animal I had startled in my first passionate search for the Time Machine. But Weena was a pleasant substitute. Yet all the same, they were soon destined to take far deadlier possession of my mind.

'I think I have said how much hotter than our own was the weather of this Golden Age. I cannot account for it. It may be that the sun was hotter, or the earth nearer the sun. It is usual to assume that the sun will go on cooling steadily in the future. But people, unfamiliar with such speculations as those of the younger Darwin,[8] forget that the planets must ultimately fall back one by one into the parent body. As these catastrophes occur, the sun will blaze with renewed energy; and it may be that some inner planet had suffered this fate. Whatever the reason, the fact remains that the sun was very much hotter than we know it.

'Well, one very hot morning—my fourth, I think—as I was seeking shelter from the heat and glare in a colossal ruin near the great house where I slept and fed, there happened this strange thing. Clambering among these heaps of masonry, I found a narrow gallery, whose end and side windows were blocked by fallen masses of stone. By contrast with the brilliancy outside, it seemed at first impenetrably dark to me.

6. A group of three, usually referring to animals.
7. The popular novelist and essayist Grant Allen (1848–1899), a friend of Wells, often drew on his background as a natural scientist in his writing. The "queer notion" referred to here is put forth in his short story "Pallinghurst Barrow" (1892).
8. Charles Darwin's second son, Sir George Howard Darwin (1845–1912), was a prominent astronomer and mathematician best known for his work on tidal effects.

I entered it groping, for the change from light to blackness made spots of colour swim before me. Suddenly I halted spellbound. A pair of eyes, luminous by reflection against the daylight without, was watching me out of the darkness.

'The old instinctive dread of wild beasts came upon me. I clenched my hands and steadfastly looked into the glaring eyeballs. I was afraid to turn. Then the thought of the absolute security in which humanity appeared to be living came to my mind. And then I remembered that strange terror of the dark. Overcoming my fear to some extent, I advanced a step and spoke. I will admit that my voice was harsh and ill-controlled. I put out my hand and touched something soft. At once the eyes darted sideways, and something white ran past me. I turned with my heart in my mouth, and saw a queer little ape-like figure, its head held down in a peculiar manner, running across the sunlit space behind me. It blundered against a block of granite, staggered aside, and in a moment was hidden in a black shadow beneath another pile of ruined masonry.

'My impression of it is, of course, imperfect; but I know it was a dull white, and had strange large greyish-red eyes; also that there was flaxen hair on its head and down its back. But, as I say, it went too fast for me to see distinctly. I cannot even say whether it ran on all fours, or only with its forearms held very low. After an instant's pause I followed it into the second heap of ruins. I could not find it at first; but, after a time in the profound obscurity, I came upon one of those round well-like openings of which I have told you, half closed by a fallen pillar. A sudden thought came to me. Could this Thing have vanished down the shaft? I lit a match, and, looking down, I saw a small, white moving creature, with large bright eyes which regarded me steadfastly as it retreated. It made me shudder. It was so like a human spider! It was clambering down the wall, and now I saw for the first time a number of metal foot- and hand-rests forming a kind of ladder down the shaft. Then the light burned my fingers and fell out of my hand, going out as it dropped, and when I had lit another the little monster had disappeared.

'I do not know how long I sat peering down that well. It was not for some time that I could succeed in persuading myself that the thing I had seen was human. But, gradually, the truth dawned on me: that Man had not remained one species, but had differentiated into two distinct animals: that my graceful children of the Upper World were not the sole descendants of our generation, but that this bleached, obscene, nocturnal Thing, which had flashed before me, was also heir to all the ages.[9]

---

9. An allusion to Alfred Tennyson's poem "Locksley Hall" (1842), line 178, in which the speaker refers to himself as "the heir of all the ages, in the foremost files of time."

'I thought of the flickering pillars and of my theory of an underground ventilation. I began to suspect their true import. And what, I
wondered, was this Lemur[1] doing in my scheme of a perfectly balanced organization? How was it related to the indolent serenity of
the beautiful Overworlders? And what was hidden down there,
at the foot of that shaft? I sat upon the edge of the well telling
myself that, at any rate, there was nothing to fear, and that there I
must descend for the solution of my difficulties. And withal I was
absolutely afraid to go! As I hesitated, two of the beautiful upper-
world people came running in their amorous sport across the daylight into the shadow. The male pursued the female, flinging flowers
at her as he ran.

'They seemed distressed to find me, my arm against the overturned pillar, peering down the well. Apparently it was considered
bad form to remark these apertures; for when I pointed to this one,
and tried to frame a question about it in their tongue, they were still
more visibly distressed and turned away. But they were interested by
my matches, and I struck some to amuse them. I tried them again
about the well, and again I failed. So presently I left them, meaning
to go back to Weena, and see what I could get from her. But my
mind was already in revolution; my guesses and impressions were
slipping and sliding to a new adjustment. I had now a clue to the
import of these wells, to the ventilating towers, to the mystery of the
ghosts: to say nothing of a hint at the meaning of the bronze gates
and the fate of the Time Machine! And very vaguely there came a
suggestion towards the solution of the economic problem that had
puzzled me.

'Here was the new view. Plainly, this second species of Man was
subterranean. There were three circumstances in particular which
made me think that its rare emergence above ground was the outcome
of a long-continued underground habit. In the first place, there was
the bleached look common in most animals that live largely in the
dark—the white fish of the Kentucky caves, for instance.[2] Then, those
large eyes, with that capacity for reflecting light, are common features of nocturnal things—witness the owl and the cat. And last of
all, that evident confusion in the sunshine, that hasty yet fumbling
and awkward flight towards dark shadow, and that peculiar carriage
of the head while in the light—all reinforced the theory of an extreme
sensitiveness of the retina.

'Beneath my feet then the earth must be tunnelled enormously, and
these tunnellings were the habitat of the New Race. The presence of

1. A lemur is a ghost or spirit of the dead; it is also a small nocturnal mammal, thought by
   Charles Darwin to be one of mankind's more distant primate ancestors.
2. The carp indigenous to the sunless lakes of Kentucky's Mammoth Cave are colorless (not
   white) and blind.

ventilating-shafts and wells along the hill slopes—everywhere, in fact, except along the river valley—showed how universal were its ramifications. What so natural, then, as to assume that it was in this artificial Underworld that such work as was necessary to the comfort of the daylight race was done? The notion was so plausible that I at once accepted it, and went on to assume the *how* of this splitting of the human species. I dare say you will anticipate the shape of my theory, though, for myself, I very soon felt that it fell far short of the truth.

'At first, proceeding from the problems of our own age, it seemed clear as daylight to me that the gradual widening of the present merely temporary and social difference between the Capitalist and the Labourer, was the key to the whole position. No doubt it will seem grotesque enough to you—and wildly incredible!—and yet even now there are existing circumstances to point that way. There is a tendency to utilize underground space for the less ornamental purposes of civilization; there is the Metropolitan Railway in London, for instance, there are new electric railways, there are subways, there are underground workrooms and restaurants, and they increase and multiply.[3] Evidently, I thought, this tendency had increased till Industry had gradually lost its birthright in the sky. I mean that it had gone deeper and deeper into larger and ever larger underground factories, spending a still-increasing amount of its time therein, till, in the end—! Even now, does not an East-end[4] worker live in such artificial conditions as practically to be cut off from the natural surface of the earth?

'Again, the exclusive tendency of richer people—due, no doubt, to the increasing refinement of their education, and the widening gulf between them and the rude violence of the poor—is already leading to the closing, in their interest, of considerable portions of the surface of the land. About London, for instance, perhaps half the prettier country is shut in against intrusion. And this same widening gulf— which is due to the length and expense of the higher educational process and the increased facilities for and temptations towards refined habits on the part of the rich—will make that exchange between class and class, that promotion by intermarriage which at present retards the splitting of our species along lines of social stratification, less and less frequent. So, in the end, above ground you must have the Haves, pursuing pleasure and comfort and beauty, and below ground the Have-nots; the Workers getting continually

3. London's Metropolitan Railway, the world's first underground railway, opened in 1863. The first electric underground railway in the city opened in 1890. "Subways" refers not to train lines but to pedestrian underpasses, such as the famous walkway opened in 1843 under the Thames at Greenwich.
4. The East End of London was known for its squalid slums and the appalling working conditions in its sweatshops, many of which were located in basements.

adapted to the conditions of their labour. Once they were there, they would, no doubt, have to pay rent, and not a little of it, for the ventilation of their caverns; and if they refused, they would starve or be suffocated for arrears. Such of them as were so constituted as to be miserable and rebellious would die; and, in the end, the balance being permanent, the survivors would become as well adapted to the conditions of underground life, and as happy in their way, as the Overworld people were to theirs. As it seemed to me, the refined beauty and the etiolated pallor followed naturally enough.

'The great triumph of Humanity I had dreamed of took a different shape in my mind. It had been no such triumph of moral education and general co-operation as I had imagined. Instead, I saw a real aristocracy, armed with a perfected science and working to a logical conclusion the industrial system of today. Its triumph had not been simply a triumph over nature, but a triumph over nature and the fellow-man. This, I must warn you, was my theory at the time. I had no convenient cicerone[5] in the pattern of the Utopian books. My explanation may be absolutely wrong. I still think it is the most plausible one. But even on this supposition the balanced civilization that was at last attained must have long since passed its zenith, and was now fallen into decay. The too-perfect security of the Overworlders had led them to a slow movement of degeneration, to a general dwindling in size, strength, and intelligence. That I could see clearly enough already. What had happened to the Undergrounders I did not yet suspect; but, from what I had seen of the Morlocks—that, by the bye, was the name by which these creatures were called—I could imagine that the modification of the human type was even far more profound than among the "Eloi," the beautiful race that I already knew.

'Then came troublesome doubts. Why had the Morlocks taken my Time Machine? For I felt sure it was they who had taken it. Why, too, if the Eloi were masters, could they not restore the machine to me? And why were they so terribly afraid of the dark? I proceeded, as I have said, to question Weena about this Underworld, but here again I was disappointed. At first she would not understand my questions, and presently she refused to answer them. She shivered as though the topic was unendurable. And when I pressed her, perhaps a little harshly, she burst into tears. They were the only tears, except my own, I ever saw in that Golden Age. When I saw them I ceased abruptly to trouble about the Morlocks, and was only concerned in banishing these signs of her human inheritance from Weena's eyes. And very soon she was smiling and clapping her hands, while I solemnly burnt a match.

5. A tour guide.

IX. The Morlocks

'It may seem odd to you, but it was two days before I could follow up the new-found clue in what was manifestly the proper way. I felt a peculiar shrinking from those pallid bodies. They were just the half-bleached colour of the worms and things one sees preserved in spirit in a zoological museum. And they were filthily cold to the touch. Probably my shrinking was largely due to the sympathetic influence of the Eloi, whose disgust of the Morlocks I now began to appreciate.

'The next night I did not sleep well. Probably my health was a little disordered. I was oppressed with perplexity and doubt. Once or twice I had a feeling of intense fear for which I could perceive no definite reason. I remember creeping noiselessly into the great hall where the little people were sleeping in the moonlight—that night Weena was among them—and feeling reassured by their presence. It occurred to me, even then, that in the course of a few days the moon must pass through its last quarter, and the nights grow dark, when the appearances of these unpleasant creatures from below, these whitened Lemurs, this new vermin that had replaced the old, might be more abundant. And on both these days I had the restless feeling of one who shirks an inevitable duty. I felt assured that the Time Machine was only to be recovered by boldly penetrating these mysteries of underground. Yet I could not face the mystery. If only I had had a companion it would have been different. But I was so horribly alone, and even to clamber down into the darkness of the well appalled me. I don't know if you will understand my feeling, but I never felt quite safe at my back.

'It was this restlessness, this insecurity, perhaps, that drove me further and further afield in my exploring expeditions. Going to the south-westward towards the rising country that is now called Combe Wood, I observed far off, in the direction of nineteenth-century Banstead, a vast green structure, different in character from any I had hitherto seen.[1] It was larger than the largest of the palaces or ruins I knew, and the façade had an Oriental look: the face of it having the lustre, as well as the pale-green tint, a kind of bluish-green, of a certain type of Chinese porcelain. This difference in aspect suggested a difference in use, and I was minded to push on and explore. But the day was growing late, and I had come upon the sight of the place after a long and tiring circuit; so I resolved to hold over the adventure for the following day, and I returned to the welcome and the caresses of little Weena. But next morning I perceived clearly enough that my curiosity regarding the Palace of Green Porcelain

1. Coombe (not Combe) Wood is about three and a half miles south of the Time Traveller's home base of Richmond. The area around Banstead, four miles past Coombe Wood to the southeast, would be visible due to its elevation.

was a piece of self-deception, to enable me to shirk, by another day, an experience I dreaded. I resolved I would make the descent without further waste of time, and started out in the early morning towards a well near the ruins of granite and aluminium.

'Little Weena ran with me. She danced beside me to the well, but when she saw me lean over the mouth and look downward, she seemed strangely disconcerted. "Good-bye, little Weena," I said, kissing her; and then, putting her down, I began to feel over the parapet for the climbing hooks. Rather hastily, I may as well confess, for I feared my courage might leak away! At first she watched me in amazement. Then she gave a most piteous cry, and, running to me, began to pull at me with her little hands. I think her opposition nerved me rather to proceed. I shook her off, perhaps a little roughly, and in another moment I was in the throat of the well. I saw her agonized face over the parapet, and smiled to reassure her. Then I had to look down at the unstable hooks to which I clung.

'I had to clamber down a shaft of perhaps two hundred yards. The descent was effected by means of metallic bars projecting from the sides of the well, and these being adapted to the needs of a creature much smaller and lighter than myself, I was speedily cramped and fatigued by the descent. And not simply fatigued! One of the bars bent suddenly under my weight, and almost swung me off into the blackness beneath. For a moment I hung by one hand, and after that experience I did not dare to rest again. Though my arms and back were presently acutely painful, I went on clambering down the sheer descent with as quick a motion as possible. Glancing upward, I saw the aperture, a small blue disc, in which a star was visible, while little Weena's head showed as a round black projection. The thudding sound of a machine below grew louder and more oppressive. Everything save that little disc above was profoundly dark, and when I looked up again Weena had disappeared.

'I was in an agony of discomfort. I had some thought of trying to go up the shaft again, and leave the Underworld alone. But even while I turned this over in my mind I continued to descend. At last, with intense relief, I saw dimly coming up, a foot to the right of me, a slender loophole in the wall. Swinging myself in, I found it was the aperture of a narrow horizontal tunnel in which I could lie down and rest. It was not too soon. My arms ached, my back was cramped, and I was trembling with the prolonged terror of a fall. Besides this, the unbroken darkness had had a distressing effect upon my eyes. The air was full of the throb-and-hum of machinery pumping air down the shaft.

'I do not know how long I lay. I was aroused by a soft hand touching my face. Starting up in the darkness I snatched at my matches and, hastily striking one, I saw three stooping white creatures similar to the one I had seen above ground in the ruin, hastily retreating before the light. Living, as they did, in what appeared to be impenetrable darkness, their eyes were abnormally large and sensitive, just as are the pupils of the abysmal fishes, and they reflected the light in the same way. I have no doubt they could see me in that rayless obscurity, and they did not seem to have any fear of me apart from the light. But, so soon as I struck a match in order to see them, they fled incontinently, vanishing into dark gutters and tunnels, from which their eyes glared at me in the strangest fashion.

'I tried to call to them, but the language they had was apparently different from that of the overworld people; so that I was needs left to my own unaided efforts, and the thought of flight before exploration was even then in my mind. But I said to myself, "You are in for it now," and, feeling my way along the tunnel, I found the noise of machinery grow louder. Presently the walls fell away from me, and I came to a large open space, and, striking another match, saw that I had entered a vast arched cavern, which stretched into utter darkness beyond the range of my light. The view I had of it was as much as one could see in the burning of a match.

'Necessarily my memory is vague. Great shapes like big machines rose out of the dimness, and cast grotesque black shadows, in which dim spectral Morlocks sheltered from the glare. The place, by the bye, was very stuffy and oppressive, and the faint halitus[2] of freshly-shed blood was in the air. Some way down the central vista was a little table of white metal, laid with what seemed a meal. The Morlocks at any rate were carnivorous! Even at the time, I remember wondering what large animal could have survived to furnish the red joint I saw. It was all very indistinct: the heavy smell, the big unmeaning shapes, the obscene figures lurking in the shadows, and only waiting for the darkness to come at me again! Then the match burnt down, and stung my fingers, and fell, a wriggling red spot in the blackness.

'I have thought since how particularly ill-equipped I was for such an experience. When I had started with the Time Machine, I had started with the absurd assumption that the men of the Future would certainly be infinitely ahead of ourselves in all their appliances. I had come without arms, without medicine, without anything to smoke—at times I missed tobacco frightfully!—even without enough matches. If only I had thought of a Kodak![3] I could have flashed that glimpse of the Underworld in a second, and examined it at leisure. But, as it was, I stood there with only the weapons and the powers that Nature had endowed me with—hands, feet, and teeth; these, and four safety matches that still remained to me.

2. Exhalation.
3. The portable camera using roll film invented by George Eastman was still very much a novelty in 1895.

'I was afraid to push my way in among all this machinery in the dark, and it was only with my last glimpse of light I discovered that my store of matches had run low. It had never occurred to me until that moment that there was any need to economize them, and I had wasted almost half the box in astonishing the Overworlders, to whom fire was a novelty. Now, as I say, I had four left, and while I stood in the dark, a hand touched mine, lank fingers came feeling over my face, and I was sensible of a peculiar unpleasant odour. I fancied I heard the breathing of a crowd of these dreadful little beings about me. I felt the box of matches in my hand being gently disengaged, and other hands behind me plucking at my clothing. The sense of these unseen creatures examining me was indescribably unpleasant. The sudden realization of my ignorance of their ways of thinking and doing came home to me very vividly in the darkness. I shouted at them as loudly as I could. They started away, and then I could feel them approaching me again. They clutched at me more boldly, whispering odd sounds to each other. I shivered violently, and shouted again—rather discordantly. This time they were not so seriously alarmed, and they made a queer laughing noise as they came back at me. I will confess I was horribly frightened. I determined to strike another match and escape under the protection of its glare. I did so, and eking out the flicker with a scrap of paper from my pocket, I made good my retreat to the narrow tunnel. But I had scarce entered this when my light was blown out, and in the blackness I could hear the Morlocks rustling like wind among leaves, and pattering like the rain, as they hurried after me.

'In a moment I was clutched by several hands, and there was no mistaking that they were trying to haul me back. I struck another light, and waved it in their dazzled faces. You can scarce imagine how nauseatingly inhuman they looked—those pale, chinless faces and great, lidless, pinkish-grey eyes!—as they stared in their blindness and bewilderment. But I did not stay to look, I promise you: I retreated again, and when my second match had ended, I struck my third. It had almost burnt through when I reached the opening into the shaft. I lay down on the edge, for the throb of the great pump below made me giddy. Then I felt sideways for the projecting hooks, and, as I did so, my feet were grasped from behind, and I was violently tugged backward. I lit my last match . . . and it incontinently went out. But I had my hand on the climbing bars now, and, kicking violently, I disengaged myself from the clutches of the Morlocks, and was speedily clambering up the shaft, while they stayed peering and blinking up at me: all but one little wretch who followed me for some way, and well-nigh secured my boot as a trophy.

'That climb seemed interminable to me. With the last twenty or thirty feet of it a deadly nausea came upon me. I had the greatest difficulty in keeping my hold. The last few yards was a frightful struggle against this faintness. Several times my head swam, and I felt all the sensations of falling. At last, however, I got over the well-mouth somehow, and staggered out of the ruin into the blinding sunlight. I fell upon my face. Even the soil smelt sweet and clean. Then I remember Weena kissing my hands and ears, and the voices of others among the Eloi. Then, for a time, I was insensible.

X. When the Night Came

'Now, indeed, I seemed in a worse case than before. Hitherto, except during my night's anguish at the loss of the Time Machine, I had felt a sustaining hope of ultimate escape, but that hope was staggered by these new discoveries. Hitherto I had merely thought myself impeded by the childish simplicity of the little people, and by some unknown forces which I had only to understand to overcome; but there was an altogether new element in the sickening quality of the Morlocks—a something inhuman and malign. Instinctively I loathed them. Before, I had felt as a man might feel who had fallen into a pit: my concern was with the pit and how to get out of it. Now I felt like a beast in a trap, whose enemy would come upon him soon.

'The enemy I dreaded may surprise you. It was the darkness of the new moon. Weena had put this into my head by some at first incomprehensible remarks about the Dark Nights. It was not now such a very difficult problem to guess what the coming Dark Nights might mean. The moon was on the wane: each night there was a longer interval of darkness. And I now understood to some slight degree at least the reason of the fear of the little upper-world people for the dark. I wondered vaguely what foul villainy it might be that the Morlocks did under the new moon. I felt pretty sure now that my second hypothesis was all wrong. The upper-world people might once have been the favoured aristocracy, and the Morlocks their mechanical servants; but that had long since passed away. The two species that had resulted from the evolution of man were sliding down towards, or had already arrived at, an altogether new relationship. The Eloi, like the Carlovingian kings,[1] had decayed to a mere beautiful futility. They still possessed the earth on sufferance: since the Morlocks, subterranean for innumerable generations, had come at last to find the daylit surface intolerable. And the Morlocks made their garments, I inferred, and maintained them in their habitual needs, perhaps through the survival of an old habit of service. They did it as a standing horse paws with his foot, or as a man enjoys killing animals in sport: because ancient and departed necessities had impressed it on the organism.

1. The Carlovingian line of kings descending from the Emperor Charlemagne (742–814) were proverbial for their weakness as rulers.

But, clearly, the old order was already in part reversed. The Nemesis[2] of the delicate ones was creeping on apace. Ages ago, thousands of generations ago, man had thrust his brother man out of the ease and the sunshine. And now that brother was coming back—changed! Already the Eloi had begun to learn one old lesson anew. They were becoming re-acquainted with Fear. And suddenly there came into my head the memory of the meat I had seen in the under-world. It seemed odd how it floated into my mind: not stirred up as it were by the current of any meditations, but coming in almost like a question from outside. I tried to recall the form of it. I had a vague sense of something familiar, but I could not tell what it was at the time.

'Still, however helpless the little people in the presence of their mysterious Fear, I was differently constituted. I came out of this age of ours, this ripe prime of the human race, when Fear does not paralyse and mystery has lost its terrors. I at least would defend myself. Without further delay I determined to make myself arms and a fastness where I might sleep. With that refuge as a base, I could face this strange world with some of that confidence I had lost in realizing to what creatures night by night I lay exposed. I felt I could never sleep again until my bed was secure from them. I shuddered with horror to think how they must already have examined me.

'I wandered during the afternoon along the valley of the Thames, but found nothing that commended itself to my mind as inaccessible. All the buildings and trees seemed easily practicable to such dexterous climbers as the Morlocks, to judge by their wells, must be. Then the tall pinnacles of the Palace of Green Porcelain and the polished gleam of its walls came back to my memory; and in the evening, taking Weena like a child upon my shoulder, I went up the hills towards the south-west. The distance, I had reckoned, was seven or eight miles, but it must have been nearer eighteen. I had first seen the place on a moist afternoon when distances are deceptively diminished. In addition, the heel of one of my shoes was loose, and a nail was working though the sole—they were comfortable old shoes I wore about indoors—so that I was lame. And it was already long past sunset when I came in sight of the palace, silhouetted black against the pale yellow of the sky.

'Weena had been hugely delighted when I began to carry her, but after a time she desired me to let her down, and ran along by the side of me, occasionally darting off on either hand to pick flowers to stick in my pockets. My pockets had always puzzled Weena, but at the last she had concluded that they were an eccentric kind of vases for floral decoration. At least she utilized them for that purpose. And that reminds me! In changing my jacket I found . . .'

2. The Greek goddess of vengeance.

The Time Traveller paused, put his hand into his pocket, and silently placed two withered flowers, not unlike very large white mallows, upon the little table. Then he resumed his narrative.

'As the hush of evening crept over the world and we proceeded over the hill crest towards Wimbledon,[3] Weena grew tired and wanted to return to the house of grey stone. But I pointed out the distant pinnacles of the Palace of Green Porcelain to her, and contrived to make her understand that we were seeking a refuge there from her Fear. You know that great pause that comes upon things before the dusk? Even the breeze stops in the trees. To me there is always an air of expectation about that evening stillness. The sky was clear, remote, and empty save for a few horizontal bars far down in the sunset. Well, that night the expectation took the colour of my fears. In that darkling calm my senses seemed preternaturally sharpened. I fancied I could even feel the hollowness of the ground beneath my feet: could, indeed, almost see through it the Morlocks on their ant-hill going hither and thither and waiting for the dark. In my excitement I fancied that they would receive my invasion of their burrows as a declaration of war. And why had they taken my Time Machine?

'So we went on in the quiet, and the twilight deepened into night. The clear blue of the distance faded, and one star after another came out. The ground grew dim and the trees black. Weena's fears and her fatigue grew upon her. I took her in my arms and talked to her and caressed her. Then, as the darkness grew deeper, she put her arms round my neck, and, closing her eyes, tightly pressed her face against my shoulder. So we went down a long slope into a valley, and there in the dimness I almost walked into a little river. This I waded, and went up the opposite side of the valley, past a number of sleeping-houses, and by a statue—a Faun,[4] or some such figure, *minus* the head. Here, too, were acacias. So far I had seen nothing of the Morlocks, but it was yet early in the night, and the darker hours before the old moon rose were still to come.

'From the brow of the next hill I saw a thick wood spreading wide and black before me. I hesitated at this. I could see no end to it, either to the right or the left. Feeling tired—my feet in particular, were very sore—I carefully lowered Weena from my shoulder as I halted, and sat down upon the turf. I could no longer see the Palace of Green Porcelain, and I was in doubt of my direction. I looked into the thickness of the wood and thought of what it might hide. Under that dense tangle of branches one would be out of sight of the stars. Even were there no other lurking danger—a danger I did not care to let my imagination loose upon—there would still be all the roots to

3. About five miles southeast of Richmond.
4. Part human, part goat, the faun is often associated with sensuality.

stumble over and the tree-boles to strike against. I was very tired, too, after the excitements of the day; so I decided that I would not face it, but would pass the night upon the open hill.

'Weena, I was glad to find, was fast asleep. I carefully wrapped her in my jacket, and sat down beside her to wait for the moonrise. The hill-side was quiet and deserted, but from the black of the wood there came now and then a stir of living things. Above me shone the stars, for the night was very clear. I felt a certain sense of friendly comfort in their twinkling. All the old constellations had gone from the sky, however: that slow movement which is imperceptible in a hundred human lifetimes, had long since rearranged them in unfamiliar groupings. But the Milky Way, it seemed to me, was still the same tattered streamer of star-dust as of yore. Southward (as I judged it) was a very bright red star that was new to me: it was even more splendid than our own green Sirius. And amid all these scintillating points of light one bright planet shone kindly and steadily like the face of an old friend.[5]

'Looking at these stars suddenly dwarfed my own troubles and all the gravities of terrestrial life. I thought of their unfathomable distance, and the slow inevitable drift of their movements out of the unknown past into the unknown future. I thought of the great precessional cycle that the pole of the earth describes. Only forty times had that silent revolution occurred during all the years that I had traversed.[6] And during these few revolutions all the activity, all the traditions, the complex organizations, the nations, languages, literatures, aspirations, even the mere memory of Man as I knew him, had been swept out of existence. Instead were these frail creatures who had forgotten their high ancestry, and the white Things of which I went in terror. Then I thought of the Great Fear that was between the two species, and for the first time, with a sudden shiver, came the clear knowledge of what the meat I had seen might be. Yet it was too horrible! I looked at little Weena sleeping beside me, her face white and starlike under the stars, and forthwith dismissed the thought.

'Through that long night I held my mind off the Morlocks as well as I could, and whiled away the time by trying to fancy I could find signs of the old constellations in the new confusion. The sky kept very clear, except for a hazy cloud or so. No doubt I dozed at times. Then, as my vigil wore on, came a faintness in the eastward sky, like the reflection of some colourless fire, and the old moon rose, thin

5. Sirius is the brightest star of the night sky. The "one bright planet" is Venus.
6. Due to the gravitational pull of the sun and moon, the earth wobbles slightly on its axis, which in turn makes the fixed stars appear to move in a circle in the sky. One complete circle of the earth's axis takes approximately 25,800 years and is called a precessional cycle. The Time Traveller's math is therefore a bit off: about 31 precessional cycles have occurred since he left home at the end of the nineteenth century.

and peaked and white. And close behind, and overtaking it, and overflowing it, the dawn came, pale at first, and then growing pink and warm. No Morlocks had approached us. Indeed, I had seen none upon the hill that night. And in the confidence of renewed day it almost seemed to me that my fear had been unreasonable. I stood up and found my foot with the loose heel swollen at the ankle and painful under the heel; so I sat down again, took off my shoes, and flung them away.

'I awakened Weena, and we went down into the wood, now green and pleasant instead of black and forbidding. We found some fruit wherewith to break our fast. We soon met others of the dainty ones, laughing and dancing in the sunlight as though there was no such thing in nature as the night. And then I thought once more of the meat that I had seen. I felt assured now of what it was, and from the bottom of my heart I pitied this last feeble rill[7] from the great flood of humanity. Clearly, at some time in the Long-Ago of human decay the Morlocks' food had run short. Possibly they had lived on rats and such-like vermin. Even now man is far less discriminating and exclusive in his food than he was—far less than any monkey. His prejudice against human flesh is no deep-seated instinct. And so these inhuman sons of men—! I tried to look at the thing in a scientific spirit. After all, they were less human and more remote than our cannibal ancestors of three or four thousand years ago. And the intelligence that would have made this state of things a torment had gone. Why should I trouble myself? These Eloi were mere fatted cattle, which the ant-like Morlocks preserved and preyed upon—probably saw to the breeding of. And there was Weena dancing at my side!

'Then I tried to preserve myself from the horror that was coming upon me, by regarding it as a rigorous punishment of human selfishness. Man had been content to live in ease and delight upon the labours of his fellow-man, had taken Necessity as his watchword and excuse, and in the fullness of time Necessity had come home to him. I even tried a Carlyle-like scorn of this wretched aristocracy-in-decay.[8] But this attitude of mind was impossible. However great their intellectual degradation, the Eloi had kept too much of the human form not to claim my sympathy, and to make me perforce a sharer in their degradation and their Fear.

'I had at that time very vague ideas as to the course I should pursue. My first was to secure some safe place of refuge, and to make myself such arms of metal or stone as I could contrive. That necessity

---

7. A small stream.
8. Scornful passages detailing the decline of European aristocracy occur in a number of the works of the Scottish essayist and historian Thomas Carlyle (1795–1881), most notably *Sartor Resartus* (1834), *The French Revolution* (1837), and *Past and Present* (1843). The Time Traveller could be thinking of any or all or none of these.

was immediate. In the next place, I hoped to procure some means of fire, so that I should have the weapon of a torch at hand, for nothing, I knew, would be more efficient against these Morlocks. Then I wanted to arrange some contrivance to break open the doors of bronze under the White Sphinx. I had in mind a battering-ram. I had a persuasion that if I could enter these doors and carry a blaze of light before me I should discover the Time Machine and escape. I could not imagine the Morlocks were strong enough to move it far away. Weena I had resolved to bring with me to our own time. And turning such schemes over in my mind I pursued our way towards the building which my fancy had chosen as our dwelling.

XI. *The Palace of Green Porcelain*

'I found the Palace of Green Porcelain, when we approached it about noon, deserted and falling into ruin. Only ragged vestiges of glass remained in its windows, and great sheets of the green facing had fallen away from the corroded metallic framework. It lay very high upon a turfy down, and looking north-eastward before I entered it, I was surprised to see a large estuary, or even creek, where I judged Wandsworth or Battersea must once have been.[1] I thought then— though I never followed up the thought—of what might have happened, or might be happening, to the living things in the sea.

'The material of the Palace proved on examination to be indeed porcelain, and along the face of it I saw an inscription in some unknown character. I thought, rather foolishly, that Weena might help me to interpret this, but I only learnt that the bare idea of writing had never entered her head. She always seemed to me, I fancy, more human than she was, perhaps because her affection was so human.

'Within the big valves of the door—which were open and bro-ken—we found, instead of the customary hall, a long gallery lit by many side windows. At the first glance I was reminded of a museum. The tiled floor was thick with dust, and a remarkable array of miscel-laneous objects was shrouded in the same grey covering. Then I per-ceived, standing strange and gaunt in the centre of the hall, what was clearly the lower part of a huge skeleton. I recognized by the oblique feet that it was some extinct creature after the fashion of the Megatherium.[2] The skull and the upper bones lay beside it in the thick dust, and in one place, where rainwater had dropped through a leak in the roof, the thing itself had been worn away. Further in the gallery was the huge skeleton barrel of a Brontosaurus.[3] My museum hypothesis was confirmed. Going towards the side I found what

1. Areas of London south of the Thames, a few miles east of Richmond.
2. An extinct, elephant-sized ground sloth.
3. The largest of the dinosaurs (now called apatosaurus).

appeared to be sloping shelves, and, clearing away the thick dust, I found the old familiar glass cases of our own time. But they must have been air-tight, to judge from the fair preservation of some of their contents.

'Clearly we stood among the ruins of some latter-day South Kensington![4] Here, apparently, was the Palæontological Section, and a very splendid array of fossils it must have been, though the inevitable process of decay that had been staved off for a time, and had, through the extinction of bacteria and fungi, lost ninety-nine hundredths of its force, was, nevertheless, with extreme sureness if with extreme slowness at work again upon all its treasures. Here and there I found traces of the little people in the shape of rare fossils broken to pieces or threaded in strings upon reeds. And the cases had in some instances been bodily removed—by the Morlocks as I judged. The place was very silent. The thick dust deadened our footsteps. Weena, who had been rolling a sea-urchin[5] down the sloping glass of a case, presently came, as I stared about me, and very quietly took my hand and stood beside me.

'And at first I was so much surprised by this ancient monument of an intellectual age that I gave no thought to the possibilities it presented. Even my pre-occupation about the Time Machine receded a little from my mind.

'To judge from the size of the place, this Palace of Green Porcelain had a great deal more in it than a Gallery of Palæontology; possibly historical galleries; it might be, even a library! To me, at least in my present circumstances, these would be vastly more interesting than this spectacle of old-time geology in decay. Exploring, I found another short gallery running transversely to the first. This appeared to be devoted to minerals, and the sight of a block of sulphur set my mind running on gunpowder. But I could find no saltpetre;[6] indeed, no nitrates of any kind. Doubtless they had deliquesced ages ago. Yet the sulphur hung in my mind, and set up a train of thinking. As for the rest of the contents of that gallery, though, on the whole, they were the best preserved of all I saw, I had little interest. I am no specialist in mineralogy, and I went on down a very ruinous aisle running parallel to the first hall I had entered. Apparently this section had been devoted to natural history, but everything had long since passed out of recognition. A few shrivelled and blackened vestiges of what had once been stuffed animals, desiccated mummies in jars that had once held spirit, a brown dust of departed plants: that was

---

4. The London borough of South Kensington was (and is still) famous for its museums, including the Geological Museum, the Science Museum, and the Natural History Museum. Paleontology is the study of fossils.
5. The shell of a round marine creature.
6. The primary ingredient in gunpowder.

all! I was sorry for that, because I should have been glad to trace the patient re-adjustments by which the conquest of animated nature had been attained. Then we came to a gallery of simply colossal proportions, but singularly ill-lit, the floor of it running downward at a slight angle from the end at which I entered. At intervals white globes hung from the ceiling—many of them cracked and smashed—which suggested that originally the place had been artificially lit. Here I was more in my element, for rising on either side of me were the huge bulks of big machines, all greatly corroded and many broken down, but some still fairly complete. You know I have a certain weakness for mechanism, and I was inclined to linger among these: the more so as for the most part they had the interest of puzzles, and I could make only the vaguest guesses at what they were for. I fancied that if I could solve their puzzles I should find myself in possession of powers that might be of use against the Morlocks.

'Suddenly Weena came very close to my side. So suddenly that she startled me. Had it not been for her I do not think I should have noticed that the floor of the gallery sloped at all.[7] The end I had come in at was quite above ground, and was lit by rare slit-like windows. As you went down the length, the ground came up against these windows, until at last there was a pit like the "area"[8] of a London house before each, and only a narrow line of daylight at the top. I went slowly along, puzzling about the machines, and had been too intent upon them to notice the gradual diminution of the light, until Weena's increasing apprehensions drew my attention. Then I saw that the gallery ran down at last into a thick darkness. I hesitated, and then, as I looked round me, I saw that the dust was less abundant and its surface less even. Further away towards the dimness, it appeared to be broken by a number of small narrow footprints. My sense of the immediate presence of the Morlocks revived at that. I felt that I was wasting my time in this academic examination of machinery. I called to mind that it was already far advanced in the afternoon, and that I still had no weapon, no refuge, and no means of making a fire. And then down in the remote blackness of the gallery I heard a peculiar pattering, and the same odd noises I had heard down the well.

'I took Weena's hand. Then, struck with a sudden idea, I left her and turned to a machine from which projected a lever not unlike those in a signal-box.[9] Clambering upon the stand, and grasping this

7. It may be, of course, that the floor did not slope, but that the museum was built into the side of a hill.—Ed. [*Wells's note*].
8. The small courtyard, slightly below street level, in front of the basement windows of a house.
9. The control tower in a rail yard. Switches and signals would be operated by means of large wooden or metal levers.

lever in my hands, I put all my weight upon it sideways. Suddenly Weena, deserted in the central aisle, began to whimper. I had judged the strength of the lever pretty correctly, for it snapped after a minute's strain, and I rejoined her with a mace in my hand more than sufficient, I judged, for any Morlock skull I might encounter. And I longed very much to kill a Morlock or so. Very inhuman, you may think, to want to go killing one's own descendants! But it was impossible, somehow, to feel any humanity in the things. Only my disinclination to leave Weena, and a persuasion that if I began to slake my thirst for murder my Time Machine might suffer, restrained me from going straight down the gallery and killing the brutes I heard.

'Well, mace in one hand and Weena in the other, I went out of that gallery and into another and still larger one, which at the first glance reminded me of a military chapel hung with tattered flags. The brown and charred rags that hung from the sides of it, I presently recognized as the decaying vestiges of books. They had long since dropped to pieces, and every semblance of print had left them. But here and there were warped boards and cracked metallic clasps that told the tale well enough. Had I been a literary man I might, perhaps, have moralized upon the futility of all ambition. But as it was, the thing that struck me with keenest force was the enormous waste of labour to which this sombre wilderness of rotting paper testified. At the time I will confess that I thought chiefly of the *Philosophical Transactions*[1] and my own seventeen papers upon physical optics.

'Then, going up a broad staircase, we came to what may once have been a gallery of technical chemistry. And here I had not a little hope of useful discoveries. Except at one end where the roof had collapsed, this gallery was well preserved. I went eagerly to every unbroken case. And at last, in one of the really air-tight cases, I found a box of matches. Very eagerly I tried them. They were perfectly good. They were not even damp. I turned to Weena. "Dance," I cried to her in her own tongue. For now I had a weapon indeed against the horrible creatures we feared. And so, in that derelict museum, upon the thick soft carpeting of dust, to Weena's huge delight, I solemnly performed a kind of composite dance, whistling *The Land of the Leal* as cheerfully as I could. In part it was a modest *cancan*, in part a step dance, in part a skirt dance (so far as my tail-coat permitted), and in part original.[2] For I am naturally inventive, as you know.

'Now, I still think that for this box of matches to have escaped the wear of time for immemorial years was a most strange, as for me it was a most fortunate, thing. Yet, oddly enough, I found a far unlikelier

1. The journal of the Royal Society, Great Britain's most distinguished scientific association.
2. A Scots ballad. "The Land o' the Leal" is a Scots phrase for the realm of the departed—that is, Heaven. The *cancan*, the step dance, and the skirt dance are all quite lively dances.

substance, and that was camphor.[3] I found it in a sealed jar, that by chance, I suppose, had been really hermetically sealed. I fancied at first that it was paraffin wax, and smashed the glass accordingly. But the odour of camphor was unmistakable. In the universal decay this volatile substance had chanced to survive, perhaps through many thousands of centuries. It reminded me of a sepia painting I had once seen done from the ink of a fossil Belemnite that must have perished and become fossilized millions of years ago.[4] I was about to throw it away, but I remembered that it was inflammable and burnt with a good bright flame—was, in fact, an excellent candle—and I put it in my pocket. I found no explosives, however, nor any means of breaking down the bronze doors. As yet my iron crowbar was the most helpful thing I had chanced upon. Nevertheless, I left that gallery greatly elated.

'I cannot tell you all the story of that long afternoon. It would require a great effort of memory to recall my explorations in at all the proper order. I remember a long gallery of rusting stands of arms, and how I hesitated between my crowbar and a hatchet or a sword. I could not carry both, however, and my bar of iron promised best against the bronze gates. There were numbers of guns, pistols, and rifles. The most were masses of rust, but many were of some new metal, and still fairly sound. But any cartridges or powder there may once have been had rotted into dust. One corner I saw was charred and shattered: perhaps, I thought, by an explosion among the specimens. In another place was a vast array of idols —Polynesian, Mexican, Grecian, Phoenician, every country on earth, I should think. And here, yielding to an irresistible impulse, I wrote my name upon the nose of a steatite[5] monster from South America that particularly took my fancy.

'As the evening drew on, my interest waned. I went through gallery after gallery, dusty, silent, often ruinous, the exhibits sometimes mere heaps of rust and lignite,[6] sometimes fresher. In one place I suddenly found myself near the model of a tin mine, and then by the merest accident I discovered, in an air-tight case, two dynamite cartridges! I shouted "Eureka", and smashed the case with joy. Then came a doubt. I hesitated. Then, selecting a little side gallery, I made my essay. I never felt such a disappointment as I did in waiting five, ten, fifteen minutes for an explosion that never came. Of course the things were dummies, as I might have guessed from

---

3. A whitish crystalline substance that is highly flammable.
4. Sepia is a brown pigment obtained from the ink-like secretions of cuttlefish; a Belemnite is the fossilized backbone of a long-extinct ancestor of the cuttlefish.
5. Soapstone.
6. Carbonized wood.

their presence. I really believe that, had they not been so, I should have rushed off incontinently and blown Sphinx, bronze doors, and (as it proved) my chances of finding the Time Machine, all together into non-existence.

'It was after that, I think, that we came to a little open court within the palace. It was turfed, and had three fruit trees. So we rested and refreshed ourselves. Towards sunset I began to consider our position. Night was creeping upon us, and my inaccessible hiding-place had still to be found. But that troubled me very little now. I had in my possession a thing that was, perhaps, the best of all defences against the Morlocks—I had matches! I had the camphor in my pocket, too, if a blaze were needed. It seemed to me that the best thing we could do would be to pass the night in the open, pro-tected by a fire. In the morning there was the getting of the Time Machine. Towards that, as yet, I had only my iron mace. But now, with my growing knowledge, I felt very differently towards those bronze doors. Up to this, I had refrained from forcing them, largely because of the mystery on the other side. They had never impressed me as being very strong, and I hoped to find my bar of iron not alto-gether inadequate for the work.

XII. *In the Darkness*

'We emerged from the Palace while the sun was still in part above the horizon. I was determined to reach the White Sphinx early the next morning, and ere the dusk I purposed pushing through the woods that had stopped me on the previous journey. My plan was to go as far as possible that night, and then, building a fire, to sleep in the protection of its glare. Accordingly, as we went along I gathered any sticks or dried grass I saw, and presently had my arms full of such lit-ter. Thus loaded, our progress was slower than I had anticipated, and besides Weena was tired. And I, also, began to suffer from sleepiness too; so that it was full night before we reached the wood. Upon the shrubby hill of its edge Weena would have stopped, fear-ing the darkness before us; but a singular sense of impending calamity, that should indeed have served me as a warning, drove me onward. I had been without sleep for a night and two days, and I was feverish and irritable. I felt sleep coming upon me, and the Morlocks with it.

'While we hesitated, among the black bushes behind us, and dim against their blackness, I saw three crouching figures. There was scrub and long grass all about us, and I did not feel safe from their insidious approach. The forest, I calculated, was rather less than a mile across. If we could get through it to the bare hill-side, there, as it seemed to me, was an altogether safer resting-place: I thought that with my matches and my camphor I could contrive to keep my path illuminated through the woods. Yet it was evident that if I was to flourish matches with my hands I should have to abandon my firewood: so, rather reluctantly, I put it down. And then it came into my head that I would amaze our friends behind by lighting it. I was to discover the atrocious folly of this proceeding, but it came to my mind as an ingenious move for covering our retreat.

'I don't know if you have ever thought what a rare thing flame must be in the absence of man and in a temperate climate. The sun's heat is rarely strong enough to burn, even when it is focused by dewdrops, as is sometimes the case in more tropical districts. Lightning may blast and blacken, but it rarely gives rise to wide-spread fire. Decaying vegetation may occasionally smoulder with the heat of its fermentation, but this rarely results in flame. In this decadence, too, the art of fire-making had been forgotten on the earth. The red tongues that went licking up my heap of wood were an altogether new and strange thing to Weena.

'She wanted to run to it and play with it. I believe she would have cast herself into it had I not restrained her. But I caught her up, and, in spite of her struggles, plunged boldly before me into the wood. For a little way the glare of my fire lit the path. Looking back presently, I could see, through the crowded stems, that from my heap of sticks the blaze had spread to some bushes adjacent, and a curved line of fire was creeping up the grass of the hill. I laughed at that, and turned again to the dark trees before me. It was very black, and Weena clung to me convulsively, but there was still, as my eyes grew accustomed to the darkness, sufficient light for me to avoid the stems. Overhead it was simply black, except where a gap of remote blue sky shone down upon us here and there. I lit none of my matches because I had no hands free. Upon my left arm I carried my little one, in my right hand I had my iron bar.

'For some way I heard nothing but the crackling twigs under my feet, the faint rustle of the breeze above, and my own breathing and the throb of the blood-vessels in my ears. Then I seemed to know of a pattering about me. I pushed on grimly. The pattering grew more distinct, and then I caught the same queer sounds and voices I had heard in the under-world. There were evidently several of the Morlocks, and they were closing in upon me. Indeed, in another minute I felt a tug at my coat, then something at my arm. And Weena shivered violently, and became quite still.

'It was time for a match. But to get one I must put her down. I did so, and, as I fumbled with my pocket, a struggle began in the darkness about my knees, perfectly silent on her part and with the same peculiar cooing sounds from the Morlocks. Soft little hands, too, were creeping over my coat and back, touching even my neck. Then the match scratched and fizzed. I held it flaring, and saw the white backs of the Morlocks in flight amid the trees. I hastily took a lump of camphor from my pocket, and prepared to light it as soon as the match should wane. Then I looked at Weena. She was lying clutching my feet and quite motionless, with her face to the ground. With a sudden fright I stooped to her. She seemed scarcely to breathe. I lit the block of camphor and flung it to the ground, and as it split and flared up and drove back the Morlocks and the shadows, I knelt down and lifted her. The wood behind seemed full of the stir and murmur of a great company!

'She seemed to have fainted. I put her carefully upon my shoulder and rose to push on, and then there came a horrible realization. In manœuvring with my matches and Weena, I had turned myself about several times, and now I had not the faintest idea in what direction lay my path. For all I knew, I might be facing back towards the Palace of Green Porcelain. I found myself in a cold sweat. I had to think rapidly what to do. I determined to build a fire and encamp where we were. I put Weena, still motionless, down upon a turfy bole, and very hastily, as my first lump of camphor waned, I began collecting sticks and leaves. Here and there out of the darkness round me the Morlocks' eyes shone like carbuncles.

'The camphor flickered and went out. I lit a match, and as I did so, two white forms that had been approaching Weena dashed hastily away. One was so blinded by the light that he came straight for me and I felt his bones grind under the blow of my fist. He gave a whoop of dismay, staggered a little way, and fell down. I lit another piece of camphor, and went on gathering my bonfire. Presently I noticed how dry was some of the foliage above me, for since my arrival on the Time Machine, a matter of a week, no rain had fallen. So, instead of casting about among the trees for fallen twigs, I began leaping up and dragging down branches. Very soon I had a choking smoky fire of green wood and dry sticks, and could economize my camphor. Then I turned to where Weena lay beside my iron mace. I tried what I could to revive her, but she lay like one dead. I could not even satisfy myself whether or not she breathed.

'Now, the smoke of the fire beat over towards me, and it must have made me heavy of a sudden. Moreover, the vapour of camphor was in the air. My fire would not need replenishing for an hour or so. I felt very weary after my exertion, and sat down. The wood, too, was full of a slumbrous murmur that I did not understand. I seemed just to nod and open my eyes. But all was dark, and the Morlocks had their hands upon me. Flinging off their clinging fingers I hastily felt in my pocket for the match-box, and—it had gone! Then they gripped and closed with me again. In a moment I knew what had happened. I had slept, and my fire had gone out, and the bitterness

of death came over my soul. The forest seemed full of the smell of
burning wood. I was caught by the neck, by the hair, by the arms,
and pulled down. It was indescribably horrible in the darkness to
feel all these soft creatures heaped upon me. I felt as if I was in a
monstrous spider's web. I was overpowered, and went down. I felt
little teeth nipping at my neck. I rolled over, and as I did so my hand
came against my iron lever. It gave me strength. I struggled up, shaking the human rats from me, and, holding the bar short, I thrust
where I judged their faces might be. I could feel the succulent giving
of flesh and bone under my blows, and for a moment I was free.

'The strange exultation that so often seems to accompany hard
fighting came upon me. I knew that both I and Weena were lost, but
I determined to make the Morlocks pay for their meat. I stood with
my back to a tree, swinging the iron bar before me. The whole wood
was full of the stir and cries of them. A minute passed. Their voices
seemed to rise to a higher pitch of excitement, and their movements
grew faster. Yet none came within reach. I stood glaring at the blackness. Then suddenly came hope. What if the Morlocks were afraid?
And close on the heels of that came a strange thing. The darkness
seemed to grow luminous. Very dimly I began to see the Morlocks
about me—three battered at my feet—and then I recognized, with
incredulous surprise, that the others were running, in an incessant
stream, as it seemed, from behind me, and away through the wood
in front. And their backs seemed no longer white, but reddish. As I
stood agape, I saw a little red spark go drifting across a gap of
starlight between the branches, and vanish. And at that I understood
the smell of burning wood, the slumbrous murmur that was growing
now into a gusty roar, the red glow, and the Morlocks' flight.

'Stepping out from behind my tree and looking back, I saw,
through the black pillars of the nearer trees, the flames of the burning forest. It was my first fire coming after me. With that I looked for
Weena, but she was gone. The hissing and crackling behind me, the
explosive thud as each fresh tree burst into flame, left little time for
reflection. My iron bar still gripped, I followed in the Morlocks'
path. It was a close race. Once the flames crept forward so swiftly on
my right as I ran, that I was outflanked, and had to strike off to the
left. But at last I emerged upon a small open space, and as I did so, a
Morlock came blundering towards me, and past me, and went on
straight into the fire!

'And now I was to see the most weird and horrible thing, I think,
of all that I beheld in that future age. This whole space was as bright
as day with the reflection of the fire. In the centre was a hillock or
tumulus,[1] surmounted by a scorched hawthorn. Beyond this was

1. A burial mound.

another arm of the burning forest, with yellow tongues already writhing from it, completely encircling the space with a fence of fire. Upon the hillside were some thirty or forty Morlocks, dazzled by the light and heat, and blundering hither and thither against each other in their bewilderment. At first I did not realize their blindness, and struck furiously at them with my bar, in a frenzy of fear, as they approached me, killing one and crippling several more. But when I had watched the gestures of one of them groping under the hawthorn against the red sky, and heard their moans, I was assured of their absolute helplessness and misery in the glare, and I struck no more of them.

'Yet every now and then one would come straight towards me, setting loose a quivering horror that made me quick to elude him. At one time the flames died down somewhat, and I feared the foul creatures would presently be able to see me. I was even thinking of beginning to fight by killing some of them before this should happen; but the fire burst out again brightly, and I stayed my hand. I walked about the hill among them and avoided them, looking for some trace of Weena. But Weena was gone.

'At last I sat down on the summit of the hillock, and watched this strange incredible company of blind things groping to and fro, and making uncanny noises to each one, as the glare of the fire beat on them. The coiling uprush of smoke streamed across the sky, and through the rare tatters of that red canopy, remote as though they belonged to another universe, shone the little stars. Two or three Morlocks came blundering into me, and I drove them off with blows of my fists, trembling as I did so.

'For the most part of that night I was persuaded it was a nightmare. I bit myself and screamed in a passionate desire to awake. I beat the ground with my hands, and got up and sat down again, and wandered here and there, and again sat down. Then I would fall to rubbing my eyes and calling upon God to let me awake. Thrice I saw Morlocks put their heads down in a kind of agony and rush into the flames. But, at last, above the subsiding red of the fire, above the streaming masses of black smoke and the whitening and blackening tree stumps, and the diminishing numbers of these dim creatures, came the white light of the day.

'I searched again for traces of Weena, but there were none. It was plain that they had left her poor little body in the forest. I cannot describe how it relieved me to think that it had escaped the awful fate to which it seemed destined. As I thought of that, I was almost moved to begin a massacre of the helpless abominations about me, but I contained myself. The hillock, as I have said, was a kind of island in the forest. From its summit I could now make out through a haze of smoke the Palace of Green Porcelain, and from that I could get my bearings for the White Sphinx. And so, leaving the remnant of these damned souls still going hither and thither and moaning, as the day grew clearer, I tied some grass about my feet and limped on across smoking ashes and among black stems that still pulsated internally with fire, towards the hiding-place of the Time Machine. I walked slowly, for I was almost exhausted, as well as lame, and I felt the intensest wretchedness for the horrible death of little Weena. It seemed an overwhelming calamity. Now, in this old familiar room, it is more like the sorrow of a dream than an actual loss. But that morning it left me absolutely lonely again—terribly alone. I began to think of this house of mine, of this fireside, of some of you, and with such thoughts came a longing that was pain.

'But, as I walked over the smoking ashes under the bright morning sky, I made a discovery. In my trouser pocket were still some loose matches. The box must have leaked before it was lost.

XIII. *The Trap of the White Sphinx*

'About eight or nine in the morning I came to the same seat of yellow metal from which I had viewed the world upon the evening of my arrival. I thought of my hasty conclusions upon that evening, and could not refrain from laughing bitterly at my confidence. Here was the same beautiful scene, the same abundant foliage, the same splendid palaces and magnificent ruins, the same silver river running between its fertile banks. The gay robes of the beautiful people moved hither and thither among the trees. Some were bathing in exactly the place where I had saved Weena, and that suddenly gave me a keen stab of pain. And like blots upon the landscape rose the cupolas above the ways to the under-world. I understood now what all the beauty of the over-world people covered. Very pleasant was their day, as pleasant as the day of the cattle in the field. Like the cattle, they knew of no enemies, and provided against no needs. And their end was the same.

'I grieved to think how brief the dream of the human intellect had been. It had committed suicide. It had set itself steadfastly towards comfort and ease, a balanced society with security and permanency as its watchword, it had attained its hopes—to come to this at last. Once, life and property must have reached almost absolute safety. The rich had been assured of his wealth and comfort, the toiler assured of his life and work. No doubt in that perfect world there had been no unemployed problem, no social question left unsolved. And a great quiet had followed.

'It is a law of nature we overlook, that intellectual versatility is the compensation for change, danger, and trouble. An animal perfectly in harmony with its environment is a perfect mechanism. Nature never appeals to intelligence until habit and instinct are useless. There is no intelligence where there is no change and no need of change. Only those animals partake of intelligence that have to meet a huge variety of needs and dangers.

'So, as I see it, the upper-world man had drifted towards his feeble prettiness, and the under-world to mere mechanical industry. But that perfect state had lacked one thing even for mechanical perfection—absolute permanency. Apparently as time went on, the feeding of an under-world, however it was effected, had become disjointed. Mother Necessity, who had been staved off for a few thousand years, came back again, and she began below. The under-world being in contact with machinery, which, however perfect, still needs some little thought outside habit, had probably retained perforce rather more initiative, if less of every other human character, than the upper. And when other meat failed them, they turned to what old habit had hitherto forbidden. So I say I saw it in my last view of the world of Eight Hundred and Two Thousand Seven Hundred and One. It may be as wrong an explanation as mortal wit could invent. It is how the thing shaped itself to me, and as that I give it to you.

'After the fatigues, excitements, and terrors of the past days, and in spite of my grief, this seat and the tranquil view and the warm sunlight were very pleasant. I was very tired and sleepy, and soon my theorizing passed into dozing. Catching myself at that, I took my own hint, and spreading myself out upon the turf I had a long and refreshing sleep.

'I awoke a little before sunsetting. I now felt safe against being caught napping by the Morlocks, and, stretching myself, I came on down the hill towards the White Sphinx. I had my crowbar in one hand, and the other hand played with the matches in my pocket.

'And now came a most unexpected thing. As I approached the pedestal of the sphinx I found the bronze valves were open. They had slid down into grooves.

'At that I stopped short before them, hesitating to enter.

'Within was a small apartment, and on a raised place in the corner of this was the Time Machine. I had the small levers in my pocket. So here, after all my elaborate preparations for the siege of the White Sphinx, was a meek surrender. I threw my iron bar away, almost sorry not to use it.

'A sudden thought came into my head as I stooped towards the portal. For once, at least, I grasped the mental operations of the Morlocks. Suppressing a strong inclination to laugh, I stepped through the bronze frame and up to the Time Machine. I was surprised to find it had been carefully oiled and cleaned. I have suspected since that the Morlocks had even partially taken it to pieces while trying in their dim way to grasp its purpose.

'Now as I stood and examined it, finding a pleasure in the mere touch of the contrivance, the thing I had expected happened. The bronze panels suddenly slid up and struck the frame with a clang. I was in the dark—trapped. So the Morlocks thought. At that I chuckled gleefully.

'I could already hear their murmuring laughter as they came towards me. Very calmly I tried to strike the match. I had only to fix on the levers and depart then like a ghost. But I had overlooked one little thing. The matches were of that abominable kind that light only on the box.

'You may imagine how all my calm vanished. The little brutes were close upon me. One touched me. I made a sweeping blow in the dark at them with the levers, and began to scramble into the saddle of the machine. Then came one hand upon me and then another. Then I had simply to fight against their persistent fingers for my levers, and at the same time feel for the studs over which these fitted. One, indeed, they almost got away from me. As it slipped from my hand, I had to butt in the dark with my head—I could hear the Morlock's skull ring—to recover it. It was a nearer thing than the fight in the forest, I think, this last scramble.

'But at last the lever was fixed and pulled over. The clinging hands slipped from me. The darkness presently fell from my eyes. I found myself in the same grey light and tumult I have already described.

XIV. The Further Vision

'I have already told you of the sickness and confusion that comes with time travelling. And this time I was not seated properly in the saddle, but sideways and in an unstable fashion. For an indefinite time I clung to the machine as it swayed and vibrated, quite unheeding how I went, and when I brought myself to look at the dials again I was amazed to find where I had arrived. One dial records days, another thousands of days, another millions of days, and another thousands of millions. Now, instead of reversing the levers I had pulled them over so as to go forward with them, and when I came to look at these indicators I found that the thousands hand was sweeping round as fast as the seconds hand of a watch—into futurity.

'As I drove on, a peculiar change crept over the appearance of things. The palpitating greyness grew darker; then—though I was still travelling with prodigious velocity—the blinking succession of day and night, which was usually indicative of a slower pace, returned, and grew more and more marked. This puzzled me very much at first. The alternations of night and day grew slower and slower, and so did the passage of the sun across the sky, until they seemed to stretch through centuries. At last a steady twilight brooded over the earth, a twilight only broken now and then when a comet glared across the darkling sky. The band of light that had indicated the sun had long since disappeared; for the sun had ceased to set—it simply rose and fell in the west, and grew ever broader and more red. All trace of the moon had vanished. The circling of the stars, growing slower and slower, had given place to creeping points of light. At last, some time before I stopped, the sun, red and very large, halted motionless upon the horizon, a vast dome glowing with a dull heat, and now and then suffering a momentary extinction. At one time it had for a little while glowed more brilliantly again, but it speedily reverted to its sullen red-heat. I perceived by this slowing down of its rising and setting that the work of the tidal drag was done.[1] The earth had come to rest with one face to the sun, even as in our own time the moon faces the earth. Very cautiously, for I remembered my former headlong fall, I began to reverse my motion. Slower and slower went the circling hands until the thousands one seemed motionless, and the daily one was no longer a mere mist upon its scale. Still slower, until the dim outlines of a desolate beach grew visible.

'I stopped very gently and sat upon the Time Machine, looking round. The sky was no longer blue. North-eastward it was inky black, and out of the blackness shone brightly and steadily the pale white stars. Overhead it was a deep Indian red and starless, and south-eastward it grew brighter to a glowing scarlet where, cut by the horizon, lay the huge hull of the sun, red and motionless. The rocks about me were of a harsh reddish colour, and all the trace of life that I could see at first was the intensely green vegetation that covered every projecting point on their south-eastern face. It was the same rich green that one sees on forest moss or on the lichen in caves: plants which like these grow in a perpetual twilight.

'The machine was standing on a sloping beach. The sea stretched away to the south-west, to rise into a sharp bright horizon against the wan sky. There were no breakers and no waves, for not a breath of wind was stirring. Only a slight oily swell rose and fell like a gentle breathing, and showed that the eternal sea was still moving and living. And along the margin where the water sometimes broke was a thick incrustation of salt—pink under the lurid sky. There was a sense of oppression in my head, and I noticed that I was breathing very fast. The sensation reminded me of my only experience of mountaineering, and from that I judged the air to be more rarefied than it is now.

'Far away up the desolate slope I heard a harsh scream, and saw a thing like a huge white butterfly go slanting and fluttering up into the sky and, circling, disappear into some low hillocks beyond. The sound

1. Wells is again drawing on the work of Sir George Howard Darwin (see Chapter VIII, note 8, p. 37) on the tides. Darwin argued that the "tidal drag" caused by the combined gravitational pull of the sun and the moon would eventually stop the earth's rotation.

of its voice was so dismal that I shivered and seated myself more firmly upon the machine. Looking round me again, I saw that, quite near, what I had taken to be a reddish mass of rock was moving slowly towards me. Then I saw the thing was really a monstrous crab-like creature. Can you imagine a crab as large as yonder table, with its many legs moving slowly and uncertainly, its big claws swaying, its long antennæ, like carters' whips,[2] waving and feeling, and its stalked eyes gleaming at you on either side of its metallic front? Its back was corrugated and ornamented with ungainly bosses,[3] and a greenish incrustation blotched it here and there. I could see the many palps of its complicated mouth flickering and feeling as it moved.

'As I stared at this sinister apparition crawling towards me, I felt a tickling on my cheek as though a fly had lighted there. I tried to brush it away with my hand, but in a moment it returned, and almost immediately came another by my ear. I struck at this, and caught something threadlike. It was drawn swiftly out of my hand. With a frightful qualm, I turned, and saw that I had grasped the antenna of another monster crab that stood just behind me. Its evil eyes were wriggling on their stalks, its mouth was all alive with appetite, and its vast ungainly claws, smeared with an algal slime, were descending upon me. In a moment my hand was on the lever, and I had placed a month between myself and these monsters. But I was still on the same beach, and I saw them distinctly now as soon as I stopped. Dozens of them seemed to be crawling here and there, in the sombre light, among the foliated sheets of intense green.

'I cannot convey the sense of abominable desolation that hung over the world. The red eastern sky, the northward blackness, the salt Dead Sea,[4] the stony beach crawling with these foul, slow-stirring monsters, the uniform poisonous-looking green of the lichenous plants, the thin air that hurts one's lungs: all contributed to an appalling effect. I moved on a hundred years, and there was the same red sun—a little larger, a little duller—the same dying sea, the same chill air, and the same crowd of earthy crustacea creeping in and out among the green weed and the red rocks. And in the westward sky I saw a curved pale line like a vast new moon.

'So I travelled, stopping ever and again, in great strides of a thousand years or more, drawn on by the mystery of the earth's fate, watching with a strange fascination the sun grow larger and duller in the westward sky, and the life of the old earth ebb away. At last, more than thirty million years hence, the huge red-hot dome of the sun had come to obscure nearly a tenth part of the darkling heavens.

2. Long, thin whips such as those used by drivers of horse-drawn carts.
3. Protuberant body parts.
4. The virtually lifeless lake in present-day Israel and Jordan is the saltiest body of water on Earth.

Then I stopped once more, for the crawling multitude of crabs had disappeared, and the red beach, save for its livid green liverworts and lichens, seemed lifeless. And now it was flecked with white. A bitter cold assailed me. Rare white flakes ever and again came eddying down. To the north-eastward, the glare of snow lay under the starlight of the sable sky, and I could see an undulating crest of hillocks pinkish-white. There were fringes of ice along the sea margin, with drifting masses further out; but the main expanse of that salt ocean, all bloody under the eternal sunset, was still unfrozen.

'I looked about me to see if any traces of animal-life remained. A certain indefinable apprehension still kept me in the saddle of the machine. But I saw nothing moving, in earth or sky or sea. The green slime on the rocks alone testified that life was not extinct. A shallow sandbank had appeared in the sea and the water had receded from the beach. I fancied I saw some black object flopping about upon this bank, but it became motionless as I looked at it, and I judged that my eye had been deceived, and that the black object was merely a rock. The stars in the sky were intensely bright and seemed to me to twinkle very little.

'Suddenly I noticed that the circular westward outline of the sun had changed; that a concavity, a bay, had appeared in the curve. I saw this grow larger. For a minute perhaps I stared aghast at this blackness that was creeping over the day, and then I realized that an eclipse was beginning. Either the moon or the planet Mercury was passing across the sun's disk. Naturally, at first I took it to be the moon, but there is much to incline me to believe that what I really saw was the transit of an inner planet passing very near to the earth.

'The darkness grew apace; a cold wind began to blow in freshening gusts from the east, and the showering white flakes in the air increased in number. From the edge of the sea came a ripple and whisper. Beyond these lifeless sounds the world was silent. Silent? It would be hard to convey the stillness of it. All the sounds of man, the bleating of sheep, the cries of birds, the hum of insects, the stir that makes the background of our lives—all that was over. As the darkness thickened, the eddying flakes grew more abundant, dancing before my eyes; and the cold of the air more intense. At last, one by one, swiftly, one after the other, the white peaks of the distant hills vanished into blackness. The breeze rose to a moaning wind. I saw the black central shadow of the eclipse sweeping towards me. In another moment the pale stars alone were visible. All else was rayless obscurity. The sky was absolutely black.

'A horror of this great darkness came on me. The cold, that smote to my marrow, and the pain I felt in breathing overcame me. I shivered, and a deadly nausea seized me. Then like a red-hot bow in the sky appeared the edge of the sun. I got off the machine to recover myself. I felt giddy and incapable of facing the return journey. As I stood sick and confused I saw again the moving thing upon the shoal—there was no mistake now that it was a moving thing—against the red water of the sea. It was a round thing, the size of a football perhaps, or, it may be, bigger, and tentacles trailed down from it, it seemed black against the weltering blood-red water, and it was hopping fitfully about. Then I felt I was fainting. But a terrible dread of lying helpless in that remote and awful twilight sustained me while I clambered upon the saddle.

XV. The Time Traveller's Return

'So I came back. For a long time I must have been insensible upon the machine. The blinking succession of the days and nights was resumed, the sun got golden again, the sky blue. I breathed with greater freedom. The fluctuating contours of the land ebbed and flowed. The hands spun backward upon the dials. At last I saw again the dim shadows of houses, the evidences of decadent humanity. These, too, changed and passed, and others came. Presently, when the million dial was at zero, I slackened speed. I began to recognize our own petty and familiar architecture, the thousands hand ran back to the starting-point, the night and day flapped slower and slower. Then the old walls of the laboratory came round me. Very gently, now, I slowed the mechanism down.

'I saw one little thing that seemed odd to me. I think I have told you that when I set out, before my velocity became very high, Mrs Watchett had walked across the room, travelling, as it seemed to me, like a rocket. As I returned, I passed again across that minute when she traversed the laboratory. But now her every motion appeared to be the exact inversion of her previous ones. The door at the lower end opened, and she glided quietly up the laboratory, back foremost, and disappeared behind the door by which she had previously entered. Just before that I seemed to see Hillyer[1] for a moment; but he passed like a flash.

'Then I stopped the machine, and saw about me again the old familiar laboratory, my tools, my appliances just as I had left them. I got off the thing very shakily, and sat down upon my bench. For several minutes I trembled violently. Then I became calmer. Around me was my old workshop again, exactly as it had been. I might have slept there, and the whole thing have been a dream.

'And yet, not exactly! The thing had started from the south-east corner of the laboratory. It had come to rest again in the north-west,

---

1. Hillyer is often taken to be the narrator of *The Time Machine*'s frame narrative, though he is not named elsewhere in the novel. Alternatively, Hillyer could be the name of the manservant who makes a brief appearance at the end of the next chapter.

against the wall where you saw it. That gives you the exact distance from my little lawn to the pedestal of the White Sphinx, into which the Morlocks had carried my machine.

'For a time my brain went stagnant. Presently I got up and came through the passage here, limping, because my heel was still painful, and feeling sorely begrimed. I saw the *Pall Mall Gazette*[2] on the table by the door. I found the date was indeed to-day, and looking at the timepiece, saw the hour was almost eight o'clock. I heard your voices and the clatter of plates. I hesitated—I felt so sick and weak. Then I sniffed good wholesome meat, and opened the door on you. You know the rest. I washed, and dined, and now I am telling you the story.'

XVI. *After the Story*

'I know,' he said, after a pause, 'that all this will be absolutely incredible to you, but to me the one incredible thing is that I am here to-night in this old familiar room, looking into your friendly faces, and telling you all these strange adventures.' He looked at the Medical Man. 'No. I cannot expect you to believe it. Take it as a lie—or a prophecy. Say I dreamed it in the workshop. Consider I have been speculating upon the destinies of our race, until I have hatched this fiction. Treat my assertion of its truth as a mere stroke of art to enhance its interest. And taking it as a story, what do you think of it?'

He took up his pipe, and began, in his old accustomed manner, to tap with it nervously upon the bars of the grate. There was a momentary stillness. Then chairs began to creak and shoes to scrape upon the carpet. I took my eyes off the Time Traveller's face, and looked round at his audience. They were in the dark, and little spots of colour swam before them. The Medical Man seemed absorbed in the contemplation of our host. The Editor was looking hard at the end of his cigar—the sixth. The Journalist fumbled for his watch. The others, as far as I remember, were motionless.

The Editor stood up with a sigh. 'What a pity it is you're not a writer of stories!' he said, putting his hand on the Time Traveller's shoulder.

'You don't believe it?'

'Well—'

'I thought not.'

The Time Traveller turned to us. 'Where are the matches?' he said. He lit one and spoke over his pipe, puffing. 'To tell you the truth . . . I hardly believe it myself. . . . And yet . . .'

His eye fell with a mute inquiry upon the withered white flowers upon the little table. Then he turned over the hand holding his pipe, and I saw he was looking at some half-healed scars on his knuckles.

2. A London evening newspaper to which Wells was a frequent contributor in the mid-1890s.

The Medical Man rose, came to the lamp, and examined the flow-ers. 'The gynæceum's[1] odd,' he said. The Psychologist leant forward to see, holding out his hand for a specimen.

'I'm hanged if it isn't a quarter to one,' said the Journalist. 'How shall we get home?'

'Plenty of cabs at the station,' said the Psychologist.

'It's a curious thing,' said the Medical Man; 'but I certainly don't know the natural order[2] of these flowers. May I have them?'

The Time Traveller hesitated. Then suddenly, 'Certainly not.'

'Where did you really get them?' said the Medical Man.

The Time Traveller put his hand to his head. He spoke like one who was trying to keep hold of an idea that eluded him. 'They were put into my pocket by Weena, when I travelled into Time.' He stared round the room. 'I'm damned if it isn't all going. This room and you and the atmosphere of every day is too much for my memory. Did I ever make a Time Machine, or a model of a Time Machine? Or is it all only a dream? They say life is a dream, a precious poor dream at times—but I can't stand another that won't fit. It's madness. And where did the dream come from? . . . I must look at that machine. If there *is* one!'

He caught up the lamp swiftly, and carried it, flaring red, through the door into the corridor. We followed him. There in the flickering light of the lamp was the machine sure enough, squat, ugly, and askew, a thing of brass, ebony, ivory, and translucent glimmering quartz. Solid to the touch—for I put out my hand and felt the rail of it—and with brown spots and smears upon the ivory, and bits of grass and moss upon the lower parts, and one rail bent awry.

The Time Traveller put the lamp down on the bench, and ran his hand along the damaged rail, 'It's all right now,' he said. 'The story I told you was true. I'm sorry to have brought you out here in the cold.' He took up the lamp, and, in an absolute silence, we returned to the smoking-room.

He came into the hall with us, and helped the Editor on with his coat. The Medical Man looked into his face and, with a certain hesi-tation, told him he was suffering from overwork, at which he laughed hugely. I remember him standing in the open doorway, bawling good-night.

I shared a cab with the Editor. He thought the tale a 'gaudy lie'. For my own part I was unable to come to a conclusion. The story was so fantastic and incredible, the telling so credible and sober. I lay awake most of the night thinking about it. I determined to go next day, and see the Time Traveller again. I was told he was in the

1. The pistil.
2. That is, their botanical classification.

laboratory, and being on easy terms in the house, I went up to him. The laboratory, however, was empty. I stared for a minute at the Time Machine and put out my hand and touched the lever. At that the squat substantial-looking mass swayed like a bough shaken by the wind. Its instability startled me extremely, and I had a queer reminiscence of the childish days when I used to be forbidden to meddle. I came back through the corridor. The Time Traveller met me in the smoking-room. He was coming from the house. He had a small camera under one arm and a knapsack under the other. He laughed when he saw me, and gave me an elbow to shake. 'I'm frightfully busy,' said he, 'with that thing in there.'

'But is it not some hoax?' I said. 'Do you really travel through time?'

'Really and truly I do.' And he looked frankly into my eyes. He hesitated. His eye wandered about the room. 'I only want half an hour,' he said. 'I know why you came, and it's awfully good of you. There's some magazines here. If you'll stop to lunch I'll prove you this time-travelling up to the hilt, specimens and all. If you'll forgive my leaving you now?'

I consented, hardly comprehending then the full import of his words, and he nodded and went on down the corridor. I heard the door of the laboratory slam, seated myself in a chair, and took up a daily paper. What was he going to do before lunch-time? Then suddenly I was reminded by an advertisement that I had promised to meet Richardson, the publisher, at two. I looked at my watch, and saw that I could barely save that engagement. I got up and went down the passage to tell the Time Traveller.

As I took hold of the handle of the door I heard an exclamation, oddly truncated at the end, and a click and a thud. A gust of air whirled round me as I opened the door, and from within came the sound of broken glass falling on the floor. The Time Traveller was not there. I seemed to see a ghostly, indistinct figure sitting in a whirling mass of black and brass for a moment—a figure so transparent that the bench behind with its sheets of drawings was absolutely distinct; but this phantasm vanished as I rubbed my eyes. The Time Machine had gone. Save for a subsiding stir of dust, the further end of the laboratory was empty. A pane of the skylight had, apparently, just been blown in.

I felt an unreasonable amazement. I knew that something strange had happened, and for the moment could not distinguish what the strange thing might be. As I stood staring, the door into the garden opened, and the man-servant appeared.

We looked at each other. Then ideas began to come. 'Has Mr — gone out that way?' said I.

'No, sir. No one has come out this way. I was expecting to find him here.'

At that I understood. At the risk of disappointing Richardson I stayed on, waiting for the Time Traveller: waiting for the second, perhaps still stranger, story, and the specimens and photographs he would bring with him. But I am beginning now to fear that I must wait a lifetime. The Time Traveller vanished three years ago. And, as everybody knows now, he has never returned.

Epilogue

One cannot choose but wonder. Will he ever return? It may be that he swept back into the past, and fell among the blood-drinking, hairy savages of the Age of Unpolished Stone; into the abysses of the Cretaceous Sea; or among the grotesque saurians, the huge reptilian brutes of the Jurassic times. He may even now—if I may use the phrase—be wandering on some plesiosaurus-haunted Oolitic coral reef, or beside the lonely saline seas of the Triassic Age.[1] Or did he go forward, into one of the nearer ages, in which men are still men, but with the riddles of our own time answered and its wearisome problems solved? Into the manhood of the race: for I, for my own part, cannot think that these latter days of weak experiment, fragmentary theory, and mutual discord are indeed man's culminating time! I say, for my own part. He, I know—for the question had been discussed among us long before the Time Machine was made— thought but cheerlessly of the Advancement of Mankind, and saw in the growing pile of civilization only a foolish heaping that must inevitably fall back upon and destroy its makers in the end. If that is so, it remains for us to live as though it were not so. But to me the future is still black and blank—is a vast ignorance, lit at a few casual places by the memory of his story. And I have by me, for my comfort, two strange white flowers—shrivelled now, and brown and flat and brittle—to witness that even when mind and strength had gone, gratitude and a mutual tenderness still lived on in the heart of man.

1. The narrator imagines the Time Traveller visiting first the earliest stages of human development (the Age of Unpolished Stone, approximately 2 million years ago) and then continuing backward through the three geologic periods of earth's Mesozoic period: the Cretaceous (roughly 145 to 65 million years ago), the Jurassic (roughly 200 to 145 million years ago), and the Triassac (roughly 250 to 200 million years ago). "Grotesque saurians" presumably are dinosaurs. Oolite is a limestone in which many marine fossils have been found, including that of the long-necked, seal-like plesiosaurus.

BACKGROUNDS
AND CONTEXTS

The Evolution of
The Time Machine

The Chronic Argonauts†

I. *The Story from an Exoteric Point of View*

BEING THE ACCOUNT OF DR. NEBOGIPFEL'S SOJOURN
IN LLYDDWDD

About half-a-mile outside the village of Llyddwdd by the road that goes up over the eastern flank of the mountain called Pen-y-pwll to Rwstog is a large farm-building known as the Manse.[1] It derives this title from the fact that it was at one time the residence of the minister of the Calvinistic Methodists. It is a quaint, low, irregular erection, lying back some hundred yards from the roadway, and now fast passing into a ruinous state.

Since its construction in the latter half of the last century this house has undergone many changes of fortune, having been abandoned long since by the farmer of the surrounding acres for less pretentious and more commodious headquarters. Among others Miss Carnot, "the Gallic Sappho,"[2] at one time made it her home, and later on an old man named Williams became its occupier. The foul murder of this tenant by his two sons was the cause of its remaining for some considerable period uninhabited; with the inevitable consequence of its undergoing very extensive dilapidation.

---

† From *Science Schools Journal* (April, May, June 1888). *The Chronic Argonauts*, Wells's earliest effort at a story centered on time travel, was serialized over three issues of the student magazine of the Normal School (later the Royal College) of Science in South Kensington, London, where Wells studied between 1884 and 1887. In his *Experiment in Autobiography* (1934), Wells wrote that the serial, begun "very much under the influence of Hawthorne," was broken off after three installments "because I could not go on with it. That I realized I could not go on with it marks a stage in my education in the art of fiction." In Greek mythology, the Argonauts accompanied Jason on his many heroic adventures, the most famous being the retrieval of the Golden Fleece. Their ship was named the Argo.

1. Though the place names are fictive, the setting is obviously Wales. Later it is specified as Caernarvonshire, on the northwest coast of the country. The house occupied by the minister of a Nonconformist congregation (such as a "Calvinistic Methodist" minister) is often called the Manse.
2. An intriguing allusion to an evidently fictitious person.

The house had got a bad name, and adolescent man and Nature combined to bring swift desolation upon it. The fears of the Williamses which kept the Llyddwdd lads from gratifying their propensity to invade its deserted exterior, manifested itself in unusually destructive resentment against its external breakables. The missiles with which they at once confessed and defied their spiritual dread, left scarcely a splinter of glass, and only battered relics of the old-fashioned leaden frames, in its narrow windows; while numberless shattered tiles about the house, and four or five black apertures yawning behind naked rafters in the roof, also witnessed vividly to the energy of their trajection. Rain and wind thus had free way to enter the empty rooms and work their will there, old Time abiding and abetting. Alternately soaked and desiccated, the planks of flooring and wainscot warped apart strangely, split here and there, and tore themselves away in paroxysms of rheumatic pain from the rust-devoured nails that had once held them firm. The plaster of walls and ceiling, growing green-black with a rain-fed crust of lowly life, parted slowly from the fermenting laths; and large fragments thereof falling down inexplicably in tranquil hours, with loud concussion and clatter, gave strength to the popular superstition that old Williams and his sons were fated to re-enact their fearful tragedy until the final judgment. White roses and daedal[3] creepers, that Miss Carnot had first adorned the walls with, spread now luxuriantly over the lichen-filmed tiles of the roof, and in slender graceful sprays timidly invaded the ghostly cobweb-draped apartments. Fungi, sickly pale, began to displace and uplift the bricks in the cellar floor; while on the rotting wood everywhere they clustered, in all the glory of purple and mottled crimson, yellow-brown and hepatite.[4] Woodlice and ants, beetles and moths, winged and creeping things innumerable, found each day a more congenial home among the ruins; and after them in ever-increasing multitudes swarmed the blotchy toads. Swallows and martins built every year more thickly in the silent, airy, upper chambers. Bats and owls struggled for the crepuscular[5] corners of the lower rooms. Thus, in the Spring of the year eighteen hundred and eighty-seven, was Nature taking over, gradually but certainly, the tenancy of the old Manse. "The house was falling into decay," as men who do not appreciate the application of human derelicts to other beings' use would say, "surely and swiftly." But it was destined nevertheless to shelter another human tenant before its final dissolution.

There was no intelligence of the advent of a new inhabitant in quiet Llyddwdd. He came without a solitary premonition out of the vast

3. Elaborately entwined.
4. Liver-colored.
5. Dimly lit.

unknown into the sphere of minute village observation and gossip. He
fell into the Llyddwdd world, as it were, like a thunderbolt falling in
the daytime. Suddenly, and out of nothingness, he *was*. Rumour,
indeed, vaguely averred that he was seen to arrive by a certain train
from London, and to walk straight without hesitation to the old
Manse, giving neither explanatory word nor sign to mortal as to his
purpose there: but then the same fertile source of information also
hinted that he was first beheld skimming down the slopes of steep
Pen-y-pwll with exceeding swiftness, riding, as it appeared to the intelligent observer, upon an instrument not unlike a sieve[6] and that he
entered the house by the chimney. Of these conflicting reports, the
former was the first to be generally circulated, but the latter, in view of
the bizarre presence and eccentric ways of the newest inhabitant,
obtained wider credence. By whatever means he arrived, there can
be no doubt that he was in, and in possession of the Manse, on the
first of May; because on the morning of that day he was inspected
by Mrs. Morgan ap Lloyd Jones, and subsequently by the numerous
persons her report brought up the mountain slope, engaged in the
curious occupation of nailing sheet-tin across the void window sockets
of his new domicile—"blinding his house," as Mrs. Morgan ap Lloyd
Jones not inaptly termed it.

He was a small-bodied, sallow-faced little man, clad in a close-
fitting garment of some stiff, dark material, which Mr. Parry Davies,
the Llyddwdd shoemaker, opined was leather. His aquiline nose,
thin lips, high cheek-ridges, and pointed chin, were all small and
mutually well proportioned; but the bones and muscles of his face
were rendered excessively prominent and distinct by his extreme
leanness. The same cause contributed to the sunken appearance of
the large eager-looking grey eyes, that gazed forth from under his
phenomenally wide and high forehead. It was this latter feature that
most powerfully attracted the attention of an observer. It seemed to
be great beyond all preconceived ratio to the rest of his countenance.
Dimensions, corrugations, wrinkles, venation,[7] were alike abnormally
exaggerated. Below it his eyes glowed like lights in some cave at a
cliff's foot. It so over-powered and suppressed the rest of his face as
to give an *unhuman* appearance almost, to what would otherwise
have been an unquestionably handsome profile. The lank black hair
that hung unkempt before his eyes served to increase rather than
conceal this effect, by adding to unnatural altitude a suggestion of
hydrocephalic[8] projection: and the idea of something ultra human
was furthermore accentuated by the temporal arteries that pulsated
visibly through his transparent yellow skin. No wonder, in view even

6. Witches were said to sail on the water in sieves.
7. The pattern of veins visible through the skin.
8. Characteristic of hydrocephalus, an abnormal enlargement of a portion of the head.

of these things, that among the highly and over-poetical Cymric[9] of Llyddwdd the sieve theory of arrival found considerable favour.

It was his bearing and actions, however, much more than his personality, that won over believers to the warlock notion of matters. In almost every circumstance of life the observant villagers soon found his ways were not only not *their* ways, but altogether inexplicable upon any theory of motives they could conceive. Thus, in a small matter at the beginning, when Arthur Price Williams, eminent and famous in every tavern in Caernarvonshire for his social gifts, endeavoured, in choicest Welsh and even choicer English, to inveigle the stranger into conversation over the sheet-tin performance, he failed utterly. Inquisitional supposition, straightforward enquiry, offer of assistance, suggestion of method, sarcasm, irony, abuse, and at last, gage of battle,[1] though shouted with much effort from the road hedge, went unanswered and apparently unheard. Missile weapons, Arthur Price Williams found, were equally unavailing for the purpose of introduction, and the gathered crowd dispersed with unappeased curiosity and suspicion. Later in the day, the swarth apparition was seen striding down the mountain road towards the village, hatless, and with such swift width of step and set resolution of countenance, that Arthur Price Williams, beholding him from afar from the "Pig and Whistle" doorway was seized with dire consternation, and hid behind the Dutch oven in the kitchen till he was past. Wild panic also smote the school-house as the children were coming out, and drove them indoors like leaves before a gale. He was merely seeking the provision shop, however, and erupted thencefrom after a prolonged stay, loaded with a various armful of blue parcels, a loaf, herrings, pigs' trotters, salt pork, and a black bottle, with which he returned in the same swift projectile gait to the Manse. His way of shopping was to name, and to name simply, without solitary other word of explanation, civility or request, the article he required.

The shopkeeper's crude meteorological superstitions and inquisitive commonplaces, he seemed not to hear, and he might have been esteemed deaf if he had not evinced the promptest attention to the faintest relevant remark. Consequently it was speedily rumoured that he was determined to avoid all but the most necessary human intercourse. He lived altogether mysteriously, in the decaying manse, without mortal service[2] or companionship, presumably sleeping on planks or litter, and either preparing his own food or eating it raw. This, coupled with the popular conception of the haunting parricides, did much to strengthen the popular supposition of some vast gulf between the newcomer and common humanity. The only thing that

9. Welsh.
1. A challenge to engage in single combat.
2. That is, he doesn't keep a servant.

was inharmonious with this idea of severance from mankind was a
constant flux of crates filled with grotesquely contorted glassware,
cases of brazen and steel instruments, huge coils of wire, vast iron and
fire-clay implements, of inconceivable purpose, jars and phials labelled
in black and scarlet—POISON, huge packages of books, and gargan-
tuan rolls of cartridge paper,[3] which set in towards his Llyddwdd
quarters from the outer world. The apparently hieroglyphic inscrip-
tions on these various consignments revealed at the profound
scrutiny of Pugh Jones that the style and title of the new inhabitant
was Dr. Moses Nebogipfel, Ph.D., F.R.S., N.W.R., PAID;[4] at which
discovery much edification was felt, especially among the purely
Welsh-speaking community. Further than this, these arrivals, by the
evident unfitness for any allowable mortal use, and inferential diabol-
icalness, filled the neighbourhood with a vague horror and lively
curiosity, which were greatly augmented by the extraordinary phenomena, and still more extraordinary accounts thereof, that followed
their reception in the Manse.

The first of these was on Wednesday, the fifteenth of May, when
the Calvinistic Methodists of Llyddwdd had their annual commemo-
ration festival; on which occasion, in accordance with custom,
dwellers in the surrounding parishes of Rwstog, Peu-y-garn, Caer-
gyllwdd, Llanrdd, and even distant Llanrwst flocked into the village.
Popular thanks to Providence were materialized in the usual way, by
means of plumb-bread and butter, mixed tea, *terza*, consecrated flir-
tations, kiss-in-the-ring, rough-and-tumble football, and vitupera-
tive political speechmaking.[5] About half-past eight the fun began to
tarnish, and the assembly to break up; and by nine numerous
couples and occasional groups were wending their way in the darkling along the hilly Llyddwdd and Rwstog road. It was a calm warm
night; one of these nights when lamps, gas and heavy sleep seem
stupid ingratitude to the Creator. The zenith sky was an ineffable
deep lucent blue, and the evening star hung golden in the liquid
darkness of the west. In the north-north-west, a faint phosphores-
cence marked the sunken day. The moon was just rising, pallid and
gibbous[6] over the huge haze-dimmed shoulder of Pen-y-pwll. Against
the wan eastern sky, from the vague outline of the mountain slope,
the Manse stood out black, clear, and solitary. The stillness of the
twilight had hushed the myriad murmurs of the day. Only the
sounds of footsteps and voices and laughter, that came fitfully rising
and falling from the roadway, and an intermittent hammering in the

3. Paper specially prepared for use in drafting.
4. Dr. Nebogipfel holds the degree of Doctor of Philosophy (Ph.D.), and he is a Fellow of the
   prestigious Royal Society (F.R.S.). Pugh Jones apparently takes N.W.R. for another of the
   doctor's titles, but it is instead a postal designation, standing for North West Region.
5. A terza is a song in three parts. Kiss in the ring is a version for adults of the children's
   game duck duck goose; it involves kissing.
6. The moon is in its gibbous phase when it is between half and full.

darkened dwelling, broke the silence. Suddenly a strange whizzing, buzzing whirr filled the night air, and a bright flicker glanced across the dim path of the wayfarers. All eyes were turned in astonishment to the old Manse. The house no longer loomed a black featureless block but was filled to overflowing with light. From the gaping holes in the roof, from chinks and fissures amid tiles and brickwork, from every gap which Nature or man had pierced in the crumbling old shell, a blinding blue-white glare was streaming, beside which the rising moon seemed a disc of opaque sulphur. The thin mist of the dewy night had caught the violet glow and hung, unearthly smoke, over the colourless blaze. A strange turmoil and outcrying in the old Manse now began, and grew ever more audible to the clustering spectators, and therewith came clanging loud impacts against the window-guarding tin. Then from the gleaming roof-gaps of the house suddenly vomited forth a wondrous swarm of heteromerous[7] living things—swallows, sparrows, martins, owls, bats, insects in visible multitudes, to hang for many minutes a noisy, gyring, spreading cloud over the black gables and chimneys, . . . and then slowly to thin out and vanish away in the night.

As this tumult died away the throbbing humming that had first arrested attention grew once more in the listeners' hearing, until at last it was the only sound in the long stillness. Presently, however, the road gradually awoke again to the beating and shuffling of feet, as the knots of Rwstog people, one by one, turned their blinking eyes from the dazzling whiteness and, pondering deeply, continued their homeward way.

The cultivated reader will have already discerned that this phenomenon, which sowed a whole crop of uncanny thoughts in the minds of these worthy folk, was simply the installation of the electric light in the Manse. Truly, this last vicissitude of the old house was its strangest one. Its revival to mortal life was like the raising of Lazarus.[8] From that hour forth, by night and day, behind the tin-blinded windows, the tamed lightning illuminated every corner of its quickly changing interior. The almost frenzied energy of the lank-haired, leather-clad little doctor swept away into obscure holes and corners and common destruction, creeper sprays, toadstools, rose leaves, birds' nests, birds' eggs, cobwebs, and all the coatings and lovingly fanciful trimmings with which that maternal old dotard, Dame Nature, had tricked out the decaying house for its lying in state. The magneto-electric apparatus whirred incessantly amid the vestiges and the wainscoted dining-room, where once the eighteenth century tenant had piously read morning prayer and eaten his Sunday dinner;

7. Varied.
8. The biblical story of Jesus raising Lazarus from the dead is in John 11:41–44.

and in the place of his sacred symbolical sideboard was a nasty heap of coke.[9] The oven of the bakehouse supplied substratum and material for a forge, whose snorting, panting bellows, and intermittent, ruddy, spark-laden blast made the benighted, but Bible-lit Welsh women murmur in liquid Cymric, as they hurried by: "Whose breath kindleth coals, and out of his mouth is a flame of fire."[1] For the idea these good people formed of it was that a tame, but occasionally restive, leviathan had been added to the terrors of the haunted house. The constantly increasing accumulation of pieces of machinery, big brass castings, block tin, casks, crates, and packages of innumerable articles, by their demands for space, necessitated the sacrifice of most of the slighter partitions of the house; and the beams and flooring of the upper chambers were also mercilessly sawn away by the tireless scientist in such a way as to convert them into mere shelves and corner brackets of the atrial space between cellars and rafters. Some of the sounder planking was utilized in the making of a rude broad table, upon which files and heaps of geometrical diagrams speedily accumulated. The production of these latter seemed to be the object upon which the mind of Dr. Nebogipfel was so inflexibly set. All other circumstances of his life were made entirely subsidiary to this one occupation. Strangely complicated traceries of lines they were—plans, elevations, sections by surfaces and solids, that, with the help of logarithmic mechanical apparatus and involved curvigraphical machines, spread swiftly under his expert hands over yard after yard of paper. Some of these symbolized shapes he dispatched to London, and they presently returned, *realized*,[2] in forms of brass and ivory, and nickel and mahogany. Some of them he himself translated into solid models of metal and wood; occasionally casting the metallic ones in moulds of sand, but often laboriously hewing them out of the block for greater precision of dimension. In this second process, among other appliances, he employed a steel circular saw set with diamond powder and made to rotate with extraordinary swiftness, by means of steam and multiplying gear. It was this latter thing, more than all else, that filled Llyddwdd with a sickly loathing of the Doctor as a man of blood and darkness. Often in the silence of midnight—for the newest inhabitant heeded the sun but little in his incessant research—the awakened dwellers around Pen-y-pwll would hear, what was at first a complaining murmur, like the groaning of a wounded man, "gurr-urr-urr-URR," rising by slow gradations

9. Coal residue.
1. The women are quoting from Job 41:21–22. The leviathan—a monstrous mythic sea-creature—mentioned in the next sentence is also found in the book of Job (41:1). In the context of Wells's narrative it refers to the powerful machines the doctor appears to be constructing.
2. Made real.

in pitch and intensity to the likeness of a voice in despairing passionate protest, and at last ending abruptly in a sharp piercing shriek that rang in the ears for hours afterwards and begot numberless grewsome dreams.

The mystery of all these unearthly noises and inexplicable phenomena, the Doctor's inhumanly brusque bearing and evident uneasiness when away from his absorbing occupation, his entire and jealous seclusion, and his terrifying behaviour to certain officious intruders, roused popular resentment and curiosity to the highest, and a plot was already on foot to make some sort of popular inquisition (probably accompanied by an experimental ducking[3]) into his proceedings, when the sudden death of the hunchback Hughes in a fit, brought matters to an unexpected crisis. It happened in broad daylight, in the roadway just opposite the Manse. Half a dozen people witnessed it. The unfortunate creature was seen to fall suddenly and roll about on the pathway, struggling violently, as it appeared to the spectators, with some invisible assailant. When assistance reached him he was purple in the face and his blue lips were covered with a glairy[4] foam. He died almost as soon as they laid hands on him.

Owen Thomas, the general practitioner, vainly assured the excited crowd which speedily gathered outside the "Pig and Whistle," whither the body had been carried, that death was unquestionably natural. A horrible zymotic[5] suspicion had gone forth that deceased was the victim of Dr. Nebogipfel's imputed aerial powers. The contagion was with the news that passed like a flash though the village and set all Llyddwdd seething with a fierce desire for action against the worker of this iniquity. Downright superstition, which had previously walked somewhat modestly about the village, in the fear of ridicule and the Doctor, now appeared boldly before the sight of all men, clad in the terrible majesty of truth. People who had hitherto kept entire silence as to their fears of the imp-like philosopher suddenly discovered a fearsome pleasure in whispering dread possibilities to kindred souls, and from whispers of possibilities their sympathy-fostered utterances soon developed into unhesitating asserverations in loud and even high-pitch tones. The fancy of a captive leviathan, already alluded to, which had up to now been the horrid but secret joy of a certain conclave of ignorant old women, was published to all the world as indisputable fact; it being stated, on her own authority, that the animal had, on one occasion, chased Mrs. Morgan ap Lloyd

---

3. Ducking a person—immersing him or her in cold water—was a popular form of "correction" for acts of anger, passion, or violence. It was also used to identify witches, whose bodies were thought to be repelled by water and therefore to float. Ducking had long since gone out of practice in Great Britain by the end of the nineteenth century.
4. Slimy.
5. Infectious. The idea is that rumors are spreading like a contagious disease.

Jones almost into Rwstog. The story that Nebogipfel had been heard within the Manse chanting, in conjunction with the Williamses, horrible blasphemy, and that a "black flapping thing, of the size of a young calf," had thereupon entered the gap in the roof, was universally believed in. A grisly anecdote, that owed its origination to a stumble in the churchyard, was circulated, to that effect that the Doctor had been caught ghoulishly tearing with his long white fingers at a new-made grave. The numerously attested declarations that Nebogipfel and the murdered Williams had been seen hanging the sons on a ghostly gibbet, at the back of the house, was due to the electric illumination of a fitfully wind-shaken tree. A hundred like stories hurtled thickly about the village and darkened the moral atmosphere. The Reverend Elijah Ulysses Cook, hearing of the tumult, sallied forth to allay it, and narrowly escaped drawing on himself the gathering lightning.

By eight o'clock (it was Monday the twenty-second of July) a grand demonstration had organized itself against the "necromancer." A number of bolder hearts among the men formed the nucleus of the gathering, and at nightfall Arthur Price Williams, John Peters, and others brought torches and raised their spark-raining flames aloft with curt ominous suggestions. The less adventurous village manhood came straggling late to the rendezvous, and with them the married women came in groups of four or five, greatly increasing the excitement of the assembly with their shrill hysterical talk and active imaginations. After these the children and young girls, overcome by undefinable dread, crept quietly out of the too silent and shadowy houses into the yellow glare of pine knots, and the tumultuary[6] noise of the thickening people. By nine, nearly half the Llyddwdd population was massed before the "Pig and Whistle." There was a confused murmur of many tongues, but above all the stir and chatter of the growing crowd could be heard the coarse, cracked voice of the bloodthirsty old fanatic, Pritchard, drawing a congenial lesson from the fate of the four hundred and fifty idolators of Carmel.[7]

Just as the church clock was beating out the hour, an occultly originated movement up hill began,[8] and soon the whole assembly, men, women, and children, was moving in a fear-compacted mass, towards the ill-fated doctor's abode. As they left the brightly-lit public house behind them, a quavering female voice began singing one

---

6. Confused and discordant. "The yellow glare of pine knots" refers to the light of burning torches made of pine wood.
7. In 1 Kings 18, 450 priests of the false god Baal ascend Mount Carmel and offer a sacrifice to their deity in vain, while the prophet Elijah's prayer to God is immediately answered.
8. By "an occultly originated movement" Wells seems to mean that the collective impulse to begin marching up the hill could not easily be traced to its source.

of those grim-sounding canticles that so satisfy the Calvinistic ear. In a wonderfully short time, the tune had been caught up, first by two or three, and then by the whole procession, and the manifold shuffling of heavy shoon[9] grew swiftly into rhythm with the beats of the hymn. When, however, their goal rose, like a blazing star, over the undulation of the road, the volume of the chanting suddenly died away, leaving only the voices of the ringleaders, shouting indeed now somewhat out of tune, but, if anything, more vigorously than before. Their persistence and example nevertheless failed to prevent a perceptible breaking and slackening of the pace, as the Manse was neared, and when the gate was reached, the whole crowd came to a dead halt. Vague fear for the future had begotten the courage that had brought the villagers thus far: fear for the present now smothered its kindred birth. The intense blaze from the gaps in the deathlike silent pile lit up rows of livid, hesitating faces: and a smothered, frightened sobbing broke out among the children. "Well," said Arthur Price Williams, addressing Jack Peters, with an expert assumption of modest discipleship, "what do we do *now*, Jack?" But Peters was regarding the Manse with manifest dubiety, and ignored the question. The Llyddwdd witch-find seemed to be suddenly aborting.

At this juncture old Pritchard suddenly pushed his way forward, gesticulatng weirdly with his bony hands and long arms. "*What!*" he shouted, in broken notes, "fear ye to smite when the Lord hateth? *Burn* the warlock!" And seizing a flambeau from Peters, he flung open the rickety gate and strode on down the drive, his torch leaving a coiling trail of scintillant sparks on the night wind. "Burn the warlock," screamed a shrill voice from the wavering crowd, and in a moment the gregarious human instinct had prevailed. With an outburst of incoherent, threatening voice, the mob poured after the fanatic.

Woe betide the Philosopher now! They expected barricaded doors; but with a groan of conscious insufficiency, the hinge-rusted portals swung wide at the push of Pritchard. Blinded by the light, he hesitated for a second on the threshold, while his followers came crowding up behind him.

Those who were there say that they saw Dr. Nebogipfel, standing in the toneless electric glare, on a peculiar erection of brass and ebony and ivory; and that he seemed to be smiling at them, half pityingly and half scornfully, as it is said martyrs are wont to smile. Some assert, moreover, that by his side was sitting a tall man, clad in ravenswing, and some even aver that this second man—whom others deny—bore on his face the likeness of the Reverend Elijah Ulysses Cook, while others declare that he resembled the description of the

9. Shoes.

murdered Williams. Be that as it may, it must now go unproven for
ever, for suddenly a wondrous thing smote the crowd as it swarmed
in through the entrance. Pritchard pitched headlong on the floor
senseless. Wild shouts and shrieks of anger, changed in mid utter-
ance to yells of agonizing fear, or to the mute gasp of heart-stopping
horror: and then a frantic rush was made for the doorway.

For the calm, smiling doctor, and his quiet, black-clad companion, and the polished platform which upbore them, had vanished
before their eyes!

HOW AN ESOTERIC STORY BECAME POSSIBLE

A silvery-foliaged willow by the side of a mere. Out of the cress-
spangled waters below, rise clumps of sedge-blades, and among them
glows the purple fleur-de-lys, and sapphire vapour of forget-me-nots.
Beyond is a sluggish stream of water reflecting the intense blue of the
moist Fenland sky; and beyond that a low osier-fringed eyot.[1] This
limits all the visible universe, save some scattered pollards and spear-
like poplars showing against the violet distance. At the foot of the willow reclines the Author watching a copper butterfly fluttering from
iris to iris.

Who can fix the colours of the sunset? Who can take a cast of
flame? Let him essay to register the mutations of mortal thought as it
wanders from a copper butterfly to the disembodied soul, and thence
passes to spiritual motions and the vanishing of Dr. Moses Nebogipfel
and the Rev. Elijah Ulysses Cook from the world of sense.

As the author lay basking there and speculating, as another once
did under the Budh tree,[2] on mystic transmutations, a presence
became apparent. There was a somewhat on the eyot between him
and the purple horizon—an opaque reflecting entity, making itself
dimly perceptible by reflection in the water to his averted eyes. He
raised them in curious surprise.

What was it?

He stared in stupefied astonishment at the apparition, doubted,
blinked, rubbed his eyes, stared again, and believed. It was solid, it
cast a shadow, and it upbore two men. There was white metal in it
that blazed in the noontide sun like incandescent magnesium, ebony
bars that drank in the light, and white parts that gleamed like polished ivory. Yet withal it seemed unreal. The thing was not square as
a machine ought to be, but all awry: it was twisted and seemed
falling over, hanging in two directions, as those queer crystals called
triclinic[3] hang; it seemed like a machine that had been crushed or

---

1. A small island
2. In Buddhist tradition, the tree associated with the Buddha's achieving enlightenment.
3. Triclinic crystals have the least symmetry of any crystal systems.

warped; it was suggestive and not confirmatory, like the machine of a disordered dream. The men, too, were dreamlike. One was short, intensely sallow, with a strangely-shaped head, and clad in a garment of dark olive green; the other was grotesquely out of place, evidently a clergyman of the Established Church, a fair-haired, pale-faced respectable-looking man.

Once more doubt came rushing in on the author. He sprawled back and stared at the sky, rubbed his eyes, stared at the willow wands that hung between him and the blue, closely examined his hands to see if his eyes had any new things to relate about them, and then sat up again and stared at the eyot. A gentle breeze stirred the osiers; a white bird was flapping its way through the lower sky. The machine of the vision had vanished! It was an illusion—a projection of the subjective—an assertion of the immateriality of mind. "Yes," interpolated the sceptic faculty, "but *how comes it that the clergyman is still there?*"

The clergyman had not vanished. In intense perplexity the author examined this black-coated phenomenon as he stood regarding the world with hand-shaded eyes. The author knew the periphery of that eyot by heart, and the question that troubled him was, "Whence?" The clergyman looked as Frenchmen look when they land at Newhaven[4]—intensely travel-worn; his clothes showed rubbed and seamy in the bright day. When he came to the edge of the island and shouted a question to the author, his voice was broken and trembled. "Yes," answered the author, "it is an island. *How did you get there?*"

But the clergyman, instead of replying to this, asked a very strange question.

He said "Are you in the nineteenth century?" The author made him repeat that question before he replied. "Thank heaven," cried the clergyman rapturously. Then he asked very eagerly for the exact date.

"August the ninth, eighteen hundred and eighty-seven," he repeated after the author. "Heaven be praised!" and sinking down on the eyot so that the sedges hid him, he audibly burst into tears.

Now the author was mightily surprised at all this, and going a certain distance along the mere, he obtained a punt,[5] and getting into it he hastily poled to the eyot where he had last seen the clergyman. He found him lying insensible among the reeds, and carried him in his punt to the house where he lived, and the clergyman lay there insensible for ten days.

Meanwhile, it became known that he was the Rev. Elijah Cook, who had disappeared from Llyddwdd with Dr. Moses Nebogipfel three weeks before.

---

4. A port on the southern coast of England, between Brighton and Eastbourne.
5. A shallow, flat-bottomed boat.

On August 19th, the nurse called the author out of his study to speak to the invalid. He found him perfectly sensible, but his eyes were strangely bright, and his face was deadly pale. "Have you found out who I am?" he asked.

"You are the Rev. Elijah Ulysses Cook, Master of Arts, of Pembroke College, Oxford, and Rector of Llyddwdd, near Rwstog, in Caernarvon."

He bowed his head. "Have you been told anything of how I came here?"

"I found you among the reeds," I said. He was silent and thoughtful for a while. "I have a deposition to make. Will you take it? It concerns the murder of an old man named Williams, which occurred in 1862, this disappearance of Dr. Moses Nebogipfel, the abduction of a ward in the year 4003—"

The author stared.

"The year of our Lord 4003," he corrected. "She would come. Also several assaults on public officials in the years 17,901 and 2."

The author coughed.

"The years 17,901 and 2, and valuable medical, social, and physiographical data for all time."

After a consultation with the doctor, it was decided to have the deposition taken down, and this is what constitutes the remainder of the story of the Chronic Argonauts.

On August 29th 1887, the Rev. Elijah Cook died. His body was conveyed to Llyddwdd, and buried in the churchyard there.

II. The Esoteric Story Based on the Clergyman's Depositions

THE ANACHRONIC[6] MAN

Incidentally it has been remarked in the first part, how the Reverend Elijah Ulysses Cook attempted and failed to quiet the superstitious excitement of the villagers on the afternoon of the memorable twenty-second of July. His next proceeding was to try and warn the unsocial philosopher of the dangers which impended. With this intent he made his way from the rumour-pelted village, through the silent, slumbrous heat of the July afternoon, up the slopes of Pen-y-pwll, to the old Manse. His loud knocking at the heavy door called forth dull resonance from the interior, and produced a shower of lumps of plaster and fragments of decaying touchwood from the rickety porch, but beyond this the dreamy stillness of the summer mid-day remained unbroken. Everything was so quiet as he stood there expectant, that the occasional speech of the haymakers a mile away in the fields, over towards Rwstog, could be distinctly heard. The reverend gentleman waited long, then knocked again, and

6. Out of its proper position in time.

waited again, and listened, until the echoes and the patter of rub-
bish had melted away into the deep silence, and the creeping in the
blood-vessels of his ears had become oppressively audible, swelling
and sinking with sounds like the confused murmuring of a distant
crowd, and causing a suggestion of anxious discomfort to spread
slowly over his mind.

Again he knocked, this time loud, quick blows with his stick, and
almost immediately afterwards, leaning his hand against the door,
he kicked its panels vigorously. There was a shouting of echoes, a
protesting jarring of hinges, and then the oaken door yawned and
displayed, in the blue blaze of the electric light, vestiges of partitions, piles of planking and straw, masses of metal, heaps of papers
and overthrown apparatus, to the rector's astonished eyes. "Doctor
Nebogipfel, excuse my intruding," he called out, but the only
response was a reverberation among the black beams and shadows
that hung dimly above. For almost a minute he stood there, leaning
forward over the threshold, staring at the glittering mechanisms,
diagrams, books, scattered indiscriminately with broken food, packing cases, heaps of coke, hay, and microcosmic lumber, about the
undivided house cavity; and then, removing his hat and treading
stealthily, as if the silence were a sacred thing, he stepped into the
apparently deserted shelter of the Doctor.

His eyes sought everywhere, as he cautiously made his way through
the confusion, with a strange anticipation of finding Nebogipfel
hidden somewhere in the sharp black shadows among the litter, so
strong in him was an indescribable sense of a perceiving presence.
This feeling was so vivid that, when, after an abortive exploration, he
seated himself upon Nebogipfel's diagram-covered bench, it made
him explain in a forced hoarse voice to the stillness—"He is not here. I
have something to say to him. I must wait for him." It was so vivid, too,
that the trickling of some grit down the wall in the vacant corner
behind him made him start round in a sudden perspiration. There was
nothing visible there, but turning his head back, he was stricken rigid
with horror by the swift, noiseless apparition of Nebogipfel, ghastly
pale, and with red stained hands, crouching upon a strange-looking
metallic platform, and with his deep grey eyes looking intently into the
visitor's face.

Cook's first impulse was to yell out his fear, but his throat was
paralysed, and he could only stare fascinated at the bizarre countenance that had thus crashed suddenly into visibility. The lips were
quivering and the breath came in short convulsive sobs. The unhuman forehead was wet with perspiration, while the veins were
swollen, knotted and purple. The Doctor's red hands, too, he
noticed, were trembling, as the hands of slight people tremble after
intense muscular exertion, and his lips closed and opened as if he,

too, had a difficulty in speaking as he gasped, "Who—what do you do here?"

Cook answered not a word, but stared with hair erect, open mouth, and dilated eyes, at the dark red unmistakeable smear that streaked the pure ivory and gleaming nickel and shining ebony of the platform.

"What are you doing here?" repeated the doctor, raising himself. "What do you want?"

Cook gave a convulsive effort. "In Heaven's name, *what* are you?" he gasped; and then black curtains came closing in from every side, sweeping the squatting, dwarfish phantasm that reeled before him into rayless, voiceless night.

The Reverend Elijah Ulysses Cook recovered his perceptions to find himself lying on the floor of the old Manse, and Doctor Nebogipfel, no longer blood-stained and with all trace of his agitation gone, kneeling by his side and bending over him with a glass of brandy in his hand. "Do not be alarmed, sir," said the philosopher with a faint smile, as the clergyman opened his eyes. "I have not treated you to a disembodied spirit, or anything nearly so extraordinary . . . May I offer you this?"

The clergyman submitted quietly to the brandy, and then stared perplexed into Nebogipfel's face, vainly searching his memory for what occurrences had preceded his insensibility. Raising himself at last into a sitting posture, he saw the oblique mass of metals that had appeared with the doctor, and immediately all that happened flashed back upon his mind. He looked from this structure to the recluse, and from the recluse to the structure.

"There is absolutely no deception, sir," said Nebogipfel with the slightest trace of mockery in his voice. "I lay no claim to work in matters spiritual. It is a *bona fide* mechanical contrivance, a thing emphatically of this sordid world. Excuse me—just one minute." He rose from his knees, stepped upon the mahogany platform, took a curiously curved lever in his hand and pulled it over. Cook rubbed his eyes. There certainly was no deception. The doctor and the machine had vanished.

The reverend gentleman felt no horror this time, only a slight nervous shock, to see the doctor presently re-appear "in the twinkling of an eye" and get down from the machine. From that he walked in a straight line with his hands behind his back and his face downcast, until his progress was stopped by the intervention of a circular saw; then, turning round sharply on his heel, he said:

"I was thinking while I was . . . away . . . Would you like to come? I should greatly value a companion."

The clergyman was still sitting, hatless, on the floor. "I am afraid," he said slowly, "you will think me stupid—"

"Not at all," interrupted the doctor. "The stupidity is mine. You desire to have all this explained . . . wish to know where I am going first. I have spoken so little with men of this age for the last ten years or more that I have ceased to make due allowances and concessions for other minds. I will do my best, but that I fear will be very unsatisfactory. It is a long story . . . Do you find that floor comfortable to sit on? If not, there is a nice packing case over there, or some straw behind you, or this bench—the diagrams are done with now, but I am afraid of the drawing pins. You may sit on the Chronic Argo!"

"*No*, thank you," slowly replied the clergyman, eyeing that deformed structure thus indicated, suspiciously; "I am *quite* comfortable here."

"Then I will begin. Do you read fables? Modern ones?"

"I am afraid I must confess to a good deal of fiction," said the clergyman depreciatingly. "In Wales the ordained ministers of the sacraments of the Church have perhaps too large a share of leisure—"

"Have you read the Ugly Duckling?"

"Hans Christian Andersen's—yes—in my childhood."

"A wonderful story—a story that has ever been full of tears and heart swelling hopes for me, since first it came to me in my lonely boyhood and saved me from unspeakable things. That story, if you understand it well, will tell you almost all that you should know of me to comprehend how that machine came to be thought of in a mortal brain . . . Even when I read that simple narrative for the first time, a thousand bitter experiences had begun the teaching of my isolation among the people of my birth—I knew the story was for me. The ugly duckling that proved to be a swan, that lived through all contempt and bitterness, to float at last sublime. From that hour forth, I dreamt of meeting with my kind, dreamt of encountering that sympathy I knew was my profoundest need. Twenty years I lived in that hope, lived and worked, lived and wandered, loved even, and, at last, despaired. Only once among all those millions of wondering, astonished, indifferent, contemptuous, and insidious faces that I met with in that passionate wandering, looked *one* upon me as I desired . . . looked—"

He paused. The Reverend Cook glanced up into his face, expecting some indication of the deep feeling that had sounded in his last words. It was downcast, clouded, and thoughtful, but the mouth was rigidly firm.

"In short, Mr. Cook, I discovered that I was one of those superior Cagots[7] called a genius—a man born out of my time—a man thinking the thoughts of a wiser age, doing things and believing things that men now cannot understand, and that in the years ordained to me

---

7. During the fourteenth and fifteenth centuries, the Cagot people of southern France were accused at various times of being heretics, lepers, sorcerers, and cannibals. Unsurprisingly, they were treated as pariahs.

there was nothing but silence and suffering for my soul—unbroken solitude, man's bitterest pain. I knew I was an Anachronic Man; my age was still to come. One filmy hope alone held me to life, a hope to which I clung until it had become a certain thing. Thirty years of unremitting toil and deepest thought among the hidden things of matter and form and life, and then *that*, the Chronic Argo, the ship that sails through time, and now I go to join my generation, to journey through the ages till my time has come."

THE CHRONIC ARGO

Dr. Nebogipfel paused, looking in sudden doubt at the clergyman's perplexed face. "You think that sounds mad," he said, "to travel through time?"

"It certainly jars with accepted opinions," said the clergyman, allowing the faintest suggestion of controversy to appear in his intonation, and speaking apparently to the Chronic Argo. Even clergymen of the Church of England you see can have a suspicion of illusions at times.

"It certainly does jar with accepted opinions," agreed the philosopher cordially. "It does more than that—it defies accepted opinions to mortal combat. Opinions of all sorts, Mr. Cook,—Scientific Theories, Laws, Articles of Belief, or, to come to elements, Logical Premises, Ideas, or whatever you like to call them,—all are, from the infinite nature of things, so many diagrammatic caricatures of the ineffable,—caricatures altogether to be avoided save where they are necessary in the shaping of results—as chalk outlines are necessary to the painter and plans and sections to the engineer. Men, from the exigencies of their being, find this hard to believe."

The Rev. Elijah Ulysses Cook nodded his head with the quiet smile of one whose opponent has unwittingly given a point.

"It is as easy to come to regard ideas as complete reproductions of entities as it is to roll off a log. Hence it is that almost all civilized men believe in the *reality* of the Greek geometrical conceptions."

"Oh! pardon me, sir," interrupted Cook. "Most men know that a geometrical point has no existence in matter, and the same with a geometrical line. I think you underrate . . ."

"Yes, yes, *those* things are recognized," said Nebogipfel calmly; "but now . . . a cube. Does that exist in the material universe?"

"Certainly."

"An instantaneous cube?"

"I don't know what you intend by that expression."

"Without any other sort of extension; a body having length, breadth, and thickness, exists?"

"What other sort of extension *can* there be?" asked Cook, with raised eyebrows.

"Has it never occurred to you that no form can exist in the material universe that has no extension in time? . . . Has it never glimmered upon your consciousness that nothing stood between men and a geometry of four dimensions—length, breadth, thickness, and *duration*—but the inertia of opinion, the impulse from the Levantine philosophers of the bronze age?"[8]

"Putting it that way," said the clergyman, "it does look as though there was a flaw somewhere in the notion of tridimensional being; *but* . . ." He became silent, leaving that sufficiently eloquent "but" to convey all the prejudice and distrust that filled his mind.

"When we take up this new light of a fourth dimension and reexamine our physical science in its illumination," continued Nebogipfel, after a pause, "we find ourselves no longer limited by hopeless restriction to a certain beat of time—to our own generation. Locomotion along lines of duration—chronic navigation comes within the range, first, of geometrical theory, and then of practical mechanics. There was a time when men could only move horizontally and in their appointed country. The clouds floated above them unattainable things, mysterious chariots of those fearful gods who dwelt among the mountain summits. Speaking practically, man in those days was restricted to motion in two dimensions; and even there circumambient ocean and hypoborean fear bound him in.[9] But those times were to pass away. First, the keel of Jason cut its way between the Symplegades, and then in the fulness of time, Columbus dropped anchor in a bay of Atlantis. Then man burst his bidimensional limits, and invaded the third dimension, soaring with Montgolfier into the clouds, and sinking with the diving bell into the purple treasure-caves of the waters.[1] And now another step, and the hidden past and unknown future are before us. We stand upon a mountain summit with the plains of the ages spread below."

Nebogipfel paused and looked down at his hearer.

The Reverend Elijah Cook was sitting with an expression of strong distrust on his face. Preaching much had brought home certain truths to him very vividly, and he always suspected rhetoric. "Are

---

8. The reference is not to any particular philosopher or school of philosophy, but instead gestures toward the origins of Western philosophy in the eastern Mediterranean in the second millennium BCE.
9. In Greek mythology, the hypoborean race lived in a land of sunshine beyond the north wind. By "hypoborean fear" Nebogipfel could mean a fear of the unknown, here exemplified by the hypoboreans' extreme northern home; or he could mean something like a fear of high altitudes.
1. In Greek mythology, the Symplegades were a pair of rocks at the entrance to the Hellespont (the Dardanelles) in Asia Minor that clashed together at random intervals. Jason and the Argonauts successfully passed between the Symplegades during their quest for the Golden Fleece. One location proposed during the Middle Ages for the lost continent of Atlantis was the unexplored ocean west of the Canary Islands; when Christopher Columbus landed in the Bahamas in October 1492, he may well have wondered whether he had discovered Atlantis. The brothers Montgolfier, Joseph-Michel (1740–1810) and Jacques-Étienne (1745–1799), were responsible for the first manned flight, in a hot-air balloon.

those things figures of speech," he asked; "or am I to take them as precise statements? Do you speak of travelling through time in the same way as one might speak of Omnipotence making His pathway in the storm, or do you—a—mean what you say?"

Dr. Nebogipfel smiled quietly. "Come and look at these diagrams," he said, and then with elaborate simplicity he commenced to explain again to the clergyman the new quadridimensional geometry. Insensibly Cook's aversion passed away, and seeming impossibility grew possible, now that such tangible things as diagrams and models could be brought forward in evidence. Presently he found himself asking questions, and his interest grew deeper and deeper as Nebogipfel slowly and with precise clearness unfolded the beautiful order of his strange invention. The moments slipped away unchecked, as the Doctor passed on to the narrative of his research, and it was with a start of surprise that the clergyman noticed the deep blue of the dying twilight through the open doorway.

"The voyage," said Nebogipfel concluding his history, "will be full of un-dreamt of dangers—already in one brief essay I have stood in the very jaws of death—but it is also full of the divinest promise of undreamt-of joy. Will you come? Will you walk among the people of the Golden Years? . . ."

But the mention of death by the philosopher had brought flooding back to the mind of Cook, all the horrible sensations of that first apparition.

"Dr. Nebogipfel . . . one question?" He hesitated. 'On your hands . . . *Was it blood?*"

Nebogipfel's countenance fell. He spoke slowly.

"When I had stopped my machine, I found myself in this room as it used to be. *Hark!*"

"It is the wind in the trees towards Rwstog."

"It sounded like the voices of a multitude of people singing . . . When I had stopped I found myself in this room as it used to be. An old man, a young man, and a lad were sitting at a table—reading some book together. I stood behind them unsuspected. 'Evil spirits assailed him,' read the old man; 'but it is written, "to him that overcometh shall be given life eternal." They came as entreating friends, but he endured through all their snares. They came as principalities and powers, but he defied them in the name of the King of Kings. Once even it is told that in his study, while he was translating the New Testament into German, the Evil One himself appeared before him . . .'[2] Just then the lad glanced timorously round, and with a fearful wail fainted away . . ."

2. The old man appears to be reading from a life of Martin Luther (1483–1546), whose translations of the Old and New Testaments into German were among the first and most influential vernacular editions of the Bible.

"The others sprang at me . . . It was a fearful grapple . . . The old man clung to my throat, screaming 'Man or Devil, I defy thee . . .'"

"I could not help it. We rolled together on the floor . . . the knife his trembling son had dropped came to my hand . . . *Hark!*"

He paused and listened, but Cook remained staring at him in the same horror-stricken attitude he had assumed when the memory of the blood-stained hands had rushed back over his mind.

"Do you hear what they are crying? *Hark!*"

Burn the warlock! Burn the murderer!

"Do you hear? There is no time to be lost."

Slay the murderer of cripples. Kill the devil's claw!

"Come! Come!"

Cook, with a convulsive effort, made a gesture of repugnance and strode to the doorway. A crowd of black figures roaring towards him in the red torchlight made him recoil. He shut the door and faced Nebogipfel.

The thin lips of the Doctor curled with a contemptuous sneer. "They will kill you if you stay," he said; and seizing the unresisting visitor by the wrist, he forced him towards the glittering machine. Cook sat down and covered his face with his hands.

In another moment the door was flung open, and old Pritchard stood blinking on the threshold.

A pause. A hoarse shout changing suddenly into a sharp shrill shriek. A thunderous roar like the bursting forth of a great fountain of water.

The voyage of the Chronic Argonauts had begun.

END OF PART II OF THE CHRONIC ARGONAUTS

How did it end? How came it that Cook wept with joy to return once more to this nineteenth century of ours? Why did not Nebogipfel remain with him? All that, and more also, has been written, and will or will never be read, according as Fate may have decreed to the Curious Reader.[3]

Revising *The Chronic Argonauts*[†]

In the first rewriting Dr. Nebogipfel and the Rev. Elijah Ulysses Cook still appear, but the scene shifts to a village on the South Downs. They arrive in a future much less changed from our time than that portrayed

---

3. The story ends abruptly here.

† From Geoffrey West, *H. G. Wells: A Sketch for a Portrait* (London: Gerald Howe, 1930), pp. 291–92. Wells continued to work on his time-travel story in the years following its appearance in the *Science Schools Journal*. Between 1889 and 1892 he produced two complete revisions. The manuscripts for both are lost. In his 1930 biography of Wells, Geoffrey West quotes the recollections of Wells's college friend A. Morley Davies concerning these lost versions of the story.

in *The Time Machine*. The upper and lower worlds exist, but their inhabitants are not yet two distinct species. A scientific aristocracy still survives in a decadent form as a red-robed priesthood, and art and literature are cultivated in a very dilettante manner. The Chronic Argonauts stir up these weary idlers, and even make it fashionable to read books. The priests take their visitors to see a vast museum, but themselves grow bored and leave the pair to explore alone, warning them against the passages which lead "down." They go "down," and discover an underworld working to support the upper world. Eventually some compunction is aroused among the aristocracy, and some kindly disposed persons descend to sing and play to the workers. At this the underworld explodes into revolution, kills them, and rushes up in a mob to carry out a general massacre. In the ensuing panic the argonauts make for their machine. Cook has become fascinated by a certain Lady Dis, and tries to take her with him, but in the excitement of the escape he discovers that all her beauty is artificial, and flings her off as he climbs into the machine. They travel back to our own time, but overshoot the mark and are nearly killed by a party of paleolithic men. At last they hit the nineteenth century, when Nebogipfel drops Cook and then vanishes with the machine.

In the third version, of which fragments only were read to me, Nebogipfel and Cook are cut out. There is no such underworld as in the earlier version and *The Time Machine*, the future being one in which a ruling class governs by hypnotism, but the end of the story is somewhat similar to that given above. One of the priests determines to put an end to the hypnotism and calls to the people to awake. They awake and kill him, and march with his head on a pole to slay his fellows. In the panic the same revelation is made of the artificial means by which the ruling class had hidden the physical degeneration resulting from their idle life.

National Observer *Time Machine*[†]

Time Travelling

POSSIBILITY OR PARADOX

The Philosophical Inventor was expounding a recondite matter to his friends. The fire burnt brightly, and the soft radiance of the

---

† From *National Observer* (March–June 1894). The seven installments appeared in the issues of March 17, 24, and 31, April 21 and 28, May 19, and June 23. After he abandoned *The Chronic Argonauts*, Wells continued to work intermittently on a time-travel story. In response to an invitation from the editor William Ernest Henley in early 1894, Wells submitted a series of pieces to the *National Observer* that, with subsequent further revision, eventually became *The Time Machine*. The installments abruptly ended when Henley left the *National Observer* and the journal's new editor discontinued the series.

incandescent lights in the lilies of silver, caught the bubbles that flashed and passed in our glasses of amber fluid.[1] Our chairs, being his patents, embraced and caressed us rather than submitted to be sat upon, and there was that luxurious after-dinner atmosphere, when thought runs gracefully free of the trammels of precision. And he put it to us in this way, as we sat and lazily admired him and his fecundity.

"You must follow me carefully here. For I shall have to controvert one or two ideas that are almost universally accepted. The geometry, for instance, they taught you at school is founded on a misconception."

"Is not that rather a large thing to expect us to begin upon?" said the argumentative person with the red hair.

"I do not mean to ask you to accept anything without reasonable ground for it. But you know of course that a mathematical line, a line of thickness *nil*, has no real existence. They taught you that. Neither has a mathematical plane. These things are mere abstractions."

"That is all right," said the man with the red hair.

"Nor can a cube, having only length, breadth, and thickness, have a real existence."

"There I object," said the red-haired man. "Of course a solid body may exist. All real things—"

"So most people think. But wait a moment. Can an *instantaneous* cube exist?"

"Don't follow you," said the red-haired man.

"Can a cube that does not last for any time at all, have a real existence?"

The red-haired man became pensive.

"Clearly," the Philosophical Inventor proceeded; "any real body must have extension in four directions: it must have length, breadth, thickness, and—duration. But through a natural infirmity of the flesh, which I will explain to you in a moment, we incline to overlook the fact. There are really four dimensions, three which we call the three planes of space, and a fourth, time. There is, however, a tendency to draw an unreal difference between the former three and the latter, because it happens that our consciousness moves intermittently in one direction along the latter from the beginning to the end of our lives."

"That," said the very young man, making spasmodic efforts to relight a cigar over the lamp, "that . . . very clear indeed."

"Now it is very remarkable that this is so extensively overlooked," continued the Philosophical Inventor with a slight accession of cheerfulness. "Really this is what I meant by the fourth dimension, though some people who talk about the fourth dimension do not know they mean it. It is only another way of looking at time. *There is*

1. "Lilies of silver" could refer either to silver fittings shaped like lilies attached to the electric light fixtures or to a lily pattern engraved on the silverware. In either case the reflected light sparkles in the bubbles of the company's after-dinner drinks.

no difference between time and any of the three dimensions of space except that our consciousness moves along it. But some foolish people have got hold of the wrong side of the idea. You have all heard what they have to say about this fourth dimension."

"*I* have not," said the provincial mayor.

"It is simply this. That space, as our mathematicians have it, is spoken of as having three dimensions, which one may call length, breadth, and thickness, and is always definable by reference to three planes, each at right angles to the others. But some philosophical people have been asking why *three* dimensions particularly—why not another direction at right angles to the other three?—and have even tried to construct a four-dimensional geometry. Professor Simon Newcombe was expounding this to the New York Mathematical Society only a month or so ago.[2] You know how on a flat surface which has only two dimensions we can represent a figure of a three-dimensional solid, and similarly they think that by models of three dimensions they could represent one of four—if they could master the perspective of the thing. See?"

"I think so," murmured the provincial mayor, and knitting his brows he lapsed into an introspective state, his lips moving as one who repeats mystic words. "Yes, I think I see it now," he said after some time, brightening in a quite transitory manner.

"Well, I do not mind telling you I have been at work upon this geometry of four dimensions for some time. Some of my results are curious. For instance, here is a portrait of a man at eight years old, another at the age of fifteen, another seventeen, another of twenty-three, and so on. All these are evidently sections, as it were, three-dimensional representations of his four-dimensional being, which is a fixed and unalterable thing."

"Scientific people," proceeded the philosopher after the pause required for the proper assimilation of this, "know very well that time is only a kind of space. Here is a popular scientific diagram, a weather record. This line I trace with my finger shows the movement of the barometer. Yesterday it was so high, yesterday night it fell, then this morning it rose again, and so gently upward to here. Surely the mercury did not trace this line in any of the dimensions of space generally recognised? But certainly it traced such a line, and that line, therefore, we must conclude was along the time-dimension."

"But," said the red-haired man, staring hard at a coal in the fire; "if time is really only a fourth dimension of space, why is it, and why has it always been, regarded as something different? And why cannot we

2. Simon Newcomb, not Newcombe (1835–1909), was professor of mathematics and astronomy at Johns Hopkins University. He raised (only to reject) the possibility of constructing a four-dimensional geometry during an address delivered at the annual meeting of the New York Mathematical Society in December 1893.

move about in time as we move about in the other dimensions of space?"

The philosophical person smiled with great sweetness. "Are you so sure we can move freely in space? Right and left we can go, backward and forward freely enough, and men have always done so. I admit we move freely in two dimensions. But how about up and down? Gravitation limits us there."

"Not exactly," said the red-haired man. "There are balloons."

"But before the balloons, man, save for spasmodic jumping and the inequalities of the surface, had no freedom of vertical movement."

"Still they could move a little up and down," said the red-haired man.

"Easier, far easier, down than up."

"And you cannot move at all in time, you cannot get away from the present moment."

"My dear sir, that is just where you are wrong. That is just where the whole world has gone wrong. We are always getting away from the present moment. Our consciousnesses, which are immaterial and have no dimensions, are passing along the time-dimension with a uniform velocity from the cradle to the grave. Just as we should travel *down* if we began our existence fifty miles above the earth's surface."

"But the great difficulty is this," interrupted the red-haired man. "You can move about in all directions of space, but you cannot move about in time."

"That is the germ of my great discovery. But you are wrong to say that we cannot move about in time. For instance, if I am recalling an incident very vividly I go back to the instant of its occurrence, I become absentminded as you say. I jump back for a moment. Of course we have no means of staying back for any length of time any more than a savage or an animal has of staying six feet above the ground. But a civilised man knows better. He can go up against gravitation in a balloon, and why should he not be able to stop or accelerate his drift along the time-dimension; or even turn about and travel the other way?"

"Oh, *this*," began the common-sense person "is all—"

"Why not?" said the Philosophical Inventor.

"It's against reason," said the common-sense person.

"What reason?" said the Philosophical Inventor.

"You can show black is white by argument," said the common-sense person; 'but you will never convince me."

"Possibly not," said the Philosophical Inventor. "But now you begin to see the object of my investigations into the geometry of four dimensions. I have a vague inkling of a machine—"

"To travel through time!" exclaimed the very young man.

"That shall travel indifferently in any direction of space and time as the driver determines."

The red-haired man contented himself with laughter.

"It would be remarkably convenient. One might travel back, and witness the Battle of Hastings!"[3]

"Don't you think you would attract attention?" said the red-haired man. "Our ancestors had no great tolerance for anachronisms."

"One might get one's Greek from the very lips of Homer and Plato!"

"In which case they would certainly plough you for the Little-go. The German scholars have improved Greek so much."[4]

"Then there is the future," said the very young man. "Just think! one might invest all one's money, leave it to accumulate at interest, and hurry on ahead!"

"To discover a society," said the red-haired man, "erected on a strictly communist basis."

"It will be very confusing, I am afraid," said the common-sense person. "But I suppose your machine is hardly complete yet?"

"Science," said the philosopher, "moves apace."

The Time Machine

"The last time I saw you, you were talking about a machine to travel through time," said the red-haired man.

The common-sense person groaned audibly. "Don't remind him of *that*," he said.

"My dear Didymus,[5] it is finished," said the Philosophical Inventor.

With violence, the red-haired man wanted to see it, and at once.

"There is no fire in the workshop," said the Philosophical Inventor, becoming luxuriously lazy in his pose, "and besides, I am in my slippers. No; I had rather be doubted."

"You are," said the red-haired man. "But tell us: Have you used it at all?"

"To confess the simple truth, even at my own expense, I have been horribly afraid. But I tried it, nevertheless. The sensations are atrocious—atrocious."

---

3. The defeat of the Saxons under King Harold by Norman forces under William the Conqueror at Hastings in 1066, which led to the conquest of England, is arguably the most famous battle in British history.
4. "To plough" was slang for "to fail." The first examination towards the B.A. degree at Cambridge University was colloquially called "the Little-go." The correct pronunciation of ancient Greek was a lively topic of debate throughout the nineteenth century. By the 1890s German scholars had long led the field of classical studies; the implied joke here is that they would have corrected the pronunciation of Homer and Plato themselves.
5. In the Gospel of John, the name Didymus is used on several occasions to refer to the apostle Thomas, who doubted the Resurrection until he saw Jesus with his own eyes.

His eye rested for a moment on the very young man, who with a moist white face was gallantly relighting the cigar the German officer had offered him.

"You see, when you move forward in time with a low velocity of (say) thirty in one, you get through a full day of twenty-four hours in about forty-eight minutes. This means dawn, morning, noon, evening, twilight, night, at about ordinary stage pace. After a few days are traversed, the alternations of light and gloom give one the sensations of London on a dismal day of drifting fog. Matters get very much worse as the speed is increased. The maximum of inconvenience is about two thousand in one; day and night in less than a minute. The sun rushes up the sky at a sickening pace, and the moon with its changing phases makes one's brain reel. And you get a momentary glimmer of the swift stars swinging in circles round the pole. After that, the faster you go the less you seem to feel it. The sun goes hop, hop, each day; the night is like the flapping of a black wing; the moon opens and shuts—full to new and new to full; the stars trace at last faint circles of silver in the sky. Then the sun, through the retention of impressions by the eye, becomes a fiery band in the heavens, with which the ghostly fluctuating belt of the moon interlaces, and the tint of the sky becomes a flickering deep blue. At last even the flickering ceases, and the only visible motion in all the universe is the swaying of the sun-belt as it dips towards the winter solstice and rises again to the summer. The transitory sickness is over. So under the burning triumphal arch of the sun, you sweep through the ages. One has all the glorious sensations of a swooping hawk or a falling man—for one of those trapeze fellows told me the sense of falling is very delicious—and much the same personal concern about the end of it."

The Philosophical Inventor stopped abruptly, and began to knock the ashes out of the filthy pipe he smokes.

"Not a bad description of the Cosmic Clock with the pendulum taken off," said the very young man after an interval.

"Plausible so far," said the red-haired man; "but we have to come to earth now. Or were you entirely engaged by the heavenly bodies?"

"No," said the Inventor; "I noticed a few things. For instance, when I was going at a comparatively slow pace, Mrs. Watchet came into the workshop by the door next to the house and out by the one into the yard. Really she took a minute or so, I suppose, to traverse the room, but to me she appeared to shoot across like a rocket. And so soon as the pace became considerable, the apparent velocity of people became so excessively great that I could no more see them than a man can see a cannonball flying through the air."

The common-sense person shivered and drew the air in sharply through his teeth.

"Then it is odd to see a tree grow up, flash its fan of green at you for a few score of summers, and vanish—all in the space of half an hour. Houses too shot up like stage buildings, stayed a while, and disappeared, and I noticed the hills grow visibly lower through the years with the wear of the gust and rain."

"It is odd," said the red-haired man, pursuing a train of thought, "that you were not interfered with by people. You see, you have been, I understand, through some hundred thousand years or so"—the Philosopher nodded—"and all that time you have been on one spot. People must have noticed you, even if you did not notice them. A gentlemen in a easy attitude, dressed in anachronisms, and meditating fixedly upon the celestial sphere, must in the course of ages, have palled upon the species. I wonder they did not try to remove you to a museum or make you . . ."

This amused the German officer very much. Without warning he filled the room with laughter, and some of it went upstairs and woke the children. "*Sehr gut!* Ha, ha! You are axplodet, mein friendt!"

"The same difficulty puzzled me—for a minute or so," said the Philosopher, as the air cleared. "But it is easily explained."

"*Gott in Himmel!*"[6] said the German officer.

"I don't know if you have heard the expression of 'presentation below the threshold.' It is a psychological technicality. Suppose, for instance, you put some red pigment on a sheet of paper, it excites a certain visual sensation, does it not? Now halve the amount of pigment, the sensation diminishes. Halve it again, the impression of red is still weaker. Continue the process. Clearly there will always be some pigment left, but a time will speedily arrive when the eye will refuse to follow the dilution, when the stimulus will be insufficient to excite the sensation of red. The presentation of red pigment to the senses is then said to be 'below the threshold.' Similarly my rapid passage through time, traversing a day in a minute fraction of a second, diluted the stimulus I offered to the perception of these excellent people of futurity far below . . ."

"Yes," said the red-haired man, interrupting after his wont. "You have parried that. And now another difficulty. I suppose while you were slipping thus invisibly through the ages, people walked about in the space you occupied. They may have pulled down your house about your head and built a brick wall in your substance. And yet, you know, it is generally believed that two bodies cannot occupy the same space."

"What an old-fashioned person you are!" said the Philosophical Inventor. "Have you never heard of the Atomic Theory? Don't you know that every body, solid, liquid, or gaseous, is made up of molecules with empty spaces between them? That leaves plenty of room

6. *Sehr gut*: very good. *Gott in Himmel*: good heavens (German).

to slip through a brick wall, if you only have momentum enough. A slight rise of temperature would be all one would notice and of course if the wall lasted too long and the warmth became uncomfortable one could shift the apparatus a little in space and get out of the inconvenience." He paused.

"But pulling up is a different matter. That is where the danger comes in. Suppose yourself to stop while there is another body in the same space. Clearly all your atoms will be jammed in with unparalleled nearness to the atoms of the foreign body. Violent chemical reactions would ensue. There would be a tremendous explosion. Hades! how it would puzzle posterity! I thought of this as I was sailing away thousands of years ahead. I lost my nerve. I brought my machine round in a whirling curve and started back full pelt. And so I pulled up again in the very moment and place of my start, in my workshop, and this afternoon. And ended my first time journey. Valuable, you see, chiefly as a lesson in the method of such navigation."

"Will you go again?" said the common-sense person.

"Just at present," said the Philosophical Inventor; "I scarcely know."

A.D. 12,203

A GLIMPSE OF THE FUTURE

He rose from his easy chair and took the little bronze lamp in his hand, when we reverted to the topic of his Time Machine. He smiled, "I know you will never believe me," he said, "until you see it with your own eyes." So speaking he led us down the staircase and along the narrow passage to his workshop. "I have had another little excursion since I saw you last," he remarked over his shoulder.

"It is an ill thing if one stop it too suddenly," said he as he stood holding the lamp for us to see; "though my life was happily spared."

"What happened?" said the sceptical man, staring suspiciously at the squat framework of aluminium, brass and ebony, that stood in the laboratory. It was an incomprehensible interlacing of bars and tubes, oddly awry, heeling over into the black shadows of the corner as if to elude our scrutiny. By the side of the leather saddle it bore, were two dials and three small levers curiously curved.

"You see how this rail is bent?" said the philosopher.

"I see you have bent it."

"And that rod of ivory is cracked."

"It is."

"The thing fell over as I stopped and flung me headlong."

He paused but no one spoke. He seemed to take it as acceptance, and proceeded to narrative.

"There was the sound of a clap of thunder in my ears. I may have been stunned for a moment. A pitiless hail was hissing around me, and I was sitting on soft turf beside the overturned Time Machine. I was on what seemed to be a little lawn in a garden, surrounded by rhododendron bushes, and I noticed that their mauve and purple blossoms were dropping in a shower under the beating of the hail-stones. Over the machine, the rebounding dancing hail hung in a little cloud, and it drove along the ground like smoke. In a moment I was wet to the skin. 'Fine hospitality,' said I, 'to a man who has trav-elled innumerable years to see you.' I stood up and looked round me. A colossal figure, carved apparently of some white stone, loomed indistinctly beyond the bushes through the hazy downpour. But all else of the world was invisible."

"H'm," said the sceptic, "this is interesting. May I ask the date?"

Our host pointed silently to the little dials.

"*Years*, ten—these divisions are thousands? I see now. Ten thou-sand, three hundred and nine,' said the common-sense person, read-ing. "*Days*, two hundred and forty-one. That is counting from now?"

"From now," said the Inventor. The common-sense person seemed satisfied by these figures, and the flavour of intelligent incredulity that had survived even the Inventor's exhibition of the machine, began to fade from his expression.

"Go on," said the doubter, looking hard into the machine.

"My sensations would be hard to describe. As the columns of hail grew thinner I saw the white figure more distinctly. It was very large, for a silver birch tree touched its shoulder. It was of white marble in shape something like a winged sphinx,[7] but the wings instead of being carried vertically over the back were spread on either side. It chanced that the face was towards me, the sightless eyes seemed to watch me. There was the faint shadow of a smile on the lips. I stood looking into this enigmatical countenance for a little space, half a minute, perhaps, or half an hour. As the hail drove before it, denser or thinner, it seemed to advance and recede. At last I tore my eyes far away from it for a moment, and saw that the hail curtain had worn threadbare, and that the sky was lightening with the promise of the sun. I looked up again at the crouching white shape, and suddenly the full temerity of my voyage came upon me. What might appear when that hazy curtain was altogether withdrawn? What might not have happened to men? What if cruelty had grown into a common passion? What if in this interval the race had lost its manliness, and had grown into something inhuman, unsympathetic and over-whelmingly powerful? To them I might seem some old-world savage animal only the more dreadful and disgusting for my likeness to themselves, a foul creature to be incontinently slain. I was seized with a panic fear. Already I saw other vast shapes, huge buildings

---

7. A mythical creature with the body of a winged lion and the head of a woman.

with intricate parapets, and a wooded hillside dimly creeping in upon me through the lessening storm. I turned in frantic mood to the Time Machine, and strove hard to readjust it.

"As I did so the shafts of the sun smote through the thunder-storm. The grey downpour was swept aside, and vanished like the trailing garments of a ghost. Above me was the intense blue of the summer sky with some faint brown shreds of cloud whirling into nothingness. The great buildings about me now stood out clear and distinct, shining with the wet of the thunderstorm and picked out in white by the unmelted hailstones piled along their courses. I felt nakedly exposed to a strange world. I felt as perhaps a bird may feel in the clear air, knowing the hawk wings above and will swoop. My fear grew to frenzy. I took a breathing space, set my teeth, and again grappled fiercely, wrist and knee, with the machine. It gave under my desperate onset and turned over. My chin was struck violently. With one hand on the saddle and the other on this lever I stood, panting heavily, in attitude to mount again.

"But with this recovery of a prompt retreat my courage recovered. I looked more curiously and less fearfully at this world of the remote future. In a circular opening high up in the wall of the nearer house I saw a group of figures, clad in robes of rich soft colour. They had seen me, and their faces were directed towards me. From some distant point behind this building a thin blade of colour shot into the blue air and went skimming in a wide ascending curve overhead. A white thing, travelling crow-fashion with a rare flap of the wings, may have been a flying machine. My attention was called from this to earth again by voices shouting. Coming through the bushes by the white sphinx could be seen the heads and shoulders of several men run-ning. One of these emerged in a pathway leading straight to the little lawn upon which I stood with my machine. His was a slight figure clad in a purple tunic, girdled at the waist with a leather belt. A kind of sandals or buskins seemed to be upon his feet—I could not clearly distinguish which. His legs were bare to the knees, and his head was bare. For the first time I noticed how warm the air was. He struck me as being a very beautiful and graceful figure, but indescribably frail. His flushed face reminded me of the more beautiful kind of con-sumptive, that hectic beauty of which we used to hear so much . . ."

"That," said the medical man, "entirely discredits your story." He was sitting on the bench near the circular saw. "It is so absolutely opposed to the probabilities of our hygienic science—"

"That you disbelieve an eye witness!" said the Philosophical Investigator.

"Well, you must admit the suggestion of pthisis,[8] coupled with a warm climate—"

---

8. Tuberculosis or any wasting pulmonary disease.

"Don't interrupt," said the red-haired man. "Have we not this battered machine here to settle our doubts?"

I turned to the Philosopher again, but he had taken the lamp and stood as if he would light us back through the passage. Apparently he was offended at the attempt to dispose of his story from internal evidence. The curtain fell abruptly upon our brief glimpse of A.D. 12,203, and the rest of the evening passed in an unsuccessful attempt on the part of the doctor to show that the physique of civilised man was better than that of the savage. I agreed with a remark of the Philosopher's: that even if this were the case, it was slender inference that the improvement would continue for the next ten thousand years.

The Refinement of Humanity

A.D. 12,203

This man, who said he had travelled through time, refrained, after our first scepticism, from any further speech of his experiences, and in some subtle way his silence, with perhaps a certain change we detected in his manner and in his expressed opinion of existing things, won us at last to a doubt of our own certain incredulity. Besides, even if he had not done as he said, even if he had not, by some juggling along the fourth dimension, glimpsed the world ten thousand years ahead, yet there might still be a sufficiently worthy lie wasting in his brain. So that some conversational inducements began to be thrown towards him, and at last he partially forgave us and produced some few further fragments of his travel story.

"Of the fragile beauty of these people of the distant future," said he, "I bear eye-witness, but how that beauty came to be, I can only speculate. You must not ask me for reasons."

"But did they not explain things to you?" asked the red-haired man.

"Odd as it may seem, I had no cicerone.[9] In all the narratives of people visiting the future that I have read, some obliging scandalmonger appears at an early stage, and begins to lecture on constitutional history and social economy, and to point out the celebrities. Indeed so little had I thought of the absurdity of this that I had actually anticipated something of the kind would occur in reality. In my day-dreams, while I was making the machine, I had figured myself lecturing and being lectured to about the progress of humanity, about the relations of the sexes, and about capital and labour, like a dismal Demological Congress.[1] But they didn't explain anything. They couldn't. They were the most illiterate people I ever met.

9. Tour guide.
1. A "Demological Congress" would be the elected governing body of a small town or community. The Philosophical Inventor seems to picture to himself a group of orators delivering long-winded speeches to one another.

"Yes, I was disappointed. On the other hand there were compensations. I had been afraid I might have to explain the principles of the Time Machine, and send a perfected humanity on experimental rides, with some chance of having my apparatus stolen or lost centuries away from me. But these people took it for granted I was heaven-descended, a meteoric man, coming as I did in a thunderstorm, and so soon as they saw me appear ran violently towards me, and some prostrated themselves and some knelt at my feet. 'Come,' said I, as I saw perhaps fifty of these dainty people engaged in this pleasing occupation; "this at least is some compensation for contemporary neglect." A feeling of fatherly exaltation replaced the diffidence of my first appearance. I made signs to them that they should rise from the damp turf, and therewith they stood smiling very fearlessly and pleasantly at me. The height of them was about four feet, none came much higher than my chest, and I noticed at once how exquisitely fine was the texture of their light garments, and how satin smooth their skins. Their faces—I must repeat—were distinctly of the fair consumptive type, with flushed cheeks, and without a trace of fulness. The hair was curled."

The medical man fidgeted in his chair. He began in a tone of protest: "But *a priori*—"[2]

The Philosophical Investigator anticipated his words. "You would object that this is against the drift of sanitary science. You believe the average height, average weight, average longevity will all be increased, that in the future humanity will breed and sanitate itself into human Megatheria.[3] I thought the same until this trip of mine. But, come to think, what I saw is just what one might have expected. Man, like other animals, has been moulded, and will be, by the necessities of his environment. What keeps men so large and strong as they are? The fact that if any drop below a certain level of power and capacity for competition, they die. Remove dangers, render physical exertion no longer a necessity but an excrescence upon life, abolish competition by limiting population: in the long run—"

"But," said the medical man, "even if man in the future no longer needs strength to fight against other men or beasts, he will still need a sufficient physique to resist disease."

"That is the queer thing," said the Time Traveller; "there was no disease. Somewhen between now and then your sanitary science must have won the battle it is beginning now. Bacteria, or at least all disease causing bacteria, must have been exterminated. I can explain it in no other way.

2. By definition; presumptively (Latin).
3. Giant ground sloths, now extinct; colloquially, the word refers to anything that has become large and ungainly.

"Certainly there had been a period of systematic scientific earth culture between now and then. Gnats, flies, and midges were gone, all troublesome animals, and thistles and thorns. The fruits of this age had no seeds, and the roses no prickles. Their butterflies were brilliant and abundant, and their dragonflies flying gems. It must have been done by selective breeding. But these delicious people had kept no books and knew no history. The world, I could speedily see, was perfectly organised—finished. It was still working as a perfect machine, had been so working for ages, but its very perfection had abolished the need of intelligence. What work was needed was done out of sight, and modesty, delicacy, had spread to all the necessary apparatus of life. The inquiries about their political economy I subsequently tried to make by signs, and by so much of their language as I learnt, were not understood or were gently parried. I saw no one eating. Indeed for some time I was in the way of starvation till I found a furtive but very pleasant and welcome meal of nuts and apples provided me in an elegant recess. They were entirely frugivorous, I found—like the Lemuridae.[4] There was no great physical difference in the sexes, and they dressed exactly alike."

The medical man would have demurred again.

"You are so unscientific," said the Philosophical Inventor. "The violent strength of a man, the distinctive charm and relative weakness of a woman, are the outcome of a period when the species survived by force and was ever in the face of danger. Marriage and the family were militant necessities before the world was conquered. But humanity has passed the zenith of its fierceness, and with an intelligent and triumphant democracy, willing to take over the care of offspring and only anxious to save itself from suffocation by its own increase, the division of a community into so many keenly competitive households elbowing one another for living room must sooner or later cease. And even now there is a steady tendency to assimilate the pursuits of the sexes. A very little refinement in our thinking, and even we should see that distinctive costume is an indelicate advertisement of facts it is the aim of all polite people to ignore.

"The average duration of life was about nineteen or twenty years. Well—what need of longer? People live nowadays to threescore and ten because of their excessive vitality, and because of the need there has been of guarding, rearing, and advising a numerous family. But a well-organised civilisation will change all that. At any rate, explain it as you will, these people about the age of nineteen or twenty, after a period of affectionate intercourse, fell into an elegant and painless

---

4. "Lemuridae" could refer to the family of frugivorous (fruit-eating) mammals that includes lemurs. More likely, though, the Time Traveller is referring to the lemuridae or "souls of the departed" in Roman mythology, which subsist on offerings of fruit nectar.

decline, experienced a natural Euthanasia, and were dropped into certain perennially burning furnaces wherein dead leaves, broken twigs, fruit peel, and other refuse were also consumed.

"Their voices, I noticed, even at the outset, were particularly soft and their inflections of the tongue, subtle. I did a little towards learning their language." He made some peculiar soft cooing sounds. "The vocabulary is not very extensive."

The red-haired man laughed and patted his shoulder.

"But I am anticipating. To return to the Time Machine. I felt singularly reassured by the aspect of these people and by their gentle manner. Many of them were children, and these seemed to me to take a keener interest in me than the fully grown ones. Presently one of these touched me, at first rather timidly, and then with more confidence. Others followed his or her example. They were vastly amused at the coarseness of my skin and at the hair upon the back of my hands, particularly the little ones. As I stood in the midst of a small crowd of them, one came laughing towards me, carrying a chain of some beautiful flowers altogether new to me, and put it about my neck. The idea was received with melodious applause; and presently they were running to and fro for flowers, and laughingly flinging them upon me until I was almost smothered with blossom. You, who have never seen the like, can scarcely imagine what delicate and wonderful flowers ten thousand years of culture had created. A flying machine, with gaily painted wings, came swooping down, scattering the crowd right and left, and its occupant joined the throng about me. Then someone suggested, it would seem, that their new plaything should be exhibited in the nearest building; and so I was beckoned and led and urged, past the Sphinx of white marble, towards a vast grey edifice of fretted stone. As I went with them, the memory of my confident anticipations of a profoundly grave and intellectual posterity came, with irresistible merriment, to my mind."

The Sunset of Mankind

"We have no doubt of the truth of your story," said the red-haired man to him that travelled through time; "but there is much in it that is difficult to understand."

"On the surface," said the Time Traveller.

"For instance, you say that the men of the year twelve thousand odd were living in elaborate luxury, in a veritable earth garden; richly clothed they were and sufficiently fed. Yet you present them as beautiful—well!—idiots. Some intelligence and some labour, some considerable intelligence I should imagine, were surely needed to keep this world garden in order."

"They had some intelligence," said the Time Traveller, "and besides—"

"Very little though; they spoke with a limited vocabulary, and foolishly took you and your Time Machine for a meteorite. Yet they were the descendants of the men who had organised the world so perfectly, who had exterminated disease, evolved flowers and fruits of indescribable beauty, and conquered the problem of flying. Those men must have had singularly powerful minds—"

"You confuse, I see, original intelligence and accumulated and organised knowledge. It is a very common error. But look the thing squarely in the face. Were you to strip the man of to-day of all the machinery and appliances of his civilisation, were you to sponge from his memory all the facts which he knows simply as facts, and leave him just his coddled physique, imperfect powers of observation, and ill-trained reasoning power, would he be the equal in wit or strength of the paleolithic savage? We do, indeed, make an innumerable multitude of petty discoveries nowadays, but the fundamental principles of thought and symbolism upon which our minds travel to these are immeasurably old. We live in the thought edifice of space, time and number, that our forefathers contrived. Look at it fairly: we invent by recipe, by Bacon's patent method for subduing the earth.[5] The world is moving now to comfort and absolute security, not so much from its own initiative as from the impetus such men as he gave it. Then the more we know the less is our scope for the exercise of useful discovery, and the more we advance in civilisation the less is our need of a brain for our preservation. Man's intelligence conquers nature, and in undisputed empire is the certain seed of decay. The energy revealed by security will run at first into art—or vice. Our descendants will give the last beautifying touch to the edifice of this civilisation with the last gleam of their waning intelligences. With perfect comfort and absolute security, the energy of advance must needs dwindle. That has been the history of all past civilisations and it will be the history of all civilisations. Civilisation means security for the weak and indolent, panmyxia[6] of weakness and indolence, and general decline. The tradition of effort that animates us will be forgotten in the end. What need for education when there is no struggle for life? What need of thought or strong desires? What need of books, or what need of stimulus to creative effort? As well take targe and dirk and mail underclothing into a City office.[7] Men who retain any vestige of intellectual activity will be restless, irked

5. The name of Sir Francis Bacon (1561–1626) is associated with the rise of modern scientific experimentation and the use of inductive reasoning.
6. Random mating within a species; the opposite of eugenics.
7. A targe is small shield, a dirk a small dagger. Medieval soldiers often wore protective clothing made of chain mail. The City is the central area of London.

by their weapons, inharmonious with the serene quiescence which will fall upon mankind. They will be ill company with their mysterious questionings, unprosperous in their love-making, and will leave no offspring. So an end comes at last to all these things."

"I don't believe that," said the common-sense person; "I don't believe in this scare about the rapid multiplication of the unfit, and all that."

"Nor do I," said the Time Traveller. "I never yet heard of the rapid multiplication of the unfit. It is the fittest who survive. The point is that civilisation—any form of civilisation—alters the qualifications of fitness, because the organisation it implies and the protection it affords, discounts the adventurous, animal, and imaginative, and puts a premium upon the mechanical, obedient, and vegetative. An organised civilisation is like Saturn, and destroys the forces that begat it."[8]

"Of course that is very plausible," said the common-sense person, in the tone of one who puts an argument aside, and proceeded to light a cigar without further remark.

"When do you conceive this civilising process ceased?" asked the red-haired man.

"It must have ceased for a vast period before the time of my visit. The great buildings in which these beautiful little people lived, a multitude together, were profoundly time-worn. Several I found collapsed through the rusting of the iron parts, and abandoned. One colossal ruin of granite, bound with aluminium, was not very distant from the great house wherein I sheltered, and among its precipitous masses and confusion of pillars were crowded thickets of nettles— nettles robbed of their stinging hairs and with leaves of purple brown. There had been no effort apparently to rebuild these places. It was in the dark recesses of this place, by-the-by, that I met my first morlock."

"*Morlock*! What is a morlock?" asked the medicine man.

"A new species of animal, and a very peculiar one. At first I took it for some kind of ape—"

"But you slip from my argument," interrupted the red-haired man. "These people were clothed in soft and beautiful raiment, which seems to me to imply textile manufactures, dyeing, cutting out, skilled labour involving a certain amount of adaptation to individual circumstance."

"Precisely. Skilled labour of a certain traditional sort—you must understand there were no changes of fashion—skill much on the level

---

8. The Time Traveller may be misremembering what he knows of Roman mythology. Saturn was himself overthrown by the gods he begat. In any case, Saturn was commonly identified with the Greek god Chronos, which may be why he is on the mind of Wells's achronic time traveller.

of that required from a bee when it builds its cell. That occurred to me. It puzzled me very much at first to account for it. I certainly found none of the people at any such work. But the explanation— that is so very grotesque that I really hesitate to tell you."

He paused, looked at us doubtfully. "Suppose you imagine machines—"

"Put your old shoes in at one end and a new pair comes out at the other," laughed the red-haired man. "Frankenstein Machines that have developed souls, while men have lost theirs! The created servant steals the mind of its creator; he puts his very soul into it, so to speak. Well, perhaps it is possible. It is not a new idea, you know. And you have said something about flying-machines. I suppose they were repaired by similar intelligent apparatus. Did you have a chat with any of these machine-beasts?"

"That seems rather a puerile idea to me," said the Time Traveller, "knowing what I do. But to realise the truth, you must bear in mind that it is possible to do things first intelligently and afterwards to make a habit of them. Let me illustrate by the ancient civilisation of the ants and bees. Some ants are still intelligent and originative; while other species are becoming mere automatic creatures, to repeat what were once intelligent actions. The working bees, naturalists say, are almost entirely automatic. Now, among these men—"

"Ah, these morlocks of yours!" said the red-haired man. "Something ape-like! Human neuters! But—"

"Look here!" suddenly interrupted the very young man. He had been lost in profound thought for some minute or so, and now rushed headlong into the conversation, after his manner. "Here is one thing I cannot fall in with. The sun, you say, was hotter than it is now, or at any rate the climate was warmer. Now the sun is really supposed to be cooling and shrinking, and so is the earth. The mean temperature ought to be colder in the future. And besides this, the Isthmus of Panama will wear through at last, and the Gulf Stream no longer impinge upon our shores with all its warmth."[9]

"There," said the Time Traveller, "I am unable to give you an explanation. All I know is that the climate was very much warmer than it is now, and that the sun seemed brighter. There was a strange and beautiful thing, too, about the night, and that was the multitude of shooting stars. Even during the November showers of our epoch I have never seen anything quite so brilliant as an ordinary night of this coming time. The sky seemed alive with them, especially towards midnight, when they fell chiefly from the zenith. Besides this the brilliance of the night was increased by a number of luminous clouds

9. Great Britain owes its temperate climate to the warm waters of the Atlantic Gulf Stream, which originates in the Caribbean and flows past Britain's western shores.

and whisps, many of them as bright or brighter than the Milky Way; but, unlike the Milky Way, they shifted in position from night to night. The fall of meteorites, too, was a comparatively common occurrence. I think it was the only thing these delightful people feared, or had any reason to fear. Possibly this meteoric abundance had something to do with the increased warmth. A quantity of such bodies in the space through which the solar system travelled might contribute to this in two ways: by retarding the tangential velocity of the earth in its orbit, and so accelerating its secular[1] approach to the sun, and by actually falling into the sun and so increasing its radiant energy. But these are guesses of mine. All I can certainly say is that the climate was very much warmer, and had added its enervating influence to their too perfect civilisation."

"Warmth and colour, ruins and decline," said the red-haired man. "One might call this age of yours the Sunset of Mankind."

The Underworld

"I have already told you," said the Time Traveller, "that it was customary on the part of the delightful people of the upper world to ignore the existence of these pallid creatures of the caverns, and consequently when I descended among them I descended alone.

"I had to clamber down a shaft of perhaps two or three hundred yards. The descent was effected by means of hooks projecting from the sides of the well, and since they were adapted to the needs of a creature much smaller and lighter than myself I was speedily cramped and fatigued by the descent. And not simply fatigued. My weight suddenly bent one of the hooks and almost swung me off it into the darkness beneath. For a moment I hung by one hand, and after that experience I did not dare to rest again, and though my arms and back were presently acutely painful, I continued to climb with as quick a motion as possible down the sheer descent. Glancing upward I saw the aperture a mere small blue disc above me, in which a star was visible. The thudding sound of some machine below grew louder and more oppressive. Everything save that minute circle above was profoundly dark. I was in an agony of discomfort. I had some thought of trying to get up the shaft again, and leave the underworld alone. But while I turned this over in my mind I continued to descend.

"It was with intense relief that I saw very dimly coming up a foot to the right of me a long loophole in the wall of the shaft, and, swinging myself in, found it was the aperture of a narrow horizontal tunnel in which I could lie down and rest. My arms ached, my back

---

1. "Secular" in this context means "pertaining to the earth."

was cramped, and I was trembling with the prolonged fear of falling. Besides this the unbroken darkness had a distressing effect upon my eyes. The air was full of the throbbing and hum of machinery.

"I do not know how long I lay in that tunnel. I was roused by a soft hand touching my face. Starting up in the darkness I snatched at my matches, and, hastily striking one, saw three grotesque white creatures similar to the one I had seen above ground in the ruin, hastily retreating before the light. Living as they did, in what appeared to me impenetrable darkness, their eyes were abnormally large and sensitive, just as are the eyes of the abyss fishes or of any purely nocturnal creatures, and they reflected the light in the same way. I have no doubt that they could see me in that rayless obscurity, and they did not seem to have any fear of me apart from the light. But so soon as I struck a match in order to see them, they fled incontinently, vanishing up dark gutters and tunnels from which their eyes glared at me in the strangest fashion.

"I tried to call them, but what language they had was apparently a different one from that of the overworld people. So that I was left to my own unaided exploration.

"Feeling my way along this tunnel of mine, the confused noise of machinery grew louder, and presently the wall receded from my hand, and I felt I had come to an open space, and striking another match saw I had entered an arched cavern, so vast that it extended into darkness at last beyond the range of my light. Huge machines with running belts and whirling fly-wheels rose out of the obscurity, and the grey bodies of the Morlocks dodged my light among the unsteady shadows. Several of the machines near me were disused and broken down. They appeared to be weaving machines, and were worked by leather belts running over drums upon great rotating shafts that stretched across the cavern. I could not see how the shafts were worked. And very soon my match burned out."

"That was a pity," said the red-haired man.

"I was afraid to push my way down this avenue of throbbing machinery in the dark, and with my last glimpse I discovered that my store of matches had run low. It had never occurred to me until that moment that there was any need to economise them, and I had wasted almost half the box in astonishing the above-ground people, to whom fire was a novelty. I had four left then. As I stood in the dark a hand touched mine, then some lank fingers came feeling over my face. I fancied I detected the breathing of a number of these little beings about me. I felt the box of matches in my hand being gently disengaged, and other hands behind me plucking at my clothing.

"The sense of these unseen creatures examining me was indescribably unpleasant. The sudden realisation of my ignorance of their ways of thinking and possible actions came home to me very vividly in the darkness. I shouted at them as loudly as I could. They started away from me, and then I could feel them approaching me again. They clutched at me more boldly, whispering odd sounds to each other. I shivered violently and shouted again, rather discordantly. This time they were not so seriously alarmed, and made a queer laughing noise as they came towards me again.

"I will confess I was frightened. I determined to strike another match and escape under its glare. Eking it out with a scrap of paper from my pocket, I made good my retreat to the narrow tunnel. But hardly had I entered this when my light was blown out, and I could hear them in the blackness rustling like wind among leaves, and pattering like rain as they hurried after me. In a moment I was clutched by several hands again, and there was no mistake now that they were trying to draw me back. I struck another light and waved it in their dazzled faces. You can scarcely imagine how nauseatingly unhuman those pale chinless faces and great pinkish grey eyes seemed as they stared stupidly, suddenly blinded by the light.

"So I gained time and retreated again, and when my second match had ended struck my third. That had almost burnt through as I reached the opening of the tunnel upon the well. I lay down upon the edge, for the throbbing whirl of the air-pumping machine below made me giddy, and felt sideways for the projecting hooks. As I did so, my feet were grasped from behind, and I was tugged violently backwards. I lit my last match . . . and it incontinently went out. But I had my hand on the climbing bars now, and, kicking violently, disengaged myself from the clutches of the Morlocks, and was speedily clambering up the shaft again. One little wretch followed me for some way, and captured the heel of my boot as a trophy."

"I suppose you could show us that boot without the heel," said the red-haired man, "if we asked to see it?"

"What do you think they wanted with you?" asked the common-sense person.

"I don't know. That was just the beastliness of it."

"And is that all you saw of the Morlocks?" said the very young man.

"I saw some once again. Frankly, I was afraid of them. I did not even look down one of those wells again."

"Have you no explanation to offer of those creatures?" said the red-haired man. "What were they really? In particular, what was their connection with the upperworld people, and how had they been developed?"

"I am a traveller, and I tell you a traveller's tale. I am not an annotated edition of myself."

"Cannot you hazard something? I am puzzled by your statement, that human beings will differentiate into two species without any separation. Would not intermarriage prevent this?"

"Oh no! a species may split up into two without any separation into different districts. This matter has been worked out by Gulick.[2] He uses the very convenient word 'segregation' to express his idea. Imagine, for instance, the more refined and indolent class of people to intermarry mainly among themselves, and the operative or business class—the class of operatives aspiring to rise to business influence and finding their interests mainly in the satisfaction of a taste for industrial and business pursuits—also marrying mainly in their own class. Might there not be a widening separation? Indeed, since this time-journey of mine I have fancied that there is such a split going on even now in our English society, a split that began some two hundred and fifty years ago or more. I do not mean any split between working people and rich—families drop and rise from toil to wealth continually—but between the sombre, mechanically industrious, arithmetical, inartistic type, the type of the Puritan and the American millionaire and the pleasure-loving, witty, and graceful type that gives us our clever artists, our actors and writers, some of our gentry, and many an elegant rogue. Conceive such types drifting away from one another each in its own direction. Along the former line we should get at last a colourless love of darkness, dully industrious and productive, and along the latter, brilliant weakness and gay silliness. But this is a mere theory of mine. The fact remains that humanity had differentiated into two very distinct species in the coming time, explain it as you will. Such traditional industries as still survived remained among the Morlocks, but the sun of man's intelligence had set and the night of humanity was creeping on apace."

The Time-Traveller Returns

"After my glimpse of the underworld my mind turned incessantly towards this age again. The upper-world people, who had at first charmed me with their light beauty, began to weary and then to irritate me by their insubstantiality. And there was something in the weird inhumanity of the undermen that robbed me of my sense of security. I could not imagine that they regarded me as their fellow creature, or that any of the deep reasonless instincts that keep man the servant of his fellow man would intervene in my favour. I was to them a strange beast. When I thought of the soft cold hands clutching me in the subterranean darkness I was filled with horrible imaginings of what might have been my fate.

2. John Thomas Gulick (1832–1923) was an American missionary and committed Darwinian naturalist whose pioneering studies of the effects of geographical isolation (or "segregation") on the evolution of species dealt primarily with the landsnails of the Hawaiian Islands.

"Then these creatures, being now aware of my existence, and possessing far more curiosity than the upper-world people, began to trouble my nights. Their excessive sensibility to light kept me safe from them during the days, but after the twilight I found it advisable to avoid the deep shadows of the buildings and to sleep out under the stars. And even in the open, when the sky was overcast, these pallid little monsters ventured to approach me.

"I could see very dimly their grey forms approaching through the black masses of the bushes, and could hear the murmuring noises that stood to them in the place of articulate speech.

"I think they were far more powerfully attracted by the Time Machine than by myself. Their minds were essentially mechanical. That, indeed, was one of the dismal thoughts that came to me—that possibly they would try to take me to pieces and investigate my construction. The only thing that kept me in the future age after I had begun to realise what had happened to humanity was my interest in the present one. I was reluctant to go until I had seen enough to tell you some definite facts about your descendants. But the near approach of these Morlocks was too much for me. As one came forward in the obscurity and laid his hand upon the bars of the time Machine, I cried aloud and vaulted into the saddle, and in another moment that strange world of the future had swept into nothingness, and I was reeling down the time dimension to this age of ours again. And so my visit to the year 12,203 came to an end."

He paused. For some minute or so there was silence.

"I do not like your vision," said the common-sense person.

"It seems to me just the Gospel of Despair," said the financial journalist.

The Time Traveller lit a cigar.

"Why there should be any particular despair for you in the contemplation of a time when our kind of beast—" he glanced round the room with a faint smile—"has ceased to exist, I fail to see."

"We have always been accustomed to consider the future as in some peculiar way ours," said the red-haired man. "Your story seems to rob us of our birthright."

"For my part I have always believed in a steady Evolution towards something Higher and Better," said the common-sense person; and added, "and I still do."

"But still essentially human in all respects?" asked the Time Traveller.

"Decidedly," said the common-sense person.

"In the past," said the Time Traveller, "the evolution has not always been upward. The land animals, including ourselves, zoologists say, are the descendants of almost amphibious mudfish that were hunted out of the seas by the ancestors of the modern sharks."

"But what will become of Social Reform? You would make out that everything that ameliorates human life tends to human degeneration."

"Let us leave social reform to the professional philanthropist," said the Time Traveller. "I told you a story; I am not prepared to embark upon a political discussion. The facts remain . . ."

"*Facts!*" said the red-haired man *sotto voce*.[3]

"That man has been evolved from the inhuman in the past—to go no further back, even the paleolithic men were practically inhuman—and that in the future he must sooner or later be modified beyond human sympathy."

"Leaving us," said the red-haired man, "a little island in time and a little island in space, the surface of the little globe out of all the oceans of space, and a few thousands of years out of eternity."

"The limits are still large enough for me to be mean in," said the Time Traveller.

"And after man?" said the medical man.

"A world with a continually longer day and a continually shorter year, so the astronomers tell us. For the drag of the tides upon the spin of the earth will bring this planet at last to the plight of Mercury, with one face turned always to the sun.[4] And the gradual diminution of the centrifugal component of the earth's motion due to interplanetary matter will cause it to approach the sun slowly and surely as the sun cools, until the parent body has recovered its offspring again. During the last stages of the sunward movement over those parts of the earth that are sunward there will be an unending day, and a vast red sun growing ever vaster and duller will glow motionless in the sky. Twice already it will have blazed into a transient period of brilliance as the minor planets, Mercury and Venus, melted back into its mass. On the further side of the earth will be perpetual night and the bitterest cold, and between these regions will be belts of twilight, of perpetual sunset, and perpetual afternoon. Whether there will be any life on the earth then we can scarcely guess. Somewhere in the belts of intermediate temperature, it may be that strange inconceivable forms of life will still struggle on against the inevitable fate that awaits them. But an end comes. Life is a mere eddy, an episode, in the great stream of universal being, just as man with all his cosmic mind is a mere episode in the story of life—"

He stopped abruptly. "There is that kid of mine upstairs crying. He always cries when he wakes up in the dark. If you don't mind, I will just go up and tell him it's all right."

---

3. In a soft voice (Italian).
4. The Time Traveller is here drawing on the work of Charles Darwin's second son, Sir George Howard Darwin (1845–1912), a prominent astronomer and mathematician best known for his work on tidal effects. Darwin argued that the "tidal drag" caused by the combined gravitational pull of the sun and the moon would eventually stop the earth's rotation.

Alternate Ending[†]

The Last Voyage of the Time Machine

The Philosophical Inventor had seemed well ~~on the~~ *when we had left his house in the small hours of that* Thursday ~~of our previous meeting and we had anticipated no misfortune~~. *Save for our concern for his mind we had no anxiety for him. The medical man came part of the way with me & made light of his fancy; A mere hectic*[1] *phase of his romancing tendency. We must get him away from that machine. It is the result of incessant study & speculation.* But on the Friday came a hastily pencilled ~~note~~ *card* from ~~him~~ *the Philosopher, brought by the hand of his housemaid. In three words,* he was dying. And when I reached his house he was dead.

His death greatly exercised the doctors for there was not a solitary symptom of any illness that they could put their fingers upon. There was an inquest, & in the end a dubious suggestion of stoppage of the heart, through some nervous lesion in the medulla. I fancy they made out some local disturbance there, but I may perhaps express my private doubt of the verdict.

His affairs were in some confusion, and I and ~~the red-haired man~~ *Bayliss* whom he had elected as his executors, found much to occupy us. He was a widower, and the bulk of his property was devised to his sister and his two little boys. It became advisable to dispose of the house at Richmond Hill where we had ~~so often~~ listened to ~~him~~ *his true story*, and meeting one day on business there, a common impulse directed us to the workshop. There we found the grotesque mass of metallic castings which he had shewn us as the Time Machine.

"What an oddly inventive brain it was, of his," said ~~the red-haired man~~ *Bayliss*, standing and staring, hands in pockets, at this oblique contrivance.

"~~He was~~ *The fact is he was* a humorist. I suppose he faked up this affair in an idle afternoon. It gave his yarn such a flavour of realistic evidence—is not the machine here even unto this day?" ~~that fool Killick really believes he did travel about in time with it. And Waterlow is a little doubtful. Do you know I sometimes fancied he half believed his story himself. And yet . . . . no, he could not really have believed that rigmarole."~~

~~The red-haired man~~ *Bayliss* laughed.

---

† The H. G. Wells collection at the University of Illinois includes the draft of a chapter Wells may have intended to use as the concluding installment of his *National Observer* story. The typescript draft is reprinted here, with Wells's autograph corrections and additions given in italics

1. Feverish or overly excited.

"He has put it together in such a delightfully credible way, too. Come to look into it, it is rivetted and jointed together in a singularly careful and workmanlike fashion for a jest. But even his jests were carefully done."

I put out my hand to one of the levers. Hesitated oddly and drew back. The thing had such an odd squint in the twist of its parts.

"I believe you are afraid of it," said ~~the red-haired man~~ *Bayliss*.

We looked at one another. Then he exclaimed abruptly, "<u>Rubbish!</u>" and without more ado grasped the bars of the machine and swung himself into the saddle.

"Behold me," said he, "mounted on the Chronic Argo,[2] the link of the ages! If it were only true. If one might only sail away into time. I would travel to and fro, until I could pick out the golden age, and end my days there. There must be a golden age, somewhere in the destiny of men. What have I done that I am out of it? If this little lever—."

He touched it lightly as he spoke and the machine swayed like a tree bough in the wind.

He looked oddly at me and down at the machine. "Our friend made a queer machine that would give at a touch like that. This thing squats heavily enough to all appearance, but just then methought I was on some ancient rocking stone. It feels unsafe—unsafe." Very gingerly he began to shift his leg over the saddle. I think he slipped slightly and he gripped the little lever instinctively, his full weight falling suddenly upon it.

I can hardly describe what followed. I saw his face white and scared and heard the beginning of a cry that seemed suddenly stifled, as though a hand had been clapped upon the mouth that uttered it. There was a thud, a rush of air around me, and a ring of breaking glass. One of the panes in the window had been blown in, I found afterwards. His horror-struck face and gesticulating form grew rapidly fainter and fainter, became transparent, and vanished. The whirling bars and curves of the Time Machine grew into a glimmering eddy of ghostly whisps, and became invisible as a dusty beam of sunlight athwart the laboratory. The floor was vacant. Save for a subsiding stir of dust everything was still. The Time Machine had after all proved itself no jest. Machine and man had vanished for ever from my ken. I stood gaping and then an irresistible tendency to hysterical laughter relieved me.

It goes without saying that I did not attempt to explain the disappearance of ~~the red-haired man~~ *Bayliss* to the general public. He is, I believe, still being sought by his family. *The details of the inquiry that followed his disappearance I shall not give here, for as the book began I must end with the Time Machine. I will say nothing of the suspicions*

---

2. In Greek mythology, the *Argo* was the name of the ship used by Jason and the Argonauts.

that clustered round myself, or the futile inquiries of the acute people who set themselves upon the problem. I & I alone held the clue. I made one attempt to broach the topic to the medical man but his manner convinced me of the wisdom of silence & silent I have remained. Even now, this story is presented without names or dates. And I have been half disposed to follow the example of the Time Traveller & avow [it] is a mere invention of my dreaming leisure. I have sometime tried to figure to myself what ~~his~~ the fate of ~~of the red haired man~~ Bayliss may have been as he swept with ever increasing velocity into time to come. Did he in some way discover the principle by which the machine was stopped, and manipulating the other lever find himself ~~suddenly~~ flung headlong into some strange unsympathetic age? Or stopping suddenly in futurity, and with some other substance in the space he sought to occupy, did a far reaching explosion terminate his involuntary voyage and him and the time machine together? Or was he rushed helpless and struggling into that fiery catastrophe ~~from which the Philosophical Inventor so narrowly escaped~~, the falling of the earth into the sun, which must terminate our planetary career?

Waking I cannot figure his fate to myself. But sometimes in my sleep I seem to realize what that headlong fall down a shaft of ten thousand years may be. I feel then that I too am slipping out of time, dropping out of this phantasmagoria of reality along some hitherto unsuspected dimension into strange and incredible existence *through the cooling solar system and the swiftly aging stars.*

It may be good to wake up again from such a dream. *To feel things under my fleshly hands again, to touch the familiar watches & see the watch & hear it tick. To look round & behold the human world again holding me in safety upon every side.* Some day it may be that waking will not come.

From New Review *Time Machine*[†]

I

THE INVENTOR

The man who made the Time Machine—the man I shall call the Time Traveller—was well known in scientific circles a few years since, and the fact of his disappearance is also well known. He was a

---

[†] From the *New Review* (January and May 1895). A revised version of Wells's *National Observer* story was serialized in five installments in the *New Review*, whose editorship was taken up by William Ernest Henley at the end of 1894. Reprinted here are two chapters (I and XII) which differ significantly from their counterparts in both the earlier *National Observer* serial and the later Heinemann first edition of the novel.

mathematician of peculiar subtlety, and one of our most conspicuous
investigators in molecular physics. He did not confine himself to
abstract science. Several ingenious and one or two profitable patents
were his: very profitable they were, these last, as his handsome house
at Richmond[1] testified. To those who were his intimates, however, his
scientific investigations were as nothing to his gift of speech. In the
after-dinner hours he was ever a vivid and variegated talker, and at
times his fantastic, often paradoxical, conceptions came so thick and
close as to form one continuous discourse. At these times he was as
unlike the popular conception of a scientific investigator as a man
could be. His cheeks would flush, his eyes grow bright; and the
stranger the ideas that sprang and crowded in his brain, the happier
and the more animated would be his exposition.

Up to the last there was held at his house a kind of informal gathering, which it was my privilege to attend, and where, at one time or
another, I have met most of our distinguished literary and scientific
men. There was a plain dinner at seven. After that we would adjourn
to a room of easy chairs and little tables, and there, with libations of
alcohol and reeking pipes, we would invoke the God. At first the
conversation was mere fragmentary chatter, with some local *lacu-
nae*[2] of digestive silence; but towards nine or half-past nine, if the
God was favourable, some particular topic would triumph by a kind
of natural selection, and would become the common interest. So it
was, I remember, on the last Thursday but one of all—the Thursday
when I first heard of the Time Machine.

I had been jammed in a corner with a gentleman who shall be disguised as Filby. He had been running down Milton[3]—the public
neglects poor Filby's little verses shockingly; and as I could think of
nothing but the relative status of Filby and the man he criticised,
and was much too timid to discuss that, the arrival of that moment
of fusion, when our several conversations were suddenly merged
into a general discussion, was a great relief to me.

"What's that nonsense?" said a well-known Medical Man, speaking across Filby to the Psychologist.

"He thinks," said the Psychologist, "that Time's only a kind of
Space."

"It's not thinking," said the Time Traveller; "it's knowledge."

"Foppish affectation," said Filby, still harping upon his wrongs;
but I feigned a great interest in this question of Space and Time.

"Kant,"[4] began the Psychologist.

---

1. A prosperous residential suburb west of London.
2. Gaps.
3. The English poet John Milton (1608–1674).
4. The German philosopher and metaphysician Immanuel Kant (1724–1804).

"Confound Kant!" said the Time Traveller. "I tell you I'm right. I've got experimental proof of it. I'm not a metaphysician." He addressed the Medical Man across the room, and so brought the whole company into his own circle. "It's the most promising departure in experimental work that has ever been made. It will simply revolutionise life. Heaven knows what life will be when I've carried the thing through."

"As long as it's not the water of Immortality I don't mind," said the distinguished Medical Man. "What is it?"

"Only a paradox," said the Psychologist.

The Time Traveller said nothing in reply, but smiled and began tapping his pipe upon the fender curb. This was the invariable presage of a dissertation.

"You have to admit that time is a spatial dimension," said the Psychologist, emboldened by immunity and addressing the Medical Man, "and then all sorts of remarkable consequences are found inevitable. Among others, that it becomes possible to travel about in time."

The Time Traveller chuckled: "You forget that I'm going to prove it experimentally."

"Let's have your experiment," said the Psychologist.

"I think we'd like the argument first," said Filby.

"It's this," said the Time Traveller: "I propose a wholly new view of things based on the supposition that ordinary human perception is an hallucination. I'm sorry to drag in predestination and free-will, but I'm afraid those ideas will have to help. Look at it in this way— this, I think, will give you the gist of it: Suppose you knew fully the position and the properties of every particle of matter, of everything existing in the universe at any particular moment of time: suppose, that is, that you were omniscient. Well, that knowledge would involve the knowledge of the condition of things at the previous moment, and at the moment before that, and so on. If you knew and perceived the present perfectly, you would perceive therein the whole of the past. If you understood all natural laws the present would be a complete and vivid record of the past. Similarly, if you grasped the whole of the present, knew all its tendencies and laws, you would see clearly all the future. To an omniscient observer there would be no forgotten past—no piece of time as it were that had dropped out of existence—and no blank future of things yet to be revealed. Perceiving all the present, an omniscient observer would likewise perceive all the past and all the inevitable future at the same time. Indeed, present and past and future would be without meaning to such an observer: he would always perceive exactly the same thing. He would see, as it were, a Rigid Universe filling space and time—a Universe in which things were always the same. He would see one sole unchanging series of cause and effect to-day and to-morrow and always. If 'past' meant anything, it would mean looking in a certain direction; while 'future' meant looking the opposite way."

"H'm," said the Rector, "I fancy you're right. So far."

"I know I am," said the Time Traveller. "From the absolute point of view the universe is a perfectly rigid unalterable apparatus, entirely predestinate, entirely complete and finished. Now, looking at things, so far as we can, from this standpoint, how would a thing like this box appear? It would still be a certain length and a certain breadth and a certain thickness, and it would have a definite mass; but we should also perceive that it extended back in time to a certain moment when it was made, and forward in time to a certain moment when it was destroyed, and that during its existence it was moved about in space. An ordinary man, being asked to describe this box, would say, among other things, that it was in such a position, and that it measured ten inches in depth, say, three in breadth, and four in length. From the absolute point of view it would also be necessary to say that it began at such a moment, lasted so long, measured so much in time, and was moved here and there meanwhile. It is only when you have stated its past and its future that you have completely described the box. You see, from the absolute standpoint—which is the true scientific standpoint—time is merely a dimension, quite analogous to the three dimensions in space. Every particle of matter has length, breadth, thickness, and—duration."

"You're perfectly right," said the Rector. "Theologians threshed all that out ages ago."

"I beg your pardon," said the Psychologist, "nothing of the sort. Our first impression, the very foundation of our mental life, is order in time. I am supported—"

"I tell you that psychology cannot possibly help us here," said the Time Traveller, "because our minds do not represent the conditions of the universe—why should they?—but only our necessities. From my point of view the human consciousness is an immaterial something falling through this Rigid Universe of four dimensions, from the direction we call 'past' to the direction we call 'future.' Just as the sun is a material something falling through the same universe towards the constellation of Hercules."

"This is rather abstruse," said Filby under his breath to me.

"I begin to see your argument," said the Medical Man. "And you go on to ask, why should we continue to drift in a particular direction? Why should we drive through time at this uniform pace? Practically you propose to study four-dimensional geometry with a view to loco-motion in time."

"Precisely. Have studied it to that end."

"Of all the wild extravagant theories!" began the Psychologist.

"Yes, so it seemed to me, and so I never talked of it until—"

"Experimental verification!" cried I. "You are going to verify *that*?"

"The experiment!" cried Filby, who was getting brain-weary.

"Let's see your experiment anyhow," said the Psychologist, "though it's all humbug, you know."

The Time Traveller smiled round at us. Then, still smiling faintly, and with his hands deep in his trousers pockets, he walked slowly out of the room, and we heard his slippers shuffling down the long passage to his laboratory.

XII

THE FURTHER VISION

"I have already told you of the sickness and confusion that comes with time travelling. And this time I was not seated properly in the saddle, but sideways and in an unstable fashion. For an indefinite time I clung to the machine as it swayed and vibrated, quite unheeding how I went, and when I brought myself to look at the dials again I was amazed to find where I had arrived. One dial records days, another thousands of days, another millions of days, and another thousands of millions. Now, instead of reversing the levers I had pulled them over so as to go forward with them, and when I came to look at these indicators I found that the thousands hand was sweeping round as fast as the seconds hand of a watch—into futurity. Very cautiously, for I remembered my former headlong fall, I began to reverse my motion. Slower and slower went the circling hands until the thousands one seemed motionless and the daily one was no longer a mere mist upon its scale. Still slower, until the grey haze around me became distincter and dim outlines of an undulating waste grew visible.

"I stopped. I was on a bleak moorland, covered with a sparse vegetation, and grey with a thin hoarfrost. The time was midday, the orange sun, shorn of its effulgence, brooded near the meridian in a sky of drabby grey. Only a few black bushes broke the monotony of the scene. The great buildings of the decadent men among whom, it seemed to me, I had been so recently, had vanished and left no trace, not a mound even marked their position. Hill and valley, sea and river—all, under the wear and work of the rain and frost, had melted into new forms. No doubt, too, the rain and snow had long since washed out the Morlock tunnels. A nipping breeze stung my hands and face. So far as I could see there were neither hills, nor trees, nor rivers: only an uneven stretch of cheerless plateau.

"Then suddenly a dark bulk rose out of the moor, something that gleamed like a serrated row of iron plates, and vanished almost immediately in a depression. And then I became aware of a number of faint-grey things, coloured to almost the exact tint of the frost-bitten soil, which were browsing here and there upon its scanty grass, and running to and fro. I saw one jump with a sudden start, and then my eye detected perhaps a score of them. At first I thought they were rabbits, or some small breed of kangaroo. Then, as one came hopping near me, I perceived that it belonged to neither of these groups. It was plantigrade,[5] its hind legs rather the longer; it was tailless, and covered with a straight greyish hair that thickened about the head into a Skye terrier's mane. As I had understood that in the Golden Age man had killed out almost all the other animals, sparing only a few of the more ornamental, I was naturally curious about the creatures. They did not seem afraid of me, but browsed on, much as rabbits would do in a place unfrequented by men; and it occurred to me that I might perhaps secure a specimen.

"I got off the machine, and picked up a big stone. I had scarcely done so when one of the little creatures came within easy range. I was so lucky as to hit it on the head, and it rolled over at once and lay motionless. I ran to it at once. It remained still, almost as if it were killed. I was surprised to see that the thing had five feeble digits to both its fore and hind feet—the fore feet, indeed, were almost as human as the fore feet of a frog. It had, moreover, a roundish head, with a projecting forehead and forward-looking eyes, obscured by its lank hair. A disagreeable apprehension flashed across my mind. As I knelt down and seized my capture, intending to examine its teeth and other anatomical points which might show human characteristics, the metallic-looking object, to which I have already alluded, reappeared above a ridge in the moor, coming towards me and making a strange clattering sound as it came. Forthwith the grey animals about me began to answer with a short, weak yelping—as if of terror—and bolted off in a direction opposite to that from which this new creature approached. They must have hidden in burrows or behind bushes and tussocks, for in a moment not one of them was visible.

"I rose to my feet, and stared at this grotesque monster. I can only describe it by comparing it to a centipede. It stood about three feet high, and had a long segmented body, perhaps thirty feet long, with curiously overlapping greenish-black plates. It seemed to crawl upon a multitude of feet, looping its body as it advanced. Its blunt round head with a polygonal arrangement of black eye spots, carried two flexible, writhing, hornlike antennae. It was coming along, I should judge, at a pace of about eight or ten miles an hour, and it left me little time for thinking. Leaving my grey animal, or grey man, whichever it was, on the ground, I set off for the machine. Halfway I paused, regretting that abandonment, but a glance over my shoulder

---

5. Plantigrade animals (such as bears, raccoons, and rabbits) walk on the soles of their feet.

destroyed any such regret. When I gained the machine the monster was scarce fifty yards away. It was certainly not a vertebrated animal. It had no snout, and its mouth was fringed with jointed dark-coloured plates. But I did not care for a nearer view.

"I traversed one day and stopped again, hoping to find colossus gone and some vestige of my victim; but, I should judge, the giant centipede did not trouble itself about bones. At any rate both had vanished. The faintly human touch of these little creatures per-plexed me greatly. If you come to think, there is no reason why a degenerate humanity should not come at last to differentiate into as many species as the descendants of the mud fish who fathered all the land vertebrates. I saw no more of any insect colossus, as to my thinking the segmented creature must have been. Evidently the physiological difficulty that at present keeps all the insects small had been surmounted at last, and this division of the animal kingdom had arrived at the long awaited supremacy which its enormous energy and vitality deserve. I made several attempts to kill or capture another of the greyish vermin, but none of my missiles were so suc-cessful as my first; and, after perhaps a dozen disappointing throws, that left my arm aching, I felt a gust of irritation at my folly in com-ing so far into futurity without weapons or equipment. I resolved to run on for one glimpse of the still remoter future—one peep into the deeper abysm of time—and then to return to you and my own epoch. Once more I remounted the machine, and once more the world grew hazy and grey.

"As I drove on, a peculiar change crept over the appearance of things. The unwonted greyness grew lighter; then—though I was travelling with prodigious velocity—the blinking succession of day and night, which was usually indicative of a slower pace, returned, and grew more and more marked. This puzzled me very much at first. The alternations of night and day grew slower and slower, and so did the passage of the sun across the sky, until they seemed to stretch through centuries. At last a steady twilight brooded over the earth, a twilight only broken now and then when a comet glared across the darkling sky. The band of light that had indicated the sun had long since disappeared; for the sun had ceased to set—it simply rose and fell in the west, and grew ever broader and more red. All trace of the moon had vanished. The circling of the stars, growing slower and slower, had given place to creeping points of light. At last, some time before I stopped, the sun, red and very large, halted motionless upon the horizon, a vast dome glowing with a dull heat, and now and then suffering a momentary extinction. At one time it had for a little while glowed more brilliantly again, but it speedily reverted to its sullen red-heat. I perceived by this slowing down of its rising and setting that the work of the tidal drag was done. The earth had come to rest with one face to the sun, even as in our own time the moon faces the earth.

"I stopped very gently and sat upon the Time Machine, looking round."

Cancelled Episode[†]

XIV

THE RETURN OF THE TIME TRAVELLER

When I recovered I found myself upon the machine & with my hand resting upon the dials. The old confusion and tumult was around me, the old blinking alternations of night & day. But now that I was hurling back in time the sun was hopping from west to east, from its setting to its rising, and the circle of the stars spun in the reverse direction.

My sole object was now to return. My curiosity was sated, I was in pain. I longed for this age, for this time, for you human beings that I have known, with an almost passionate longing.

I turned to the dials. For a moment I could scarcely credit my eyes. Then I remembered that my hand had rested upon the slender rod connecting them with the rest of the machine. This was displaced. The dials simply recorded the extent of my voyage.

Now to you that may seem an inconvenient accident, a little trouble to meet. To me it was—not even excepting the visit to the Morlocks & the fight in the forest—the most awful thing of all that happened in my time journey. The strange sickness that had come upon me by that desolate beach of the dying Earth, still clung to me. Now I was lost in time! It was weak of me, no doubt—the fact of it is I was horribly weak physically at that time—but I began to cry like a child. So conceive me, the Time Traveller, the discoverer of Futurity, clinging senseless to his Time Machine, choking with sobs & with the tears streaming down his face, full of a terrible fear that he would never see humanity again or enter again into the delights of life. In my passion I drove back, I do not know how far. A childish persuasion came to my mind that I should stop when the country was submerged, & sink plump into the waters of some of those vanished oceans whose sediments form the dry land of today.

---

† From a manuscript in the H. G. Wells collection at the University of Illinois. Wells appears to have written this episode sometime in 1894; it is unclear whether he intended it for the *National Observer* or the *New Review* serialization of the story. Either way, it was not included in any of the published versions of *The Time Machine* that appeared during Wells's lifetime.

So I travelled back through time. At last my heaping wretchedness grew to agony. Anything was better than that horrible suspense. In a suicidal mood I turned to the levers. Slower & slower I travelled. I began to see a flat greensward about me & the leaden gleam of waters. This gave me heart. I stopped completely & the Time Machine subsided with a succulent sound upon a bed of marshy gamboge[1] & green weeds. Around me were shapely trees not unlike willows. The sky was clear & very blue, the air hazy & the glowing western sky betokened a recent sunset. The yellow ground upon which I stood was perfectly flat & but a little raised above the level of the waters that flowed on either side. A smell of decaying vegetation was in the air, & the soil that showed below the litter of green weed was black. I judged I stood on a part of the delta of some large river.

A number of small white birds were moving about on the green, a few score yards away. They were picking about amidst the slime, & carried their wings, which appeared to me to be webbed, extended. Now & then one would flutter up in the air. They were not unlike gulls. I saw some shells like large water snails. Beyond this I saw at first no living things.

Then I felt thirsty & descending from the machine I went to the edge of the water, stooped down & taking some in the hollow of my hand tasted it. It was brackish but quite drinkable. I took a draught & bathing my hands and face, felt very commendably refreshed.

I stood up & as I did so saw a pair of brown bodies swimming towards me & perhaps forty yards away. They looked like floating lumps of brown leather. For a moment I wondered what these might be & then as they approached I saw they were the protuberant eyes and nostrils of a large hippopotamus. At that I hastily retreated to my machine. The monster came partly out of the water, then stopped & stared at me. Then with a grunt he turned back into the water & swam away.

I was hungry but saw no means of satisfying my hunger on that desolate spot. My courage was creeping back to me by slow degrees. I looked the facts squarely in the face. So far as my knowledge of geology went[2] this river might be the great flood that deposited what is now the London Clay.[3]

I sat under the warm sunset musing upon my position. I peered through the thin haze to see any forms of life that I could identify from

1. A reddish yellow.
2. "The Time Traveller's knowledge of geology was scarcely on a level with his mechanical acquirements. A distinguished geologist assures me that this supposition was quite inaccurate. The birds puzzled this authority, but the hippopotamus—if it was a true hippopotamus—would indicate the much more recent epoch of the Pliocene period" [*Wells's note*]. (The Pliocene period extended from roughly 5.5 million to roughly 2 million years ago.)
3. The thick layer (as much as 600 feet) of clay beneath the greater London area was deposited between 35 and 55 million years ago.

my geological reading & that would give me some idea of my position in time. Far away through the drifting mist some huge grey creatures followed one another in a line but I could not imagine what they were. I looked at the fluttering birds & at the willows. Then I remembered that the deciduous trees came after the Cretaceous[4] period. At any rate I had not that oceanic period between me & my own time.

I determined to travel forward two million years & see what came of it. I connected the dials with the mechanism again & pulled over the levers.

When I stopped again it was very cold. It was night & the stars were shining, & a softly undulating mantle of white lay upon the earth. I was on a hillside & a river gleamed dimly among the black tree stems below. Then suddenly as I looked at the sky my heart came into my throat. For high above circled the old familiar constellation of the Great Bear.

I shouted at that & held out my arms to the dear old stars. For I knew from that grouping I was nearing my own time.

I began calling their names to them & pointing to them. "Cassiopeia," I cried; "with your chair there! back again in the sky! The Swan! Polaris! The white streams of the Milky Way!"

Then suddenly I heard a crackling among the bushes & footsteps. "Hallo!" said a voice hoarsely.

I turned my head and saw coming through the trees the black figure of a man carrying a many-paned lantern. The pink light from this lay in a circle on the snow round him & showed his nearer leg, clad in a kind of ruffled knee breeches, black hose, & buckled shoes.

"Hallo!" cried I.

He stopped abruptly and lifted the lantern to the level of his head. The pink light fell on his ear & I saw his hair was close cropped & his hat square of outline & straight of brim. An expression of extreme astonishment came upon his face as he saw me.

I wanted to say something but I was speechless with excitement. I tried to gesticulate.

Abruptly he dropped the lantern, which was extinguished as it hit the ground. I heard his heels clattering up the hill & I saw the sparks fly from the pebbles. I sat there in silence under the starlight for some time, speculating how the thing might seem to this worthy. I judged him a seventeenth century puritan[5] so that I had nearly hit the mark—quite by accident as it happened. My impression had been that I was thirty or forty million years away from our time. That is the period I think some geologists give for the London Clay.[6] I was

4. The Cretaceous period ended about 65 million years ago.
5. The man's clothing, hat, and haircut conform to conventional depictions of seventeenth-century Puritans.
6. "The Time Traveller's geology was extremely elementary" [*Wells's note*].

thinking of going on another hundred years & stopping. But now I was in no great hurry or anxiety. There were now no nameless terrors in the air.

Then I saw a pink glimmer coming through the trees & heard several voices, & the noise of stumbling feet. Several voices seemed shouting together. Scraps of their talk came drifting down to me.

"Lead's no good, brother, a fair silver button—"

"We must go forward with the lantern for me to take my aim by."

"But we—"

"Even so are all warlocks."

I saw their lights now, a pink cylindrical lantern, & two torches showering sparks and carried by boys. In front of the advancing crowd came a tall man whose head glinted like metal in the flickering light. He had a sandy coloured jacket drawn in at the waist by a leather belt, big leather gloves, & huge riding boots. He carried a lumpish piece of artillery with a heavy stock & a brass barrel, broadening at the muzzle.

They became silent when they saw me & halted. Then one stood a little in front of the rest—a tall man with white bands under his chin—& lifting up his right hand to heaven & pointing his left to me this person began shouting at me in a loud voice.

"Hence Satan! I command thee. Get thee hence & be no more seen!"

I shouted back. "Can you tell me the date please?"

This seemed to disconcert him a little. He began again. "Avaunt.[7] You spirit of mischief!"

I put my hands to the sides of my mouth. "I am no spirit of mischief, but an honest English gentleman, I tell you. I ask you a simple question."

He lowered his hand. A man standing in the shadow behind him said something I did not catch & the preacher—for such I judge he was—turned & began to argue with him, every now & then glancing at me. The soldier fumbled with his musket. The boys with the torches drew near each other.

The night was bitterly cold. I felt my teeth were chattering. "Cannot you answer a plain question?" I said.

"Who be you?" said the soldier sullenly.

"What are you doing out here at midnight with that devilry?" said the preacher pointing to my machine.

"I tell you I am an honest English gentleman & this is no devilry at all. Will you, in the name of charity, tell me the date?"

"It's some devilish trick—" began the preacher.

---

7. "Avaunt" can mean "to go forward." The preacher evidently is urging the soldier to charge the Time Traveller.

"New Year's Eve, sixteen hundred & forty five," piped out one of the little boys. "*Now*, who are you?"

The preacher gripped him by the collar.

"Well I," said I, "am a Chronic Argonaut, an explorer of epochs, a man for all time, a Morlock fighter, a—"

"*Hor*rible blasphemy!" screamed the preacher gesticulating. "Shoot him! Avaunt! Avaunt!"

The soldier hastily clapped his gun to his shoulder & as hastily I pulled on the lever. I heard the dull bang of the musket & the twang of the silver button by my ear.

But I didn't care what they thought I said or did. I was coming home now. I rushed headlong down through the intervening two hundred & fifty years & in my excitement overshot the mark by a decade. I swung round & came back more deliberately. The hands on the dials ran back again.

Wells's Scientific Journalism (1891–94)

From The Rediscovery of the Unique[†]

The neat little picture of a universe of souls made up of passions and principles in bodies made of atoms, all put together so neatly and wound up at the creation, fades in the series of dissolving views that we call the march of human thought. We no longer believe, whatever creed we may affect, in a Deity whose design is so foolish and little that even a theological bishop can trace it and detect a kindred soul. Some of the most pious can hardly keep from scoffing at Milton's world— balanced just in the middle of those crystalline spheres that hung by a golden chain from the battlements of heaven.[1] We no longer speculate
  "What varied being peoples ev'ry star,"[2]
because we have no reason at all to expect life beyond this planet. We are a century in front of that Nuremberg cosmos,[3] and in place of it there looms a dim suggestion of the fathomlessness of the unique mystery of life. The figure of a roaring loom with unique threads flying and interweaving beyond all human following, working out a pattern beyond all human interpretation, we owe to Goethe, the intellectual father of the nineteenth century.[4] Number, order, seems now the least law in the universe; in the days of our greatgrandfathers it was heaven's first law.

[†] From *Fortnightly Review* n.s. 50 (July 1891): 106–11. These are the final two paragraphs of the essay.
1. In pre-Copernican cosmologies, the earth was placed at the center of a series of concentric crystalline spheres, upon which were fixed the moon, sun, planets, and stars. The entire universe was hung from heaven by a golden chain. John Milton refers to the golden chain in Book 2 of *Paradise Lost* (1674), to the crystalline spheres in Book 7.
2. Alexander Pope, *Essay on Man. Epistle 1* (1733), 1. 27. This portion of the poem is concerned with man's place in what Pope describes as a divinely ordered and beneficent universe.
3. A reference to the depictions in the fifteenth century *Nuremberg Chronicle* of God's creation of a perfectly ordered cosmos, a view that, according to Wells, has not been tenable for a century or more.
4. "'Tis thus at the roaring loom of Time I ply, / And weave for God the garment thou seest Him by," from a song of the Earth-spirit in Johann Wolfgang von Goethe's *Faust* (1808).

Science is a match that man has just got alight. He thought he was in a room—in moments of devotion, a temple—and that his light would be reflected from and display walls inscribed with wonderful secrets and pillars carved with philosophical systems wrought into harmony. It is a curious sensation, now that the preliminary splutter is over and the flame burns up clear, to see his hands lit and just a glimpse of himself and the patch he stands on visible, and around him, in place of all that human comfort and beauty he anticipated—darkness still.

From Zoological Retrogression[†]

Perhaps no scientific theories are more widely discussed or more generally misunderstood among cultivated people than the views held by biologists regarding the past history and future prospects of their province—life. Using their technical phrases and misquoting their authorities in an invincibly optimistic spirit, the educated public has arrived in its own way at a rendering of their results which it finds extremely satisfactory. It has decided that in the past the great scroll of nature has been steadily unfolding to reveal a constantly richer harmony of forms and successively higher grades of being, and it assumes that this "evolution" will continue with increasing velocity under the supervision of its extreme expression—man. This belief, as effective, progressive, and pleasing as transformation scenes at a pantomime, receives neither in the geological record nor in the studies of the phylogenetic embryologist any entirely satisfactory confirmation.

On the contrary, there is almost always associated with the suggestion of advance in biological phenomena an opposite idea, which is its essential complement. The technicality expressing this would, if it obtained sufficient currency in the world of culture, do much to reconcile the naturalist and his traducers. The toneless glare of optimistic evolution would then be softened by a shadow; the monotonous reiteration of "Excelsior"[1] by people who did not climb would cease; the too sweet harmony of the spheres would be enhanced by a discord, this evolutionary antithesis—degradation.

Isolated cases of degeneration have long been known, and popular attention has been drawn to them in order to point well-meant moral lessons, the fallacious analogy of species to individual being employed. It is only recently, however, that the enormous importance of degeneration as a plastic[2] process in nature has been suspected and its entire parity with evolution recognised.

---

† From *Gentleman's Magazine* 271 (September 1891): 246–53.
1. "Excelsior," which can be loosely translated as "onward and upward," is the refrain of a popular 1841 poem of the same title by Henry Wadsworth Longfellow.
2. By "plastic," Wells means "formative."

It is no libel to say that three-quarters of the people who use the phrase, "organic evolution," interpret it very much in this way:—Life began with the amæba, and then came jelly-fish, shell-fish, and all those miscellaneous invertebrate things, and then *real* fishes and amphibia, reptiles, birds, mammals, and man, the last and first of creation. It has been pointed out that this is very like regarding a man as the offspring of his first cousins; these, of his second; these, of his relations at the next remove, and so forth—making the remotest living human being his primary ancestor. Or, to select another image, it is like elevating the modest poor relation at the family gathering to the unexpected altitude of fountain-head—a proceeding which would involve some cruel reflections on her age and character. The sounder view is, as scientific writers have frequently insisted, that living species have varied along divergent lines from intermediate forms, and, as it is the object of this paper to point out, not necessarily in an upward direction.

In fact, the path of life, so frequently compared to some steadily-rising mountain-slope, is far more like a footway worn by leisurely wanderers in an undulating country. Excelsior biology is a popular and poetic creation—the *real* form of a phylum, or line of descent, is far more like the course of a busy man moving about a great city. Sometimes it goes underground, sometimes it doubles and twists in tortuous streets, now it rises far overhead along some viaduct, and, again, the river is taken advantage of in these varied journeyings to and fro. Upward and downward these threads of pedigree inter-weave, slowly working out a pattern of accomplished things that is difficult to interpret, but in which scientific observers certainly fail to discover that inevitable tendency to higher and better things with which the word "evolution" is popularly associated.

* * *

The ascidian, though a pronounced case of degradation, is only one of an endless multitude.[3] Those shelly warts that cover every frag-ment of sea-side shingle are degraded crustaceans; at first they are active and sensitive creatures, similar essentially to the earlier phases of the lift-history of a prawn. Other Cirripeds and many Copepods sink down still deeper, to almost entire shapelessness and loss of organization.[4] The corals, sea-mats, the immobile oysters and mus-sels are undoubtedly descended from free-living ancestors with eye-spots and other sense-organs. Various sea-worms and holothurians[5] have also taken to covering themselves over from danger, and so have

3. In the previous section of this essay, Wells traces the devolutionary arc of the ascidian or sea squirt over several millennia.
4. Cirripeds are sea barnacles. Copepods are minute parasitic crustaceans.
5. The genus holothuria includes sea worms.

deliberately foregone their dangerous birthright to a more varied and active career. The most fruitful and efficient cause of degradation, however, is not simply cowardice, but that loathsome tendency that is so closely akin to it—an aptness for parasitism. There are whole orders and classes thus pitifully submerged. The *Acarina*, or Mites, include an immense array of genera profoundly sunken in this way, and the great majority of both the flat and round worms are parasitic degeneration forms. The vile tapeworm, at the nadir, seems to have lost even common sensation; it has become an insensible mechanism of evil—a multiplying disease-spot, living to that extent, and otherwise utterly dead.

Such evident and indisputable present instances of degeneration alone would form a very large proportion of the catalogue of living animals. If we were to add to this list the names of all those genera the ancestors of which have at any time sunk to rise again, it is probable that we should have to write down *the entire roll of the animal kingdom*!

* * *

These brief instances of degradation may perhaps suffice to show that there is a good deal to be found in the work of biologists quite inharmonious with such phrases as "the progress of the ages," and the "march of mind." The zoologist demonstrates that advance has been fitful and uncertain; rapid progress has often been followed by rapid extinction or degeneration, while, on the other hand, a form lowly and degraded has in its degradation often happened upon some fortunate discovery or valuable discipline and risen again, like a more fortunate Antæos, to victory.[6] There is, therefore, no guarantee in scientific knowledge of man's permanence or permanent ascendency. He has a remarkably variable organisation, and his own activities and increase cause the conditions of his existence to fluctuate far more widely than those of any animal have ever done. The presumption is that before him lies a long future of profound modification, but whether that will be, according to present ideals, upward or downward, no one can forecast. Still, so far as any scientist can tell us, it may be that, instead of this, Nature is, in unsuspected obscurity, equipping some now humble creature with wider possibilities of appetite, endurance, or destruction, to rise in the fulness of time and sweep *homo* away into the darkness from which his universe arose. The Coming Beast must certainly be reckoned in any anticipatory calculations regarding the Coming Man.

---

6. In Greek mythology, King Antaeos (or Antaeus) challenged any visitor to a wrestling match to the death. He was finally defeated by Hercules, who, realizing that Antaeos derived his strength from contact with the earth, lifted him off the ground.

On Extinction[†]

The passing away of ineffective things, the entire rejection by Nature of the plans of life, is the essence of tragedy. In the world of animals, that runs so curiously parallel with the world of men, we can see and trace only too often the analogies of our grimmer human experiences; we can find the equivalents to the sharp tragic force of Shakespeare, the majestic inevitableness of Sophocles, and the sordid dreary tale, the middle-class misery, of Ibsen. The life that has schemed and struggled and committed itself, the life that has played and lost, comes at last to the pitiless judgment of time, and is slowly and remorselessly annihilated. This is the saddest chapter of biological science—the tragedy of Extinction.

In the long galleries of the geological museum are the records of judgments that have been passed graven upon the rocks. Here, for instance, are the huge bones of the 'Atlantosaurus,' one of the mightiest land animals that this planet has ever seen. A huge terrestrial reptile this, that crushed the forest trees as it browsed upon their foliage, and before which the pigmy ancestors of our present denizens of the land must have fled in abject terror of its mere might of weight. It had the length of four elephants, and its head towered thirty feet—higher, that is, than any giraffe—above the world it dominated. And yet this giant has passed away, and left no children to inherit the earth. No living thing can be traced back to these monsters; they are at an end among the branchings of the tree of life. Whether it was through some change of climate, some subtle disease, or some subtle enemy, these titanic reptiles dwindled in numbers, and faded at last altogether among things mundane. Save for the riddle of their scattered bones, it is as if they had never been.

Beside them are the pterodactyls, the first of vertebrated animals to spread a wing to the wind, and follow the hunted insects to their last refuge of the air. How triumphantly and gloriously these winged lizards, these original dragons, must have floated through their new empire of the atmosphere! If their narrow brains could have entertained the thought, they would have congratulated themselves upon having gained a great and inalienable heritage for themselves and their children for ever. And now we cleave a rock and find their bones, and speculate doubtfully what their outer shape may have been. No descendants are left to us. The birds are no offspring of theirs, but lighter children of some clumsy 'deinosaurs.' The pterodactyls also have heard the judgment of extinction, and are gone altogether from the world.

† From *Chambers's Journal* 10 (30 September 1893): 623–24.

The long roll of palæontology is half filled with the records of exter-mination; whole orders, families, groups, and classes have passed away and left no mark and no tradition upon the living fauna of the world. Many fossils of the older rocks are labelled in our museums, 'of doubtful affinity.' Nothing living has any part like them, and the baffled zoologist regretfully puts them aside. What they mean, he cannot tell. They hint merely at shadowy dead sub-kingdoms, of which the form eludes him. Index fingers are they, pointing into unfathomable darkness, and saying only one thing clearly, the word 'Extinction.'

In the living world of to-day the same forces are at work as in the past. One Fate still spins, and the gleaming scissors cut.[1] In the last hundred years the swift change of condition throughout the world, due to the invention of new means of transit, geographical discovery, and the consequent 'swarming' of the whole globe by civilised men, has pushed many an animal to the very verge of destruction. It is not only the dodo that has gone; for dozens of genera and hundreds of species, this century has witnessed the writing on the wall.[2]

In the fate of the bison extinction has been exceptionally swift and striking. In the 'forties' so vast were their multitudes that sometimes, 'as far as the eye could reach,' the plains would be covered by a gal-loping herd. Thousands of hunters, tribes of Indians, lived upon them. And now! It is improbable that one specimen in an altogether wild state survives. If it were not for the merciful curiosity of men, the few hundred that still live would also have passed into the dark-ness of non-existence. Following the same grim path are the seals, the Greenland whale, many Australian and New Zealand animals and birds ousted by more vigorous imported competitors, the black rat, endless wild birds.[3] The list of destruction has yet to be made in its completeness. But the grand bison is the statuesque type and example of the doomed races.

Can any of these fated creatures count? Does any suspicion of their dwindling numbers dawn upon them? Do they, like the Red Indian, perceive the end to which they are coming? For most of them, unlike the Red Indian, there is no alternative of escape by interbreed-ing with their supplanters. Simply and unconditionally, there is writ-ten across their future, plainly for any reader, the one word 'Death.'

Surely a chill of solitude must strike to the heart of the last strag-glers in the rout, the last survivors of the defeated and vanishing

---

1. The three Fates of Greek mythology are typically represented as spinning, measuring, and snipping the Thread of Life.
2. The dodo was hunted to extinction in the 1680s.
3. The bison, the Greenland whale, and several varieties of seal were nearly extinct by the 1890s, though all have made partial recoveries since. In this paragraph Wells also alludes to the havoc caused by the introduction by Europeans of non-native predators (such as the black rat) to the islands of the South Pacific.

species. The last shaggy bison, looking with dull eyes from some western bluff across the broad prairies, must feel some dim sense that those wide rolling seas of grass were once the home of myriads of his race, and are now his no longer. The sunniest day must shine with a cold and desert light on the eyes of the condemned. For them the future is blotted out, and hope is vanity.

These days are the days of man's triumph. The awful solitude of such a position is almost beyond the imagination. The earth is warm with men. We think always with reference to men. The future is full of men to our preconceptions, whatever it may be in scientific truth. In the loneliest position in human possibility, humanity supports us. But Hood, who sometimes rose abruptly out of the most mechanical punning to sublime heights, wrote a travesty, grotesquely fearful, of Campbell's 'The Last Man.'[4] In this he probably hit upon the most terrible thing that man can conceive as happening to man: the earth desert through a pestilence, and two men, and then one man, looking extinction in the face.

The Man of the Year Million[†]

A Scientific Forecast

Accomplished literature is all very well in its way, no doubt, but much more fascinating to the contemplative man are the books that have not been written. These latter are no trouble to hold; there are no pages to turn over. One can read them in bed on sleepless nights without a candle. Turning to another topic, primitive man, in the works of the descriptive anthropologist, is certainly a very entertaining and quaint person; but the man of the future, if we only had the facts, would appeal to us more strongly. Yet where are the books? As Ruskin has said somewhere, apropos of Darwin, it is not what man has been, but what he will be, that should interest us.

The contemplative man in his easy chair, pondering this saying, suddenly beholds in the fire, through the blue haze of his pipe, one of these great unwritten volumes. It is large in size, heavy in lettering, seemingly by one Professor Holzkopf, presumably Professor at Weissnichtwo.[1] "The Necessary Characters of the Man of the Remote Future deduced from the Existing Stream of Tendency," is the title.

---

4. Thomas Campbell's poem "The Last Man" (1823) is a dream-vision in which the title figure, fortified by his Christian faith, contemplates humanity's demise. In Thomas Hood's grotesquely fearful poem of the same title, a hangman executes a beggar for theft, leaving himself the last man on earth.
† From *Pall Mall Gazette* 57 (6 November 1893): 3–4.
1. That is, Professor Wooden Head of the University of Who-Knows-Where.'

The worthy Professor is severely scientific in his method, and deliberate and cautious in his deductions, the contemplative man discovers as he pursues his theme, and yet the conclusions are, to say the least, remarkable. We must figure the excellent Professor expanding the matter at great length, voluminously technical, but the contemplative man—since he has access to the only copy—is clearly at liberty to make such extracts and abstracts as he chooses for the unscientific reader. Here, for instance, is something of practicable lucidity that he considers admits of quotation.

"The theory of evolution," writes the Professor, "is now universally accepted by zoologists and botanists, and it is applied unreservedly to man. Some question, indeed, whether it fits his soul, but all agree it accounts for his body. Man, we are assured, is descended from ape-like ancestors, moulded by circumstances into men, and these apes again were derived from ancestral forms of a lower order, and so up from the primordial protoplasmic jelly. Clearly, then, man, unless the order of the universe has come to an end, will undergo further modification in the future, and at last cease to be man, giving rise to some other type of animated being. At once the fascinating question arises, What will this being be? Let us consider for a little the plastic[2] influences at work upon our species.

"Just as the bird is the creature of the wing, and is all moulded and modified to flying, and just as the fish is the creature that swims, and has had to meet the inflexible conditions of a problem in hydrodynamics, so man is the creature of the brain; he will live by intelligence, and not by physical strength, if he live at all. So that much that is purely 'animal' about him is being and must be, beyond all question, suppressed in his ultimate development. Evolution is no mechanical tendency making for perfection according to the ideas current in the year of grace 1892; it is simply the continual adaptation of plastic life, for good or evil, to the circumstances that surround it. . . . We notice this decay of the animal part around us now, in the loss of teeth and hair, in the dwindling hands and feet of men, in their smaller jaws, and slighter mouths and ears. Man now does by wit and machinery and verbal agreement what he once did by bodily toil; for once he had to catch his dinner, capture his wife, run away from his enemies, and continually exercise himself, for love of himself, to perform these duties well. But now all this is changed. Cabs, trains, trams, render speed unnecessary, the pursuit of food becomes easier; his wife is no longer hunted, but rather, in view of the crowded matrimonial market, seeks him out. One needs wits now to live, and physical activity

2. By "plastic," a word he uses often in his essays of the 1890s, Wells generally means "formative" or "creative."

is a drug, a snare even; it seeks artificial outlets and overflows in games. Athleticism takes up time and cripples a man in his competitive examinations, and in business. So is your fleshly man handicapped against his subtler brother. He is unsuccessful in life, does not marry. The better adapted survive."

The coming man, then, will clearly have a larger brain, and a slighter body than the present. But the Professor makes one exception to this. "The human hand, since it is the teacher and interpreter of the brain, will become constantly more powerful and subtle as the rest of the musculature dwindles."

Then in the physiology of these children of men, with their expanding brains, their great sensitive hands and diminishing bodies, great changes were necessarily worked. "We see now," says the Professor, "in the more intellectual sections of humanity an increasing sensitiveness to stimulants, a growing inability to grapple with such a matter as alcohol, for instance. No longer can men drink a bottle full of port; some cannot drink tea; it is too exciting for their highly-wrought nervous systems. The process will go on, and the Sir Wilfrid Lawson of some near generation may find it his duty and pleasure to make the silvery spray of his wisdom tintinnabulate against the tea-tray.[3] These facts lead naturally to the comprehension of others. Fresh raw meat was once a dish for a king. Now refined persons scarcely touch meat unless it is cunningly disguised. Again, consider the case of turnips; the raw root is now a thing almost uneatable, but once upon a time a turnip must have been a rare and fortunate find, to be torn up with delirious eagerness and devoured in ecstacy. The time will come when the change will affect all the other fruits of the earth. Even now only the young of mankind eat apples raw—the young always preserving ancestral characteristics after their disappearance in the adult. Some day, boys even will regard apples without emotion. The boy of the future, one must believe, will gaze on an apple with the same unspeculative languor with which he now regards a flint"—in the absence of a cat.

"Furthermore, fresh chemical discoveries came into action as modifying influences upon men. In the prehistoric period even, man's mouth had ceased to be an instrument for grasping food; it is still growing continually less prehensile, his front teeth are smaller, his lips thinner and less muscular; he has a new organ, a mandible not of irreparable tissue, but of bone and steel—a knife and fork. There is no reason why things should stop at partial artificial division thus afforded; there is every reason, on the contrary, to believe

3. Sir Wilfred Lawson (1829–1906) was a well-known temperance campaigner and tee-totaler. Wells's joke is that tea itself will be an intoxicant for the man of the future. "Tintinnabulate": to ring.

my statement that some cunning exterior mechanism will presently masticate and insalivate his dinner, relieve his diminishing salivary glands and teeth, and at last altogether abolish them."

Then what is not needed disappears. What use is there for external ears, nose, and brow ridges now? The two latter once protected the eye from injury it conflict and in falls, but in these days we keep on our legs, and at peace. Directing his thoughts in this way, the reader may presently conjure up a dim, strange vision of the latter-day face: "Eyes large, lustrous, beautiful, soulful; above them, no longer separated by rugged brow ridges, is the top of the head, a glistening, hairless dome, terete[4] and beautiful; no craggy nose rises to disturb by its unmeaning shadows the symmetry of that calm face, no vestigial ears project; the mouth is a small, perfectly round aperture, toothless and gumless, jawless, unanimal, no futile emotions disturbing its roundness as it lies, like the harvest moon or the evening star, in the wide firmament of face." Such is the face the Professor beholds in the future.

Of course parallel modifications will also affect the body and limbs. "Every day so many hours and so much energy are required for digestion; a gross torpidity, a carnal lethargy, seizes on mortal men after dinner. This may and can be avoided. Man's knowledge of organic chemistry widens daily. Already he can supplement the gastric glands by artificial devices. Every doctor who administers physic implies that the bodily functions may be artificially superseded. We have pepsine, pancreatine, artificial gastric acid—I know not what like mixtures.[5] Why, then, should not the stomach be ultimately superannuated altogether? A man who could not only leave his dinner to be cooked, but also leave it to be masticated and digested, would have vast social advantages over his food-digesting fellow. This is, let me remind you here, the calmest, most passionless, and scientific working out of the future forms of things from the data of the present. At this stage the following facts may perhaps stimulate your imagination. There can be no doubt that many of the arthropods, a division of animals more ancient and even now more prevalent than the vertebrata, have undergone more phylogenetic[6] modification"—a beautiful phrase—"than even the most modified of vertebrated animals. Simple forms like the lobsters display a primitive structure parallel with that of the fishes. However, in such a form as the degraded "Chondracanthus,"[7] the structure has diverged far more widely from its original type than in man. Among some of

4. Smooth and round.
5. Pepsin and pancreatin are digestive enzymes.
6. Pertaining to the pattern of relationships between species that results from evolutionary changes.
7. A species of minute parasitic crustaceans.

these most highly modified crustaceans the whole of the alimentary canal—that is, all the food-digesting and food-absorbing parts—form a useless solid cord: the animal is nourished—it is a parasite—by absorption of the nutritive fluid in which it swims. Is there any absolute impossibility in supposing man to be destined for a similar change; to imagine him no longer dining, with unwieldy paraphernalia of servants and plates, upon food queerly dyed and distorted, but nourishing himself in elegant simplicity by immersion in a tub of nutritive fluid?

"There grows upon the impatient imagination a building, a dome of crystal, across the translucent surface of which flushes of the most glorious and pure prismatic colours pass and fade and change. In the centre of this transparent chameleon-tinted dome is a circular white marble basin filled with some clear, mobile, amber liquid, and in this plunge and float strange beings. Are they birds?

"They are the descendants of man—at dinner. Watch them as they hop on their hands—a method of progression advocated already by Bjornsen[8]—about the pure white marble floor. Great hands they have, enormous brains, soft, liquid, soulful eyes. Their whole muscular system, their legs, their abdomens, are shrivelled to nothing, a dangling, degraded pendant to their minds."

The further visions of the professor are less alluring.

"The animals and plants die away before men, except such as he preserves for his food or delight, or such as maintain a precarious footing about him as commensals and parasites.[9] These vermin and pests must succumb sooner or later to his untiring inventiveness and incessantly growing discipline. When he learns (the chemists are doubtless getting towards the secret now) to do the work of chlorophyll without the plant, then his necessity for other animals and plants upon the earth will disappear. Sooner or later, where there is no power of resistance and no necessity, there comes extinction. In the last days man will be alone on the earth, and his food will be won by the chemist from the dead rocks and the sunlight.

"And—one may learn the full reason in that explicit and painfully right book, the 'Data of Ethics'[1]—the irrational fellowship of man will give place to an intellectual co-operation, and emotion fall within the scheme of reason. Undoubtedly it is a long time yet, but a long time is nothing in the face of eternity, and every man who thinks of these things must look eternity in the face."

8. Unidentified.
9. A commensal is an animal or plant that attaches itself to another and shares its food, whereas a parasite feeds on its host.
1. In *The Data of Ethics* (1879), the prominent social philosopher and psychologist Herbert Spencer (1828–1903) emphasizes the effects of reason and cooperation in the processes of human evolution.

Then the earth is ever radiating away heat into space, the Professor reminds us. And so at last comes a vision of earthly cherubim, hopping heads, great unemotional intelligences, and little hearts, fighting together perforce and fiercely against the cold that grips them tighter and tighter. For the world is cooling—slowly and inevitably it grows colder as the years roll by. "We must imagine these creatures," says the Professor, "in galleries and laboratories deep down in the bowels of the earth. The whole world will be snow-covered and piled with ice; all animals, all vegetation vanished, except this last branch of the tree of life. The last men have gone even deeper, following the diminishing heat of the planet, and vast steel shafts and ventilators make way for the air they need."

So with a glimpse of these human tadpoles, in their deep close gallery, with their boring machinery ringing away, and artificial lights glaring and casting black shadows, the professor's horoscope concludes. Humanity in dismal retreat before the cold, changed beyond recognition. Yet the Professor is reasonable enough, his facts are current science, his methods orderly. The contemplative man shivers at the prospect, starts up to poke the fire, and the whole of this remarkable book that is not written vanishes straightway in the smoke of his pipe. This is the great advantage of this unwritten literature: there is no bother in changing the books. Our contemplative man consoles himself for the destiny of the species with the lost portion of Kubla Khan.[2]

The Extinction of Man[†]

Some Speculative Suggestions

It is part of the excessive egotism of the human animal that the bare idea of its extinction seems incredible to it. "A world without *us*!" it says, as a heady young Cephalapsis might have said it in the old Silurian sea. But since the Cephalapsis and the Coccostens many a fine animal has increased and multiplied upon the earth, lorded it over land or sea without a rival, and passed at last into the night.[1] Surely it is not so unreasonable to ask why man should be an exception to the rule. From the scientific standpoint at least any reason for such exception is hard to find.

No doubt man is undisputed master at the present time—at least of most of the land surface; but so it has been before with other

---

2. Samuel Taylor Coleridge claimed that he was interrupted while composing his poem "Kubla Khan, or a Vision in a Dream. A Fragment" (published 1816), and so it was left unfinished.

† From *Pall Mall Gazette* 59 (25 September 1894): 3.

1. Cephalapsis and coccosteid are fish that became extinct over 400 million years ago.

animals. Let us consider what light geology has to throw upon this. The great land and sea reptiles of the Mesozoic period, for instance, seem to have been as secure as humanity is now in their pre-eminence. But they passed away and left no descendants when the new orders of the mammals emerged from their obscurity. So, too, the huge Titanotheria of the American continent, and all the powerful mammals of Pleistocene South America, the sabre-toothed lion, for instance, and the Machrauchenia suddenly came to a finish when they were still almost at the zenith of their rule.[2] And in no case does the record of the fossils show a really dominant species succeeded by its own descendants. What has usually happened in the past appears to be the emergence of some type of animal hitherto rare and unimportant, and the extinction, not simply of the previously ruling species, but of most of the forms that are at all closely related to it. Sometimes, indeed, as in the case of the extinct giants of South America, they vanished without any considerable rivals, victims of pestilence, famine, or, it may be, of that cumulative inefficiency that comes of a too undisputed life. So that the analogy of geology, at any rate, is against this too acceptable view of man's certain tenure of the earth for the next few million years or so.

And after all even now man is by no means such a master of the kingdoms of life as he is apt to imagine. The sea, that mysterious nursery of living things, is for all practical purposes beyond his control. The low-water mark is his limit. Beyond that he may do a little with seine and dredge, murder a few million herrings a year as they come in to spawn, butcher his fellow air-breather, the whale, or haul now and then an unlucky king crab or strange sea urchin out of the deep water in the name of science; but the life of the sea as a whole knows him not, plays out its slow drama of change and development unheeding him, and may in the end, in mere idle sport, throw up some new terrestrial denizen, some new competitor for space to live in and food to live upon, that will sweep him and all his little contrivances out of existence, as certainly and inevitably as he has swept away auk, bison, and dodo during the last two hundred years.[3]

For instance, there are the crustacea. As a group the crabs and lobsters are confined below the high-water mark. But experiments in air-breathing are no doubt in progress in this group—we already have tropical land crabs—and as far as we know there is no reason why in the future these creatures should not increase in size and terrestrial capacity. In the past we have the evidence of the fossil *Paradoxides*

2. The Mesozoic Era lasted approximately from 250 million to 65 million years ago. Titano-theria resembled rhinoceri, machrauchenia camels or llamas; along with saber-toothed cats, they went extinct during the Pleistocene period, which ended less than a million years ago.
3. The dodo and the great auk were hunted to extinction; the former disappeared in the 1680s, the latter in the 1840s. The American bison or buffalo narrowly escaped the same fate in the mid-nineteenth century.

that creatures of this kind may at least attain a length of six feet, and, considering their intense pugnacity, a crab of such dimensions would be as formidable a creature as one could well imagine. And their amphibious capacity would give them an advantage against us such as at present is only to be found in the case of the alligator or crocodile. If we imagine a shark that could raid out upon the land, or a tiger that could take refuge in the sea, we should have a fair suggestion of what a terrible monster a large predatory crab might prove. And so far as zoological science goes we must, at least, admit that such a creature is an evolutionary possibility.

Then, again, the order of the Cephalopods, to which belong the cuttle-fish and the octopus (sacred to Victor Hugo), may be, for all we can say to the contrary, an order with a future.[4] Their kindred, the Gasteropods, have, in the case of the snail and slug, learnt the trick of air-breathing. And not improbably there are even now genera of this order that have escaped the naturalist, or even well-known genera whose possibilities in growth and dietary are still unknown. Suppose some day a specimen of a new species is caught off the coast of Kent. It excites remark at a Royal Society[5] soirée, engenders a Science Note or so, "A Huge Octopus!" and in the next year or so three or four other specimens come to hand and the thing becomes familiar. "Probably a new and larger variety of Octopus so-and-so, hitherto supposed to be tropical," says Professor Gargoyle, and thinks he has disposed of it. Then conceive some mysterious boating accidents and deaths while bathing. A large animal of this kind coming into a region of frequent wrecks might so easily acquire a preferential taste for human nutriment, just as the Colorado beetle acquired a new taste for the common potato and gave up its old food-plants some years ago. Then perhaps a school or pack or flock of Octopus Gigas would be found busy picking the sailors off a stranded ship, and then in the course of a few score years it might begin to stroll up the beaches and batten on excursionists. Soon it would be a common feature of the watering-places. Possibly at last commoner than excursionists. Suppose such a creature were to appear—and it is, we repeat, a possibility, if perhaps a remote one— how could it be fought against? Something might be done by torpedoes; but so far as our past knowledge goes man has no means of seriously diminishing the numbers of any animal of the most rudimentary intelligence that made its fastness in the sea.

4. In "Octopus with the Initials V. H.," a pen-and-ink drawing from around 1866, the renowned French writer Victor Hugo offers a comic if still mildly disturbing self-portrait. Octopuses make more than token appearances in his novel Les Travailleurs de la Mer (Toilers of the Sea), also published in 1866.
5. Great Britain's preeminent scientific society.

Even on land it is possible to find creatures that with a little modification might become excessively dangerous to the human ascendency. Most people have read of the migratory ants of Central Africa, against which no man can stand. On the march they simply clear out whole villages, drive men and animals before them in headlong rout, and kill and eat every living creature they can capture. One wonders why they do not already spread the area of their devastations. But at present no doubt they have their natural checks, of ant-eating birds, or what not. In the near future it may be that the European immigrant, as he sets the balance of life swinging in his vigorous manner, may kill off these ant-eating animals, or otherwise unwittingly remove the checks that now keep these terrible little pests within limits. And once they begin to spread in real earnest it is hard to see how their advance could be stopped. A world devoured by ants seems incredible now, simply because it is not within our experience; but a naturalist would have a dull imagination who could not see in the numerous species of ants, and in their already high intelligence, far more possibility of strange developments than we have in the solitary human animal. And no doubt the idea of the small and feeble organism of man triumphant and omnipresent would have seemed equally incredible to an intelligent mammoth or a palæolithic cave bear.

And finally there is always the prospect of a new disease. As yet science has scarcely touched more than the fringe of the probabilities associated with the minute fungi that constitute our zymotic[6] diseases. But the bacilli have no more settled down into their final quiescence than have men; like ourselves, they are adapting themselves to new conditions and acquiring new powers. The plagues of the Middle Ages, for instance, seem to have been begotten of a strange bacillus engendered under conditions that sanitary science, in spite of its panacea of drainage, still admits are imperfectly understood, and for all we know even now we may be quite unwittingly evolving some new and more terrible plague—a plague that will not take ten or twenty or thirty per cent., as plagues have done in the past, but the entire hundred.

No; man's complacent assumption of the future is too confident. We think, because things have been easy for mankind as a whole for a generation or so, we are going on to perfect comfort and security in the future. We think that we shall always go to work at ten and leave off at four and have dinner at seven for ever and ever. But these four suggestions out of a host of others must surely do a little against this complacency. Even now, for all we can tell, the coming terror may be crouching for its spring and the fall of humanity be at hand. In the case of every other predominant animal the world has ever seen,

6. Infectious.

we repeat, the hour of its complete ascendency has been the beginning of its decline.

From The "Cyclic" Delusion[†]

Nothing is more deeply impressed upon the human mind than the persuasion of a well-nigh universal cyclic quality in things, of an inevitable disposition to recur in the long run to a former phase. In great things and in small we see it; we are, indeed, like men in a workshop full of whirling machinery, who, wherever they turn, see a wheel, until at last this rotation is so dinned into the texture of our minds that the whole world spins. Every moment the heart goes through its cycle from dilatation to contraction and so back to dilatation; for every four heart-beats the lungs expand and contract; then hunger comes, is satisfied, recurs; the sun rises and sets, and sleep follows activity. Other bodily functions run in longer periods, as the moon changes from new to full and from full to new, and spring-tide follows neap;[1] in still larger circles spins the succession of seed-time and harvest. Yet larger again is the circle of the lifetime from birth to begetting, and so again to birth. The planetary cycles accomplish themselves in still longer periods, and, greatest and slowest of all, the pole of the earth completes its gigantic precessional revolution through the constellations.[2]

It is scarcely wonderful if the human mind is inclined to look for, and ready to discover, the circle—the recurrence—in everything it deals with. A few years ago that happily departed phrase, "the inevitable reaction," was alive to witness to the facility of this persuasion. We find it in history, in poetry, in mathematics. A straight line is an arc of a circle of infinite radius, says the mathematician; and a ring is the world-wide symbol of eternity. This idea lies implicitly at the base of countless scientific researches and theories.

* * *

In geological literature the idea that Glacial periods have occurred time after time is constantly cropping up, in spite of the absence of any satisfactory corroboration. It is one of the commonest employments of the modern astronomer to discover pairs of stars revolving round one another. And both the meteoric and the nebular hypotheses—really theories of the material universe—are cyclic theories, in which cold

---

[†] From *Saturday Review* 78 (10 November 1894): 505–06.
1. During neap tides, there is the least difference between the high- and low-water marks. During spring tides, the difference is at its greatest.
2. Because the earth wobbles slightly on its axis, the constellations appear to move in a circle around the earth's pole. One complete circle of the axis through the sky takes about 25,800 years and is called a precessional cycle.

dark bodies, moving through space, collide, are rendered gaseous and incandescent by the heat of the collision, and slowly revert by radiation to the cold dark condition again.

* * *

Now, it is a curious and suggestive speculation to investigate the sources of this cyclic predisposition. In the end one is surprised by the narrowness of the base upon which this extraordinary conception has arisen. In the first place, the planetary motions, the lunar phases, the tides, the alternation of day and night, and the sequence of seasons, cease in the light of scientific analysis to be corroboratory evidence. For both the generally accepted theories of the origin of the solar system suppose a nebulous cloud rotating on its axis to begin with, from the central mass of which the planets were torn by centrifugal force, and sent spinning in widening orbits round the central sun, throwing off satellites as they spun; on which view these instances of cyclic recurrence are really only special aspects of one and the same case, consequences of an eddying motion in the original nebula. The periodicity of many animal functions, waking and sleep and the reproductive seasons, for instance, are very conceivably correlated with these.

And, with further examination, we discover that these apparent cycles seem cyclic only through the limitation of our observation. The tidal drag upon the planets slowly retards their rotation, so that every day is—though by an imperceptible amount—longer. "As certain as that the sun will rise" is a proverb for certainty, but one day the sun will rise for the last time, will become as motionless in the sky as the earth is now in the sky of the moon. According to Professor G. H. Darwin, the actual motion of a satellite is spiral; it recedes from its source and primary until a maximum distance is attained, and thence it draws nearer again, until it reunites at last with the central body.[3] Moreover, the recurrence of living things is also illusory. The naturalist tells us that the egg hatches into a hen not *quite* like the parent hen; that if we go back along the pedigree we shall come at last to creatures not hens, but to the ancestral forms of the hen. Take only a few generations, and the cycle seems perfect enough; but, as more and more are taken, we drift further and further from the starting point—drift steadily, without any disposition to return.

Then the beating of the heart, the breathing, the rhythm of muscular motion, all the physiological sequences spring probably out of one common necessity, the impossibility—or, at least, the great

---

3. The mathematician and astronomer Sir George Howard Darwin (1845–1912) postulated that the gravitational pull of a planet or a sun eventually stops the rotation of the satellites circling it. Just as the earth's moon does not rotate, Darwin argued, the earth itself will one day stop its rotation, leaving half the planet in a perpetual daytime. In the even longer view, satellites are sooner or later drawn by gravitation back into their parent bodies.

inconvenience—of living tissue acting and feeding at the same time, of loading and discharging the gun simultaneously. We have activity, fatigue, and nutritive pause, activity again; for only half its beat is the heart actively working, the remaining period is a pause during which the repair of the muscular tissue occurs. It is at least a plausible speculation that the musical sequences appeal to us as they do because of the rhythmic quality of our physiological organization. And, though one heart-beat seems to follow the next truly enough, yet a time comes when the pitcher goes no longer to the well.

So it may be that this cyclic quality that is so woven into the texture of our being, into the fundamentals of our thought, is, after all, a prejudice, the outcome of two main accidents of our existence. We live in an eddy; are, as it were, the creatures of that eddy. But the great stream of the universe flows past us and onward. Here and there is a backwater or a whirling pool, a little fretful midge of life spinning upon its axis, or a gyrating solar system. But the main course is forward, from the things that are past and done with for ever to things that are altogether new.

Wells on
The Time Machine

From Preface to the Atlantic Edition of *The Time Machine* (1924)†

In this first volume are some of the author's earliest imaginative writings. The idea of "The Time Machine" itself, a rather forced development of the idea that time is a direction in space, came when he was still a student at the Royal College of Science. He tried to make a story of it in the students' magazine. If the old numbers of that publication for the years 1889 and 1890, or thereabouts,[1] still exist, the curious may read there that first essay, written obviously under the influence of Hawthorne and smeared with that miscellaneous allusiveness that Carlyle and many other of the great Victorians had made the fashion. "Time Travellers" were not to be written of in those days of the twopence coloured style;[2] the story was called, rather deliciously, "The Chronic Argonauts" and the Time Traveller was "Mr. Nebo-gipfel." Similar pigments prevailed throughout. A cleansing course of Swift and Sterne intervened before the idea was written again for Henley's *National Observer* in 1894, and his later *New Review* in 1895, and published as a book in the spring of that latter year. That version stands here unaltered. There was a slight struggle between the writer and W. E. Henley who wanted, he said, to put a little "writing" into the tale. But the writer was in reaction from that sort of thing, the Henley interpolations were cut out again, and he had his own way with the text.

And now the writer reads this book, "The Time Machine," and can no more touch it or change it than if it were the work of an entirely different person. He reads it again after a long interval, he does not believe he has opened its pages for twenty years, and finds it hard and

† From *The Atlantic Edition of the Works of H. G. Wells* (New York: Charles Scribner's Sons, 1924), Volume 1, pp. xxi–xxii. Reprinted by permission of the Rare Book and Manuscript Library, University of Illinois at Urbana-Champaign.
1. Actually, 1888.
2. That is, Wells felt that he had to sensationalize his story "The Chronic Argonauts" to make it marketable. Cheap illustrated stories could be bought for a penny; stories with color illustrations cost twopence.

"clever" and youthful. And—what is odd, he thinks—a little unsympathetic. He is left doubting—rather irrelevantly to the general business of this Preface—whether if the Time Machine were a sufficiently practicable method of transport for such a meeting, the H. G. Wells of 1894 and the H. G. Wells of 1922 would get on very well together.

Preface to *The Time Machine: An Invention* (1931)†

The Time Machine was published in 1895. It is obviously the work of an inexperienced writer, but certain originalities in it saved it from extinction and there are still publishers and perhaps even readers to be found for it after the lapse of a third of a century. In its final form, except for certain minor amendments, it was written in a lodging at Sevenoaks in Kent. The writer was then living from hand to mouth as a journalist. There came a lean month when scarcely an article of his was published or paid for in any of the papers to which he was accustomed to contribute and since all the offices in London that would tolerate him were already amply supplied with still unused articles, it seemed hopeless to write more until the block moved. Accordingly, rather than fret at this dismaying change in his outlook, he wrote this story in the chance of finding a market for it in some new quarter. He remembers writing at it late one summer night by an open window, while a disagreeable landlady grumbled at him in the darkness outside because of the excessive use of her lamp, expanding to a dreaming world her unwillingness to go to bed while that lamp was still alight; he wrote on to that accompaniment; and he remembers, too, discussing it and the underlying notions of it, while he walked in Knole Park with that dear companion[1] who sustained him so stoutly through those adventurous years of short commons and hopeful uncertainty.

The idea of it seemed in those days to be his "one idea." He had saved it up so far in the hope that he would one day make a much longer book of it than the *Time Machine*, but the urgent need for something marketable obliged him to exploit it forthwith. As the discerning reader will perceive, it is a very unequal book: the early discussion is much more carefully planned and written than the later chapters. A slender story springs from a very profound root. The early part, the explanation of the idea had already seen the light in 1893[2] in Henley's *National Observer*. It was the latter half that was written so urgently at Sevenoaks in 1894.

---

† From *The Time Machine: An Invention* (New York: Random House, 1931), pp. vii–x. Reprinted by permission of the Rare Book and Manuscript Library, University of Illinois at Urbana-Champaign.
1. Amy Catherine Robbins ("Jane"), with whom he eloped in 1894.
2. Actually, 1894.

That one idea is now everybody's idea. It was never the writer's own peculiar idea. Other people were coming to it. It was begotten in the writer's mind by students' discussions in the laboratories and debating society of the Royal College of Science in the eighties and already it had been tried over in various forms by him before he made this particular application of it. It is the idea that Time is a fourth dimension and that the normal present is a three-dimensional section of a four-dimensional universe. The only difference between the time dimension and the others, from this point of view, lay in the movement of consciousness along it, whereby the progress of the present was constituted. Obviously there might be various "presents" according to the direction in which the advancing section was cut, a method of stating the conception of relativity that did not come into scientific use until a considerable time later, and as obviously, since the section called the "present" was real and not "mathematical," it would possess a certain depth that might vary. The "now" therefore is not instantaneous, it is a shorter or longer measure of time, a point that has still to find its proper appreciation in contemporary thought.

But my story does not go on to explore either of these possibilities; I did not in the least know how to go on to such an exploration. I was not sufficiently educated in that field, and certainly a story was not the way to investigate further. So my opening exposition escapes along the line of paradox to an imaginative romance stamped with many characteristics of the Stevenson and early-Kipling period in which it was written. Already the writer had made an earlier experiment in the pseudo-Teutonic, Nathaniel Hawthorne style, an experiment printed in the *Science Schools Journal* (1888–89) and now happily unattainable. All the gold of Mr. Gabriel Wells cannot recover that version.[3] And there was also an account of the idea, set up to be printed for the *Fortnightly Review* in 1891 and never used. It was there called "The Universe Rigid." That too is lost beyond recovery, though a less unorthodox predecessor "*The Rediscovery of the Unique*," insisting upon the individuality of atoms, saw the light in the July issue of that year. Then the editor Mr. Frank Harris woke up to the fact that he was printing matter twenty years too soon, reproached the writer terrifyingly, and broke type again. If any impression survives it must be in the archives of the *Fortnightly Review* but I doubt if any impression survives. For years I thought I had a copy but when I looked for it, it had gone.

The story of the *Time Machine* as distinguished from the idea, "dates" not only in its treatment but in its conception. It seems a very undergraduate performance to its now mature writer, as he looks it over once more. But it goes as far as his philosophy about human

---

3. Gabriel Wells (1862–1946), no relation to H. G. Wells, made his fortune dealing in rare books and manuscripts.

evolution went in those days. The idea of a social differentiation of mankind into Eloi and Morlocks, strikes him now as more than a little crude. In his adolescence Swift had exercised a tremendous fascination upon him and the naive pessimism of this picture of the human future is, like the kindred *Island of Doctor Moreau*, a clumsy tribute to a master to whom he owes an enormous debt. Moreover, the geologists and astronomers of that time told us dreadful lies about the "inevitable" freezing up of the world—and of life and mankind with it. There was no escape it seemed. The whole game of life would be over in a million years or less. They impressed this upon us with the full weight of their authority, while now Sir James Jeans in his smiling *Universe Around Us* waves us on to millions of millions of years.[4] Given as much law as that man will be able to do anything and go anywhere, and the only trace of pessimism left in the human prospect today is a faint flavour of regret that one was born so soon. And even from that distress modem psychological and biological philosophy offers ways of escape.

One must err to grow and the writer feels no remorse for this youthful effort. Indeed he hugs his vanity very pleasantly at times when his dear old *Time Machine* crops up once more in essays and speeches, still a practical and convenient way to retrospect or prophecy. *The Time Journey of Doctor Barton*, dated 1929, is upon his desk as he writes— with all sorts of things in it we never dreamt of six and thirty years ago.[5] So the *Time Machine* has lasted as long as the diamond-framed safety bicycle, which came in at about the date of its first publication. And now it is going to be printed and published so admirably that its author is assured it will outlive him. He has long since given up the practise of writing prefaces for books, but this is an exceptional occasion and he is very proud and happy to say a word or so of reminiscence and friendly commendation for that needy and cheerful namesake of his, who lived back along the time dimension, six and thirty years ago.

H. G. WELLS

4. The physicist and astronomer Sir James Jeans (1877–1946) wrote a series of often breezy books on scientific topics aimed at a popular readership, including *The Universe Around Us* (1929).
5. *The Time-Journey of Dr. Barton: An Engineering and Sociological Forecast Based on Present Possibilities* was edited by John Lawrence Hodgson.

From Preface to Seven Famous Novels (1934)[†]

These tales have been compared with the work of Jules Verne and there was a disposition on the part of literary journalists at one time to call me the English Jules Verne.[1] As a matter of fact there is no literary resemblance whatever between the anticipatory inventions of the great Frenchman and these fantasies. His work dealt almost always with actual possibilities of invention and discovery, and he made some remarkable forecasts. The interest he evoked was a practical one. . . . But these stories of mine collected here do not pretend to deal with possible things; they are exercises of the imagination in a quite different field. They belong to a class of writing which includes the *Golden Ass of Apuleius*, the *True Histories of Lucian*, *Peter Schlemil* and the story of *Frankenstein*.[2] . . . They are all fantasies; they do not aim to project a serious possibility; they aim indeed only at the same amount of conviction as one gets in a good gripping dream. They have to hold the reader to the end by art and illusion and not by proof and argument, and the moment he closes the cover and reflects he wakes up to their impossibility.

In all this type of story the living interest lies in their non-fantastic elements and not in the invention itself. They are appeals for human sympathy quite as much as any "sympathetic" novel, and the fantastic element, the strange property or the strange world, is used only to throw up and intensify our natural reactions of wonder, fear or perplexity. The invention is nothing in itself and when this kind of thing is attempted by clumsy writers who do not understand this elementary principle nothing could be conceived more silly and extravagant. Anyone can invent human beings inside out or worlds like dumb-bells or a gravitation that repels. The thing that makes such imaginations interesting is their translation into commonplace terms and a rigid exclusion of other marvels from the story. Then it becomes human. "How would you feel and what might not happen to you," is the typical question, if for instance pigs could fly and one

† From *Seven Famous Novels. With a Preface by the Author* (New York: Alfred A. Knopf, 1934), pp. vii–viii. By permission of AP Watt Ltd. on behalf of The Literary Executors of the Estate of H. G. Wells.
1. Jules Verne (1828–1905), prolific, popular, and influential novelist and originator of modern science fiction.
2. Lucius Apuleius's *Metamorphosis, or The Golden Ass* and Lucian of Samosata's *True History*, prose narratives dating from the second century CE, are full of fabulous incidents and adventures. The title character of Adelbert von Chamisso's *Peter Schlemihl's Remarkable Story* (1814) sells his soul to the devil. Mary Shelley's *Frankenstein* was first published in 1818.

came rocketing over a hedge at you. How would you feel and what might not happen to you if suddenly you were changed into an ass and couldn't tell anyone about it? Or if you became invisible? But no one would think twice about the answer if hedges and houses also began to fly, or if people changed into lions, tigers, cats and dogs, left and right, or if everyone could vanish anyhow. Nothing remains interesting where anything may happen.

For the writer of fantastic stories to help the reader play the game properly, he must help him in every possible unobtrusive way to *domesticate* the impossible hypothesis.

Scientific and Social Contexts

EDWIN RAY LANKESTER

From Degeneration

A CHAPTER IN DARWINISM[†]

* * *

It is a very general popular belief at the present day that the Darwinian theory is simply no more than a capricious and anti-theological assertion that mankind are the modified descendants of ape-like ancestors.

Though most of my readers, I do not doubt, know how imperfect and erroneous a conception this is, yet I shall not, I think, be wasting time in stating what the Darwinian theory really is. In fact, it is so continuously misrepresented and misunderstood, that no opportunity should be lost of calling attention to its real character. Bit by bit, naturalists had succeeded in discovering the order of nature—so far that all the great facts of the universe, the constitution and movements of the heavenly bodies, the form of our earth, and all the peculiarities of its crust, had been successfully assigned to one set of causes—*the properties of matter*, which are set forth in what we know by the name of the "laws of physics and chemistry." Whilst geologists, led by Lyell,[1] had shown that the strata of the earth's crust and its mountains, rivers, and seas were due to the long-continued operation of the very same general causes—the physico-chemical causes—which at this moment are in operation and are continuing their work of change, yet the living matter on the crust of the earth had to be excluded from the grand uniformity which was elsewhere complete.

---

† From Edwin Ray Lankester, *Degeneration: A Chapter in Darwinism* (London: Macmillan and Co., 1880), pp. 11–17, 28–30, 32–33, 58–62. An eminent zoologist, in 1880 Lankester (1847–1929) was chair of zoology at University College, London (1875–80).
1. Sir Charles Lyell's seminal *Principles of Geology* (1830–33) had a profound influence on the work of, among many others, Charles Darwin.

The first hypothesis, then, which was present to Mr. Darwin's mind, as it had been to that of other earlier naturalists, was this: "Have not all the varieties or species of living things (man, of course, included) been produced by the continuous operation of the *same* set of physico-chemical causes which alone we can discover, and which alone have been proved sufficient to produce everything else?" "If this be so," Mr. Darwin must have argued (and here it was that he boldly stepped beyond the speculations of Lamarck[2] and adopted the method by which Lyell had triumphantly established Geology as a science), "these causes must still be able to produce new forms, and are doing so wherever they have opportunity." He had accordingly to bring the matter to the test of observation by seeking for some case of the production of new forms of plants, or of animals, by natural causes at the present day. Such cases he found in the production of new forms or varieties of plants and animals, by breeders. Breeders (the persons who make it their business to produce new varieties of flowers, of pigeons, of sheep, or what not) make use of two fundamental properties of living things in order to accomplish their purpose. These two properties are, firstly, that no two animals or plants, even when born of the same parents, are *exactly* alike; this is known as Variation: secondly, that an organism, as a rule, inherits, that is to say, is born with the peculiarities of its parents; this is known as Transmission, and is simply dependent on the fact that the offspring of any plant or animal is only a detached portion of the parents—a chip of the old block, as the saying is. The breeder selects from a number of specimens of a plant or animal a variety which comes nearest to the form he wishes to produce. Supposing he wished to produce a race of oxen with short horns, he would select from his herd bulls and cows with the shortest horns, and allow these only to breed; they would *transmit* their relatively short horns to their offspring, and from these again the cattle with the shortest horns would be selected by the breeder for propagation, and so on through several generations. In the end a very short-horned generation would be obtained, differing greatly in appearance from the cattle with which the breeder started.

Now we know of no facts which forbid us to suppose that could a breeder continue his operations indefinitely for any length of time—say for a few million years—he could convert the short-horned breed into a hornless breed; that he could go on and thicken the tail, could shorten the legs, get rid of the hind limbs altogether by a series of insensible gradations, and convert the race into forms like the Sirenia, or sea-cows. But if he could do this, you have only to give him a longer time still and there is no obstacle remaining to the conversion, by the same kind of process, of a polyp into a worm, or of a worm into a fish, or even of a monkey into a man.

2. In *Philosophie Zoologique* (1809), the French naturalist Jean-Baptiste Lamarck (1744–1829) outlined a theory of evolution that anticipated and influenced that of Darwin.

So far we have supposed the interference of a breeder who selects and determines the varieties which shall propagate themselves; so far we have not got a complete explanation, for we must find a substitute in nature for the *human selection* exercised by the breeder. The question arises, then, "Is there any necessary selective process in nature which could have operated through untold ages, and so have represented the selective action of the breeder, during an immense period of time?" Strangely enough, Mr. Darwin was led to the discovery of such a cause existing necessarily in the mechanical arrangements of nature, by reading the celebrated book of an English clergyman, the Rev. Mr. Malthus, *On Population*.[3] On happening to read this book, Mr. Darwin himself tells us that the idea of "natural selection" flashed upon him. That idea is as follows. Not only among mankind, but far more largely among other kinds of animals and of plants, the number of offspring produced by every pair is immensely in excess of the available amount of the food appropriate to the particular species in question. Accordingly, there is necessarily a struggle for existence—a struggle among all those born for the possession of the small quantum of food. The result of this struggle is to pick out, or select, a few who survive and propagate the species, whilst the majority perish before reaching maturity. The fact that no two members of a species are alike has already been shown to be the starting-point which enables the breeder to make *his* selection. So, too, with *natural* selection in the struggle for existence; the fact that all the young born of one species are not exactly alike—but some larger, some smaller, some lighter, some darker, some short-legged, some big-eyed, some long-tongued, some sharp-toothed, and so on—furnishes the opportunity for a selection. Those varieties which are best fitted to obtain food and to baffle their competitors, gain the food and survive, the rest perish.

We have, then, to note that the hypothesis that there *must be a selection*—which was framed or deduced as a "test hypothesis" from the earlier hypothesis that species have arisen by the action of causes still competent to produce new forms—led Mr. Darwin to the discovery of this great cause—the *"natural selection,"* or "survival of the fittest," in the struggle for existence. Just as the breeder can slowly change the proportions of the animals or plants on which he operates, so in inconceivably long periods of time has this struggling of varieties, and the consequent natural selection of the fittest, led to the production, from shapeless primitive living matter, of all the endless varieties of complicated plants and animals which now

3. In *An Essay on the Principle of Population* (1798), Thomas Robert Malthus (1766–1834) argued that populations tend to increase more rapidly than available food supplies. The resulting struggle for survival often leads to great misery, Malthus acknowledged, but such struggle is finally part of God's plan, since it serves to stimulate human creativity and development.

people the world. Countless varieties have died out, leaving only their modified descendants to puzzle the ingenuity of the biologist.

* * *

It is clearly enough possible for a set of forces such as we sum up under the head "natural selection" to so act on the structure of an organism as to produce one of three results, namely these; to keep it *in statu quo;* to increase the complexity of its structure; or lastly, to diminish the complexity of its structure. We have as possibilities either BALANCE, or ELABORATION, or DEGENERATION.

Owing, as it seems, to the predisposing influence of the systems of classification in ascending series proceeding steadily upwards from the "lower" or simplest forms to the "higher" or more complex forms,—systems which were prevalent before the doctrine of transformism had taken firm root in the minds of naturalists, there has been up to the present day an endeavour to explain every existing form of life on the hypothesis that it has been maintained for long ages in a state of Balance; or else on the hypothesis that it has been Elaborated, and is an advance, an improvement, upon its ancestors. Only one naturalist—Dr. Dohrn, of Naples[4]—has put forward the hypothesis of Degeneration as capable of wide application to the explanation of existing forms of life; and his arguments in favour of a general application of this hypothesis have not, I think, met with the consideration which they merit.

The statement that the hypothesis of Degeneration has not been recognised by naturalists generally as an explanation of animal forms, requires to be corrected by the exception of certain kinds of animals, namely, those that are parasitic or quasi-parasitic. With regard to parasites, naturalists have long recognised what is called *retrogressive metamorphosis*; and parasitic animals are as a rule admitted to be instances of Degeneration. It is the more remarkable whilst the possibility of a degeneration—a loss of organisation making the descendant far *simpler* or *lower* in structure than its ancestor—has been admitted for a few exceptional animals, that the same hypothesis should not have been applied to the explanation of other simple forms of animals. The hypothesis of Degeneration will, I believe, be found to render most valuable service in pointing out the true relationships of animals which are a puzzle and a mystery when we use only and exclusively the hypothesis of Balance, or the hypothesis of Elaboration. It will, as a true scientific hypothesis, help us to discover causes.

* * *

Degeneration may be defined as a gradual change of the structure in which the organism becomes adapted to *less* varied and *less* complex

---

4. Anton Dohrn (1840–1909), German zoologist and founder of the zoological laboratory in Naples, Italy.

conditions of life; whilst Elaboration is a gradual change of structure in which the organism becomes adapted to more and more varied and complex conditions of existence. In Elaboration there is a new *expression* of form, corresponding to new perfection of work in the animal machine. In Degeneration there is *suppression* of form, corresponding to the cessation of work. Elaboration of some one organ *may* be a necessary accompaniment of Degeneration in all the others; in fact, this is very generally the case; and it is only when the total result of the Elaboration of some organs, and the Degeneration of others, is such as to leave the whole animal in a *lower* condition, that is, fitted to less complex action and reaction in regard to its surroundings, than was the ancestral form with which we are comparing it (either actually or in imagination) that we speak of that animal as an instance of Degeneration.

Any new set of conditions occurring to an animal which render its food and safety very easily attained, seem to lead as a rule to Degeneration; just as an active healthy man sometimes degenerates when he becomes suddenly possessed of a fortune; or as Rome degenerated when possessed of the riches of the ancient world. The habit of parasitism clearly acts upon animal organisation in this way. Let the parasitic life once be secured, and away go legs, jaws, eyes, and ears; the active, highly-gifted crab, insect, or annelid may become a mere sac, absorbing nourishment and laying eggs.

* * *

The traditional history of mankind furnishes us with notable examples of degeneration. High states of civilisation have decayed and given place to low and degenerate states. At one time it was a favourite doctrine that the savage races of mankind were degenerate descendants of the higher and civilised races. This general and sweeping application of the doctrine of degeneration has been proved to be erroneous by careful study of the habits, arts, and beliefs of savages; at the same time there is no doubt that many savage races as we at present see them are actually degenerate and are descended from ancestors possessed of a relatively elaborate civilisation. As such we may cite some of the Indians of Central America, the modern Egyptians, and even the heirs of the great oriental monarchies of præ-Christian times. Whilst the hypothesis of universal degeneration as an explanation of savage races has been justly discarded, it yet appears that degeneration has a very large share in the explanation of the condition of the most barbarous races, such as the Fuegians, the Bushmen, and even the Australians. They exhibit evidence of being descended from ancestors more cultivated than themselves.

With regard to ourselves, the white races of Europe, the possibility of degeneration seems to be worth some consideration. In accordance with a tacit assumption of universal progress—an unreasoning optimism—we are accustomed to regard ourselves as necessarily progressing, as necessarily having arrived at a higher and more elaborated condition than that which our ancestors reached, and as destined to progress still further. On the other hand, it is well to remember that we are subject to the general laws of evolution, and are as likely to degenerate as to progress. As compared with the immediate forefathers of our civilisation—the ancient Greeks—we do not appear to have improved so far as our bodily structure is concerned, nor assuredly so far as some of our mental capacities are concerned. Our powers of perceiving and expressing beauty of form have certainly *not* increased since the days of the Parthenon and Aphrodite of Melos. In matters of the reason, in the development of intellect, we may seriously inquire how the case stands. Does the reason of the average man of civilised Europe stand out clearly as an evidence of progress when compared with that of the men of bygone ages? Are all the inventions and figments of human superstition and folly, the self-inflicted torturing of mind, the reiterated substitution of wrong for right, and of falsehood for truth, which disfigure our modern civilisation—are these evidences of progress? In such respects we have at least reason to fear that we may be degenerate. Possibly we are all drifting, tending to the condition of intellectual Barnacles or Ascidians.[5] It is possible for us—just as the Ascidian throws away its tail and its eye and sinks into a quiescent state of inferiority—to reject the good gift of reason with which every child is born, and to degenerate into a contented life of material enjoyment accompanied by ignorance and superstition. The unprejudiced, all-questioning spirit of childhood may not inaptly be compared to the tadpole tail and eye of the young Ascidian: we have to fear lest the prejudices, pre-occupations, and dogmatism of modern civilisation should in any way lead to the atrophy and loss of the valuable mental qualities inherited by our young forms from primæval man.

There is only one means of estimating our position, only one means of so shaping our conduct that we may with certainty avoid degeneration and keep an onward course. We are as a race more fortunate than our ruined cousins—the degenerate Ascidians. For us it is possible to ascertain what will conduce to our higher development, what will favour our degeneration. To us has been given the power to *know the causes of things*, and by the use of this power it is possible for us to control our destinies. It is for us by ceaseless and ever hopeful labour to try to gain a knowledge of man's place in the order of nature. When we have gained this fully and minutely, we shall be able by the light of the past to guide ourselves in the future. In proportion as the whole of the past evolution of civilised man, of which we at present perceive the outlines, is assigned to its causes, we and our successors on the

5. Earlier in his essay, Lankester had traced the devolutionary history of the Ascidian, a kind of mollusk.

globe may expect to be able duly to estimate that which makes for, and that which makes against, the progress of the race. The full and earnest cultivation of Science—the Knowledge of Causes—is that to which we have to look for the protection of our race—even of this English branch of it—from relapse and degeneration.

THOMAS HENRY HUXLEY

From The Struggle for Existence: A Programme[†]

The vast and varied procession of events which we call Nature affords a sublime spectacle and an inexhaustible wealth of attractive problems to the speculative observer. If we confine our attention to that aspect which engages the attention of the intellect, nature appears a beautiful and harmonious whole, the incarnation of a fault-less logical process, from certain premises in the past to an inevitable conclusion in the future. But if she be regarded from a less elevated, but more human, point of view; if our moral sympa-thies are allowed to influence our judgment, and we permit ourselves to criticise our great mother as we criticise one another;—then our verdict, at least so far as sentient nature is concerned, can hardly be so favourable.

In sober truth, to those who have made a study of the phenomena of life as they are exhibited by the higher forms of the animal world, the optimistic dogma that this is the best of all possible worlds will seem little better than a libel upon possibility. It is really only another instance to be added to the many extant, of the audacity of à priori speculators who, having created God in their own image, find no difficulty in assuming that the Almighty must have been actuated by the same motives as themselves. They are quite sure that, had any other course been practicable, He would no more have made infinite suffering a necessary ingredient of His handiwork than a respectable philosopher would have done the like.

But even the modified optimism of the time-honoured thesis of physico-theology, that the sentient world is, on the whole, regulated by principles of benevolence, does but ill stand the test of impartial confrontation with the facts of the case. No doubt it is quite true that sentient nature affords hosts of examples of subtle contrivances directed towards the production of pleasure or the avoidance of pain; and it may be proper to say that these are evidences of benevolence.

† From *The Nineteenth Century* 23 (February 1888): 161–63, 165–66, 168–69. Huxley (1825–1895), the great Victorian champion of science, taught at the Normal School (later the Royal College) of Science. Wells attended his lectures and for the remainder of his life acknowledged Huxley's influence.

But if so, why is it not equally proper to say of the equally numerous arrangements, the no less necessary result of which is the production of pain, that they are evidences of malevolence?

If a vast amount of that which, in a piece of human workmanship, we should call skill, is visible in those parts of the organisation of a deer to which it owes its ability to escape from beasts of prey, there is at least equal skill displayed in that bodily mechanism of the wolf which enables him to track, and sooner or later to bring down, the deer. Viewed under the dry light of science, deer and wolf are alike admirable; and if both were non-sentient automata, there would be nothing to qualify our admiration of the action of the one on the other. But the fact that the deer suffers while the wolf inflicts suffering engages our moral sympathies. We should call men like the deer innocent and good, men such as the wolf malignant and bad; we should call those who defended the deer and aided him to escape brave and compassionate, and those who helped the wolf in his bloody work base and cruel. Surely, if we transfer these judgments to nature outside the world of man at all, we must do so impartially. In that case, the goodness of the right hand which helps the deer, and the wickedness of the left hand which eggs on the wolf, will neutralise one another: and the course of nature will appear to be neither moral nor immoral, but non-moral.

This conclusion is thrust upon us by analogous facts in every part of the sentient world; yet, inasmuch as it not only jars upon prevalent prejudices, but arouses the natural dislike to that which is painful, much ingenuity has been exercised in devising an escape from it.

From the theological side, we are told that this is a state of probation, and that the seeming injustices and immoralities of nature will be compensated by-and-by. But how this compensation is to be effected, in the case of the great majority of sentient things, is not clear. I apprehend that no one is seriously prepared to maintain that the ghosts of all the myriads of generations of herbivorous animals which lived during the millions of years of the earth's duration before the appearance of man, and which have all that time been tormented and devoured by carnivores, are to be compensated by a perennial existence in clover; while the ghosts of carnivores are to go to some kennel where there is neither a pan of water nor a bone with any meat on it. Besides, from the point of view of morality, the last state of things would be worse than the first. For the carnivores, however brutal and sanguinary, have only done that which, if there is any evidence of contrivance in the world, they were expressly constructed to do. Moreover, carnivores and herbivores alike have been subject to all the miseries incidental to old age, disease, and over-multiplication, and both might well put in a claim for 'compensation' on this score.

On the evolutionist side, on the other hand, we are told to take comfort from the reflection that the terrible struggle for existence tends to final good, and that the suffering of the ancestor is paid for by the increased perfection of the progeny. There would be something in this argument if, in Chinese fashion, the present generation could pay its debts to its ancestors; otherwise it is not clear what compensation the *Eohippus* gets for his sorrows in the fact that, some millions of years afterwards, one of his descendants wins the Derby.[1] And, again, it is an error to imagine that evolution signifies a constant tendency to increased perfection. That process undoubtedly involves a constant re-adjustment of the organism in adaptation to new conditions; but it depends on the nature of those conditions whether the direction of the modifications effected shall be upward or downward. Retrogressive is as practicable as progressive metamorphosis. If what the physical philosophers tell us, that our globe has been in a state of fusion, and, like the sun, is gradually cooling down, is true; then the time must come when evolution will mean adaptation to a universal winter, and all forms of life will die out, except such low and simple organisms as the Diatom of the arctic and antarctic ice and the Protococcus of the red snow.[2] If our globe is proceeding from a condition in which it was too hot to support any but the lowest living thing to a condition in which it will be too cold to permit of the existence of any others, the course of life upon its surface must describe a trajectory like that of a ball fired from a mortar; and the sinking half of that course is as much a part of the general process of evolution as the rising.

From the point of view of the moralist the animal world is on about the same level as a gladiator's show. The creatures are fairly well treated, and set to fight—whereby the strongest, the swiftest and the cunningest live to fight another day. The spectator has no need to turn his thumbs down, as no quarter is given. He must admit that the skill and training displayed are wonderful. But he must shut his eyes if he would not see that more or less enduring suffering is the meed of both vanquished and victor.

* * *

In the strict sense of the word 'nature,' it denotes the sum of the phenomenal world, of that which has been, and is, and will be; and society, like art, is therefore a part of nature. But it is convenient to distinguish those parts of nature in which man plays the part of immediate cause, as something apart; and, therefore, society, like art, is usefully to be considered as distinct from nature. It is the

---

1. Eohippus, a long-extinct ancestor of the horse, was the size of a small dog. The annual Epsom Derby is a prestigious horse race.
2. The diatom and the protococcus are forms of microscopic algae.

more desirable, and even necessary, to make this distinction, since society differs from nature in having a definite moral object; whence it comes about that the course shaped by the ethical man—the member of society or citizen—necessarily runs counter to that which the non-ethical man—the primitive savage, or man as a mere member of the animal kingdom—tends to adopt. The latter fights out the struggle for existence to the bitter end, like any other animal; the former devotes his best energies to the object of setting limits to the struggle.

In the cycle of phenomena presented by the life of man, the animal, no more moral end is discernible than in that presented by the lives of the wolf and of the deer. However imperfect the relics of prehistoric men may be, the evidence which they afford clearly tends to the conclusion that, for thousands and thousands of years, before the origin of the oldest known civilisations, men were savages of a very low type. They strove with their enemies and their competitors; they preyed upon things weaker or less cunning than themselves; they were born, multiplied without stint, and died, for thousands of generations, alongside the mammoth, the urus, the lion, and the hyæna, whose lives were spent in the same way; and they were no more to be praised or blamed, on moral grounds, than their less erect and more hairy compatriots.

As among these, so among primitive men, the weakest and stupidest went to the wall, while the toughest and shrewdest, those who were best fitted to cope with their circumstances, but not the best in any other sense, survived. Life was a continual free fight, and beyond the limited and temporary relations of the family, the Hobbesian war of each against all was the normal state of existence.[3] The human species, like others, plashed and floundered amid the general stream of evolution, keeping its head above water as it best might, and thinking neither of whence nor whither.

The history of civilisation—that is of society—on the other hand, is the record of the attempts which the human race has made to escape from this position. The first men who substituted the state of mutual peace for that of mutual war, whatever the motive which impelled them to take that step, created society. But, in establishing peace, they obviously put a limit upon the struggle for existence. Between the members of that society, at any rate, it was not to be pursued *à outrance*.[4] And of all the successive shapes which society has taken, that most nearly approaches perfection in which the war of individual against individual is most strictly limited. The primitive

3. This was indeed an oft-repeated argument of the English philosopher Thomas Hobbes (1588–1679).
4. "To the last extremity" (French).

savage, tutored by Istar,[5] appropriated whatever took his fancy, and killed whomsoever opposed him, if he could. On the contrary, the ideal of the ethical man is to limit his freedom of action to a sphere in which he does not interfere with the freedom of others; he seeks the common weal as much as his own; and, indeed, as an essential part of his own welfare. Peace is both end and means with him; and he founds his life on a more or less complete self-restraint, which is the negation of the struggle for existence. He tries to escape from his place in the animal kingdom, founded on the free development of the principle of non-moral evolution, and to found a kingdom of Man, governed upon the principle of moral evolution. For society not only has a moral end, but in its perfection, social life, is embodied morality.

But the effort of ethical man to work towards a moral end by no means abolished, perhaps has hardly modified, the deep-seated organic impulses which impel the natural man to follow his non-moral course. One of the most essential conditions, if not the chief cause, of the struggle for existence, is the tendency to multiply without limit, which man shares with all living things. It is notable that 'increase and multiply' is a commandment traditionally much older than the ten, and that it is, perhaps, the only one which has been spontaneously and *ex animo*[6] obeyed by the great majority of the human race. But, in civilised society, the inevitable result of such obedience is the re-establishment, in all its intensity, of that struggle for existence—the war of each against all—the mitigation or abolition of which was the chief end of social organisation.

* * *

Let us look at home. For seventy years, peace and industry have had their way among us with less interruption and under more favourable conditions than in any other country on the face of the earth. The wealth of Crœsus was nothing to that which we have accumulated, and our prosperity has filled the world with envy. But Nemesis did not forget Crœsus;[7] has she forgotten us?

I think not. There are now 36,000,000 of people in our island, and every year considerably more than 300,000 are added to our numbers. That is to say, about every hundred seconds, or so, a new claimant to a share in the common stock of maintenance presents him or herself among us. At the present time, the produce of the soil does not suffice to feed half its population. The other moiety has to be supplied with food which must be bought from the people of food-producing countries. That is to say, we have to offer them the

5. Earlier in the essay, Huxley identifies Istar as the Babylonian goddess of both love and war.
6. Sincerely or from the heart (Latin).
7. Crœsus, the legendarily wealthy ruler of Lydia in the sixth century BCE, lost both wealth and kingdom in a war with the Persians.

things which they want in exchange for the things we want. And the things they want and which we can produce better than they can are mainly manufactures—industrial products.

The insolent reproach of the first Napoleon had a very solid foundation. We not only are, but, under penalty of starvation, we are bound to be, a nation of shopkeepers.[8] But other nations also lie under the same necessity of keeping shop, and some of them deal in the same goods as ourselves. Our customers naturally seek to get the most and the best in exchange for their produce. If our goods are inferior to those of our competitors, there is no ground compatible with the sanity of the buyers, which can be alleged, why they should not prefer the latter. And, if that result should ever take place on a large and general scale, five or six millions of us would soon have nothing to eat. We know what the cotton famine was; and we can therefore form some notion of what a dearth of customers would be.

Judged by an ethical standard, nothing can be less satisfactory than the position in which we find ourselves. In a real, though incomplete, degree we have attained the condition of peace which is the main object of social organisation; and it may, for argument's sake, be assumed that we desire nothing but that which is in itself innocent and praiseworthy—namely, the enjoyment of the fruits of honest industry. And lo! in spite of ourselves, we are in reality engaged in an internecine struggle for existence with our presumably no less peaceful and well-meaning neighbours. We seek peace and we do not ensue it. The moral nature in us asks for no more than is compatible with the general good; the non-moral nature proclaims and acts upon that fine old Scottish family motto 'Thou shalt starve ere I want.' Let us be under no illusions then. So long as unlimited multiplication goes on, no social organisation which has ever been devised, or is likely to be devised; no fiddle-faddling with the distribution of wealth, will deliver society from the tendency to be destroyed by the reproduction within itself, in its intensest form, of that struggle for existence, the limitation of which is the object of society. And however shocking to the moral sense this eternal competition of man against man and of nation against nation may be; however revolting may be the accumulation of misery at the negative pole of society, in contrast with that of monstrous wealth at the positive pole; this state of things must abide, and grow continually worse, so long as Istar holds her way unchecked. It is the true riddle of the Sphinx; and every nation which does not solve it will sooner or later be devoured by the monster itself has generated.

* * *

8. Napoleon Bonaparte reportedly dismissed the English as "a nation of shopkeepers."

BENJAMIN KIDD

From Social Evolution†

* * *

There is no phenomenon so stupendous, so bewildering, and withal so interesting to man as that of his own evolution in society. The period it has occupied in his history is short compared with the whole span of that history; yet the results obtained are striking beyond comparison. Looking back through the glasses of modern science we behold him at first outwardly a brute, feebly holding his own against many fierce competitors. He has no wants above those of the beast; he lives in holes and dens in the rocks; he is a brute, even more feeble in body than many of the animals with which he struggles for a brute's portion. Tens of thousands of years pass over him, and his progress is slow and painful to a degree. The dim light which inwardly illumines him has grown brighter; the rude weapons which aid his natural helplessness are better shaped; the cunning with which he circumvents his prey, and which helps him against his enemies, is of a higher order. But he continues to leave little impress on nature or his surroundings; he is still in wants and instincts merely as his fellow denizens of the wilderness.

We look again, and a marvellous transformation has taken place—a transformation which is without any parallel in the previous history of life. This brute-like creature, which for long ages lurked in the woods and amongst the rocks, scarcely to all appearances of so much account as the higher carnivora with which he competed for a scanty subsistence, has obtained mastery over the whole earth. He has organised himself into great societies. The brutes are no longer his companions and competitors. He has changed the face of continents. The earth produces at his will; all its resources are his. The secrets of the universe have been plumbed, and with the knowledge obtained he has turned the world into a vast workshop where all the powers of nature work submissively in bondage to supply his wants. His power at length appears illimitable; for the source of it is the boundless wealth of knowledge which is stored up in the great civilisations he has developed and which ever continues to increase, every addition thereto but offering new opportunities for further expansion.

But when we come to examine the causes of this remarkable development we find the greatest obscurity prevailing. Man himself has hitherto viewed his progress with a species of awe; so much so

---

† From *Social Evolution* (New York and London: Macmillan and Co., 1894), pp. 29–31, 33–34, 35–36, 37–39. The sociologist Benjamin Kidd (1858–1916) was at the forefront of late-Victorian efforts to apply Darwinian paradigms to the study of human society.

that he often seems to hesitate to regard it as a natural phenomenon, and therefore under the control of natural laws. To all of us it is from its very nature bewildering; to many it is in addition mysterious, marvellous, supernatural.

In proceeding to discuss in what manner natural laws have operated in producing the advance man has made in society we must endeavour to approach the subject without bias or prejudice; if possible in the same spirit in which the historian feels it to be his duty to deal with human history so far as it extends before his more limited view, or in which the biologist has dealt with the phenomena of the development of life elsewhere. Man, since we first encounter him, has made ceaseless progress upwards, and this progress continues before our eyes. But it has never been, nor is it now, an equal advance of the whole of the race. Looking back we see that the road by which he has come is strewn with the wrecks of nations, races, and civilisations, that have fallen by the way, pushed aside by the operation of laws which it takes no eye of faith to distinguish at work amongst us at the present time as surely and as effectively as at any past period. Social systems and civilisations resemble individuals in one respect; they are organic growths, apparently possessing definite laws of health and development. Such laws science has already defined for the individual, it should also be her duty to endeavour to define them for society.

* * *

We find man in everyday life continually subject to laws and conditions which have been imposed upon him in common with all the rest of creation, and we accept these conditions and make it our business to learn all we can of them. If in following his evolution in society, we find him in like manner subject to laws which have governed the development of the lower forms of life, and which are merely operating in society under more complex conditions, it is also our duty, if we would comprehend our own history, to take these laws as we find them, and to endeavour, at the very earliest stage, to understand them as far as possible.

Now, at the outset, we find man to be in one respect exactly like all the creatures which have come before him. He reproduces his kind from generation to generation. In doing so he is subject to a law which must never be lost sight of. Left to himself, this high-born creature, whose progress we seem to take for granted, has not the slightest innate tendency to make any onward progress whatever. It may appear strange, but it is strictly true, that if each of us were allowed by the conditions of life to follow his own inclinations, the average of one generation would have no tendency whatever to rise beyond the average of the preceding one, but distinctly the reverse. This is not a peculiarity of man; it has been a law of life from the beginning, and it continues to be a universal law which we have no power to alter. How then is progress possible? The answer to this question is the starting-point of all the science of human society.

Progress everywhere from the beginning of life has been effected in the same way, and it is possible in no other way. It is the result of selection and rejection. In the human species, as in every other species which has ever existed, no two individuals of a generation are alike in all respects; there is infinite variation within certain narrow limits. Some are slightly above the average in a particular direction as others are below it; and it is only when conditions prevail which are favourable to a preponderating reproduction of the former that advance in any direction becomes possible. To formulate this as the immutable law of progress since the beginning of life has been one of the principal results of the biological science of the century.

* * *

Where there is progress there must inevitably be selection, and selection must in its turn involve competition of some kind.

But let us deal first with the necessity for progress. From time to time we find the question discussed by many who only imperfectly understand the conditions to which life is subject, as to whether progress is worth the price paid for it. But we have really no choice in the matter. Progress is a necessity from which there is simply no escape, and from which there has never been any escape since the beginning of life. Looking back through the history of life anterior to man, we find it to be a record of ceaseless progress on the one hand, and ceaseless stress and competition on the other. This orderly and beautiful world which we see around us is now, and always has been, the scene of incessant rivalry between all the forms of life inhabiting it—rivalry, too, not chiefly conducted between different species but between members of the same species. The plants in the green sward beneath our feet are engaged in silent rivalry with each other, a rivalry which if allowed to proceed without outside interference would know no pause until the weaker were exterminated. Every part, organ, or quality of these plants which calls forth admiration for its beauty or perfection, has its place and meaning in this struggle, and has been acquired to ensure success therein. The trees of the forest which clothe and beautify the landscape are in a state of nature engaged in the same rivalry with each other. Left to themselves they fight out, as unmistakable records have shown, a stubborn struggle extending over centuries in which at last only those forms most suitable to the conditions of the locality retain their places. But so far we view the rivalry under simple conditions; it is amongst the forms of animal life as we begin to watch the gradual progress upwards to higher types that it becomes many-sided and complex.

* * *

It is now coming to be recognised as a necessarily inherent part of the doctrine of evolution, that if the continual selection which is always going on amongst the higher forms of life were to be suspended, these forms would not only possess no tendency to make progress forwards, but must actually go backwards. *That is to say, if all the individuals of every generation in any species were allowed to equally propagate their kind, the average of each generation would continually tend to fall below the average of the generation which preceded it, and a process of slow but steady degeneration would ensue.* It is, therefore, an inevitable law of life amongst the higher forms, that competition and selection must not only always accompany progress, but that they must prevail amongst every form of life which is not actually retrograding. Every successful form must, *of necessity*, multiply beyond the limits which the average conditions of life comfortably provide for. Other things being equal, indeed, the wider the limits of selection, the keener the rivalry, and the more rigid the selection the greater will be the progress; but rivalry and selection in some degree there must inevitably be.

The first condition of existence with a progressive form is, therefore, one of continual strain and stress, and along its upward path this condition is always maintained. Once begun, too, there can be no pause in the advance; for if by any combination of circumstances the rivalry and selection cease, then progress ceases with them, and the species or group cannot maintain its place; it has taken the first retrograde step, and it is immediately placed at a disadvantage with other species, or with those groups of its own kind where the rivalry still goes on, and where selection, adaptation, and progress continue unchecked. So keen is the rivalry throughout, that the number of successful forms is small in comparison with the number which have failed. Looking round us at the forms of life in the world at the present day, we see, as it were, only the isolated peaks of the great range of life, the gaps and valleys between representing the number of forms which have disappeared in the wear and stress of evolution.

It would be a mistake to regard this rivalry from a very common point of view, and to think that the extinction of less efficient forms has been the same thing as the extermination of the individuals comprising them. This, as we shall see, is not so. With whatever feelings we may regard the conflict it is, however, necessary to remember that it is the first condition of progress. It leads continually onwards and upwards. From this stress of nature has followed the highest result we are capable of conceiving, namely, continual advance towards higher and more perfect forms of life. Out of it has arisen every attribute of form, colour, instinct, strength, courage, nobility, and beauty in the teeming and wonderful world of life around us. To it we owe all that is best and most perfect in life at the present day, as well as all its highest promise for the future. The law of life has been always the same from the beginning,—ceaseless and inevitable struggle and competition, ceaseless and inevitable selection and rejection, ceaseless and inevitable progress.

* * *

WILLIAM THOMSON

From On the Age of the Sun's Heat[†]

The second great law of Thermodynamics involves a certain principle of *irreversible action in nature*. It is thus shown that, although mechanical energy is *indestructible*, there is a universal tendency to its dissipation, which produces gradual augmentation and diffusion of heat, cessation of motion and exhaustion of potential energy through the material universe. The result would inevitably be a state of universal rest and death, if the universe were finite and left to obey existing laws. But it is impossible to conceive a limit to the extent of matter in the universe; and therefore science points rather to an endless progress, through an endless space, of action involving the transformation of potential energy into palpable motion and thence into heat, than to a single finite mechanism, running down like a clock, and stopping for ever. It is also impossible to conceive either the beginning or the continuance of life, without an overruling creative power; and, therefore, no conclusions of dynamical science regarding the future condition of the earth, can be held to give dispiriting views as to the destiny of the race of intelligent beings by which it is at present inhabited.

* * *

The considerations adduced above, in this paper, regarding the sun's possible specific heat, rate of cooling, and superficial temperature, render it probable that he must have been very sensibly warmer one million years ago than now; and, consequently, that if he has existed as a luminary for ten or twenty million years, he must have radiated away considerably more than the corresponding number of times the present yearly amount of loss.

It seems, therefore, on the whole most probable that the sun has not illuminated the earth for 100,000,000 years, and almost certain

---

[†] From *Macmillan's Magazine* 5 (March 1862): 388–89, 393. William Thomson (1824–1907), later Lord Kelvin, was arguably the most eminent scientist and mathematician of the nineteenth century. His essays on the inevitable "heat-death" of the universe due to the workings of the second law of thermodynamics were well known, as were his calculations concerning the date of the sun's eventual extinction.

that he has not done so for 500,000,000 years. As for the future, we may say, with equal certainty, that inhabitants of the earth cannot continue to enjoy the light and heat essential to their life, for many million years longer, unless sources now unknown to us are prepared in the great storehouse of creation.

BALFOUR STEWART AND PETER GUTHRIE TAIT

From The Unseen Universe[†]

It thus appears that at each transformation of heat-energy into work a large portion is degraded, while only a small portion is transformed into work. So that while it is very easy to change all of our mechanical or useful energy into heat, it is only possible to transform a portion of this heat-energy back again into work. After each change too the heat becomes more and more dissipated or degraded, that is, less and less available for any future transformation.

In other words, the tendency of heat is towards equalisation; heat is *par excellence* the communist of our universe, and it will no doubt ultimately bring the present system to an end. The visible universe may with perfect truth be compared to a vast heat-engine, and this is the reason why we have brought such engines so prominently before our readers. The sun is the furnace or source of high-temperature-heat of our system, just as the stars are for other systems, and the energy which is essential to our existence is derived from the heat which the sun radiates, and represents only an excessively minute portion of that heat. But while the sun thus supplies us with energy he is himself getting colder, and must ultimately, by radiation into space, part with the life-sustaining power which he at present possesses. Besides the inevitable cooling of the sun we must also suppose that owing to something analogous to ethereal friction the earth and the other planets of our system will be drawn spirally nearer and nearer to the sun, and will at length be engulfed in his mass. In each case there will be, as the result of the collision, the conversion of visible energy into heat, and a partial and temporary restoration of the power of the sun. At length, however, this process will have come to an end, and he will be extinguished until, after long but not immeasurable ages, by means of the same ethereal

† From *The Unseen Universe, or Physical Speculations on a Future State* (London: Macmillan and Co., 1885), pp. 126–28. Balfour Stewart (1828–1887) and Peter Guthrie Tait (1831–1901) were professors of natural philosophy at, respectively, Owens College, Manchester, and the University of Edinburgh.

friction his black mass is brought into contact with that of one or more of his nearer neighbours.

Not much further need we dilate on this. It is absolutely certain that life, so far as it is physical, depends essentially upon transformations of energy; it is also absolutely certain that age after age the possibility of such transformations is becoming less and less; and, so far as we yet know, the final state of the present universe must be an aggregation (into one mass) of all the matter it contains, *i.e.* the potential energy gone, and a practically useless state of kinetic energy, *i.e.* uniform temperature throughout that mass.

But the present potential energy of the solar system is so enormous, approaching in fact possibly to what in our helplessness we call infinite, that it may supply for absolutely incalculable future ages what is required for the physical existence of life. Again, the fall together, from the distance of Sirius, let us say, of the sun and an equal star would at once supply the sun with at least as much energy for future radiation to possible planets as could possibly have been acquired by his own materials in their original falling together from practically infinite diffusion as a cloud of stones or dust, or a nebula; so that it is certain that, if the present physical laws remain long enough in operation, there will be (at immense intervals of time) mighty catastrophes due to the crashing together of defunct suns—the smashing of the greater part of each into nebulous dust surrounding the remainder, which will form an intensely heated nucleus—then, possibly, the formation of a new and larger set of planets with a proportionately larger and hotter sun, a solar system on a far grander scale than the present. And so on, growing in grandeur but diminishing in number till the exhaustion of energy is complete, and after that eternal rest, so far at least as visible motion is concerned.

* * *

CRITICISM

Early Reviews

RICHARD HOLT HUTTON

In A.D. 802,701[†]

Mr. H. G. Wells has written a very clever story as to the condition of this planet in the year 802,701 A.D., though the two letters A.D. appear to have lost their meaning in that distant date, as indeed they have lost their meaning for not a few even in the comparatively early date at which we all live. The story is one based on that rather favourite speculation of modern metaphysicians which supposes *time* to be at once the most important of the conditions of organic evolution, and the most misleading of subjective illusions. It is, we are told, by the efflux of time that all the modifications of species arise on the one hand, and yet Time is so purely subjective a mode of thought, that a man of searching intellect is supposed to be able to devise the means of travelling in time as well as in space, and visiting, so as to be contemporary with, any age of the world, past or future, so as to become as it were a true "pilgrim of eternity."[1] This is the dream on which Mr. H. G. Wells has built up his amusing story of *The Time Machine*. A speculative mechanician is supposed to have discovered that the "fourth dimension," concerning which mathematicians have speculated, is Time, and that with a little ingenuity a man may travel in Time as well as in Space. The Time-traveller of this story invents some hocus-pocus of a machine by the help of which all that belongs or is affixed to that machine may pass into the Future by pressing down one lever, and into the Past by pressing down another. In other words, he can make himself at home with the society of hundreds of thousands of centuries hence, or with the chaos of hundreds of thousands of centuries past, at his pleasure. As a matter of choice, the novelist very judiciously chooses the Future only in which to disport himself. And as we have no means of testing his conceptions of the Future, he is of course at liberty to imagine

† From *Spectator* 75 (13 July 1895): 41–43. Notes are by the editor.
1. A quotation from Percy Bysshe Shelley's poem "Adonais" (1821), I. 264.

what he pleases. And he is rather ingenious in his choice of what to imagine. Mr. Wells supposes his Time-traveller to travel forward from A.D. 1895 to A.D. 802,701, and to make acquaintance with the people inhabiting the valley of the Thames (which has, of course, somewhat changed its channel) at that date. He finds a race of pretty and gentle creatures of silken organisations, as it were, and no particular interests or aims, except the love of amusement, inhabiting the surface of the earth, almost all evil passions dead, almost all natural or physical evils overcome, with a serener atmosphere, a brighter sun, lovelier flowers and fruits, no dangerous animals or poisonous vegetables, no angry passions or tumultuous and grasping selfishness, and only one object of fear. While the race of the surface of the earth has improved away all its dangers and embarrassments (including, apparently, every trace of a religion), the race of the underworld,—the race which has originally sprung from the mining population,—has developed a great dread of light, and a power of vision which can work and carry on all its great engineering operations with a minimum of light. At the same time, by inheriting a state of servitude it has also inherited a cruel contempt for its former masters, who can now resist its attacks only by congregating in crowds during the hours of darkness, for in the daylight, or even in the bright moonlight, they are safe from the attacks of their former serfs. This beautiful superior race of faint and delicate beauty is wholly vegetarian. But the inferior world of industrious dwellers in the darkness has retained its desire for flesh, and in the absence of all other animal life has returned to cannibalism; and is eager to catch unwary members of the soft surface race in order to feed on their flesh. Moreover, this is the one source of fear which disturbs the gentle pastimes of the otherwise successful subduers of natural evils. Here is Mr. Wells's dream of the two branches into which the race of men, under the laws of evolution, had diverged:—[quotes from Chapter XIII (pp. 61–62 in this Norton Critical Edition), from "I grieved to think how brief the dream" to "and as that I give it to you."] The central idea of this dream is, then, the unnerving effect of a too great success in conquering the natural resistance which the physical constitution of the world presents to our love of ease and pleasure. Let a race which has learned to serve, and to serve efficiently, and has lost the physical equality with its masters by the conditions of its servitude, coexist with a race that has secured all the advantages of superior organisation, and the former will gradually recover, by its energetic habits, at least some of the advantages which it has lost, and will unite with them the cruel and selfish spirit which servitude breeds. This is, we take it, the warning which Mr. Wells intends to give:—"Above all things avoid sinking into a condition of satisfied ease; avoid a soft and languid serenity; even evil passions which involve continuous effort, are not so absolutely deadly as the temperament of languid and harmless playfulness." We have no doubt that, so far as Mr. Wells goes, his warning is wise. But we have little fear that the languid, ease-loving, and serene temperament will ever paralyse the human race after the manner he supposes, even though there may be at present some temporary signs of the growth of the appetite for mere amusement.

In the first place, Mr. Wells assumes, what is well-nigh impossible, that the growth of the pleasure-loving temperament would not itself prevent that victory over physical obstacles to enjoyment on which he founds his dream. The pleasure-loving temperament soon becomes both selfish and fretful. And selfishness no less than fretfulness poisons all enjoyment. Before our race had reached anything like the languid grace and frivolity of the Eloi (the surface population), it would have fallen a prey to the many competing and conflicting energies of Nature which are always on the watch to crush out weak and languid organisations, to say nothing of the uncanny Morlocks (the envious subterranean population), who would soon have invented spectacles shutting out from their sensitive eyes the glare or either moon or sun. If the doctrines as to evolution have any truth in them at all, nothing is more certain than that the superiority of man to Nature will never endure beyond the endurance of his fighting strength. The physical condition of the Eloi is supposed, for instance, so to have accommodated itself to external circumstances as to extinguish that continual growth of population which renders the mere competition for food so serious a factor in the history of the globe. But even supposing such a change to have taken place, of which we see no trace at all in history or civilisation, what is there in the nature of frivolity and love of ease, to diminish, and not rather to increase, that craving to accumulate sources of enjoyment at the expense of others, which seems to be *most* visible in the nations whose populations are of the slowest growth, and which so reintroduces rivalries and wars. Let any race find the pressure of population on its energies diminishing, and the mutual jealousy amongst those who are thus placed in a position of advantage for securing wealth and ease, will advance with giant strides. The hardest-pressed populations are not the most, but on the whole the least, selfish.

In the next place Mr. Wells's fancy ignores the conspicuous fact that man's nature needs a great deal of hard work to keep it in order at all, and that no class of men or women are so dissatisfied with their own internal condition as those who are least disciplined by the necessity for industry. Find the idlest class of a nation and you certainly find the most miserable class. There would be no tranquillity or serenity at all in any population for which there were not hard tasks and great duties. The Eloi of this fanciful story would have become even more eager for the satisfaction of selfish desires than the Morlocks themselves. The nature of man must have altered not merely accidentally, but essentially, if the devotion to ease and amusement had left it sweet and serene. Matthew Arnold wrote in his unreal mood of agnosticism:—

> We, in some unknown Power's employ,
> Move on a rigorous line;
> Can neither, when we will, enjoy,
> Nor, when we will, resign.[2]

But it is not in some "unknown Power's employ" that we move on this "rigorous line." On the contrary, it is in the employ of a Power which has revealed itself in the Incarnation and the Cross. And we may expect with the utmost confidence that if the earth is still in existence in the year 802,701 A.D., either the A.D. will mean a great deal more than it means now, or else its inhabitants will be neither Eloi nor Morlocks. For in that case evil passions will by that time have led to the extinction of races spurred and pricked on by conscience and yet so frivolous or so malignant. Yet Mr. Wells's fanciful and lively dream is well worth reading, if only because it will draw attention to the great moral and religious factors in human nature which he appears to ignore.

UNSIGNED

A Pilgrim through Time[†]

No two books could well be more unlike than *The Time Machine* and *The Strange Case of Dr. Jekyll and Mr. Hyde*,[1] but since the appearance of Stevenson's creepy romance we have had nothing in the domain of pure fantasy so bizarre as this "invention" by Mr. H. G. Wells. For his central idea Mr. Wells may be indebted to some previously published narrative suggestion, but if so we must confess ourselves entirely unacquainted with it, and so far as our knowledge goes he has produced in fiction that rarity which Solomon declared to be not merely rare but non-existent—a "new thing under the sun."[2]

The narrative opens in the dining-room of the man who is known to us throughout simply as the Time Traveller, and who is expounding to his guests a somewhat remarkable theory in esoteric mathematics.

---

2. "Stanzas in Memory of the Author of 'Obermann'" (1849), ll. 77–80.
† From *Daily Chronicle* [London] (July 27, 1895): 3. Notes are by the editor.
1. Robert Louis Stevenson's novella was published in 1886.
2. Ecclesiastes 1:8.

He says:—[quotes from Chapter I (pp. 5–6 in this Norton Critical Edition), from "You know, of course, that a mathematical line" to "to the end of our lives."] By this Poe-like ingenuity of whimsical reasoning the Time Traveller leads up to his great invention—nothing less than a machine which shall convey him through time, that fourth dimension of space, with even greater facility than men are conveyed through the other three dimensions by bicycle or balloon. He can go back either to the days of his grandsires or to the days of creation; he can go forward to the days of his grandsons, or still further to that last *fin de siècle*, when the earth is moribund and man has ceased to be. The one journey of which we have a record is a voyage into far futurity, and when after a wild flight through the centuries the Time Traveller stops the machine the dial register tells him that he is in or about the year 802,000 A.D. Man is still existent, but a remarkable change has passed upon him. The fissure of cleavage between the classes and the masses instead of being bridged over or filled up has become a great gulf. In centuries of centuries the environment of the more favoured has become so exquisitely adapted to all their needs, and indeed to all their desires, that the necessity for physical or mental activity is so many generations behind them that it does not survive even as a memory; the powers of body and mind which are distinctively manly have perished in ages of disuse, and they have become frail, listless, pleasure-loving children. The workers, on the other hand, have become brutalised, bleached, ape-like creatures, who live underground and toil for their effeminate lords, taking their pay, when they can, by living upon them literally in a horrible cannibalistic fashion. The adventures of the Time Traveller among the Eloi and the Morlocks are conceived in the true spirit of fantasy—the effect of remoteness being achieved much more successfully than in such as a book, for example, as Lord Lytton's *The Coming Race*.[3] Still more weird are the further wanderings in a future where man has gone, and even nature is not what it was, because sun, moon, stars, and earth are tottering to their doom. The description of the seacoast of the dying ocean, still embracing a dying world, and of the huge, hideous creeping things which are the last remains of life on a worn-out planet has real impressiveness—it grips the imagination as it is only gripped by genuinely imaginative work. It is in what may be described literally as the "machinery" of the story that Mr. Wells's imagination plays least freely and convincingly. He constantly forgets—or seems to forget—that his Traveller is journeying simply through *time*, and records effects which inevitably suggest travel through *space*. Why, for example, should the model of

3. Lytton's 1871 novel, set in the far future, bears some superficial resemblances to *The Time Machine*.

the machine vanish from sight when in the second chapter it is set in motion? Why, in the last chapter, should the machine itself disappear when the Traveller has set out on his final journey; why on his progress through the centuries should it jar and sway as if it were moving through the air; why should he write of "slipping like a vapour through the interstices of intervening substance," or anticipate sudden contact with some physical obstacle? To these questions Mr. Wells will probably reply that it is unfair to blame an artist for not surmounting difficulties which are practically insurmountable; but the obvious rejoinder is that it is unwise to choose a scheme from which such difficulties are inseparable. Still, when all deductions are made *The Time Machine* remains a strikingly original performance.

ISRAEL ZANGWILL

[Paradoxes of Time Travel][†]

Countless are the romances that deal with other times, other manners; endless have been the attempts to picture the time to come. Sometimes the future is grey with evolutionary perspectives, with previsions of a post-historic man, bald, toothless and fallen into his second infancy; sometimes it is gay with ingenuous fore-glimpses of a renewed golden age of socialism and sentimentality. In his brilliant little romance *The Time Machine* Mr. Wells has inclined to the severer and more scientific form of prophecy—to the notion of a humanity degenerating inevitably from sheer pressure of physical comfort; but this not very novel conception, which was the theme of Mr. Besant's *Inner House*, and even partly of Pearson's *National Life and Character*,[1] Mr. Wells has enriched by the invention of the Morlocks, a differentiated type of humanity which lives underground and preys upon the softer, prettier species that lives luxuriously in the sun, a fine imaginative creation worthy of Swift, and possibly not devoid of satirical reference to "the present discontents." There is a good deal of what Tyndall would have called "scientific imagination"[2] in Mr. Wells' further vision of the latter end of all things, a vision far more sombre and impressive than the ancient imaginings of the Biblical seers. The only criticism I have to offer is that his Time Traveller,

---

† From *Pall Mall Magazine* 7 (September 1895): 153–55. Notes are by the editor.
1. Walter Besant's dystopic novel *The Inner House* was published in 1888, C. H. Pearson's socio-historical study *National Life and Character: A Forecast* in 1894.
2. The Victorian physicist John Tyndall often preached the importance of the creative imagination in scientific research.

a cool scientific thinker, behaves exactly like the hero of a common-place sensational novel, with his frenzies of despair and his appeals to fate, when he finds himself in danger of having to remain in the year eight hundred and two thousand seven hundred and one, into which he has recklessly travelled; nor does it ever occur to him that in the aforesaid year he will have to repeat these painful experiences of his, else his vision of the future will have falsified itself—though how the long dispersed dust is to be vivified again does not appear. Moreover, had he travelled backwards, he would have reproduced a Past which, in so far as his own appearance in it with his newly invented machine was concerned, would have been *ex hypothesi*[3] unveracious. Had he recurred to his own earlier life, he would have had to exist in two forms simultaneously, of varying ages—a feat which even Sir Boyle Roche would have found difficult.[4] These absurdities illustrate the absurdity of any attempt to grapple with the notion of Time; and, despite some ingenious metaphysics, worthy of the inventor of the Eleatic paradoxes,[5] Mr. Wells' *Time Machine*, which traverses time (viewed as the Fourth Dimension of Space) backwards or forwards, much as the magic carpet of *The Arabian Nights* traversed space, remains an amusing fantasy. That Time is an illusion is one of the earliest lessons of metaphysics; but, even if we could realise Time as self-complete and immovable, a vast *continuum* holding all that has happened and all that will happen, an eternal Present, even so to introduce a man travelling through this sleeping ocean is to re-introduce the notion of Time which has just been expelled. There is really more difficulty in understanding the Present than the Past or the Future into which it is always slipping; and those old Oriental languages which omitted the Present altogether displayed the keen metaphysical instinct of the East. And yet there is a sense in which the continued and continuous existence of all past time, at least, can be grasped by the human intellect without the intervention of metaphysics. The star whose light reaches us to-night may have perished and become extinct a thousand years ago, the rays of light from it having so many millions of miles to travel that they have only just impinged upon our planet. Could we perceive clearly the incidents on its surface, we should be beholding the Past in the Present, and we could travel to any given year by travelling actually through space to the point at which the rays of that year would first strike upon our consciousness. In like manner the whole Past of the earth is still playing itself out—to an eye conceived as

3. According to the premises on which the argument is based.
4. An eighteenth-century politician renowned for his Yogi Berra-esque misstatements.
5. Zeno, the most famous Greek philosopher associated with the Eleatic school founded by Parmenides, was known for his paradoxes.

stationed to-day in space, and moving now forwards to catch the Middle Ages, now backwards to watch Nero fiddling over the burning of Rome. The sounds of his fiddle are still vibrating somewhere in the infinite spaces, for this is the only "music of the spheres," these voices of vanished generations, still troubling the undulatory æther. It is all there—every plea of prayer, or cry of pain, or clamour of mad multitudes; every stave of lewd song, every lullaby in every tongue in which mothers have rocked their babes to sleep, every sob of joy or passion.

* * *

In verity, there is no Time Traveller, Mr. Wells, save Old Father Time himself. Instead of being a Fourth Dimension of Space, Time is perpetually travelling through Space, repeating itself in vibrations farther and farther from the original point of incidence; a vocal panorama moving through the universe across the infinities, a succession of sounds and visions that, having once been, can never pass away, but only on and on from point to point, permanently enregistered in the sum of things, preserved from annihilation by the endlessness of Space, and ever visible and audible to eye or ear that should travel in a parallel movement. It is true the scientists allege that only light can thus travel through the infinities, sound-waves being confined to a material medium and being quickly dissipated into heat. But light alone is sufficient to sustain my fantasy, and in any case the sounds would be æons behind the sights. Terrible, solemn thought that the Past can never die, and that for each of us Heaven or Hell may consist in our being placed at the point of vantage in Space where we may witness the spectacle of our past lives, and find bliss or bale in the panorama. How much ghastlier than the pains of the pit, for the wicked to be perpetually "moved on" by some Satanic policeman to the mathematical point at which their autobiography becomes visible, a point that moves backwards in the infinite universe each time the green curtain of the grave falls over the final episode, so that the sordid show may commence all over again, and so *ad infinitum*. Pascal[6] defined Space as a sphere whose centre is everywhere and whose circumference is nowhere. This brilliant figure helps us to conceive God as always at the centre of vision, receiving all vibrations simultaneously, and thus beholding all Past time simultaneously with the Present. We can also conceive of Future incidents being visible to a spectator, who should be moved forward to receive the impressions of them æons earlier than they would otherwise have reached him. But these "futures" would only be relative; in reality they would already have happened, and the absolute Future, the universe of things that have *not* happened, would still

6. Blaise Pascal, the seventeenth-century French philosopher.

elude our vision, though we can very faintly imagine the Future, interwoven inevitably with the Past, visible to an omniscient Being somewhat as the evolution of a story is to the man of genius upon whom past and future flash in one conception. Mr. Wells might have been plausibly scientific in engineering his Time Machine through Space and stopping at the points where particular periods of the world's past history became visible: he would then have avoided the fallacy of mingling personally in the panorama. But this would not have suited his design of "dealing in futures." For there is no getting into the Future, except by waiting. You can only sit down and see it come by, as the drunken man thought he might wait for his house to come round in the circulation of the earth; and if you lived for an eternity, the show would only be "just about to begin."

* * *

Recent Criticism

YEVGENY ZAMYATIN

[Wells's Urban Fairy Tales]†

I

The laciest, most Gothic of cathedrals are, after all, made of stone. The most marvelous, most fantastic fairy tales of any country are, after all, made of the earth, the trees, the animals of that country. In woodland tales, there is the wood goblin, shaggy and gnarled as a pine, hooting like a forest echo. In tales of the steppes, there is the magical white camel, flying like storm-driven sand. In tales of the Arctic regions, there is the shaman-whale and the polar bear with a body of mammoth tusks. But imagine a country where the only fertile soil is asphalt, where nothing grows but dense forests of factory chimneys, where the animal herds are of a single breed, automobiles, and the only fragrance in the spring is that of gasoline. This place of stone, asphalt, iron, gasoline, and machines is present-day, twentieth-century London, and, naturally, it was bound to produce its own iron, automobile goblins, and its own mechanical, chemical fairy tales. Such urban tales exist: they are told by Herbert George Wells. They are his fantastic novels.

The city, the huge modern city, full of the roar, din, and buzzing of propellers, electric wires, wheels, advertisements, is everywhere in H. G. Wells, The present-day city, with its uncrowned king, the machine—as an explicit or implicit function—is an invariable component of every fantastic novel written by Wells, of every equation in his myths; and this is precisely what his myths are—logical equations.

Wells began with the mechanism, the machine. His first novel, *The Time Machine*, is the modern city version of the tale of the flying carpet, and the fairy-tale tribes of morlocks and eloi are, of course, the

† Originally published in 1920; reprinted from *A Soviet Heretic: Essays by Yevgeny Zamyatin*, ed. and trans. Mirra Ginsburg (Chicago: University of Chicago Press, 1970), pp. 259–61.

two warring classes of the modern city, extrapolated, with their typical characteristics heightened to the point of the grotesque.

* * *

The motifs of the Wellsian urban fairy tales are essentially the same as those encountered in all other fairy tales: the invisible cap, the flying carpet, the bursting grass, the self-setting tablecloth, dragons, giants, gnomes, mermaids, and man-eating monsters. But the difference between his tales and, let us say, ours, is the difference between the psychology of a Poshekhonian[1] and that of a Londoner: our Russian Poshekhonian sits down at the window and waits until the invisible cap and the flying carpet come to him magically, "at the pike's behest"; the Londoner does not rely on "the pike's behest," he relies on himself. He sits down at the drawing board, takes the slide rule, and calculates a flying carpet. He goes to the laboratory, fires the electric furnace and invents the bursting grass. The Poshekhonian reconciles himself to his wonders happening twenty-seven lands and forty kingdoms away. The Londoner wants his wonders today, right now, right here. And therefore he chooses the trustiest road to his fairy tales—a road paved with astronomic, physical, and chemical formulas, a road rolled flat and solid by the cast-iron laws of the exact sciences. This may seem paradoxical at first—exact science and fairy tale, precision and fantasy. But it is so, and must be so. For a myth is always, openly or implicitly, connected with religion, and the religion of the modern city is precise science. Hence, the natural link between the newest urban myth, urban fairy tale, and science. And I do not know whether there is a single major branch of the exact sciences that has not been reflected in Wells's fantastic novels. Mathematics, astronomy, astrophysics, physics, chemistry, medicine, physiology, bacteriology, mechanics, electrotechnology, aviation. Almost all of Wells's fairy tales are built upon brilliant and most unexpected scientific paradoxes. All his myths are as logical as mathematical equations. And this is why we, modern men, we, skeptics, are conquered by these logical fantasies, this is why they command our attention and win our belief.

Wells brings the reader into an atmosphere of the miraculous, of the fairy tale, with extraordinary cunning. Carefully, gradually, he leads you up from one logical step to the next. The transition from step to step is quite imperceptible; trustingly, without realizing it, you mount higher and higher. And suddenly, you look back and gasp, but it is too late: you already believe what had seemed, from the title, absolutely impossible, totally absurd.

* * *

1. The Russian province of Poshekhonie is the setting for a series of folklorish tales written by the satirist M. Y. Saltykov-Shchedrin in the 1870s and '80s [Editor's note].

BERNARD BERGONZI

[Wells the Myth-Maker]†

* * *

Structually, *The Time Machine* belongs to the class of story, which includes James's *Turn of the Screw* and Conrad's *Lord Jim*, that Northrop Frye has called 'the tale told in quotation marks, where we have an opening setting with a small group of congenial people, and then the real story told by one of the members'. As Frye observes:

> The effect of such devices is to present the story through a relaxed and contemplative haze as something that entertains us without, so to speak, confronting us, as direct tragedy confronts us.[1]

This aesthetic distancing of the central narrative of *The Time Machine*, 'the time traveller's story', is carefully carried out. At the end of the book, the Traveller says:

> 'No, I cannot expect you to believe it. Take it as a lie—or a prophecy. Say I dreamed it in the workshop. Consider I have been speculating upon the destinies of our race, until I have hatched this fiction. Treat my assertion of its truth as a mere stroke of art to enhance its interest. And taking it as a story, what do you think of it?' (p. 68).

The manifest disbelief of all his friends (with the exception of the story-teller)—one of them 'thought the tale a "gaudy lie"' (p. 69)—is balanced by the apparent evidence of his sojourn in the future, the 'two strange white flowers' of an unknown species. In fact Wells demands assent by apparently discouraging it, a device he was frequently to use in his fantastic short stories.

The opening chapters of the novel show us the inventor entertaining his friends, a group of professional men, in the solid comfort of his home at Richmond. They clearly derive from the 'club-man' atmosphere with which several of Kipling's short stories open, and their function in the narrative is to give it a basis in contemporary life at its most ordinary and pedestrian: this atmosphere makes the completest possible contrast with the tale that is to come, with its account of a wholly imaginative world of dominantly paradisal and

---

† From *The Early H. G. Wells: A Study of the Scientific Romances* (Manchester: Manchester University Press, 1961), pp. 42–59. Reprinted by permission of the author. Page references to *The Time Machine* are to this Norton Critical Edition.

1. Northrop Frye, *Anatomy of Criticism: Four Essays* (Princeton: Princeton University Press, 1957), pp. 202–03.

demonic imagery, lying far outside the possible experience of the late Victorian bourgeoisie. These chapters are essential to Wells's purpose, since they prevent the central narrative from seeming a piece of pure fantasy, or a fairy story, and no more. The character of the Time Traveller himself—cheerful, erratic, and somewhat absurd, faintly suggestive of a hero of Jerome K. Jerome's—has a similar function. One may compare the work of other popular writers of fantastic romance in the nineties, such as Arthur Machen and M. P. Shiel (both deriving from Stevenson), where a 'weird' atmosphere is striven after from the very beginning and the dramatic power is correspondingly less. Wells was conscious of this technique; in a magazine interview he gave in 1897 he admitted that though there was a distinction in his own work between 'realism' and 'romance', the two could never be wholly separate, since 'the scientific episode which I am treating insists upon interesting me, and so I have to write about the effect of it upon the mind of some particular person'.[2]

Once the reader has been initiated into the group of friends, he is prepared for whatever is to come next. First the model time machine is produced—'a glittering metallic framework, scarcely larger than a small clock, and very delicately made . . . there was ivory in it, and some crystalline substance' (p. 9)—and sent off into time, never to be seen again. Then we are shown the full-scale machine, and the account of it is a brilliant example of Wells's impressionistic method:

> I remember vividly the flickering light, his queer, broad head in silhouette, the dance of the shadows, how we all followed him, puzzled but incredulous, and how there in the laboratory we beheld a larger edition of the little mechanism which we had seen vanish from before our eyes. Parts were of nickel, parts of ivory, parts had certainly been filed or sawn out of rock crystal. The thing was generally complete, but the twisted crystalline bars lay unfinished upon the bench beside some sheets of drawings, and I took one up for a better look at it. Quartz it seemed to be (p. 11).

One sees here how much Wells's narrative technique had developed since the days of *The Chronic Argonauts*. The assemblage of details is strictly speaking meaningless but nevertheless conveys very effectively a sense of the machine without putting the author to the taxing necessity of giving a direct description. As a reviewer of one of his later books was to remark, 'Precision in the unessential and vagueness in the essential are really the basis of Mr Wells's art, and convey admirably the just amount of conviction.'[3]

2. *To-day* (September 11, 1897), p. 164.
3. *Athenaeum* (June 26, 1897), p. 1.

The central narrative of *The Time Machine* is of a kind common to several of Wells's early romances; a character is transferred to or marooned in a wholly alien environment, and the story arises from his efforts to deal with the situation. This is the case with the Time Traveller, with the Angel in *The Wonderful Visit* and with Prendick in *The Island of Dr Moreau*, while Griffin in *The Invisible Man* becomes the victim of his environment in attempting to control it. In all these novels, themes and motifs frequently recur so that cross-reference is inevitable when discussing them. Though Wells is a writer of symbolic fiction—or a myth-maker—the symbolism is not of the specifically 'heraldic' kind that we associate, for instance with Hawthorne's scarlet letter, Melville's white whale, or James's golden bowl. In Wells the symbolic element is inherent in the total fictional situation and to this extent he is closer to Kafka. When, for instance, we see in *The Time Machine* a paradisal world on the surface of the earth inhabited by beautiful carefree beings leading a wholly aesthetic existence, and a diabolic or demonic world beneath the surface inhabited by brutish creatures who spend most of their time in darkness in underground machine shops, and only appear on the surface at night, and when we are told that these two races are the descendants respectively of the present-day bourgeoisie and proletariat, and that the latter live by cannibalistically preying on the former—then clearly we are faced with a symbolic situation of considerable complexity, where several different 'mythical' interpretations are possible.

The hero of *The Time Machine*—unlike his predecessor, Nebogipfel, and his successors, Moreau and Griffin—is not a solitary eccentric on the Frankenstein model, but an amiable and gregarious bourgeois. Like Wells himself, he appears to be informed and interested in the dominant intellectual movements of his age, Marxism and Darwinism. Wells had come across Marx at South Kensington, and though in later years he was to become extremely anti-Marxist, it appears that in his immediate post-student days he was prepared to uphold Marxian socialism as 'a new thing based on Darwinism'.[4] However doubtfully historical this may be, the juxtaposition of the two names is very important for Wells's early imaginative and speculative writing. The time traveller, immediately after he has arrived in the world of 802701, is full of forebodings about the kind of humanity he may discover:

> What might not have happened to men? What if cruelty had grown into a common passion? What if in this interval the race had lost its manliness, and had developed into something inhuman, unsympathetic, and overwhelmingly powerful? I might

4. Report of a debate, *Science Schools Journal* (February 1889), p. 153.

seem some old world savage animal, only the more dreadful and disgusting for our common likeness—a foul creature to be incontinently slain (pp. 19–20).

On a purely thematic level, *The Time Machine* can be considered as a development and expansion of the kind of speculation contained in 'The Man of the Year Million', though with a number of important differences. The Traveller, during his sojourn in 802701, is involved in a series of discoveries, both physical and intellectual. The more he finds out about the Eloi—and subsequently the Morlocks—and their way of life, the more radically he has to reformulate his previous theories about them. The truth, in each case, turns out to be more unpleasant than he had thought.

At first, however, his more fearful speculations are not fulfilled. Instead of 'something unhuman, unsympathetic and overwhelmingly powerful', he discovers the Eloi, who are small, frail and beautiful. He is rather shocked and then amused by their child-like ways and manifest lack of intellectual powers—'the memory of my confident anticipations of a profoundly grave and intellectual posterity came, with irresistible merriment, to my mind' (p. 22). Such a 'grave and intellectual posterity' had in fact been postulated by Bulwer Lytton in *The Coming Race* (1871), a work which, it has been suggested, had some influence on *The Time Machine*, though the resemblances are very slight.[5] But it is quite possible that Wells was here alluding to Bulwer Lytton's romance, as well as to the wider implications of optimistic evolutionary theory.

Subsequently the Traveller becomes charmed with the Eloi and the relaxed communism of their way of life. They live, not in separate houses, but in large semi-ruinous buildings of considerable architectural splendour, sleeping and eating there communally. Their only food is fruit, which abounds in great richness and variety, and they are described in a way which suggests the figures of traditional pastoral poetry: 'They spent all their time in playing gently, in bathing in the river, in making love in a half-playful fashion, in eating fruit and sleeping' (p. 35). The Traveller takes stock of their world:

> I have already spoken of the great palaces dotted about among the variegated greenery, some in ruins and some still occupied. Here and there rose a white or silvery figure in the waste garden of the earth, here and there came the sharp vertical line of some cupola or obelisk. There were no hedges, no signs of proprietary rights, no evidence of agriculture; the whole earth had become a garden (p. 26).

5. Gordon S. Haight, "H. G. Wells's 'The Man of the Year Million,'" *Nineteenth-Century Fiction* 12 (1958), p. 325.

There appear to be no animals, wild or domestic, left in the world, and such forms of life as remain have clearly been subject to a radical process of selection:

> The air was free from gnats, the earth from weeds or fungi; everywhere were fruits and sweet and delightful flowers; brilliant butterflies flew hither and thither. The ideal of preventive medicine was attained. Diseases had been stamped out. I saw no evidence of any contagious disease during all my stay. And I shall have to tell you later that even the processes of putrefaction and decay had been profoundly affected by these changes (p. 27).

Man has, in short, at some period long since past obtained complete control of his environment, and has been able to manipulate the conditions of life to his absolute satisfaction. The 'struggle for existence' has been ended, and as a result of this manipulation, the nature of the species has undergone profound modification. Not only have the apparent physical differences between male and female disappeared, but their mental powers have declined as well as their physical. The human race, as it presents itself to the Traveller, is plainly in its final decadence. Wells had already dealt in 'The Man of the Year Million' with the possible ways in which the easing of environmental conditions would modify the species; but the men of the year million, as described in that essay, though physically much altered, had been both more intelligent and less beautiful than the Eloi (whose name carries several obvious associations, suggesting not only their *elfin* looks, but also *éloigné*, and their apparent status as an *élite*: there may also be a suggestion of *eld*, meaning old age and decrepitude). The Eloi, with their childlike and sexually ambiguous appearance, and their consumptive type of beauty, are clear reflections of *fin de siècle* visual taste.[6]

In the world that the Traveller surveys, aesthetic motives have evidently long been dominant as humanity has settled down to its decline. 'This has ever been the fate of energy in security; it takes to art and to eroticism, and then come languour and decay' (p. 28). But in the age of the Eloi even artistic motives seem almost extinct. 'To adorn themselves with flowers, to dance, to sing in the sunlight; so much was left of the artistic spirit, and no more' (p. 28). The first chapter of the Time Traveller's narrative is called 'In the Golden Age', and the following chapter 'The Sunset of Mankind'; there is an ironic effect, not only in the juxtaposition, but in the very reference to a 'golden age'. Such an age, the *Saturnia regna*, when men were

---

6. It is also significant that the Traveller's first impression of the future world is dominated by the statue of the White Sphinx and that the first edition of *The Time Machine* had a sphinx upon the cover. The sphinx was a familiar object in *fin de siècle* iconography: *vide* Wilde's poem, "The Sphinx," published in 1894, and various references in [J.-K. Huysman's] *A Rebours*; also Gustave Moreau's celebrated "sphinx" paintings, described by Mario Praz in *The Romantic Agony* [1933], Chapter V.

imagined as living a simple, uncomplicated and happy existence, before in some way falling from grace, was always an object of literary nostalgia, and traditionally thought of as being at the very beginning of man's history. Wells, however, places it in the remotest future and associates it not with dawn but with sunset. The Time Traveller sees the Eloi as leading a paradisal existence, and his sense of this is imparted to the reader by the imagery of the first part of his narrative. They are thoroughly assimilated to their environment, where 'the whole earth had become a garden', and 'everywhere were fruits and sweet and delicious flowers: brilliant butterflies flew hither and thither'. Their appearance and mode of life makes a pointed contrast to the drab and earnest figure of the Traveller:

> Several more brightly-clad people met me in the doorway, and so we entered, I, dressed in dingy nineteenth-century garments, looking grotesque enough, garlanded with flowers, and surrounded by an eddying mass of bright, soft-coloured robes and shining white limbs, in a melodious whirl of laughter and laughing speech (pp. 22–23).

The writing here suggests that Wells was getting a little out of his depth, but the intention is clearly to present the Eloi as in some sense heirs to Pre-Raphaelite convention. This implicit contrast between the aesthetic and utilitarian, the beautiful and idle set against the ugly and active, shows how *The Time Machine* embodies another profound late-Victorian preoccupation, recalling, for instance, the aesthetic anti-industrialism of Ruskin and Morris. The world of the Eloi is presented as not only a golden age, but as something of a lotos land, and it begins to exercise its spell on the Traveller. After his immediate panic on discovering the loss of his machine, he settles down to a philosophic resignation:

> Suppose the worst? I said. Suppose the machine altogether lost—perhaps destroyed? It behoves me to be calm and patient, to learn the way of the people, to get a clear idea of the method of my loss, and the means of getting materials and tools; so that in the end, perhaps, I may make another. That would be my only hope, a poor hope, perhaps, but better than despair. And, after all, it was a beautiful and curious world (p. 31).

The Traveller's potential attachment to the Eloi and their world is strengthened when he rescues the little female, Weena, from drowning and begins a prolonged flirtation with her. This relationship is the biggest flaw in the narrative, for it is totally unconvincing, and tends to embarrass the reader (Pritchett has referred to 'the faint squirms of idyllic petting').[7] But though the Traveller feels the attraction of

7. V. S. Pritchett, *The Living Novel* (London: Chatto and Windus, 1946), p. 119.

the kind of life she represents, he is still too much a man of his own age, resourceful, curious and active, to succumb to it. As he says of himself, 'I am too Occidental for a long vigil. I could work at a problem for years, but to wait inactive for twenty-four hours—that is another matter' (p. 32).

But it is not long before he becomes aware that the Eloi are not the only forms of animal life left in the world, and his curiosity is once more aroused. He realizes that Weena and the Eloi generally have a great fear of darkness: 'But she dreaded the dark, dreaded shadows, dreaded black things' (p. 36). Here we have the first hint of the dominant imagery of the second half of the narrative, the darkness characteristic of the Morlocks, and the ugly shapeless forms associated with it, contrasting with the light and the brilliant colours of the Eloi and their world. Looking into the darkness one night just before dawn the Traveller imagines that he can see vague figures running across the landscape, but cannot be certain whether or not his eyes have deceived him. And a little later, when he is exploring one of the ruined palaces, he comes across a strange creature—'a queer little ape-like figure'—that runs away from him and disappears down one of the well-like shafts that are scattered across the country, and whose purpose and nature had puzzled the Traveller on his arrival: 'My impression of it is, of course, imperfect; but I know it was a dull white, and had strange large greyish-red eyes; also that there was flaxen hair on its head and down its back' (p. 38). The Traveller now has to reformulate his ideas about the way the evolutionary development of man has proceeded: 'Man had not remained one species, but had differentiated into two distinct animals' (p. 38). He has to modify his previous 'Darwinian' explanation by a 'Marxist' one: 'It seemed clear as daylight to me that the gradual widening of the merely temporary and social difference between the Capitalist and the Labourer was the key to the whole position' (p. 40). Even in his own day, he reflects, men tend to spend more and more time underground: 'There is a tendency to utilize underground space for the less ornamental purposes of civilization' (p. 40). 'Even now, does not an East-end worker live in such artificial conditions as practically to be cut off from the natural surface of the earth?' (p. 40). Similarly, the rich have tended to preserve themselves more and more as an exclusive and self-contained group, with fewer and fewer social contacts with the workers, until society has stratified rigidly into a two-class system. 'So, in the end, above the ground you must have the Haves, pursuing pleasure and comfort and beauty, and below ground the Have-nots; the Workers getting continually adapted to the conditions of their labour' (pp. 40–41). The analysis represents, it will be seen, a romantic and pessimistic variant of orthodox Marxist thought; the implications of the class-war are accepted but the possibility of the successful proletarian revolution establishing a classless society is excluded. Thus, the Traveller concludes, the social tendencies of nineteenth century industrialism have become rigidified and then built in, as it were, to the evolutionary development of the race. Nevertheless, he is orthodox enough in his analysis to assume that the Eloi, despite their physical and mental decline, are still the masters and the Morlocks—as he finds the underground creatures are called—are their slaves. It is not long before he discovers that this, too, is a false conclusion.

Soon enough, despite his dalliance with Weena, and her obvious reluctance to let him go, the Traveller decides that he must find out more about the Morlocks, and resolves to descend into their underworld. It is at this point that, in Pritchett's phrase, 'the story alters its key, and the Time Traveller reveals the foundation of slime and horror on which the pretty life of his Arcadians is precariously and fearfully resting'.[8] The descent of the Traveller into the underworld has, in fact, an almost undisplaced mythical significance: it suggests a parody of the Harrowing of Hell, where it is not the souls of the just that are released but the demonic Morlocks, for it is they who dominate the subsequent narrative. During his 'descent into hell' the Traveller is seized by the Morlocks, but he keeps them at bay by striking matches, for they recoil from light in any form (which is why they do not normally appear on the surface of the earth by day). During his brief and confused visit to their world he sees and hears great machines at work, and notices a table spread for a meal. He observes that the Morlocks are carnivorous, but does not, for a time, make the obvious conclusion about the nature of the meat they are eating. However, it is readily apparent to the reader. The Morlocks have a complex symbolic function, for they not only represent an exaggerated fear of the nineteenth century proletariat, but also embody many of the traditional mythical images of a demonic world. This is apparent if one compares Wells's account of them and their environment with the chapter on 'Demonic Imagery' in Northrop Frye's *Anatomy of Criticism*. As Frye writes:

> Images of perverted work belong here too: engines of torture, weapons of war, armour, and images of a dead mechanism which, because it does not humanize nature, is unnatural as well as inhuman. Corresponding to the temple or One Building of the apocalypse, we have the prison or dungeon, the sealed furnace of heat without light, like the City of Dis in Dante.[9]

Indeed, nothing is more remarkable about *The Time Machine* than the way in which its central narrative is polarized between opposed

8. Pritchett, p. 120.
9. Frye, p. 150.

groups of imagery, the paradisal (or, in Frye's phrase, the apocalyptic) and the demonic, representing extreme forms of human desire and repulsion.

A further significance of the Morlocks can be seen in the fact that they are frequently referred to in terms of unpleasant animal life: thus they are described as, or compared with, 'apes', 'lemurs', 'worms', 'spiders', 'ants', and 'rats'. One must compare these images with the Traveller's original discovery that all forms of non-human animal life—with the apparent exception of butterflies—had been banished from the upper-world, whether noxious or not. There is a powerful irony in his subsequent discovery that the one remaining form of animal life, and the most noxious of all, is a branch of humanity. Furthermore, this confusion of human and animal—with its origin in an imaginative perturbation over the deeper implications of Darwinism—was to provide the central theme of *The Island of Dr Moreau*.

The traveller narrowly escapes with his life from the Morlocks, and returns to the surface, to make another reappraisal of the world of 802701. The image of the 'golden age' as it had presented itself to him on his arrival has been destroyed: 'there was an altogether new element in the sickening quality of the Morlocks—a something inhuman and malign' (p. 46). He has to reject his subsequent hypothesis that the Eloi were the masters and the Morlocks their slaves. A new relationship has clearly evolved between the two races; the Eloi, who are in terror of dark and moonless nights, are in some way victims of the Morlocks, though he is still not certain precisely how. His experience underground has shattered his previous euphoria (symbolically, perhaps, an end of the paradisal innocence in which he has been participating), and his natural inventiveness and curiosity reassert themselves. He makes his way with Weena to a large green building that he has seen in the distance many miles off, which he later calls the 'Palace of Green Porcelain'. On their way they pass a night in the open: the Traveller looks at the stars in their now unfamiliar arrangements and reflects on his present isolation.

> Looking at these stars suddenly dwarfed my own troubles and all the gravities of terrestrial life. I thought of their unfathomable distance, and the slow inevitable drift of their movements out of the unknown past into the unknown future. I thought of the great precessional cycle that the pole of the earth describes. Only forty times had that silent revolution occurred during all the years that I had traversed. And during these few revolutions all the activity, all the traditions, the complex organizations, the nations, languages, literatures, aspirations, even the mere memory of Man as I knew him had been swept out of existence. Instead were these frail creatures who

had forgotten their high ancestry, and the white Things of which I went in terror. Then I thought of the Great Fear that was between the two species, and for the first time, with a sudden shiver, came the clear knowledge of what the meat I had seen might be. Yet it was too horrible! I looked at little Weena sleeping beside me, her face white and star-like under the stars, and forthwith dismissed the thought (p. 49).

The Traveller's knowledge of the world of the Eloi and the Morlocks, and the relation between them, is almost complete. When they reach the Palace of Green Porcelain, he finds, as if to belie his reflections on the disappearance of all traces of the past, a vast museum: 'Clearly we stood among the ruins of some latter-day South Kensington' (p. 52). The museum, with its semi-ruinous remains of earlier phases of human achievement, puts the Traveller once more in direct emotional relation with the past, and, by implication, with his own age. Here, the Arcadian spell is finally cast off. He remembers that he is, after all, a late-Victorian scientist with a keen interest in technology. He is intrigued by various great machines, some half destroyed and others in quite good condition:

> You know I have a certain weakness for mechanism, and I was inclined to linger among these: the more so as for the most part they had the interest of puzzles, and I could make only the vaguest guesses at what they were for. I fancied that if I could solve their puzzles I should find myself in possession of powers that might be of use against the Morlocks (p. 53).

The Morlocks, after all, are a technological race, and if he is to defend himself against them—as he has decided he must—he must match himself against their mechanical prowess. The images of machinery in this part of the narrative are sufficient to suggest to the reader the presence of the Morlocks, and before long the Traveller sees footprints in the dust around him, and hears noises coming from one end of a long gallery, which means that the Morlocks are not far away. He breaks an iron lever off one of the machines to use as a mace. By now, his feelings for the Morlocks are those of passionate loathing: 'I longed very much to kill a Morlock or so. Very inhuman, you may think, to want to go killing one's own descendants! But it was impossible, somehow, to feel any humanity in the things' (p. 54). Since the Morlocks on one level stand for the late nineteenth century proletariat, the Traveller's attitude towards them symbolizes a contemporary bourgeois fear of the working class, and it is not fanciful to impute something of this attitude to Wells himself. From his schooldays in Bromley he had disliked and feared the working class in a way wholly appropriate to the son of a small tradesman—as various Marxist critics have not been slow to remark.[1] The Traveller's gradual identification with the beautiful and aristocratic—if decadent—Eloi against the brutish Morlocks is indicative of Wells's own attitudes, or one aspect of them, and links up with a common theme in his realistic fiction: the hypergamous aspirations of a low-born hero towards genteel heroines: Jessica Milton in *The Wheels of Chance*, Helen Walsingham in *Kipps*, Beatrice Normandy in *Tono-Bungay*, and Christabel in *Mr Polly*.

Wells's imagination was easily given to producing images of mutilation and violence, and the Traveller's hatred of the Morlocks gives them free rein. The reader is further prepared for the scenes of violence and destruction which end the Traveller's expedition to the museum by his discovery of 'a long gallery of rusting stands of arms', where he 'hesitated between my crowbar and a hatchet or a sword' (p. 55). But he could not carry both and kept the crowbar. He contented himself with a jar of camphor from another part of the museum, since this was inflammable and would make a useful weapon against the Morlocks. By now we have wholly moved from the dominantly paradisal imagery of the first half of the narrative to the demonic imagery of the second. Instead of a golden age, or lotos land, we are back in the familiar world of inventiveness and struggle.

When Weena and the Traveller are once more outside the museum and are making their way homeward through the woods, he decides to keep the lurking Morlocks at bay during the coming night by lighting a fire. He succeeds only too well and before long he has set the whole forest ablaze. Several Morlocks try to attack him, but he fights them off with his iron bar. He then discovers the creatures all fleeing in panic before the advancing fire: in the confusion Weena is lost. There are some powerful descriptions of the Morlocks' plight:

> And now I was to see the most weird and horrible thing, I think, of all that I beheld in that future age. This whole space was as bright as day with the reflection of the fire. In the centre was a hillock, or tumulus, surmounted by a scorched hawthorn. Beyond this was another arm of the burning forest, with yellow tongues already writhing from it, completely encircling the space with a fence of fire. Upon the hillside were some thirty or forty Morlocks, dazzled by the light and heat, and blundering hither and thither against each other in their bewilderment. At first I did not realize their blindness, and struck furiously at them with my bar, in a frenzy of fear, as they approached me, killing one and crippling several more. But when I had watched the gestures of one of them groping under the hawthorn against

---

1. See Christopher Caudwell, *Studies in a Dying Culture* (London: John Lane, 1938), pp. 73–95; A. L. Morton, *The English Utopia* (London: Lawrence & Wishart, 1952), pp. 183–94.

the red sky, and heard their moans, I was assured of their absolute helplessness and misery in the glare, and I struck no more of them (pp. 59–60).

Eventually, on the following morning, the Traveller gets back to the neighbourhood of the White Sphinx, whence he had started. Everything is as it was when he left. The beautiful Eloi are still moving across the landscape in their gay robes, or bathing in the river. But now his disillusion with their Arcadian world and his realization of the true nature of their lives is complete.

I understood now what all the beauty of the overworld people covered. Very pleasant was their day, as pleasant as the day of the cattle in the field. Like the cattle, they knew of no enemies, and provided against no needs. And their end was the same (p. 61).

Here we have the solution to a riddle that was implicitly posed at the beginning of the Traveller's narrative. Soon after his arrival among the Eloi he had found that there were no domestic animals in their world: 'horses, cattle, sheep, dogs, had followed the Ichthyosaurus into extinction' (p. 23). Yet the life led by the Eloi is clearly that contained in conventional literary pastoral, and so the first part of the Traveller's narrative partakes of the nature of pastoral—but it is a pastoral world without sheep or cattle. And a little later, during his speculations on the possibilities of eugenic development, he had reflected:

We improve our favourite plants and animals—and how few they are—gradually by selective breeding; now a new and better peach, now a seedless grape, now a sweeter and larger flower, now a more convenient breed of cattle (p. 27).

Something of this sort, he concludes, has brought about the world of 802701. But the paradox latent in the observation is only made manifest on his return from the museum, now possessing a complete knowledge of this world. There are no sheep or cattle in the pastoral world of the Eloi because they are themselves the cattle, fattened and fed by their underground masters. They are *both* a 'sweeter and larger flower' and a 'more convenient breed of cattle'. Thus, the complex symbolism of the central narrative of *The Time Machine* is ingeniously completed on this note of diabolic irony. Such knowledge has made the Arcadian world intolerable to the Traveller. He is now able to escape from it: the Morlocks have produced his machine and placed it as a trap for him, but he is able to elude them, and travels off into the still more remote future.

* * *

KATHRYN HUME

Eat or Be Eaten: H. G. Wells's *Time Machine*†

"It is very remarkable that this is so extensively overlooked," says the Time Traveller, speaking of time as the fourth dimension (p. 6). Similarly remarkable is the way we have overlooked the comprehensive functions of oral fantasies in *The Time Machine*. They play a fourth dimension to the other three of entropy, devolution, and utopian satire. They ramify, by regular transformations, into those other three; into the social and economic worlds of consumption and exploitation; and into the realm of gender anxieties. They transform the ideological commonplaces from which the text constructs its reality. They create a network of emotional tensions that subliminally unites the three time frames: Victorian England, the Realm of the Sphinx, and the Terminal Beach. At the same time, this nexus of related images undercuts and fragments the logical, scientific arguments being carried out on the surface of the tale.

The Time Machine is the first of Wells's scientific romances to achieve canonical status.[1] In their eagerness to elevate and assimilate this text, however, critics have lost awareness that some of its parts are not explained by their normal critical strategies. One such feature to disappear from critical discourse is the failure of any coherent social message to emerge from the world of the Eloi and Morlocks. Another partly repressed feature is the disparity between the Time Traveller's violent emotions and the experiences that evoke them.[2] A third feature lost to view is the dubious logic that binds the two futuristic scenarios.

I would like to approach the text with both the oral image complex and these elided mysteries in mind. What emerges will not fill the gaps in the narrative logic; the text resists such treatment, for reasons that will be shown. Rather, I wish to explore the hidden dynamics of emotion and logic. Since the semes attached to eating, consumption, and engulfment point in so many directions, I shall start instead with the public ideologies of power, size and gender. Then we can explore their symbolic manifestations as fantasies of being eaten or engulfed; as equations involving body size, intelligence, and physical

---

† From *Philological Quarterly* 69.2 (Spring 1990): 233–42, 245–46, 247–49. Reprinted by permission of the University of Iowa and the author. Page references to *The Time Machine* are to this Norton Critical Edition.
1. Bernard Bergonzi rendered *The Time Machine* orthodox by bestowing upon it two charismatic labels: "ironic" and "myth." See "*The Time Machine*: An Ironic Myth," *Critical Quarterly* 2 (1960): 293–305.
2. See David J. Lake, "Wells's Time Traveller: An Unreliable Narrator?" *Extrapolation* 22, no. 2 (1981): 117–26.

energy; and as gender attributes projected on the world. Once sensi-
tized to these concerns, we can examine the two future scenarios
and their relationship to the Victorian frame. By exploring the inter-
play of ideology with its symbolic distortions, we will better sense
what the text represses, and why despite (or even because of) this
hidden material, the book has such disturbing power.

Ideological Assumptions

Ideology, used here in Roland Barthes' sense, means the unexamined
assumptions as to what is natural and inevitable and hence unchange-
able. One realizes these "inevitabilities" to be historical and contingent most readily by comparing cultures, for within a culture, the
ideological is taken to be "real."

The part of the general ideology relevant here consists of a nexus
of values that include power, body size, and gender. Separating the
values even to this extent is artificial; they intertwine tightly, and in
turn link to other values such as dominance, exploitation, race, physical height, and bodily strength. They also merge with political and
social and military power. The form taken by this family of assumptions in England made the British Empire possible.

Let us assume you are a nineteenth-century Briton—white, male,
and a member of the politically powerful classes. You are also nomi-
nally Christian and equipped with the latest weaponry. You could
expect to march into any country not blessed with most of these
characteristics and expropriate what you wanted, be it raw material,
cheap labor, land, or valuables. Such power gives the ability to
exploit and consume. The so-called inferior races had no choice,
since their technology was insufficient to resist British force. The
Traveller's outlook is very much that of the nineteenth-century
Briton among the aliens. His strength, technological know-how, and
culture elevate him in his own mind. He scribbles his name on a
statue, much as other nineteenth-century Britons carved theirs on
Roman and Greek temples. To the empire builders, killing Africans
or Indians was not "really" murder; they were Other and hence less
than truly human. While the Traveller controls his impulse to massacre Morlocks (and is even praised for his restraint by one critic),[3]
he smashes at their skulls in a way he would never dream of doing in
Oxford Street. He is outraged (as well as frightened) when his tres-
passing machine is impounded. In the "kangaroo" and "centipede"
episode found in the *New Review* serialization of the novel, his
immediate impulse is to hit one of the kangaroo-like creatures on

3. John Huntington sees this mastery of his actions as index to the protagonist's superiority
   over both Eloi and Morlocks, since they lack such self-control. See *The Logic of Fantasy:
   H. G. Wells and Science Fiction* (Columbia U. Press, 1982), p. 51.

the skull with a rock. When examination of the body suggests that it is of human descent, he feels only a flash of "disagreeable apprehension," evidently directed toward this proof of Man's degeneration, not at his own murderous action. His regret at leaving the body (possibly just unconscious) to the monstrous "centipede." appears to be regret at the loss, of a scientific specimen, not guilt at leaving this "grey animal . . . or grey man" to be devoured.[4] He protects himself from any acknowledgment of this self-centeredness by viewing his urges as scientific, but ultimately he sees himself as having the right to whatever he wants, and cherishes himself for being the only "real" human and therefore the only creature with rights.

Part of this superiority stems from physical size, the second element in the ideology and one closely linked to power. Size generally permits a man to feel superior to women, and a British man to feel superior to members of shorter races. In English, size is a metaphor used to indicate that which is valuable, good, desirable. "Great," "high," and "large" are normally positive markers.[5]

In the two paragraphs that encompass the narrator's first language lesson and his response to it, we find the word "little" used eight times. Attached in his mind to the littleness of the Eloi is their "chatter," their tiring easily, their being "indolent" and "easily fatigued," and their "lack of interest" (pp. 24, 21). Littleness and its associated debilities are so grotesquely prominent that one cannot help note this obsession with the inferiority attaching to bodies of small size. What the narrator thinks will shape and limit what he hears and sees. When he first hears the Eloi (p. 20), they look and sound like "men" running. Later, his senses register "children": "I heard cries of terror and their little feet running" (p. 30).

The ideological inferiority of littleness is reinforced for readers by the Traveller's reactions to artifacts of the prior civilization. He admires and wonders at the "ruinous splendor" consisting of "a great heap of granite, bound together by masses of aluminium, a vast labyrinth of precipitous walls" (p. 25). He cannot describe such a building without expressing this admiration for sheer size: the buildings are "splendid," "colossal," "tall," "big," "magnificent," "vast," "great," and "huge." He never wonders whether the size was functional and if so, how. Nor does he speculate on whether it was achieved through slave labor, as were the colossal monuments of antiquity which it resembles, with its "suggestions of old Phoenician

---

4. See p. 125 of this Norton Critical Edition for this episode in the *New Review* version of *The Time Machine* [*Editor's note*].
5. In her utopian novel, *The Dispossessed*, Ursula Le Guin calls our attention to this unthinking esteem for height by replacing commendatory terms based on size with those based on centrality.

decorations" (p. 22). He simply extends automatic admiration to such remains because of their impressive size.

The third element in the common ideology, besides power and size, is gender. Power and size support the superior status of maleness. Wells extends this prejudice to the point of defining humanity as male. Early in his narrative, the Time Traveller recounts his fear that "the race had lost its manliness" (p. 20). No sooner does he identify the Eloi as shorter than himself than they become "creatures" and are quickly feminized with such terms as "graceful," "frail," "hectic beauty," "Dresden china type of prettiness." All later descriptions use codes normally applied to women or children: mouths small and bright red, eyes large and mild, a language that sounds sweet and liquid and cooing and melodious. Ultimately, he equates loss of manliness with loss of humanity.

To sum up the ideological assumptions: the text shows as natural and inevitable the interconnection of power, size, and male gender. Wells was to prove capable of challenging the politics of power in later scientific romances. He questions the might-makes-right outlook of Empire in his reference to the Tasmanians in *The War of the Worlds* (1898), and in Dr. Moreau's parodic imposition of The Law on inferior beings (1896). Callousness towards non-British sentients is rebuked by Cavor, who is shocked by Bedford's slaughter of Selenites in *The First Men in the Moon* (1901). However, though power may be somewhat negotiable to Wells, size and maleness remain positively marked throughout the scientific romances. In *The Food of the Gods* (1904), size automatically conveys nobility of purpose, and this idealized race of giants consists so exclusively of men that it will have trouble propagating.

If this text merely echoed the ideology of its times, *The Time Machine* (1895) would be drab and predictable. The symbolic enlargements and distortions of these values are what create the images and tensions that make it interesting, so let us turn to them.

Symbolic Transformations of Ideology

Power belongs to the same family of values as "exploitation" and "consumption." These terms from the political and economic spheres take on added resonances when they emerge as oral fantasies about eating and being eaten. As Patrick A. McCarthy points out, cannibalism lies at the heart of this darkness, or so at least the Traveller asseverates.[6] Actually, the evidence for cannibalism is far from complete, as David Lake observes, and the narrator may be jumping to totally

---

6. See McCarthy's "*Heart of Darkness* and the Early Novels of H. G. Wells: Evolution, Anarchy, Entropy," *Journal of Modern Literature* 13, no. 1 (1986): 37–60.

unwarranted conclusions. However the notion of humans as fatted kine for a technologically superior group will reappear in *The War of the Worlds*, so it evidently held some fascination for Wells. The latter book certainly makes the connection between eating people and economic exploitation,[7] a parallel made famous by Swift's "Modest Proposal."

The putative cuisine of the Morlocks is only the most obvious of the oral fantasies. "Eat or be eaten" is a way of characterizing some social systems, but in Wells's futures, the words are literally applicable, and the text regales us with variations upon the theme of eating. The Time Traveller fears that the Morlocks will feed upon him as well as on Eloi. In the extra time-frame of the *New Review* version, the centipede appears to be hungry. The crabs make clear their intentions to consume the Traveller. The Sphinx traditionally devoured those who could not guess her riddle; the Traveller's entering her pedestal constitutes but a slight displacement of entering her maw. The Victorian frame features a prominent display of after-dinner satisfactions (including drinks, cigars, and feminized chairs that embrace and support the men) and a meal at which the Traveller urgently gobbles his food. Oral fantasies also take the forms of engulfment: one can be overwhelmed, drowned, swallowed by darkness, or rendered unconscious. Both in the narrator's dreams and in his physical adventures, we find several such threats of dissolution.

Norman Holland observes that "the single most common fantasy-structure in literature is phallic assertiveness balanced against oral engulfment,"[8] exactly the pattern of *The Time Machine*. Typical of the phallic stage anxieties is the exploration of dark, dangerous, and congested places. Time travel and other magic forms of travel are common omnipotence fantasies at this stage of development. So is the pre-oedipal polarization of agents into threatening and non-threatening, and the focus on a single figure. Opposing this phallic quest are oral anxieties. One such wave of anxiety oozes forth as the engulfing embraces of night (e.g., "dreaming . . . that I was drowned, and that sea-anemones were feeling over my face with their soft palps"—p. 36). Another such anxiety grips the narrator when he faces the yawning underworld; indeed, upon escaping from below, he collapses in a dead faint. The threat of being eaten, and the enfolding gloom of the Terminal Beach are two others.

The protagonist faces engulfment of body and mind. When he returns to his own time, he responds with typical defenses against oral anxieties; he eats something ("Save me some of that mutton.

7. See Kathryn Hume, "The Hidden Dynamics of *The War of the Worlds*," *PQ* 62 (1983): 279–92; Wells developed the connection more forcefully in the serialized version.
8. Norman N. Holland, *The Dynamics of Literary Response* (New York: W. W. Norton, 1975), p. 43.

I'm starving for a bit of meat"—p. 14), and he tells his tale. Holland observes that "a common defense against oral fusion and merger is putting something out of the mouth . . . usually speech" (p. 37).

This fantasy content forecloses many options for plot development. Within the economy of oral anxieties, the subject eats or is eaten; there is no third way. When the Time Traveller finds himself on the Terminal Beach, where nothing appears edible or consumable or exploitable, he cannot assert his status as eater. Evidently, he subliminally accepts power relationships in terms of this binary fantasy, and thus dooms himself to being devoured through sheer default of cultural imagination. His technological magic may permit him to withdraw physically, but psychically, he is more defeated than triumphant at the end. Like his strategic withdrawal from the underworld, his departure is a rout. We note that although he returns home, he does not long remain. He is swallowed up by past or future.[9]

The commonplace assumptions in this text about bodily size undergo equivalent amplifications and distortions that affect the plot. We find elaborate equations between bodily size, intelligence, and bodily energy. Some of these simply reflect the science of the day. Researchers were establishing averages for sizes and weights of male and female brains, and followed many dead-end theories as they tried to prove what they were looking for: superiority of men over women and of whites over darker races. Furthermore, many scientists were convinced that the First Law of Thermodynamics, conservation of energy, applied to mental "energy" as well as physical.

> Food was taken in, energy (including thought) emerged, and the energy was "an exact equivalent of the amount of food assumed and assimilated." In Hardaker's crudely quantitative universe bigger was definitely better, and men were bigger.[1]

If the human race dwindles in size, so will its brain size, so will intelligence, and so will physical energy. Thus much is good science of the day. The text moves from science to symbolism, however, in linking

9. For an argument in favor of the Traveller's being a traditional monomyth hero, and hence triumphant, see Robert J. Begiebing, "The Mythic Hero in H. G. Wells's *The Time Machine,*" *Essays in Literature,* 11 (1984): 201–10. Wells's many escape endings are analyzed by Robert P. Weeks in "Disentanglement as a Theme in H. G. Wells's Fiction," originally published in *Papers of the Michigan Academy of Science, Arts, and Letters* 39 (1954), reprinted in *H. G. Wells: A Collection of Critical Essays,* edited by Bernard Bergonzi (Englewood Cliffs, New Jersey: Prentice-Hall, 1976), pp. 25–31. Interestingly, Wells considered another kind of ending, at least in response to editorial pressures. In the version of this story serialized in *The National Observer,* the story ends with the Traveller referring to hearing his child crying upstairs because frightened by the dark. This *ad hoc* family man, however, may result from hasty termination of the serial. Henley, as editor, liked Wells's work while his replacement, Vincent, did not.
1. For the nineteenth-century science behind all the assumptions about body size and energy, see Cynthia Eagle Russett, *Sexual Science: The Victorian Construction of Womanhood* (Harvard U. Press, 1989), p. 105.

the First and Second Laws of Thermodynamics and implying that energy loss in the universe will directly diminish the mental and physical energy of humanity. Although Wells does not state this explicitly, he apparently accepted it. The loss of culture and security would otherwise have reversed the devolutionary decline as the descendants of humans had once more to struggle for existence. This reason for species degeneration remains implicit, but it clearly follows the fantastic elaboration of ideology and science.

The explicit reason given for degeneration is Darwinian. The Traveller decides that strength and size must have declined because they were no longer needed for survival: "Under the new conditions of perfect comfort and security, that restless energy, that with us is strength, would become weakness. . . . And in a state of physical balance and security, power, intellectual as well as physical, would be out of place" (p. 28). Such a safe society dismays him. He relishes swashbuckling physical action, and is loath to consider a world that would exclude it. Indeed the Morlocks provide him with a welcome excuse to exercise powers not wanted in London. "I struggled up, shaking the human rats from me, and, holding the bar short, I thrust where I judged their faces might be. I could feel the succulent giving of flesh and bone under my blows, and for a moment I was free" (p. 59). "Succulent" is highly suggestive, relating as it does to the realm of the edible.

The equivalence of body, mind, and energy determines major features of the futuristic scenarios. We find something like medieval planes of correspondence. As the cosmos runs down, men will lose energy individually—a linkage no more logical than the Fisher-King's thigh wound causing sterility to fall upon the crops of his realm. Given this as a textual assumption about reality, however, we can see that clever, efficient, and adaptive beings are impossible, although a setting like the Terminal Beach would call forth precisely such a humanity in the hands of other writers.

Gender, the third ideological element, undergoes a different kind of symbolic transformation. The traditional semes of "masculine" and "feminine"—whether culturally derived or natural—are widely familiar and even transcend cultural boundaries. Semes of the masculine include such constellated values as culture, light, the Sun, law, reason, consciousness, the right hand, land, and rulership. The feminine merges with chaos, darkness, the Moon, intuition, feeling, the left hand, water, and the unconscious.[2] The dialogue between them in some cultures involves balance; in the West, however, we find masculine consciousness fighting off or being overwhelmed by

2. In other words, Yin, Yang, and Jung. These symbolic clusters of values are discussed and illustrated throughout both the following Jungian studies by Erich Neumann: *The Origins and History of Consciousness*, Bollingen Series 42 (Princeton U. Press, 1970), and *The Great Mother: An Analysis of the Archetype*, Bollingen Series 47 (Princeton U. Press, 1972).

the feminine powers associated with unconsciousness. Thus the eat-consume-overwhelm nexus also enters the story as an attribute of gender.

Much of what troubles us in the realm of the Sphinx derives its power from the text's manipulation of these values. The grotesque is frequently formed from the mingling of characteristics from two "naturally" separate sets, man and beast, for instance. Despite cultural changes since the turn of the century, the traditional assumptions about gender are well enough ingrained in us by reading, if nothing else, to give the story's grotesques most of their original power. Wells attaches but also denies "feminine" and "masculine" attributes to both Eloi and Morlocks. The resulting contradictions prevent us from resolving the tensions roused by these grotesques into the kinds of reality that we are culturally conditioned to find comfortable.

The Eloi at first appear to be the only race, and then the superior of the two. Their life consists of a pastoral idyll, sunlight, and apparent rulership. Thanks to happiness, beauty, absence of poverty, and uninterrupted leisure, their life better fits our notion of Haves than Havenots. However, closer inspection shows them to be small, lacking in reason, deficient in strength, passively fearful, ineffectual, and ultimately just not "masculine" enough to be plausible patriarchal rulers, the standard against which they are implicitly held. In the *National Observer* version the Eloi have personal flying machines, but Wells ultimately deprived them of anything so technical. For all that they are feminized, however, they lack positive identity with the feminine, so we cannot reconcile them to our sense of the real by means of that pattern.

The Morlocks, by virtue of living in the dark and underground, seem first of all sinister, but secondarily are marked with symbolism of the unconscious and hence the feminine. Their access to the innards of the Sphinx reinforces the latter. Confusing our judgment, however, is their possible control of the machines, a power linked in Western eyes with the masculine rather than the feminine. Likewise, their apparently predatory aggression, their hunting parties (if such they be) fit "masculine" patterns. However, they seem deficient in strength and size to the Traveller, and their inability to tolerate light makes them obviously vulnerable in ways not befitting a "master" race. When comparing the two races, we find that both have traits associated with ruling and exploiting. The Eloi apparently live off the labor of the Morlocks while the latter apparently live off the flesh of the former. However, both are "feminized" in ways that render them less than masterful. These ambiguities in the cultural symbol system cannot be resolved. The traits associated with each race remain in uneasy tension, and contribute to the difficulty that critics have had in putting labels to the two races.

Power, size, and gender; oral fantasies, the laws of thermodynamics as applied to bodies and thought, and the grotesque: this peculiar
mixture propels the story and gives it much of its intensity, its disturbing power. However, these concepts are not entirely consistent
and harmonious. The conflicts they generate undermine the narrative logic and thereby dissolve the coherence of the ideas Wells was
exploring. As we move to the future scenarios, we will note the gaps
in the logic.

In the Riddling Realm of the Sphinx

Almost any way we approach this addled utopia, we find irreducible
ambiguity. Does *The Time Machine* seriously concern a possible—
albeit distant—future, or is futurity only a metaphoric disguise for
the present? Darko Suvin focuses on the biological elements of the
story, so he views the futurity as substantial and important. Others
who focus on entropy or time travel likewise assume the significance
of the futurity.[3] After all, without a real time lapse, anatomical evolution would be impossible. Alternatively, the "future" settings may
be read as versions of Wells's present. "If the novella imagines a
future, it does so not as a forecast but as a way of contemplating the
structures of our present civilization."[4] Social warnings of danger
800,000 years away will inevitably fail to grip. Hence, the reality of
time in this text—Wells's cherished fourth dimensional time—depends
upon whether readers are focusing on biological or social systems.

Even if the critic ruthlessly simplifies to one or the other, interpretations go fuzzy at the edges or lead to contradiction. The biological
reading appears at first to be straightforward. Wells asks, "what
if progress is not inevitable and devolution can happen as well as
evolution?" The Traveller decides that the Eloi degenerate because
they no longer need to fight for survival—an interesting argument to
present to the increasingly non-physical Victorian society. The need
for serious, bodily rivalry makes utopia a dangerous goal, and social
restraint unhealthy. Wells thus raises a genuine problem, but does
not develop it.

The social reading is yet more disturbing in its inability to satisfy
the expectation of coherence. Oppressing the working class is dangerous as well as inhumane, and if we continue along such lines, the
Haves will fall prey to the Havenots. At first glance, this seems like

3. Darko Suvin, *Metamorphoses of Science Fiction: On the Poetics and History of a Literary
   Genre* (Yale U. Press, 1979), chapter 10. For an analysis of time travel, see Veronica
   Hollinger, "Deconstructing the Time Machine," *Science-Fiction Studies* 14 (1987):
   201–21.
4. Huntington, p. 41. Others focusing on social issues include Patrick Parrinder, "*News from
   Nowhere, The Time Machine* and the Break-Up of Classical Realism," *Science-Fiction
   Studies* 3, no. 3 (1976): 265–74, and Wayne C. Connely, "H. G. Well's [sic] *The Time
   Machine*: It's [sic] Neglected Mythos," *Riverside Quarterly* 5, no. 3 (1972): 178–91.

an unexceptionable social warning about mistreating the Workers. Somewhat unexpectedly, Wells treats the situation not as a revolution devoutly to be desired, but as a nightmarish terror. He evidently could not work up much sense of identification with the exploited. Hence the dilemma: not improving conditions leads to nightmare, but improving them in the direction of equality gets us back to utopia and its degeneration. If one accepts the biological message—physical competition—one must ignore the social message; if one accepts the social—improved conditions—one must ignore the biological. Wells offers us no way to accept both.

* * *

What are we to make of this adventure in the realm of the Sphinx, then? A rather mixed message, at best. Utopias by most definitions eliminate competition. This proves a dangerous ideal, because so safe an environment would encourage bodily weakness, and then degeneration of mind and feminization. In other words, beware Socialism! However, the paradise of capitalists is a world in which the Great Unwashed lives underground, its misery unseen and ignored. This too leads to degeneration, as we see, because it also abolishes real struggle. Without the chance or need to compete—literally to destroy or exploit or "consume"—man devolves, according to Wells's ideology. The importance of competition comes out when we realize its relevance to power, size, and masculine behavior patterns, and its status as guarantor of intelligence. This competitive violence appears to be the most consistently upheld value in the first adventure, but even such struggle is undermined by the arguments in the second adventure, the excursion to the Terminal Beach. There entropy, by means of the planes of correspondences, cancels the energizing effect of struggling for existence.

The Terminal Beach: A Journey to the Interior

"Journey to the interior" nicely condenses what happens here. *The Time Machine* as a totality consists of a trip to the interior of some unknown land, as found in *She, Henderson the Rain King, Heart of Darkness*, and *The Lost Steps*. The foray from 800,000 to thirty million years into the future is an embedded journey to the interior, a *mise en abîme* repetition. Call the Terminal Beach a mindscape reached by being eaten. The Traveller enters the Sphinx much as Jonah or Lucian enter their respective whales. Entropy may supply the logic that links the two scenarios, but the emotional unity derives from oral fantasies.

The Terminal Beach actually consists of two scenes and several fractional visions. The crab-infested litoral comes first, then the world in which life lingers in the form of a black, flapping, tentacled "football." The eclipse and snowflakes both belong to the second scene, increasing its inhospitability. However, both form a continuum of desolation and an invitation to despair.

* * *

One's first instinct upon reading the Terminal Beach chapter is to interpret it solely as a funereal rhapsody on entropy, as a look at the inevitable death of the sun and the ramifications of this eventuality for mankind. George H. Darwin provided Wells with ideas about tidal friction and slowed rotation. The Book of Revelation contributes water-turned-blood. These simple transformations, plus the narrator's depression at what he finds, make the bleakness and hopelessness seem natural and inevitable. I would argue that to some degree they are actually cultural and ideological.

One has only to look at *The War of the Worlds* or even *The First Men in the Moon* to see very different fictional responses to apparently dead-end situations. The protagonists in those stories * * * are not foolish optimists, but a bleak and threatening situation is cause for intellectual stimulation, for forming and confirming theories, for taking pride in observing new phenomena, for striving against the environment. The Time Traveller, though, seemingly suffers an entropic loss of his own energy as he observes that life in general has lost the struggle. The point of failure, however, actually came where Wells's thermodynamic fantasy overcame his Darwinian science. When the social system eventually disintegrated, the descendents of Eloi and Morlocks should have improved through survival of the fittest. His assumptions about mind, energy, and body, though, render his fictional creations helpless long before the final scenes. That helplessness was dictated by a fantastic distortion of the laws of thermodynamics, not by the laws themselves, so here again, we find the amplifications and elaborations of basic ideologies affecting plot. Mankind disappears because of one such fantasy; the Traveller's panic takes its form from another.

In superficial regards, *The Time Machine* is obviously enough a social satire to justify our expecting a reasonably coherent warning. The doubled identities of both Eloi and Morlocks turns them into the literary equivalent of an optical illusion. Coherence can no more emerge from them than from Escher's drawing of water flowing downhill in a circle. Scientifically, *The Time Machine* explores entropic decline, but refuses to give us ingenious humanity striving ever more ferociously to put off the inevitable. Humanity has already degenerated irreversibly through the exercise of what is generally considered its higher impulses. Even that would be a warning, but Wells undercuts it with his thermodynamic fantasies, which would bring about similar degeneration in any case through the links he posits among body and mind and energy. Thus do some of the rather fierce undercurrents in this romance break up its arguments, leaving them as stimulating fragments rather than logical structures. The powerful emotions both expressed by the Traveller and generated in readers are tribute to the sub-surface currents, especially the oral-stage anxieties. The torment they represent is most clearly seen in the blind, defensive, totally illogical projection of savagery and cannibalism upon the group most apparently exploited. Like the imperialistic nations fantasizing their own humiliation at the hands of invaders, Wells's Traveller, and possibly Wells himself, are projecting behavior upon others in ways that suggest considerable repressed social guilt.

The return of the repressed is important to the dynamics of this tale. I will finish my arguments with one further variant on that theme. When the Time Traveller seeks the ruler of the pastoral realm, he seeks an Absent Father, and finds instead the Sphinx, avatar of threatening femininity. Within the classical Greek world view, "man" is the proud answer to the Sphinx's riddle, and man as Oedipus vanquishes the feminine and chaotic forces from Western civilization. In *The Time Machine*, "man" is no longer as proud an answer, and man has no power to prevent the lapse from order towards entropy. One might even argue that this time-travelling Oedipus is to some degree the criminal responsible for the status quo, for the ideologies he embodies have limited his culture's vision and rendered alternatives invisible. The Greeks and their civilization based on patriarchal structures banished the Sphinx. Here, she returns, and she succeeds in swallowing humanity after all.

ELAINE SHOWALTER

The Apocalyptic Fables of H. G. Wells[†]

In his book *Going to Miami* (1987), which is about the futuristic ethnic and cultural mix that has developed in Miami as a result of Cuban and Latino immigration, David Rieff expresses his outrage at having to share his flight from Kennedy to Miami with two students from the University of Miami, a 'muscular-looking, blond-downed' white boy and a 'tall black girl'. Although the boy is reading *Dubliners*, Rieff is convinced from overhearing their slangy conversation

† From *Fin de Siècle/Fin du Globe: Fears and Fantasies of the Late Nineteenth Century*, ed. John Stokes (New York: St. Martin's Press, 1992), pp. 69–77. Reprinted by permission of St. Martin's Press.

that 'the copy of Joyce was a bit of protective coloration' and that the students have 'a collective IQ barely above room temperature'. Indeed, they remind him of the post-apocalyptic world divided between 'the perfectly formed, brainless Eloi' and 'a hideous, competent tribe of subterraneans, the Morlocks', in H. G. Wells's *The Time Machine*. As Rieff notes, 'The Morlocks look after the Eloi, and intermittently, pause to eat them, a perfectly sensible arrangement which the traveller (played by Rod Taylor in the fifties film) screws up. These kids across from me, incapable of uttering a humane sentence, were Eloi. There was nothing whatsoever in their heads and . . . I wanted to eat them.'[1]

Armoured in an impervious intellectual snobbery, Rieff is utterly without irony, and he sees nothing awkwardly self-revealing in this burst of Morlockian desire, even later when in the Art Museum of the University of Miami, he is fascinated by a 'heartbreakingly beautiful' blond boy in 'post-apocalyptic cutoffs and faintly radioactive looking orange and green U. of M. T-shirt'. Such erotically compelling and casually dressed people obviously do not belong in museums, any more than they could actually be reading serious literature; and the sophisticated New York editor Rieff is outraged by their presence: 'I wanted to shout "Get out of here, Eloi, go back to your vacation."'[2]

The analogies between Rieff, the postmodern urban intellectual, and the Time Traveller, Wells's fin-de-siècle London scientist, bring uncannily into focus the mingled elements of class conflict, sexual hostility, cannibalistic transgression, racial fantasy, gender confusion, and apocalyptic angst that inhabit both Wells's novella, *The Time Machine* (1895) and his even more sinister story, *The Island of Dr Moreau* (1896). In these stories cannibalism is a major theme, as it would also be in Conrad's *Heart of Darkness* a few years later, signifying the final breakdown of civilised ethics.

The cannibal theme is one element of the fin-de-siècle male quest romance, the *genre* to which Wells's scientific fables and David Rieff's travel narrative both loosely belong. These stories, which flourished in England in the 1880s and 1890s, represent a yearning for escape from a confining society, which is rigidly structured in terms of gender, class, and race, to a mythologised place elsewhere, where men can be freed from the constraints of Victorian morality. In the caves, jungles,

---

1. David Rieff, *Going to Miami* (New York: Penguin, 1987) p. 18 and p. 73.
2. Ibid., p. 73. Some of Rieff's contempt for these students can be attributed to the widespread American stereotype of the University of Miami as a party school for rich surfers. When the comedian Bob Newhart refers to Miami as 'that great seat of learning,' he expects a laugh. It pleases me that the scholar who has written most brilliantly about the parallels between Conrad and Wells is Patrick McCarthy of the University of Miami in 'Heart of Darkness and the Early Novels of H. G. Wells: Evolution, Anarchy, Entropy,' *Journal of Modern Literature*, 13, March 1986.

mountains, beaches, or islands of this other place, the protagonists of male romance explore their secret selves within the framework of what they can safely call the 'primitive'. Because these stories are so closely linked to the restrictive and insular politics of the mother country, Patrick Brantlinger calls them 'imperial Gothic', and sees their main characteristics as 'individual regression, or going native; an invasion of civilisation by the forces of barbarism or demonism; and the diminution of opportunities for adventure and heroism in the real world'.[3]

Moreover, the quest stories all bear an allegorical relation to late Victorian English society. In the 1890s, after the publication of Stanley's *In Darkest Africa*, several English reformers made explicit connections between the exotic and the local. In an eloquent comparison of Stanley's vast African forest, with its pygmies, traders, and cannibals, and the labyrinth of London, with its stunted people and its predators, William Booth, the leader of the Salvation Army, asked: 'As there is a darkest Africa is there not also a darkest England?' Everything that was 'dark, labyrinthine, threatening, and benighted', Deborah Nord notes, could be located in 'the East—whether Burma, India, or the East End of London'.[4] Thus both Wells's Time Traveller and Prendick, the protagonist of *The Island of Dr Moreau*, return to see the nightmares of their voyage reflected in the London streets. This return, usually presented in a framing narrative, is one of the most important elements in the genre, for the world elsewhere is a nightmare projection of the domestic world, a doubling which is most clearly stated in Barrie's *Peter Pan*.

Quest narratives all involve a penetration into the imagined centre of an exotic civilisation, the core, Kôr, *coeur*, or heart of darkness which is a blank place on the map, a realm of the unexplored and unknown. For fin-de-siècle writers, this free space is usually Africa, the 'dark continent', or a mysterious district of the East, a place inhabited by a darker race. Sexual and racial images merged in the mythology of the dark continent and the Orient. 'Just as the various colonial possessions . . . were useful as places to send wayward sons, superfluous populations of delinquents, poor people, and other undesirables,' Edward Said points out in his important study of Orientalism, 'so the Orient was a place where one could look for sexual experience unobtainable in Europe.'[5]

Metaphorically, the dark continent was usually associated with the female body, especially the black female body, with the jungle

3. Patrick Brantlinger, *Rule of Darkness: British Literature and Imperialism, 1830–1914* (Ithaca: Cornell University Press, 1988) p. 231.
4. Deborah E. Nord, 'The Social Explorer as Anthropologist: Victorian Travellers among the Urban Poor,' in *Visions of the Modern City*, ed. William Sharpe and Leonard Wallock (New York: Columbia University Press, 1983) p. 119.
5. Edward Said, *Orientalism* (New York: Vintage, 1979) p. 190.

queen in *Heart of Darkness*, the fatal bride in Kipling's *The Man Who Would Be King*, the black girl on Rieff's flight to Miami. For a psychoanalysis having its roots in the fin de siècle, 'female sexuality', in Freud's notorious epigram, '*is* the dark continent'. Hélène Cixous has argued that the feminine dark continent is a defensive projection of male sexuality, and an evasion of its anxieties:

> Men still have everything to say about their sexuality, and every-thing to write. For what they have said so far, for the most part, stems from the opposition activity/passivity, from the power rela-tion between a fantasised obligatory virility meant to invade, to colonise, and the consequential phantasm of women as a 'dark continent' to penetrate and to 'pacify.' . . . Conquering her, they've made haste to depart from her borders, to get out of sight, out of body. The way man has of getting out of himself and into her whom he takes not for the other but for his own, deprives him, he knows, of his own bodily territory. One might understand how man, confusing himself with his penis and rushing in for the attack, might feel resentment and fear of being 'taken' by the woman, of being lost in her, absorbed or alone.[6]

Yet the quest involves access not only to women but also to other men. For example, in the 'Terminal Essay' to his translation of the *Arabian Nights* (1885–8), Richard Burton had delineated the geog-raphy of a transgressive space he called the 'Sotadic Zone' in which pederasty and perversion held sway. Ranging from the Iberian Peninsula to Italy, Greece, North and Central Africa, Asia Minor, Afghanistan, the Punjab, Kashmir, China, Japan, Turkistan, and the South Sea Islands, the Sotadic Zone became the locus of fin-de-siècle fantasies of the homoerotic, of male societies, or priesthoods where marriages are always morganatic and usually fatal, as in Kipling's *The Man Who Would Be King*.

Indeed, 'the writer of the quest romance,' Joseph Boone writes, 'dealt by definition with a world almost totally devoid of women or heterosexual social regulations, a world in which the exploration of sea or desert provided a fresh and alternate subject for one wishing to rebel against the thematic strictures of the literary marriage tradi-tion'.[7] If the woman's novel at the end of the nineteenth century is primarily about marriage, these men's novels are about 'the flight from marriage'.[8] I would argue that the racial and sexual anxieties

6. Hélène Cixous; 'The Laugh of the Medusa,' in *New French Feminisms*, eds. Elaine Marks and Isabelle de Courtivron (Amherst: University of Massachusetts Press; London: Har-vester, 1987) pp. 245–64, p. 247, n. 1.
7. Joseph Boone, *Tradition Counter Tradition: Love and the Form of Fiction* (Chicago: Uni-versity of Chicago Press, 1987) p. 231.
8. Wayne Koestenbaum, 'A Shadow on the Bed: Dr. Jekyll, Mr Hyde, and the Labouchère Amendment', *Critical Matrix: Princeton Working Papers in Women's Studies*, Spring 1988, 31–55.

displayed in these stories as the vision of the Other, the dark exogamous bride, mask the desire to evade heterosexuality altogether. Real and fictive colonialists, Judith Sensibar brilliantly argues, 'may have sought the wilderness as a place where they could more successfully mask homosexual panic . . . taboos on women . . . were also perhaps a way of avoiding the kinds of threatening encounters they felt forced to seek in the "homophobic" civilised world. In the wilderness they no longer needed to practice compulsory heterosexuality.'[9]

The bachelor heroes of Wells's scientific romances also seek freedom from domestic ties. In 1895, the year in which he wrote *The Time Machine*, Wells divorced his first wife Isabel and married his student, Amy Catherine Robbins. We might read into the Time Traveller's elegiac comments on his feeble Eloi girlfriend Weena, Wells's farewell to the marriage: 'Her distress when I left her was very great, her expostulations at the parting were sometimes frantic, and I think, altogether, I had as much trouble as comfort from her devotions.' (Amy would prove less possessive and tiresome a wife.)

Among the recurrent themes of these narratives are fantasies of replacing heterosexual reproduction with male self-creation. In men's writing of the fin de siècle, celibate male creative generation was valorised, and female powers of creation and reproduction were denigrated. Gerard Manley Hopkins, for example, writes in 1886 that 'the begetting of one's thoughts on paper' is 'a kind of male gift', clearly a gift of begetting that requires no female assistance and avoids contact with the maternal body.[1] In numerous texts, male writers imagined fantastic plots involving alternative forms of male reproduction or self-replication: splitting or cloning, as in *Dr Jekyll and Mr Hyde*; reincarnation, as in Rider Haggard's *She*; transfusion, as in *Dracula*; aesthetic duplication, as in *The Picture of Dorian Gray*; agricultural breeding, as in *The Time Machine*, or vivisection, as in *The Island of Dr Moreau*.

Above all, the quest romances are allegorised journeys into the physical and psychological male self. Their psychological complexity is marked for us by their complicated frame structure, in which a male narrator tells the story to an implied male reader or to a male audience. Structured as stories about men told to men, and organised around the formal and thematic exclusion of women, the romance narrative provided a 'safe arena where late-Victorian readers could approach subjects that were ordinarily taboo'.[2] Foreseeing a time when 'the ancient mystery of Africa will have vanished,' Rider

9. Judith L. Sensibar, 'Edith Wharton Reads the Bachelor Type,' *American Literature*, 60, December 1988, p. 582.
1. *The Correspondence of Gerard Manley Hopkins and Richard Watson*, ed. C. C. Abbott (London: Oxford University Press, 1935) p. 133.
2. See Norman Etherington, *Rider Haggard* (Boston: G.K. Hall) p. 84.

Haggard worried about the fate of the male imagination: 'where will the romance writers of future generations find a safe and secret place . . . in which to lay their plots?'[3]

In *The Time Machine*, H. G. Wells suggested that this safe and secret place might be the future, an infinite terrain of the male imagination which could never be exhausted by mapmakers, colonisers, or women. Like *Heart of Darkness*, *The Time Machine* is a frame narrative told to an audience of allegorised male professionals: the Psychologist, the Provincial Mayor, the Medical Man, the Editor and the Journalist. The Time Traveller is a man of science whose assumptions about the future reflect his political and gender ideologies, his belief in stable class and sex roles, and especially his confidence in masculine scientific rationality. But this confidence is persistently undermined by the world of 802,701. The Time Traveller repeatedly guesses wrong about the social structures of the future.

One of the ironies of the story is the pre-modern machinery available to Wells's imagination. In this era before air travel, the idea of the Time Machine, and the accompanying notions of being stranded in an island of time or castaway on a remote island were soon to be undermined by the air and space ages, of which Wells would be a leading prophet and advocate.

The Time Machine is a famous element in the narrative, a 'glittering metallic framework' with 'ivory in it and some transparent crystalline substance'. It has levers and a saddle, ivory bars, brass rails, and quartz rods, as well as ebony somewhere that makes it in motion a 'whirling mass of black'. Overall it is 'very delicately' and 'very beautifully made'. This fragmented, exotic, and elusive description is generally considered one of Wells's triumphs in the art of modem antirealist narrative. As Frank McConnell comments, 'the machine has been described, but nothing of its precise form has been given. It has . . . been made real without being at all realised.'[4]

Many readers over the century trying to visualise the Time Machine have imagined it as looking something like a bicycle. This impression is fortified by Wells's remark in his preface to the 1931 edition that *The Time Machine* had lasted 'as long as the diamond-framed safety bicycle which came in about the date of its first publication'.[5] In his study of Wells, John Batchelor draws attention to the sexual implications of this bicycle image: 'Cycling was one of Wells's great enthusiasms in the

---

3. '"Elephant Smashing" and "Lion Shooting"' (1894), quoted in Brantlinger, *Rule of Darkness*, p. 239.
4. Frank McConnell, *The Science Fiction of H. G. Wells* (Oxford: Oxford University Press, 1981) p. 82.
5. Preface to Random House edition, quoted in Harry Geduld (ed.), *The Definitive Time Machine* (Bloomington: Indiana University Press, 1987) p. 96, note 27.i

1890s . . . and he saw the bicycle as a revolutionary democratic form of transport which would initiate social change; it was one of the very few activities in which men and women could enjoy each other's company without chaperones.'[6]

The bicycle was indeed one of the new machines of the fin de siècle that seemed to subvert the conventions of sexual difference, and undermine the separation of masculine and feminine spheres. It was strongly identified with the New Woman, both in the pages of *Punch* and in the French magasine *La Plume*. In September 1895, the novelist Victor Jozé attacked the new technology and the new androgyny: 'The bicycle's triumph . . . necessitates an androgynous outfit . . . worn by its adepts of the weaker sex . . . Will we never make our skirted publishers and sociologists in dresses understand that a woman is . . . endowed with other functions by nature than the man with whom she has no business competing in social life? A woman exists only through her ovaries.'[7] (In the equally sexist films, *Back to the Future I, II, III*, the Time Machine is not a bicycle but a DeLorean, an American emblem of failed masculine aspiration.)

A second embodiment of the Time Machine is the moving picture projector. After reading the novel, the inventor Robert Paul wrote to Wells, who conferred with him at his London laboratory. Out of their talks came British Patent No. 19984, 'a novel form of exhibition whereby the spectators have presented to their view scenes which are supposed to occur in the future or past while they are given the sensation of voyaging upon a machine through time'. Paul's motion picture was demonstrated only to a scientific audience; no commercial backers came forward to support it.[8]

The third reading of the Time Machine is as a *machine célibataire* or bachelor machine. The idea of the bachelor machine follows directly from that of the film projector. The term comes from Marcel Duchamp via Michel Carrouges's book *Machines Célibataires*, which describes the literary, artistic and scientific construction between 1850 and 1925 of 'anthropomorphised machines to represent the relation of the body to the social, the relation of the sexes to each other, the structure of the psyche, or the workings of history'. Ranging from Jules Verne to Jean Tinguely, the bachelor machine is 'typically a closed, self-sufficient system. Its common themes include frictionless, sometimes perpetual motion, an ideal time of the magical

6. John Batchelor, *H. G. Wells* (Cambridge: Cambridge University Press, 1985) p. 10.
7. Quoted in Debora L. Silverman, *Art Nouveau in Fin-de-Siècle France* (Berkeley: University of California, 1989) p. 72.
8. Terry Ramsaye, 'Robert Paul and *The Time Machine*,' in Geduld, *The Definitive Time Machine*, p. 196.

possibilities of its reversal, . . . electrification, voyeurism and mas-
turbatory eroticism, the dream of the mechanical reproduction of
art, and artificial birth or reanimation'.[9] Both the Time Machine and
the cinematic apparatus are exemplary bachelor machines.

Furthermore, the bachelor machine has obvious associations with
the male body. Michel de Certeau notes that 'It does not tend to
write the woman . . . the machine's chief distinction is its being
male.' In *The Interpretation of Dreams*, Freud claims 'it is highly
probable that all complicated machinery and apparatus occurring in
dreams stands for the genitals and as a rule the male ones.'[1] In this
vehicle of masculine fantasy the Time Traveller ventures into the
world of 802,701. If the time machine is the emblem of self-fathering,
celibatary reproduction, the White Sphinx of the future represents
another image of reproduction. A pocked and weatherworn colossus, it looms over the world of the future with 'an unpleasant suggestion of disease'. John Huntington sees the White Sphinx as the sign
of Oedipus speculating about the riddle of birth and death, human
and animal, male and female, identity and difference. Half woman
and half lion, the Sphinx is a 'union of sexual opposition', which suggests that experience will go beyond the binary opposites of the Time
Traveller's training.[2]

The most immediate answer to the riddle of sexual differerence
posed by the Sphinx is the split between the Eloi and the Morlocks.
The 'pretty little' Eloi, with their 'little pink hands', consumptive
beauty, vegetarianism, and perpetual leisure, seem hyperfeminised,
and the Time Traveller frequently comments on the absence of sexual difference which he regards as the product of an advanced civilisation: 'Where violence came but rarely and offspring are secure,
there is less necessity . . . for an efficient family and the specialisation of the sexes . . . disappears.'

But this is in fact a world of intense sexual specialisation. When
he penetrates into the underground labyrinths of the Morlocks, the
Time Traveller seems to be leaving the femininity of the surface and
entering the male body itself. He is surrounded by the 'throb and
hum' of machinery, by the 'heavy smell' of blood, and by the sense of
disgusting physical contact. The loathsome Morlocks are one vision
of extreme sexual differentation, beings who are hypermasculinised,

9. Constance Penley, 'Feminism, Film Theory, and the Bachelor Machines,' *The Future of an
    Illusion* (Minneapolis: University of Minnesota Press; London: Routledge, 1989) p. 57.
1. 'Arts de Mourir: Écritures anti-mystiques,' *Les machines célibitaires*, ed. Jean Clair and
    H. Szeeman (Venice: Alfieri, 1975) p. 94; and Sigmund Freud, 'The Interpretation of
    Dreams' (1900), *Standard Edition of the Collected Works*, Volume V (London: Hogarth
    Press, 1955) p. 356.
2. John Huntington, *The Logic of Fantasy* (New York: Columbia University Press, 1982) p. 45.

technological, rapacious, and cannibalistic, embodying both upper-class fears of working-class revolution, and feminist dread of male violence and lust. The world of the Morlocks is a fin-de-siècle leather bar, the Mine Shaft or the Mother Lode. These creatures do not seem to reproduce independently of their raids on the Eloi.

As he contemplates the Sphinx, the Time Traveller asks one of his rhetorical questions: 'What if in this interval the race had lost its manliness and had developed into something inhuman, unsympathetic, and overwhelmingly powerful?' The Oedipal and self-referential riddles of the Sphinx are made more explicit in the Time Traveller's descent to this underworld. He enters it through circular and waterless 'wells . . . of a very great depth,' which he discovers during his explorations of the landscape. 'I thought in a transitory way', he comments, 'of the oddness of wells still existing.' Like Wilde punning on the 'wildness' of Dorian Gray, Wells emphasises the wells that lead into the unconscious, into the subterranean corridors of the creative, violent, and sexual self where the stories start.[3] Furthermore, as John Batchelor points out, the Sphinx's riddles lead directly to the Morlocks, for 'the Sphinx caps one of the shafts leading down to their subterranean world'.[4]

The dark continent of the Morlocks corresponds not only to a guiltily rapacious male sexuality, but also to the writing process, by which, like dreaming, Wells descended into his own unconscious and retrieved primitive images. He described this process in the metaphors of his own fin-de-siècle fiction:

> I found that, taking almost anything as a starting-point, and letting my thoughts play about with it, there would presently come out of the darkness, in a manner quite inexplicable, some absurd or vivid little nucleus. Little men in canoes upon sunlit oceans would come floating out of nothingness, incubating the eggs of prehistoric monsters unawares; violent conflicts would break out amidst the flower beds of suburban gardens; I would discover I was peering into remote and mysterious worlds ruled by an order logical indeed but other than our common sanity.[5]

* * *

3. William Bellamy is the only other critic I have found who notices this pun. See *The Novels of Wells, Bennett and Galsworthy: 1890–1910* (London: Routledge & Kegan Paul, 1971) p. 67.
4. Batchelor, *H. G. Wells*, p. 16.
5. Wells, quoted in Norman and Jeanne Mackenzie, *The Time Traveller: The Life of H. G. Wells* (London: Weidenfeld & Nicolson, 1973) p. 118.

JOHN HUNTINGTON

The Time Machine and Wells's Social Trajectory[†]

As Lionel Stevenson observed almost thirty years ago, H. G. Wells "emerged from the lowest stratum of the middle class, which had previously produced only one major English novelist—Dickens."[1] Wells enthusiasts have tended not to make much of that exceptional origin, but we miss something of Wells's accomplishment if we slight the difficulties of his social trajectory. *The Time Machine* is an important book because it manages to voice Wells's social aspirations and his deep social angers, while still maintaining the decorum required for its author to become a successful writer. It is an intricate stylistic feat, not to be accomplished in a single try.

That the Time Traveller "hated to have servants waiting at dinner" (p. 14) is a clue to the complexity of class awareness behind *The Time Machine*. The comment is one of the remarkably few signs in this parable of class difference of an awareness in the present—that is, in the Time Traveller's 1895—of the powerful social distinctions that will become genetic in the next eight hundred millennia. The remark shows that even before he saw the future and the consequences of class oppression, the Time Traveller had a social conscience. Yet, though he feels some unhappiness about the master-servant relationship, the Time Traveller accepts the privileges of the master position. He salves his conscience by keeping the servants out of sight in certain public rituals, such as meals. Before we hastily condemn him as a hypocrite on this account, however, we need to remind ourselves that the delicate subtleties of class awareness and behavior in eras other than our own are very difficult to reconstruct and evaluate. People born into families with servants—and in 1895 this does not mean only the aristocracy but also people of quite modest economic standing—take servants for granted. Indeed, the Karl Marx family had a servant.[2]

I would suggest that at the end of the nineteenth century, unease with servants waiting at dinner is, in fact, not so much a sign of "conscience" as it is a sign of a person who has been in the servant class. Ann Kipps shares exactly the same sentiment, preferring a house that

---

[†] From *H. G. Wells's Perennial Time Machine*, ed. George Slusser, Patrick Parrinder, and Danièle Chatelain (Athens: University of Georgia Press, 2001), pp. 97–100, 103–06. Reprinted by permission of the University of Georgia Press. References to *The Time Machine, The Chronic Argonauts*, and the *National Observer Time Machine* are to this Norton Critical Edition.

1. Lionel Stevenson, *The History of the English Novel*, Volume 11, *Yesterday and After* (New York: Barnes and Noble, 1967), p. 11.
2. The much beloved Helene ("Lenchen") Demuth. See Franz Mehring, *Karl Marx: The Story of His Life*, trans. Edward Fitzgerald (1935; reprint, New York: Humanities, 1962), p. 174.

does not require servants at all.[3] The Time Traveller is working out a difficult negotiation with what Pierre Bourdieu would label his *habitus*; a transposable set of expectations and values that one internalizes early in life and which one brings to bear in new social and economic situations.[4] The Time Traveller's upbringing has conditioned him to rise in class, but he has difficulty behaving the way people born to the higher position do. And Wells himself, here in his first published novel, is working out a similar difficulty. The nervousness about how servants should be handled is Wells's as much as the Time Traveller's. The position of privilege, to which Wells very much aspires and ultimately receives due to the success of *The Time Machine,* is also, thanks to his disadvantaged upbringing, an object of resentment.

For many years it has been commonplace to discuss Wells's hostility toward the working class.[5] The fear of, and antipathy toward, the Morlocks is taken as an expression of this class attitude. But we miss much of Wells's complexity and power if we simplify his attitudes into simple positives and negatives. His attitude toward the Morlocks as expressed in the text itself is a very complicated one, mixed, as I have suggested elsewhere, with sexual and sadistic feelings.[6] Now I want to pursue this question further by asking what "fear of the working class" might mean *socially*. I should note that arguments for Wells's class attitude often refer to the underground servants' quarters at Uppark. But underground is an emotionally double-valued icon: if it identifies a contemptible social inferiority, it also identifies a source of deep and righteous anger. Anthony West speaks of Wells's outrage at first seeing the underground quarters about which his mother had boasted:[7] such rage is evidence of sympathy rather than

---

3. H. G. Wells. *Kipps: The Story of a Simple Soul* (New York: Scribner's, 1924), p. 386.
4. To understand Wells's own social practice I propose to rely on some basic concepts of Pierre Bourdieu, who seems to me our most acute and important analyst of the sociology of culture. Three of Bourdieu's terms that I find particularly useful (in addition to the emphasis on *practice*) are: *habitus*, which accounts for how attitudes appropriate to the class of origin persist in new class situations; *distance from necessity*, a synonym in many cases for *wealth* but nuanced to allow for various kinds of wealth and various stances; and *misrecognition*, for Bourdieu the reason style has social importance, since the injustice of the social system could never seem so rational were it not that style transforms and disguises the material facts. *Misrecognition* is something like *ideology*, and it accounts for Wells's conscious and resolute rejection of class. These terms recur throughout Bourdieu's work, but the central text for the present analysis is *Distinction: A Social Critique of the Judgment of Taste*, trans. Richard Nice (Cambridge: Harvard University Press, 1984).
5. Bernard Bergonzi, *The Early H. G. Wells* (Manchester: Manchester University Press, 1961), p. 56; Darko Suvin, *Metamorphoses of Science Fiction* (New Haven: Yale University Press, 1979), p. 240; Alex Eisenstein, "Very Early Wells: Origins of Some Major Physical Motifs in The Time Machine and The War of the Worlds," *Extrapolation* 13 (1972), 119–26.
6. See my *The Logic of Fantasy: H. G. Wells and Science Fiction* (New York: Columbia University Press, 1982), p. 44.
7. Anthony West, *H. G. Wells: Aspects of a Life* (New York: Random House, 1984), pp. 226–27. West's meditation on Uppark is complex and includes Wells's anger at his mother's acceptance of servitude and her willingness to commit Wells himself to such a life along with a more general critique of the serene injustice implicit in the architecture of the house.

horror and fear. To settle Wells's attitude by quoting out of context Bernard Bergonzi's statement that he "disliked and feared the working class"[8] is to oversimplify and thereby distort a very intricate and conflicted social moment and to obscure an important aspect of *The Time Machine*'s success.

By turning class difference into species difference, Wells both foregrounds the fact of class separation, making *The Time Machine* one of the great statements of social outrage, and hides the way class actually operates. This contradiction runs through Wells's work and, I would suggest, defines one of the special qualities of his art. It is also a particularly difficult issue to deal with because Wells himself, even as he depicted class issues in his fiction, persistently sought to deny the importance of class as a meaningful analytical category. He repeatedly expressed irritation at Marx for basing his theories on class hostility.[9] We need to realize that Wells's denial of class is itself a social strategy and that at this point Wells himself cannot help us theoretically. In *Kipps*, Arthur Kipps's experience is generalizable: a person coming from low on the social scale, however wealthy he or she may become, can never be comfortable in anything but very modest circumstances. Wells knows from his own experience how class background (*habitus*) complicates success. Yet, if his success is to be rewarding and worth the effort, Wells cannot accept Kipps as his model. His denial of the reality of class may well be a way of assuring himself that it is possible to rise out of his class of origin. In this reading, *Kipps* is an exorcism of sorts, written when Wells himself was safely famous.

In 1894, when he is finishing *The Time Machine*, Wells is in the midst of an enormous social gamble. We should take very seriously his remark to Elizabeth Healey as *The Time Machine* was about to appear in the *New Review*: "It's my trump card and if it does not come off very much I shall know my place for the rest of my career."[1] To "know one's place" conventionally means to accept one's class position and to give up ambitions of rising in class. *The Time Machine* is, in fact, a gambit in Wells's strategy to escape his mother's class. As such, it can never ignore class even as it is careful never to be "vulgar" about class by mentioning it in a resentful way.

---

8. Bergonzi, p. 56. Bergonzi remarks that Wells "had disliked and feared the working class in a way wholly appropriate to the son of a small tradesman." A sign of how such social dynamics can be misunderstood later is that in Harry Geduld's introduction to *The Definitive Time Machine*, this passage is twice misquoted and the fear and dislike are said to be "wholly *in*appropriate" (*The Definitive Time Machine*, ed. Harry M. Geduld [Bloomington: Indiana University Press, 1987], pp. 3, 21).
9. H. G. Wells, *Experiment in Autobiography* (New York: Macmillan, 1934), pp. 143, 207, 215, 626.
1. This letter is often quoted. See Bernard Loing, *H. G. Wells à l'oeuvre: Les débuts d'un écrivain* 1894–1900 (Paris: Didier, 1984), pp. 416–17; Bergonzi, p. 40; Geduld, p. 7.

Vulgarity is itself a complex and interesting social judgment. It ingeniously turns plain speaking and a refusal to participate in the euphemisms that hide the violence of culture and by which a society rationalizes its structure and distinctions (Bourdieu terms these euphemisms "misrecognitions") into social gaffes.[2] Any analysis of social differences, insofar as it exposes misrecognitions that constitute the language and style with which the game of culture is played, will risk vulgarity. Vulgarity is a social crime not because it is false— quite the contrary!—but because those who employ it bluntly refuse to play the game. Yet the charge of vulgarity is more potent than the accusation of falsehood, and any aspiring writer will take great pains to avoid the charge.

By writing a popular story about class catastrophe, Wells is playing a risky and delicate game. Even as it tells an angry and vengeful parable of the consequences of class division, *The Time Machine* avoids appearing vulgar about class by ignoring—except for the very brief and casual mentions of servants—class division in the present. Paradoxically, by talking about class difference in terms of species, Wells obviates the most subtle dimension of the class issue: style, which would upset his audience and would cause him the most anxiety. The Morlocks may be lower class by their genealogy, but they are identified symbolically rather than realistically. They are creatures from a zoo, not people from a slum. One reason it takes the Time Traveller a while to realize the nature of the situation is that the Morlocks do not immediately suggest a class style. The Eloi, on the contrary, as others have frequently observed, are depicted somewhat more precisely in terms of fin-de-siècle aesthetic icons.[3] The elegant upper class aestheticism is a sign of the mocker's own superiority. If by making the Morlocks inhuman Wells evades the vulgarity of depicting lower-class style, by making the criticism of the Eloi stylistic he avoids the opposite vulgarity of seeming to resent upper-class privilege. *The Time Machine*, thus, may explicitly raise the issue of class division and oppression, but it sanitizes it with an allegory of sorts. It does not commit the vulgarity of showing the lower classes as they are. The actual servants are kept out of sight.

* * *

The utopian space of the Time Traveller's parlor is balanced against the appalling divisions of the grim 802,701 pastoral. This stylistic economy, which involves matching generic styles and narrative

2. Bourdieu himself is very concerned with the problem of vulgarity. At the very beginning of *Distinction*, he addresses the way the accusation of vulgarity is commonly used to deny the importance of sociological insights. And he concludes *Distinction* with an essay entitled "A Vulgar Critique of Pure Critiques," in which he argues that philosophizing itself (his main examples are Kant and Derrida) is a social strategy.

3. Bergonzi, pp. 49–50.

oppositions, did not come quickly or easily to Wells. It is an important invention that evolves somewhat awkwardly through the different drafts of *The Time Machine*. In its evolution, we can see Wells the artist solving the problem of how to give voice to his strong class awareness without losing the gamble with fame by becoming vulgar.

A crucial change between Wells's first version of the novel, "The Chronic Argonauts," and *The Time Machine* is in the motive for time travel. Dr Nebogipfel, the Time Traveller in the very first version, is, by contrast, a mad, driven scientist of the Frankensteinian tradition.[4] Time travel is, for him, a desperate necessity. In the midst of his explanations of time, Dr Nebogipfel tells the Reverend Elijah Ulysses Cook the story of "The Ugly Duckling" in pointed detail:

> Even when I read that simple narrative for the first time, a thousand bitter experiences had begun the teaching of my isolation among the people of my birth—I knew the story was for me. The ugly duckling that proved to be a swan, that lived through all contempt and bitterness, to float at last sublime. [. . .] In short, Mr Cook, I discovered that I was one of those superior Cagots called a genius—a man born out of my time. [. . .] (p. 90)

The anachronistic man is analogous to the lower-class man who feels his "isolation among the people of [his] birth" and resolves to escape. The anguish we hear in this passage is, importantly, absent from the final version. The Time Traveller is in a utopian situation, and he invents time travel the way an author invents a story, as a display of ingenuity, as a paradox befitting a cultivated parlor. He is motivated by a pure intellectual drive, not the kind of ugly-duckling loneliness of which the Doctor complains. As Wells rewrites the story, the anguishing consequences of class division become distanced (in time and in urgency), and the true utopia of the tale becomes not some future world hospitable to genius but that 1895 parlor in which all men are economically indistinguishable and the only criterion of discrimination is intelligence.

In the *National Observer* version of *The Time Machine* we can see how nervous Wells is about bringing up class at all. It is significant that here, in his first rendering of the Eloi-Morlock split, he explicitly denies its class basis.[5]

> I do not mean any split between working people and rich— families drop and rise from toil to wealth continually—but

---

4. Bergonzi, p. 35, first noted the Frankensteinian aspects of Nebogipfel and the importance of the ugly duckling story.
5. Here the year is 12,203, a good deal earlier than the final version's 802,701. Loing, p. 91, suggests that at this point Wells had not thought of the final interpretation and that is why the *National Observer* version is "slightly different" ("en des termes légèrement différents").

between the sombre, mechanically industrious, arithmetical, inartistic type, the type of the Puritan and the American millionaire and the pleasure-loving, witty, and graceful type that gives us our clever artists, our actors and writers, some of our gentry, and many an elegant rogue. (p. 115)

In this early version of *The Time Machine*, Wells even goes so far as to suggest that servitude may be a chosen condition, lamenting "the deep reasonless instincts that keep man the servant of his fellow man" (p. 115). Only in the *New Review* version of *The Time Machine* does Wells come out and interpret the split between Eloi and Morlock as originating precisely and explicitly in class exploitation. Such change suggests not intellectual growth or confusion but social anxiety. The point is that Wells is both animated by class anger and unsure about his ability to "pass" as cultivated. The *National Observer* version is an attempt to deny the class anger that has created the fantasy. The great accomplishment of *The Time Machine* we are familiar with is its success in overcoming the inhibitions of the earlier version while maintaining the tone of objective neutrality. That neutrality is the great gamble of *The Time Machine*: Wells puts his success as a science writer, who speaks soberly in that special realm of technical discourse in which class is irrelevant,[6] to work in fiction, a discourse in which issues of class are inescapable. In terms of the traditions of literature, this strategy is the opposite of Poe, whose Dupin aspires to a literary place by emphasizing his extraordinary competence in the art of allusion (think of the importance of his familiarity with Crebillon). Wells, who is well-read in the English and French literary classics, works with a palette almost entirely devoid of explicit allusion. The exception, to be sure, is the White Sphinx. But the final obscurity of that allusion may paradoxically testify to the nonliterary nature of Wells's narrative.

Bernard Loing has described this style well: it is free from specific ideology, a prose that describes physical realities and immediate sensations.[7] What I want to emphasize is the way the style conceals Wells's deepest concerns while rendering a tale that speaks to them with a power and an anger that he himself will publicly deny. It is this style that prevents the descriptions of the Morlocks from being only an expression of hostility to proletarians, even as it prevents the descriptions of the Eloi from being simply a W. H. Hudson–like erotic fantasy. In its striking surface neutrality, so different from

6. Bourdieu argues (especially in Pierre Bourdieu and Jean-Claude Passeron's *Reproduction in Education, Society, and Culture*, trans. Richard Nice [London: Sage, 1990], pp. 107–38) that the scientific fields are the choice of lower class students because they do not depend on the preliminary education into subtleties of allusion and style that are available only to students from privileged educations and family backgrounds.
7. Loing, p. 55.

Poe's extravagance, this style allows Wells to sympathize with the generally repulsive Morlocks and to feel a profound lack of interest in the Eloi, a lack of interest that becomes contempt.

Despite the openness about class that Wells achieves in *The Time Machine*, there are still moments when he blurs what for a moment seem clear formulations. Bourdieu's "distance from necessity," his measure of economic rank and security, in a rather remarkable way echoes a concern that recurs a number of times late in *The Time Machine*. The Time Traveller explains that it is necessity, that grim grindstone, that keeps us keen. What is telling in the present context is that in his final theory of the *value* of "Mother Necessity" (p. 62) the Time Traveller opens the way to a critique of the dominant and leisure classes and then deflects it. No sooner has he suggested a class criticism than he shifts to apply it to the whole system, to all classes. "I understood now what all the beauty of the Upper-world people covered" (p. 61) might seem an insight into the dialectic of class domination whereby domination weakens the dominators and strengthens the dominated. But instead it turns into a critique of the complacency of the whole culture: "Once, life and property must have reached almost absolute safety. The rich had been assured of his wealth and comfort, the toiler assured of his life and work. No doubt in that perfect world there had been no unemployed problem, no social question left unsolved. And a great quiet had followed" (p. 61).

Despite what he says here, some part of Wells cannot believe this world of the secure rich and the permanently employed toiler is stable and "perfect." At another time the Time Traveller will begin to indulge in a specific criticism of the upper classes:

> Then I tried to preserve myself from the horror that was coming upon me, by regarding it as a rigorous punishment of human selfishness. Man had been content to live in ease and delight upon the labours of his fellow man [here the complacency of "the toiler assured of his life and work" is exploded], had taken Necessity as his watchword and excuse, and in the fulness of time Necessity had come home to him. I even tried a Carlyle-like scorn of this wretched aristocracy in decay. (p. 50)

But again, the class criticism is deflected, this time by sympathy:

> But this attitude of mind was impossible. However great their intellectual degradation, the Eloi had kept too much of the human form not to claim my sympathy, and to make me perforce a sharer in their degradation and their Fear. (p. 50)

In this shift away from class back to species, we see exactly Wells's own double consciousness as he aspires to become a successful writer. He is filled with anger at the inequalities that his mother accepted, but his ambitions are not revolutionary or anarchistic. Success as a writer means becoming a member of the dominant class he condemns, and it is important to his conception of success that the social structure, so offensive at one level, remain in place so that he can secure his "place" in it. . . .

PAUL A. CANTOR AND PETER HUFNAGEL

The Empire of the Future: Imperialism and Modernism in H. G. Wells[†]

H. G. Wells's scientific romances of the 1890s are remarkably innovative in form and subject matter, and the first in the series, *The Time Machine*, may be the most original of them all. It virtually inaugurated the genre of science fiction, and has been shamelessly imitated by aspiring authors in the field ever since. And yet as forward-looking as Wells's first novel is, it is deeply rooted in the Victorian era. As we shall see, in *The Time Machine*, he takes us 800,000 years into the future, and he finds the Victorian class system still intact. Its extremes have of course been exaggerated, but, as many commentators have noted, in the Eloi and the Morlocks, we can still recognize Disraeli's "two nations," the rich and the poor of Victorian England. But another Victorian aspect of *The Time Machine* has not been as thoroughly analyzed—the way in which Wells drew upon his experience of the British Empire to shape his vision of the future. And yet some of the most modern and even modernist aspects of *The Time Machine* grow out of precisely this engagement with the very Victorian theme of empire. . . .

Wells's many false starts and the number of versions he went through before he published *The Time Machine* as we know it testify to the difficulty of his enterprise.[1] It is therefore understandable that when he was trying to imagine a journey into the future, he ended up modeling it on something more familiar, a journey to the imperial frontier. Imperialist narratives—either factual or fictional—became very popular in Britain in the nineteenth century, and had reached the level of a fad in the mid-1880s with the publication of H. Rider

---

† From *Studies in the Novel* 38.1 (Spring 2006): 36–46, 49–51. Reprinted by permission of the University of North Texas. References to *The Time Machine* are to this Norton Critical Edition.

1. For the complicated history of the composition of *The Time Machine* and an account of the many versions Wells went through, see Geduld 5–9 and Ruddick 22–30.

Haggard's bestsellers, *King Solomon's Mines* and *She*. Drawing upon Robert Louis Stevenson's *Treasure Island*, Haggard crystallized the form of the imperialist romance as a journey to a remote corner of European dominion, where a group of intrepid British explorers encounter an exotic civilization, with strange and often bizarre customs that seem the antithesis of the European way of life.

This formula would in itself have been useful to Wells, preparing as he was to create a new form of exoticism in his first science fiction novel. But Haggard prepared the way for Wells even further by adding a new twist to the imperialist romance, or at least highlighting an element that had been latent in the form. In *King Solomon's Mines* and *She* the journey to the imperial frontier becomes a journey into the past; for Haggard space travel becomes time travel. That is, in both works Haggard's British heroes leave the world of modern Europe behind and enter what he views as a historically backward land. Haggard's British heroes are associated with modern science and technology, whereas the African natives they encounter are associated with magic and superstition. Indeed the British use their scientific knowledge and their modern weapons to awe the African natives into submission. Moreover, the British explorers represent the principles of modern politics as Haggard understands them—limited government and the rule of law—whereas the African natives represent the principles of the old regime, autocracy and the rule of priests and witches. Thus in Haggard the journey to the imperial frontier becomes imaginatively a journey into the past of Europe. That is why Haggard goes out of his way to link contemporary Africa to the ancient heritage of Europe, finding Biblical connections with the African civilization in *King Solomon's Mines* and Egyptian and Classical Greek connections with the one in *She*.

Haggard's fiction thus reveals the peculiar way in which the imperialist expansion of Europe in the nineteenth century opened up the imaginative possibility of time travel. The relentless European drive to occupy all corners of the earth made it for the first time a regular occurrence for cultures at very different stages of historical development to come into contact and be forced to co-exist. Travelers to remote corners of empire often had the impression that they were entering the world of the past. Perhaps the most famous literary expression of this feeling can be found in Conrad's *Heart of Darkness*, where Marlow views his voyage up the Congo as a journey into a prehistoric age: "Going up that river was like travelling back to the earliest beginnings of the world" (Conrad 35). All Wells had to do was reverse this perspective and imagine how things might look going in the opposite direction in order to come up with the possibility of journeying to the future. *The Time Machine* begins with a remarkable anticipation of Einstein and Minkowski (Russell 54–55), as Wells has his hero articulate a theory of four dimensions and in particular the equivalence of time and space: *"There is no difference between Time and any of the three dimensions of Space except that our consciousness moves along it"* (p. 6). Thus Wells's theory of time travel rests on the idea that it is only a form of space travel, or as Wells has his hero put it: "Time is only a kind of Space" (p. 7). If time travel as space travel is the formula for Wells's first novel, then he is following a path already adumbrated by Rider Haggard in *King Solomon's Mines* and *She*. We do not wish to call into question Wells's genuine originality in *The Time Machine*—only to point out that to the extent that he had any experiential basis for time travel it was provided by the imperialist romances spawned by the expansion of the British Empire in the nineteenth century.

This hypothesis is borne out by the actual form the plot of *The Time Machine* takes. In many respects Wells's book is simply a Rider Haggard romance in science fiction dress and his hero is a sort of Richard Burton or Henry Stanley of the future. The imperialist coloring of Wells's scientific romance is perhaps most clearly evident in the nature of the natives the Time Traveller meets. The Eloi and the Morlocks are of course, as we have already suggested, based on the social divisions of the Victorian Britain Wells knew (Stover 4–12). But they also come straight out of the pages of imperialist romance; they are the two tribes the European explorer usually meets when he enters a strange land: a good tribe and an evil tribe.[2] The good tribe is peaceful, docile, and friendly to the explorers; indeed it demonstrates its goodness by its willingness and even eagerness to submit to European rule. The evil tribe is beastly, warlike, and hostile to the explorers; far from being submissive to European rule, it tries to kill the explorers, and sometimes even to eat them (the evil tribe is frequently marked as cannibalistic). This archetype in imperialist literature can be traced back at least as far as Defoe's *Robinson Crusoe*, where Friday plays the role of the good, submissive native and Crusoe has to save him from a group of evil cannibals. Whatever the origins of this motif, it clearly flourished in nineteenth-century imperialist romances. In *King Solomon's Mines*, for example, Haggard's British heroes ally themselves with a good faction of natives against an evil faction, as they seek to restore the rightful ruler of an African people to a throne occupied by a villainous usurper, and thereby to establish a European form of rule of law in place of native autocracy. Since imperialist romances generally sought to provide an ideological justification for European rule over non-Europeans, the reason

---

2. For the way Wells drew upon accounts of African exploration in creating the "tribes" of the Eloi and the Morlocks, see Pagetti 123. Pagetti points out that in his book *In Darkest England* (1890), General William Booth had drawn parallels between African tribes and the urban poor in London (Booth 11–12).

for the "two tribes" motif is obvious. If the natives are docile, they are asking to be ruled by Europeans; if they are warlike and even cannibalistic, they cannot be trusted to rule themselves and must still be brought under European control.

Wells's Morlocks seem to have been ordered up by central casting to play the role of the evil tribe in his romance. They are several times referred to as "ape-like" and the Time Traveller speaks of "how nauseatingly inhuman they looked" (p. 45). And of course the Time Traveller's shocking discovery about the Morlocks is that they feed upon the Eloi, which, in view of their common descent from human beings, makes the Morlocks cannibals (Wells's hero compares them to "our cannibal ancestors" p. 50). In his visceral revulsion against the Morlocks, the Time Traveller allies himself with the Eloi, who are equally suited to play the role of the good tribe of imperialist romance. Wells's hero describes them as docile: "there was something in these pretty little people that inspired confidence—a graceful gentleness, a certain childlike ease" (p. 21). The non-European natives in imperialist romance are frequently pictured as children as part of the attempt to portray Europeans as their natural superiors, and the Time Traveller picks up the same motif: "I felt like a schoolmaster amidst children" (p. 24). In an archetypal scene from imperialist romance, the Eloi even take Wells's hero for a god descended from the sky:

> Then one of them suddenly asked me a question that showed him to be on the intellectual level of one of our five-year-old children—asked me, in fact, if I had come from the sun in a thunderstorm! . . . I nodded, pointed to the sun, and gave them such a vivid rendering of a thunderclap as startled them. They all withdrew a pace or so and bowed. (p. 22)

The Eloi conform to a specific archetype of the good native in imperialist romance, what might be called the "South Seas Islander" motif. As if they had stepped out of a Gauguin painting, they appear to live in a kind of paradise, where all things are held in common and enjoyed without labor: "There were no hedges, no signs of proprietary rights, no evidences of agriculture; the whole earth had become a garden" (p. 26). Later the Time Traveller's description of the Eloi even more clearly resembles the kind of South Seas idyll European travelers liked to conjure up: "They spent all their time in playing gently, in bathing in the river, in making love in a half-playful fashion, in eating fruit and sleeping" (p. 35). The "eroticism" (p. 28) of the Eloi particularly links them with places like Tahiti and Samoa in the European colonial imagination, especially in one scene the Time Traveller describes: "two of the beautiful Upper-world people came running in their amorous sport across the daylight into the shade. The male pursued the female, flinging flowers at her as he ran" (p. 39).

The mention of eroticism leads us to another familiar motif from imperialist romance that Wells drew upon, the love affair between the European explorer and a native woman. In what might be labeled the "Pocahontas motif," the European explorer typically falls in love with a native woman, who comes to embody all that is submissive in the good tribe. She is totally devoted to the explorer, caters to his every desire, and in particular often supplies him with the information he needs to survive in the strange world he has entered. All that attracts the European explorer to the exotic non-European world becomes concentrated in the figure of his native lover, who threatens to seduce him away from his European way of life and get him to go native. In the racial discourse that is basic to imperialist romance, the native woman poses the threat of miscegenation. She therefore usually has to be killed off by the end of the story, in order to free the explorer to return to Europe and perhaps even to a racially suitable European fiancé or wife. Often the native woman must sacrifice her life to save the explorer in a gesture that validates the superiority of the European to the non-European. *King Solomon's Mines* offers a textbook example of the Pocahontas motif in the romance between John Good and the Kukuana woman Foulata. In a variant of the motif, Rider Haggard made it the center of his plot in *She* in the romance between Leo Vincey and Ayesha.[3] The motif survives in the sophisticated imperialist narratives of Conrad; it is at the heart of *Lord Jim*, for example, in the hero's love for Jewel and can even be detected in *Heart of Darkness* in the juxtaposition of Kurtz's native mistress with his Intended back in Belgium.

The Eloi woman Weena is of course the Pocahontas of *The Time Machine*. Given the physical and mental feebleness of the Eloi, she cannot be of much help to the Time Traveller, and in fact their romance begins when he has to save her from drowning. But almost as if he has been reading imperialist romances himself, the Time Traveller expects Weena to perform the usual role of the native informant when he turns to her to translate a puzzling inscription: "I thought, rather foolishly, that Weena might help me to interpret this, but I only learned that the bare idea of writing had never entered her head" (p. 51). But although she lacks the competence of the typical female companion of imperialist romance, Weena makes up for it by her total devotion to the Time Traveller:

> She received me with cries of delight and presented me with a big garland of flowers—evidently made for me and me alone. . . .
> The creature's friendliness affected me exactly as a child's

3. That Wells was quite aware of this pattern in imperialist romance is evident from the fact that he makes fun of it in his May 30, 1896, *Saturday Review* comment on Haggard's *Heart of the World* (Parrinder and Philmus 98).

might have done. We passed each other flowers, and she kissed
my hands. . . . She was exactly like a child. She wanted to be
with me always. She tried to follow me everywhere. (p. 35)

Weena is a perfect distillation of the childish character of the natives
that makes them subject to European rule, and indeed the Time
Traveller assumes that she wants him to have dominion over her.
Accordingly he becomes tempted by the prospect of a kind of
intertemporal miscegenation: "Weena I had resolved to bring with
me to our own time" (p. 51). Thus, following the logic of imperialist
romance, Wells has to kill off his native heroine—she apparently
dies in a forest fire ironically set by the Time Traveller himself.[4]

If the fate of Weena is not enough to establish that Wells was following the pattern of imperialist romance in *The Time Machine*, one
might point to a really unexpected element in the book that cannot
otherwise be explained—its orientalism. Orientalism is the tendency
for the West to define itself in opposition to the East in a series of
binaries that always place the West on top: reason vs. passion, science vs. superstition, representative government vs. despotism, and
so on (Said 40). We have already seen how these binary oppositions
are at work in imperialist romances such as *King Solomon's Mines*
and *She*; it is necessary only to point out that the supposedly inferior
characteristics of the non-European natives in these stories are
clearly associated with the East. Recalling that in the nineteenth
century the "orient" began with the Levant, what we would call the
Middle East today, we can see that the way Haggard associates his
Africans with figures out of the Bible and ancient Egypt stamps
them as "oriental." It is thus significant that virtually the first object
the Time Traveller sees when he arrives in the future is a giant
sphinx.[5] The sphinx of course suggests Egypt and was a chief symbol
of the East in the British colonial imagination.

Confronted with the strangely easternized world of the future, the
Time Traveller defines himself in opposition to it as a Westerner:
"I was too Occidental for a long vigil" (p. 32).[6] Wells's hero views
himself as active in contrast to the passive Eloi—exactly one of the
binary oppositions by which the West sought to distinguish itself from
the East. Just like the explorers in *King Solomon's Mines*, the Time
Traveller finds "suggestions of old Phœnecian decorations" (p. 22) in

---

4. There is some question about the exact manner of Weena's death, but most commentators assume that she died in the fire. Wells's carelessness about this important detail in a
sense reveals the generic character of the event; Wells knows that according to the formula of imperialist romance, Weena must die; he does not trouble himself too much over
how it happens.

5. For a variety of interpretations of this sphinx, see Stover 2–4, Hammond 78, and Geduld,
101–102 (n.12).

6. For the importance of Wells's use of the word *occidental* here, see Stover 87 (n. 112),
Geduld 105 (n. 6), and Pagetti 125.

the buildings he observes.[7] He names the most impressive structure he finds "the Palace of Green Porcelain" and remarks that "the façade had an Oriental look: the face of it having the lustre, as well as the pale-green tint, a kind of bluish-green, of a certain type of Chinese porcelain" (p. 42). Even the plants in Wells's future are "pagoda-like" (p. 25).[8] What makes the orientalizing touches in *The Time Machine* all the more interesting is that Wells is at the same time mapping the landscape against the familiar contours of Greater Metropolitan London. When the Time Traveller correlates his movements with such locations as "Wimbledon" (p. 48), "Battersea" (p. 51), and "South Kensington" (p. 52), one is tempted to get out a London tube map in order to follow the action. The result is that Wells is not just orientalizing the future; he is orientalizing the future of *Britain*. In this respect, *The Time Machine* is truly prophetic, although a glance at London today would suggest that Wells was off by about 800,000 years in his prediction of when the city would take on an Eastern look.

In a weird way, then, Wells anticipates one of the principal motifs of postcolonial literature, the idea that the Empire Strikes Back.[9] In the course of its imperialist expansion in the nineteenth century, Britain believed that it was conquering the world, but in certain respects it actually surrendered to the forces it assumed it had under its control. Britain thought that it was imposing its language, its literature, its educational system, and other British traditions on its colonial subjects—and to some extent it surely was—but at the same time they had almost as much impact in changing Britain as Britain had in changing them. The way the English language has absorbed words with Indian, African, and Caribbean origins is one measure of this countermovement. One might also cite the way writers from the periphery of the Empire moved to the center of the English literary tradition in the twentieth century, beginning with Rudyard Kipling and continuing down to Salman Rushdie. In both his fiction and his essays, Rushdie has documented how Britain's colonial subjects have worked to transform the mother country of the Empire.[1] His *Satanic Verses* portrays the experience of so-called Third World immigrants in Britain, and one of the novel's themes is the orientalizing

7. In the corresponding moment in *King Solomon's Mines*, Sir Henry Curtis observes several giant statues and comments: "Perhaps these colossi were designed by some Phœnecian official who managed the mine" (Haggard 259).
8. See Geduld 110–11 (n. 4) for an account of Wells's experience of pagodas in London, at the Victoria and Albert Museum, the Royal Albert Hall, and the Royal Botanical Gardens at Kew.
9. On this general subject, see Ashcroft, et al.
1. See, for example, a number of essays in Rushdie's *Imaginary Homelands*, including the title essay, "The New Empire Within Britain," and "*Hobson-Jobson*."

of London—the way the very food that Londoners eat has taken on an Eastern flavor.

The many orientalizing touches in *The Time Machine* combine to portray a Britain that has in effect gone native, that has succumbed to the seductive forces it hoped to subdue on the imperial frontier. Going native was one of the great fears of imperial Britain. The British Empire based its right to rule its subjects on the claim that the British were disciplined and the natives undisciplined, and therefore only British dominion could maintain order in the colonial lands. But the British continually worried that the example of the free and easy life of the natives would prove too attractive to the British masters sent over to rule them, that the natives would infect the British with their supposed laziness and lack of self-control. The fear of going native seems to stand behind Tennyson's poem "The Lotos-Eaters," which may have provided one of Wells's models for the Eloi. That would suggest that a kind of imperialist anxiety informs Wells's vision of the future of Britain in *The Time Machine*.

We have been talking about the Time Traveller as if he were journeying to the imperial frontier, but now we are suggesting that Wells's genius is to map the imperial frontier back onto the homeland of Britain in *The Time Machine*. One of the ways in which Wells accomplishes this reversal is to tropicalize the Britain of the future; in the words of his hero: "I think I have said how much hotter than our own was the weather of this Golden Age. I cannot account for it. It may be that the sun was hotter, or the earth nearer the sun" (p. 37). The "Golden Age" aspects of the life of the Eloi follow from this change of climate—passing from the temperate to the tropic zone, they get to lead the idyllic existence of South Seas islanders. But in Wells's account, the happiness of the Eloi is purchased at the price of their moral fiber and their intellectual development. One might read this aspect of *The Time Machine* as a comment on the British belief that they were by nature entitled to rule the world. Wells in effect says: "Put the British in a tropical climate and you will soon see the famous British pluck that conquered the world disappear; the British will degenerate to the level of the natives they despise." The British believed that their bracing northern climate made them into a hardier race and assured their ability to conquer any people reared in the enervating environment of a tropical climate. Wells seems to be playing with this notion in *The Time Machine*—if the British really owe their superiority and their imperial conquests to their harsh climate, then meteorological developments over vast stretches of geological time may well fundamentally alter the nature of the British and eventually turn them into a subject race themselves.

Wells thus anticipates the remarkable passage in *The Satanic Verses* in which Rushdie describes the tropicalization of London. Raise the temperature of London, Rushdie suggests, and you will soon see the Londoners loosening up, enjoying "spicier food" and "higher-quality popular music," and even relaxing their sexual inhibitions ("No more British reserve; hot-water bottles to be banished forever, replaced in the foetid nights by the making of slow and odourous love" 355). Rushdie is having fun at the expense of the proverbially uptight British, but he and Wells may be making a similar serious point: the British pride themselves on being British in every sense of the term, but that very Britishness may be more an accident of climate than anything inherent in the British national character. We began by discussing the Time Traveller as the archetypal European encountering non-Europeans on the imperial frontier. But because the country he comes to is in fact Britain, Wells reverses perspectives for his readers, and thus reduces the British to the level of the natives they regard as their natural inferiors. At the end of the nineteenth century, the British seemed to be on top of the world and at the peak of their imperial power. Wells wished to warn his countrymen that they might not remain this powerful forever, and that time in its infinite duration might eventually bring about a reversal of their position of superiority. The revenge of the Morlocks upon the Eloi has been read—quite rightly–as the lower classes of Victorian Britain turning the tables on the upper classes. But viewing *The Time Machine* in the context of imperialism, one might also read the Morlocks as the long oppressed colonial subjects of Britain finally having their revenge on their imperial masters.

Thus *The Time Machine* may be interpreted as a parable of the doom of empire. Looking back to the example of Rome, eighteenth- and nineteenth-century thinkers began to view empires as inevitably going through a cycle of rise and fall. In particular, empires were said to reach a peak of power, and then go into decline precisely because of the stagnation bred by a position of unchallenged supremacy.[2] At their height, empires were said to go soft, eventually leaving them prey to the onslaught of barbarians, who retained their natural energy and aggressiveness.[3] In the Time Traveller's hypothetical account of the development of the Eloi, he seems to have something like this process in mind, especially in the parallels he draws to European history. At one point he says that "the Eloi, like the Carlovingian kings, had decayed to a mere beautiful futility" (p. 46)

2. For an example of this kind of thinking, see Montesquieu's *Considerations on the Causes of the Greatness of the Romans and Their Decline*.
3. For a striking visual representation of this cycle, see Thomas Cole's five paintings entitled "The Course of Empire" (Truettner and Wallach 90–95).

and he later comments: "I even tried a Carlyle-like scorn of this wretched aristocracy in decay" (p. 50). Although the terms of the Time Traveller's analysis of the Eloi's fate are generally economic and biological, at times he speaks like a historian of imperial decline: "the balanced civilisation that was at last attained must have long since passed its zenith, and was now far fallen into decay. The too-perfect security of the Upper-worlders had led them to a slow movement of degeneration, to a general dwindling in size, strength, and intelligence" (p. 41). Although even this passage has a Darwinian ring to it, it is also very much in the spirit of Edward Gibbons's *Decline and Fall of the Roman Empire*, one of Wells's favorite books.[4] Through the historical references in *The Time Machine*, Wells touched a raw nerve in the Victorian sensibility, a widespread fear that Britain might be degenerating the way Rome once did and thus be on the brink of its decline as an imperial power.

Wells conveys a sense of empire in decline in *The Time Machine* in the haunting scene of a museum in ruins: "The tiled floor was thick with dust, and a remarkable array of miscellaneous objects was shrouded in the same grey covering. . . . Clearly we stood among the ruins of some latter-day South Kensington" (p. 52). The South Kensington museum complex in London was a showcase of the British Empire, proudly exhibiting artifacts and natural history specimens brought back to the metropolitan center from all around the globe.[5] Thus Wells can powerfully suggest the fall of the British Empire by showing such an imperial museum in ruins.[6] But Wells deploys an even more potent symbol of imperial decline in *The Time Machine*. The most Tennysonian aspect of the novel is the prevailing mood of the setting sun Wells creates. A rough count suggests that there are seven references to sunsets in the main part of the narrative, but, more importantly, when the Time Traveller journeys further into the future, he comes upon the sunset to end all sunsets, the moment when as a result of "tidal drag," "the earth had come to rest with one face to the sun" (p. 64), thus producing an "eternal sunset" (p. 66). The most famous line associated with Victorian imperialism was of course: "The sun never sets on the British Empire." In his final dark vision of the future in *The Time Machine*, Wells seems to go out of his way to suggest that the sun would someday set on the British Empire with a vengeance.

---

4. For the relevance of Gibbon to *The Time Machine*, see Parrinder (1995) 65–68.
5. This aspect of the Victorian museum is reflected in the Time Traveller's observation: "In another place was a vast array of idols—Polynesian, Mexican, Grecian, Phœnecian, every country on earth I could think of" (p. 55).
6. The classic visual representation of such a scene is Hubert Robert's "Imaginary View of the Grande Galerie in Ruins," a painting both in and of the Louvre Museum in Paris. For the significance of the ruined museum in *The Time Machine*, see Parrinder (1995) 53–55 and Parrinder (2001) 111–12.

Even though Wells himself acknowledged how much *The Time Machine* was rooted in its imperialistic age (Ruddick 250), the book aggressively breaks out of Victorian horizons. Wells refuses to accept Victorian complacency and self-satisfaction—he does not think that the British by virtue of some kind of racial superiority are entitled to rule the world, or that their empire will last forever. Here is the core of Wells's modernism. Indeed he was as thoroughgoing a critic of Victorian pieties as any of the famous modernists, and shared their contempt for Victorian smugness, as becomes evident in his portrayal of the Time Traveller as an explorer.

Just as the Eloi and the Morlocks are modeled on the two tribes of imperialist romance, Wells developed the character of the Time Traveller according to the standard pattern of the intrepid Victorian explorer. Wells's hero displays the same sense of adventure that drove real explorers like Burton and Stanley, but he also shares their darker side. Although he has a few moments of doubt, he basically assumes that he is superior to any being he encounters, and therefore believes that he has a right to appropriate anything he needs or desires, including, as we have seen, a native woman. He does not feel bound by the laws or customs of the lands he enters. Indeed, since he is separated from his homeland, he apparently no longer feels bound by its laws either. In the exotic world of the future, the Time Traveller feels liberated from the fundamental civilized prohibition against murder: "I longed very much to kill a Morlock or so. Very inhuman, you may think, to want to go killing one's own descendants! But it was impossible, somehow, to feel any humanity in the things" (p. 54). Wells's hero seems to operate according to the Kurtzian principle: "Exterminate all the brutes" (Conrad 51).

Like his real and fictional prototypes, Wells's hero is a kind of anthropologist. He understands that knowledge is power, and if he is to survive in and master the world of the future, he must first come to understand it. In particular, in a scene familiar from imperialist romance, the Time Traveller sets out to learn the language of the Eloi, which turns out to be childishly simple (p. 24). The idea that native languages are primitive and incapable of expressing sophisticated ideas was a cliché of imperialist romance (Pagetti 125).

In his activity as an anthropologist the Time Traveller displays his cultural arrogance. He has entered a world totally unfamiliar to him, and yet he believes that he can figure out by his own efforts exactly how it works. His typical procedure is to observe something in the world of the future and immediately try to erect a grand speculative theory to explain how it came about. In this, he resembles Victorian explorers in fact and fiction, who were equally eager to theorize about the native cultures they encountered, often on the basis of very limited knowledge. Given the number of mistakes Wells shows the Time Traveller making, he seems to be criticizing his hero for precisely this overconfidence and overeagerness in thinking that native society is simply transparent to him.

Wells develops this critique by showing how long it takes the Time Traveller to understand the world of the future. *The Time Machine* is structured around a series of progressive revelations. At each stage, confronted by a certain set of phenomena, the Time Traveller offers an explanation for them, always revising his theories in light of new data, and thus coming closer to the truth about the future world. Wells carefully marks the progressive nature of this process by having his hero warn us about the limited character of his knowledge at each stage. For example, "This, I must remind you, was my speculation of the time. Later, I was to appreciate how far it fell short of the reality" (p. 26). At first, trying to explain the seemingly idyllic life of the Eloi, the Time Traveller theorizes that sometime in the future, humanity achieved perfection of social organization, solved all its problems, and eventually began to degenerate and lose its strength as a result of no longer having to face any challenges or threats. When the Time Traveller learns of the existence of the Morlocks, he is forced to come up with a "new view" (p. 39), and spins out a theory of how humanity could eventually evolve into two distinct species in the distant future. He suggests that a deepening of the class conflicts already evident in the Victorian period would lead to the aristocracy and proletariat evolving along separate paths. But the Time Traveller must make one last revision of his theory of the future, when he finally realizes how the Morlocks have turned the tables on their former masters, the Elois; the Morlocks have become cannibals and now treat the Eloi as their cattle.

This structure of progressive revelations makes a powerful statement about what is often called Eurocentrism today. In his efforts to understand an alien world, Wells's hero is all too eager to impose categories derived from his homeland, to explain the unfamiliar in terms of the familiar. If he repeatedly misunderstands what is going on among the Eloi and the Morlocks, the reason is that he assumes that he can view them on the model of the English men and women he knows. Of course the joke of Wells's story is that the Eloi and the Morlocks are in fact English men and women at an advanced stage of evolution. And yet in the Time Traveller's eagerness to jump to conclusions about the future world, Wells seems to be satirizing the way the typical Victorian explorer assumed that he could easily solve the mysteries of native life any place on the globe. In this respect, *The Time Machine* becomes a prototypical modernist narrative. By its structure, it raises serious questions about our access to truth, in particular, whether our view of the world is colored by our distinct perspective on it.

* * *

As we have been seeing, the way Wells's hero jumps back and forth between different time periods corresponds to the way an imperial explorer jumps back and forth between communities at different stages of historical development. In either case, this kind of back and forth movement is culturally disorienting, since it involves a constant shifting of perspectives and hence a questioning of traditional assumptions. The equivalent in fictional terms of this constant decentering movement would be the temporal and other shifts characteristic of modernist narrative. By destabilizing the narrative framework of fiction, the modernist author hopes to undermine traditional notions of reality and in particular to reveal the perspectival nature of truth. The progressive revelations of a modernist narrative keep readers off balance, forcing them continually to revise their understanding of the story and perhaps eventually to realize that no one view can ever encompass the whole truth about reality.

That is how the imperialist romance helped prepare the way for modernist fiction; by exploring shifting perspectives as a narrative principle, imperialist authors such as Kipling served as models for modernist authors such as Conrad. (Kipling's experiments with native narrators in such stories as "Gemini" and "In Flood Time" are especially pertinent here.) Such considerations in turn explain the paradox of *The Time Machine*—how a novel that seems at first to reflect Wells's inability to think outside the categories of British imperialist romance turns into a searching critique of those very categories—in short, how a Victorian thriller turns into a modernist interrogation of Victorian culture. For Wells, time travel itself becomes a fundamentally modernist experience. Indeed there is something distinctively modern about the way the Time Traveller approaches his whole enterprise: "with a kind of madness growing upon me, I flung myself into futurity" (p. 18). This is of course literally true of Wells's hero, but it is also symbolically true of his generation, which may have been the first to orient itself by the future, rather than by the past, as humanity had done for millennia.

Being guided by the future rather than the past is almost the defining characteristic of modernity. *Victorian* has become for us a by-word for "old-fashioned," but in fact the British in the second half of the nineteenth century, with their faith in progress and their remarkable record of economic, technological, and scientific achievements, were embracing the future with an unprecedented eagerness. Throughout history, humanity had lived in a basically stable world, in which changes of course happened, but they tended to happen slowly and thus pass unnoticed. In the course of the nineteenth century in Britain the pace of change increased at an exponential rate, and as a result for the first time in human history change became a way of life. The building of the great medieval cathedrals certainly changed the urban landscape of Europe, but these massive construction projects took decades and sometimes hundreds of years. By contrast, nineteenth-century observers were startled by the speed with which London grew, and frequently remarked about how new housing developments were springing up seemingly overnight (Pagetti 122). One of the defining events of the Victorian Era was the erection in 1851 of the famous Crystal Palace, a huge edifice of iron and glass, which, because of prefabrication and other new building techniques, was, to the amazement of the British public, put up in only four months; even more remarkably, it was taken down in three (Auerbach 207).

It is on precisely this spectacle of rapid change that Wells concentrates in trying to capture the nature of the Time Traveller's experience—the radical transitoriness of the modern landscape:

> I saw trees growing and changing like puffs of vapour, now brown, now green; they grew, spread, shivered, and passed away. I saw huge buildings rise up faint and fair, and pass like dreams. The whole surface of the earth seemed changed—melting and flowing under my eyes. . . . I saw great and splendid architecture rising about me, more massive than any building of our own time, and yet, as it seemed, built of glimmer and mist. (pp. 17–18)

Here Wells almost seems to be echoing the famous characterization of modernity in Marx and Engels: "All that is solid melts into air" (Feuer 10). The Crystal Palace was probably Wells's inspiration for this vision of architecture "built of glimmer and mist,"[7] but, more generally, in his hero's experience of time travel, Wells was trying to convey a sense of how the world had suddenly begun to look to observant people in the late nineteenth century; he marked the emergence of the modern sensibility, with its acute awareness that nothing humanity creates is built to last. Indeed it is a real question whether this passage could have been written by anyone living much before the 1890s. Wells was drawing upon the Victorian's new sense of geological time, developed by Lyell and others in mid-century— the idea that the natural landscape is always changing—gradually but radically over long intervals.[8] But Wells was also impressed by the new mutability of the urban landscape in Victorian London—a tribute to humanity's emerging power to alter its own environment.

* * *

---

7. In his introduction to his edition of *The Time Machine*, Parrinder points out: "Wells as a child was taken to see the life-size plaster reproductions of the dinosaurs at the Crystal Palace in Sydenham" (xviii).
8. On the importance of the new geological thinking in the Victorian era, see Gillispie and Gould.

Works Cited

Ashcroft, Bill, Gareth Griffiths, and Helen Tiffin. *The Empire Writes Back: Theory and Practice in Post-Colonial Literatures*. London: Routledge, 1989.

Auerbach, Jeffrey A. *The Great Exhibition of 1851: A Nation on Display*. New Haven: Yale UP, 1999.

Booth, William. *In Darkest England and The Way Out*. New York: Funk & Wagnalls, 1890.

Conrad, Joseph. *Heart of Darkness*. 1902. New York: Norton, 1988.

Feuer, Lewis S., ed. *Marx & Engels: Basic Writings on Politics & Philosophy*. Garden City, NY: Doubleday, 1959.

Galassi, Susan Grace. *Picasso's Variations on the Masters*. New York: Abrams, 1996.

Geduld, Harry M., ed. *The Definitive Time Machine*. Bloomington: Indiana UP, 1987.

Gillispie, Charles Coulston. *Genesis and Geology*. Cambridge: Harvard UP, 1957.

Gould, Stephen Jay. *Time's Arrow/Time's Cycle: Myth and Metaphor in the Discovery of Geological Time*. Cambridge: Harvard UP, 1987.

Haggard, H. Rider. *King Solomon's Mines*. Oxford: Oxford UP, 1989.

Hammond, J. R. *H. G. Wells and the Modern Novel*. London: Macmillan, 1988.

Leslie, Richard. *Pablo Picasso: A Modern Master*. New York: Smithmark, 1996.

Pagetti, Carlo. "Change in the City: The Time Traveller's London and the 'Baseless Fabric' of His Vision." *H. G. Wells's Perennial Time Machine*. Eds. George Slusser, Patrick Parrinder, and Danièle Chatelain. Athens, GA: U of Georgia P, 2001.

Parrinder, Patrick. *Shadows of the Future: H. G. Wells, Science Fiction and Prophecy*. Liverpool: Liverpool UP, 1995

———. "From Rome to Richmond: Wells, Universal History, and Prophetic Time." *H. G. Wells's Perennial Time Machine*. Ed. George Slusser, Patrick Parrinder, and Danièle Chatelain. Athens, GA: U of Georgia P, 2001.

Parrinder, Patrick and Robert Philmus, eds. *H. G. Wells's Literary Criticism*. Brighton: Harvester, 1980.

Pater, Walter. *The Renaissance*. (1873). Oxford: Oxford UP, 1986.

Ruddick, Nicholas, ed. *The Time Machine*. Peterborough: Broadview, 2001.

Rushdie, Salman. *Imaginary Homelands*. New York: Viking, 1991.

———. *The Satanic Verses*. New York: Viking, 1989.

Russell, W. M. S. "Time Before and After *The Time Machine*." *H. G. Wells's Perennial Time Machine*. Ed. George Slusser, Patrick Parrinder, and Danièle Chatelain. Athens, GA: U of Georgia P, 2001.

Said, Edward W. *Orientalism*. New York: Vintage, 1979.

Stover, Leon, ed. *The Time Machine: An Invention*. Jefferson, NC: McFarland, 1996.

Truettner, William H. and Alan Wallach. *Thomas Cole: Landscape into History*. New Haven: Yale UP, 1994.

Watt, Ian. *Conrad in the Nineteenth Century*. Berkeley: U of California P, 1979.

Wells, H. G. *The Time Machine* (1895) and *The Island of Doctor Moreau* (1896). Ed. Patrick Parrinder. New York: Oxford UP, 1996.

COLIN MANLOVE

H. G. Wells and the Machine in Victorian Fiction[†]

* * *

Where the machine appears in the Victorian novel—scarcely any poetry of significance deigns to admit it, aside from Kipling's—it is rarely central to the work as fiction.[1] Disraeli in *Coningsby* (1844) is

---

[†] From "Charles Kingsley, H. G. Wells, and the Machine in Victorian Fiction," *Nineteenth-Century Literature* 48.2 (September 1993): 213–15, 224–32. Reprinted by permission of the University of California Press. References to *The Time Machine* are to this Norton Critical Edition.

1. See Herbert L. Sussman, *Victorians and the Machine: The Literary Response to Technology* (Cambridge, Mass.: Harvard Univ. Press, 1968), esp. pp. 1–12, 228–33.

happy to have it occasionally, but in a context of extraliterary sermonizing: the young aristocrat Coningsby, on a visit to Manchester, views a factory as a wonder out of Arabian fable and descants on the more-than-human abilities of the machines and the apparent contentment of their operatives.[2] Mrs. Gaskell in *North and South* (1854–55), when rarely she mentions actual machinery rather than the condition of underpaid or alienated workers, uses the valetudinarian and Southern English Hale to wonder at "the energy which conquered immense difficulties with ease; the power of the machinery of Milton [again Manchester]."[3] Dickens is prepared to give the ironmaster Rouncewell in *Bleak House* (1853) a future of industrial amelioration beyond the narrative of his novel; in *Dombey and Son* (1848) he equates the rush of the railway locomotive with "Death" (chap. 20); and in *Hard Times* he shows us the effect of the machine making people mechanical.[4] In Hardy's novels the machine is subsumed in the workings of fate against the central characters, its progressive and scientific nature sweeping aside the old rural methods of Henchard in *The Mayor of Casterbridge* (1886), or, in the shape of the threshing-machine on the bleak fields of Flintcomb Ash, grinding down still further the blighted and ill-starred spirit of the heroine of *Tess of the d'Urbervilles* (1891). For Zola in *Germinal* (1895), the machinery is summed up in the name of the focal coal mine, Le Voreux, and is itself devoured by a man-engineered cataclysm at the end.[5]

And yet the Victorian period is an age that is most truly founded on the machine and the progressivism that its powers invoke. Darwin's theory of evolution might not have been formulated without the medium of mechanical amelioration in which he lived.[6] And it is fair too to say that an element of mechanism creeps back into the nineteenth-century novel despite itself. In the eighteenth-century novel the protagonist often finds out what he or she is, while in the nineteenth-century novel the process is one of learning what one may become. But that "becoming" is circumscribed by the factory of Christian teaching, and bound down as to a bench by Victorian evangelical principles. The optimism behind many Victorian novels, in which there is a tendency to turn out perfect moral products after they have been shaped in the furnace of experience or turned on the lathe of self-knowledge, makes them into spiritual manufactories in

2. Disraeli, *Coningsby; or, The New Generation* (Leipzig: Tauchnitz, 1844); pp. 144–45.
3. Gaskell, *North and South* (London: Oxford Univ. Press, 1973), p. 69; cf. pp. 80–81.
4. Equally Butler in his "Book of the Machines" in *Erewhon* (1872) portrays an Erewhonian argument that machines have all the attributes of people and are therefore a dangerous threat that must be removed. He is actually by inversion satirizing the Huxleyan notion of likening organic life to the machine.
5. Charles Reade's *Put Yourself in His Place* (1870), which portrays improved machinery as the key to social betterment, is a lonely exception here.
6. See, e.g., Peter J. Bowler, *Evolution: The History of an Idea*, rev. ed. (Berkeley: Univ. of California Press, 1989), pp. 103–4.

which each item of apparently contingent vicissitude is part of a production line designed to generate admiration in man and acceptability to God.

What we are dealing with, of course, is the "two nations" and the "two cultures" mentality so characteristic of Britain. *North and South* in a sense sums up one side of it: the major part of industrialism was well away from southern and metropolitan England and thus could be felt as northern and vulgar, a sentiment that persists today. But there was also the feeling among the cultured—most sharply voiced by Matthew Arnold—that machinery, with its concomitant progressivist and acquisitive philosophy, was a threat to man's human nature: "The idea of perfection as an *inward* condition of the mind and spirit is at variance with the mechanical and material civilisation in esteem with us."[7] Thus, while writers such as Carlyle, Mill, Macaulay, or Frederic Harrison might extol the wonders of the machine and its promise, and while the increased comforts and intercommunication that many Victorian poets and novelists benefited from sprang from mechanical advance,[8] there is everywhere among the "cultured" this sense of antagonism to the progress of their age, and indeed often to science itself. The emphasis of criticism is on the machine as a brutalizer of the human sensibility, the agent of a repressive society that, while it goes forward materially, is the enemy of the individual human spirit. For all those who, like Macaulay, could proclaim that "every improvement of the means of locomotion benefits mankind morally and intellectually as well as materially," or that education, sanitation, and care for the arts of life made man happier and morally better,[9] there were as many who scorned such views as philistine, as a confusion of material with spiritual goods. Yet there is real evidence that not only disease but also vice and crime were lessened by these methods.[1]

Scientifically adventurous though the age was, it was often spiritually reactionary: no accommodation of the machine to the artistic sensibility seemed possible. The result was frequent nostalgia or flight into pastoral or the past in poetry—witness Morris's escape from "six counties" of "snorting steam and piston stroke" at the start of *The Earthly Paradise*—and in the novel a reliance for amelioration solely on individual human effort rather than on any collective or mechanical aid. It seemed only at the level of analogy that a bridge could be

7. Arnold, *Culture and Anarchy* (1869), ed. J. Dover Wilson (Cambridge: Cambridge Univ. Press, 1960), p. 49.
8. See, e.g., Walter E. Houghton, *The Victorian Frame of Mind, 1830–1870* (New Haven: Yale Univ. Press, 1957), pp. 27–45.
9. See Macaulay, *History of England*, in *The Complete Works of Lord Macaulay*, ed. Lady Trevelyan, 8 vols. (London: Longmans, Green, 1866), I, 290–91 (quoted in Houghton, p. 41). See also Houghton, pp. 35–41.
1. See Houghton, p. 41.

made between the machine and human values, as in Marx's concept of a new communist society in which, via the abolition of private property, all parts would drive and be sustained by the greater whole.

* * *

The bulk of the Victorian cultural elite, of course, shares Dickens's more negative view of the machine.[2] Its only literary home seems to be the proto-science-fictional novel, and even there (apart from a certain class of post-1871 works on the possibilities of future war between Britain and another country)[3] it is only in Verne and Wells that we find much attention given to the machine itself.[4] In other works we have the creative surgery of Frankenstein in Mary Shelley's 1818 novel, the mesmeric powers utilized in Poe's "Facts in the Case of M. Valdemar" (1845), the electrical force of *vril* in Bulwer-Lytton's *The Coming Race* (1871), or the transformative properties of the chemical powder in Stevenson's *Dr. Jekyll and Mr. Hyde* (1886). And we may note that in all these works, including those of Wells, admiration of scientific advance goes together with warning of its risks. For these novels are different from those of Kingsley and Dickens: they deal with inventions, not with machines that already exist in the form of the steam engine. They speak of what may be, while Kingsley and Dickens depict their view of what already *is*, what exists in the "real" outer world. The other works are concerned with speculative machines of the future, and thus they are inherently transgressive in content—and thereby, in their period, self-critical in orientation.

Wells writes about machines at a point when their possibilities are becoming unquantifiable. The steam engine performs evident tasks—drives ships or locomotives, drains mines, powers looms or smelters. Its actions are known, its required fuels measurable, its pressures subject to regulation. And it is this one type of engine that powers Victorian industry, through pistons, cogs, levers, belts, and ratchets. But by the time of Wells, with the discovery of the electromagnetic spectrum and the beginnings of atomic physics, a whole new generation of machines based on the seemingly invisible and immense powers of radio, electricity, magnetism, or even particle

2. The excised portion of this essay considered the representation of machinery in Charles Kingsley's novel *Alton Locke* (1850) and Charles Dickens's novel *Hard Times* (1854) [*Editor's note*].
3. On which see I. F. Clarke, *Voices Prophesying War, 1763–1984* (London: Oxford Univ. Press, 1966), esp. chap. 2.
4. On pre-Wellsian science fiction, see Darko Suvin, *Victorian Science Fiction in the UK: The Discourses of Knowledge and Power* (Boston: G. K. Hall, 1983).
5. See Peter Nicholls, ed., *The Encyclopaedia of Science Fiction: An Illustrated A to Z* (London: Granada, 1981), p. 371. Useful accounts of technical change in the Victorian period are Lewis Mumford, *Technics and Civilization* (London: Routledge, 1934); and Charles Singer, E. J. Holmyard, A. R. Hall, and Trevor I. Williams, eds., *A History of Technology*, 5 vols. (Oxford: Clarendon Press, 1958), vol. V, *The Late Nineteenth Century, c. 1850 to c. 1900*. For the way technological change altered the understanding of time and space in the period, see Stephen Kern, *The Culture of Space and Time, 1880–1918* (Cambridge, Mass.: Harvard Univ. Press, 1983).

physics was poised for discovery and application.[5] Concomitant with this was an enormous excitement at the sheer boundlessness of possible invention. If Kingsley and the pro-scientific writers of his age could be thrilled still at the possibilities of the use of machines to establish a heaven on earth, or as functionaries in social better-ment,[6] science by the close of the century had often leapt "beyond" such ideals to a sense of its own untested and immense powers. In Wells we see science become capable of being a law unto itself, its invented products thrown off like dangerous sparks that can threaten, not subserve, the social system.

In fact what we have here is a situation in which, from being a danger to the human individual or the soul, the machine can now be seen as a potential menace to society as a whole. From being identi-fied with a society that variously demanded the subjection of all indi-viduals to its collective purposes, it is now the society that becomes human and the machine that is at war with it. This to a large extent expresses the less optimistic and in particular *fin-de-siècle* view of social development; but there is also the beginnings of the modern sense that man's inventions may not work for his betterment alone, but may in ways unknown to him work rather to undermine the whole fabric of his existence on the planet.[7] There is, in short, a much greater sense of human frailty, at least registered by some of those who made it their business to speculate on the possibilities of human development.

In Wells the scientist is separate from the social fabric. Where Brunel followed the engineering demands made upon him by the rev-olution in public transport, or Charles Babbage sought continually to apply new science and technology to British industry, or Darwin set man among the whole society of living creatures, the inventors we find in Wells are either alone—like the invisible Griffin, the islanded Moreau, or the solitary Time Traveller—or else alien and a threat to society, in the shape of the Martians of *The War of the Worlds*. Their inventions serve to make them either more independent of their environment or able to shape it as they wish. The Time Traveller's machine flits through the lattice of the future, the changing world shimmering about it like a ghost; the invisibility of Griffin makes him free to slip through space and do as he wishes without notice; the powers of Moreau enable him to subvert Darwin and turn beasts into part-men under his control; the Martian machines are able utterly to subdue man.

6. See, e.g., Kingsley, *Sermons on National Subjects*, in *The Works of Charles Kingsley*, 28 vols. (London: Macmillan, 1879–84), XXII (1880), 109–10.
7. See Langdon Winner, *Autonomous Technology: Technics-out-of-Control as a Theme in Political Thought* (Cambridge, Mass.: MIT Press, 1977), esp. pp. 1–43.

With Wells we have moved on from Newtonian to pre-Einsteinian physics, expressing now a less stable reality. A literary form of the theory of relativity informs the very postulated existence of a fourth dimension in *The Time Machine*, extending reality and altering the purview on it. Indeed, much of Wells's work here is "perspectivist":[8] in *The War of the Worlds* the complacency of man is mocked in relation to the undreamed-of designs of the far-off Martians, and we are told that the Martians' treatment of man is no worse than European man's own treatment of the Tasmanian natives;[9] here too men have become as Eloi to the blood-sucking Martians. In *The Time Machine* the traveler to the future finds a baffling society for which he offers a series of hypothetical explanations until at last he thinks he arrives at the right one, but even then he has to admit, "It may be as wrong an explanation as mortal wit could invent. It is how the thing shaped itself to me, and as that I give it to you" (p. 62). Nothing is certain: reality is plastic and elusive, shimmering and mutating as the time machine passes through it, changing form and habit as the beasts are made to do in *The Island of Dr. Moreau* (1896). The very fact that Wells writes science fiction, creating a universe of possibilities alternative to our own, and that he writes not one but many of these tales, is a literary mode of this relativism. And of course relativism is precisely one of the purposes of Wells's invented machines: he wants to throw ironic light on our own technological pride by imagining infinitely superior technology, and equally to highlight our temporal provincialism against the perspectives revealed by a machine that may enact for the future the same Olympian view that was to be applied to the far past in his *Short History of the World* (1922).

In *The Time Machine* we also have relativism contained within the form of the journey and the story. The Time Traveller returns to the Victorian present of the book (which is now our past) to tell his tale of the future: the whole of his adventure is contained within a temporal loop within the story, where on a Thursday morning he sets off on his machine and by Thursday evening is back for supper and explanations, after having traveled thirty million years into the future. In that sense his colossal journey is contained within about ten hours of our time. Further, the futurity that he has experienced is recounted as a past event. And beyond that is the fact that the adventures the Traveller has had via the time-leaping powers of his machine may still await him: wherever he is, dead or alive, he may have to relive the future he experienced with the Eloi and the

---

8. "Perspectivism" was first promoted by Nietzsche in 1887, and formulated as a theory by the Spanish philosopher José Ortega y Gasset, who in a 1916 lecture also linked it to the theory of relativity (see Kern, pp. 150–52).
9. See *The War of the Worlds* (London: William Heinemann, 1898), pp. 4–5.

Morlocks in 802,701 and beyond as "natural" time grinds its way through to these eras; for he is now inexorably a part of that future.

Unless . . . unless it is not the *only* or "the real" future—which, given relativity, may not be unreasonable. That it is contingent is implied in the Awful Warning to Victorian man in the very existence of the divided races of Eloi and Morlocks, which are the end-point of the brutal division of capitalist from laborer that to Wells had increased throughout the nineteenth century. The Time Traveller points to the dangers of the rich "haves" dividing themselves from the poor, who are increasingly thrust underground to work, and sees a "widening gulf" that will "make that exchange between class and class, that promotion by intermarriage that at present retards the splitting of our species along lines of social stratification, less and less frequent" (p. 40). Clearly the point is that the future is alterable if the dangers exposed in present conditions can be corrected. Further, it is an interesting feature of the future the Time Traveller visits that one of the few buildings in it that he enters is a museum, a museum containing no identified artifact later than the late-Victorian period from which the story began (pp. 52–56). And of course we now know that the earth and sun will not run out of heat thirty million years hence, as Kelvin's second law of thermodynamics (1868) predicted and as most scientists of the time—with the important exception of Darwin—came to believe.[1]

We can take this point further. Suppose the *machine itself* in a sense makes this future? Certainly, without it, it would never have been seen. And inevitably, at certain points in the story, the movements of the machine become assimilated to those of future history itself: "I saw trees growing and changing like puffs of vapour, now brown, now green; they grew, spread, shivered, and passed away. I saw huge buildings rise up faint and fair, and pass like dreams. The whole surface of the earth seemed changed—melting and flowing under my eyes" (p. 40); "So I came back. . . . The blinking succession of the days and nights was resumed, the sun got golden again, the sky blue. . . . The fluctuating contours of the land ebbed and flowed. The hands spun backward upon the dials" (p. 67). In 1909 E. M. Forster wrote (partly in answer to Wells) a story called "The Machine Stops": suppose that in *The Time Machine* the verb "stops"

1. In his "Another Basis for Life" (22 Dec. 1894; repr. *H. G. Wells: Early Writings in Science and Science Fiction*, ed. Robert M. Philmus and David Y. Hughes [Berkeley: Univ. of California Press, 1975], pp. 144–47), Wells accepted the theory, "On the supposition, accepted by all scientific men, that the earth is undergoing a steady process of cooling . . ." (p. 145): he clearly had the perspective to see that this position might be challenged in the future. See also Philmus and Hughes, pp. 4, 89–90 nn. 1, 3, 102 n. 1; and Bowler, *Evolution*, pp. 137–38, 206–7, on Kelvin and his influence.

is considered as transitive? It has frequently been observed that the future the Time Traveller visits is "run down," approaching entropy. In a year whose descending numbers can be symbolic—802,701— he finds near-exhausted remnants of humankind in the disjoined segments of the effete Eloi on the one hand and the brute, near-monkey Morlocks on the other. This "civilization" is close to terminus, with the Eloi as the last and now vacuous remnants of the former ruling class, kept perhaps as cattle by a brutalized race of now purposeless workers; indeed the two could be said to be the pieces of a broken social machine. Further on into the future, life has devolved still more, with a beach populated by giant crabs: further still, life itself has shrunk to a dubious tentacled polyp flopping in the twilight by an ice-rimmed sea. The future has retraced the past, right back from the most sophisticated to the most primitive forms of life—in a sense it has swallowed itself. We may here note that eating and devouring imagery is recurrent in the story and present in its very form, whereby the story of the future is almost literally digested in the Victorian past, as the Time Traveller recounts his experience while his mutton dinner is absorbed in his stomach. More than this, we may note that the journey of the time machine is accompanied by the progressive slowing of the sun, until it becomes stationary and massively red in the sky. The further and faster the machine goes, the slower moves that symbol and stimulus of organic life, the sun. May there not be enough of a suggestion here that the transgressive technology involved in the time machine devours and deracinates the future as it traverses it?

In a sense, then, *The Time Machine* becomes an awful warning about technology even while, like much early science fiction, it also glorifies it. It is the very success of future technology that destroys man. By utterly conquering nature it renders man helpless, because he no longer has to struggle to survive, can no longer continually fashion himself on "the grindstone of pain and necessity" (p. 28). When mind has done all it can to subdue matter, it atrophies for want of material, and stasis and then decline result. There can be no question that the Time Traveller, simply by moving, by inventing a machine that transgresses the bounds of known possibility, is a kind of technological hero in the story: without his machine the future of the book would have been unplumbed. Yet technology, while it witnesses to intellectual daring, witnesses also to technical voracity: as his machine proceeds, technology declines to fading pastoral, and pastoral to the collapse of organic life altogether.

The condition of the built machine is duality. It is there from the first, even in Swift, whose adamant-driven Laputa's flight above the earth figures the dissociation of mind from body; a condition further figured in the total disconnection of the minds of Laputan thinkers from the world about them. As human construct, the machine is opposed to the organic and to nature. As product of mind, it ultimately figures the continued struggle of mind to dominate the physical and to make the universe intelligible. The mind of the Time Traveller is amply deployed in his story: first as synthetic, in the construction of the time machine; and then as analytic, in his layered interpretations of the diminished human society he encounters. In the latter role, his attempt at comprehending the future race he meets is conducted first in idealistic and pastoral terms; but later he is forced continually to modify his theories under the impact of brutal fact. Finally he is driven toward pure brutality itself, in his belief that the Eloi are the cattle of the Morlocks. Dualism remains: the last conclusion is still presented as a hypothesis (p. 62). And throughout the story, the Time Traveller glides above and through the material world, untouched by it as his machine surges through its numerous contingent manifestations, a classic image of mind's dominance of the material—if here to the point possibly of absorbing the material.

The point is put in the Traveller's own late reflection, "an animal perfectly in harmony with its environment is a perfect mechanism" (pp. 00). When mind and world are at one we have a perfect machine: Wells here approaches the notion of an organic machine, which at once recalls Kingsley and looks forward to his own later yearning for an organic world-state.[3] But the crux is the overcoming of duality. The Time Traveller *has* no environment: he simply travels. His inventiveness, which in itself continually throws his mind out of the present into future projections and plans, becomes, as it were, symbolized in the time machine itself. But it means that he must be perpetually mobile, with no real home. He is forced to leave the year 802,701, he makes brief forays to the "final" future, and in the end he disappears again. Through his dependence on the machine he lacks a hold on reality: it may in fact be a mere accidental disturbance of the machine by the narrator that ensures that when the Traveller next climbs aboard it he finds himself driven once more into time, never to return. ("I . . . put out my hand and touched the lever. At that the squat substantial-looking mass swayed like a bough shaken by the wind. Its instability startled me extremely, and I had a queer reminiscence of the childish days when I used to be forbidden to meddle"; and then, "I heard an exclamation, oddly truncated at the end, and a click and a thud" [p. 61].) We know the machine was heavy from the Traveller's difficulties in righting it when he first arrived in 802,701. All this takes place just when the Traveller is

2. E.g. in "The World Organism" (1902, 1914; repr. in *H. G. Wells: Journalism and Prophecy, 1893 1916*, ed. W. Warren Wagar [London. The Bodley Head, 1964], pp. 273–76).

about to give the narrator incontrovertible proof regarding time travel, something he strangely failed to do earlier with his prodigal party trick with the model he sent into the future (pp. 10). And arguably one "reason" for this is that the time machine has to remain improbable, cut off from a basis in reality, just as is its owner. And that of course could explain why the machine itself is given so little scientific explanation within the novel, but left as an uncertain and "aesthetic" construct, "a glittering metallic framework" of which "parts were of nickel, parts of ivory, parts had certainly been filed or sawn out of rock crystal" (pp. 11). And beyond the Time Traveller's mind we have that of Wells himself, inventor of this book and of the explorations in it: a book that has been described as "a finely fashioned aesthetic machine,"[3] and has been presented by Wells as a mere fantasy, without the slightest basis in possible fact.[4]

* * *

ROGER LUCKHURST

The Scientific Romance
and the Evolutionary Paradigm[†]

* * *

Narrowly defined conceptions of SF [science fiction] applied retrospectively to Wells in the *fin de siècle* can be used to filter and simplify not only his literary context and possible influences, but also Wells's own work. The Wells of the 1890s did not write just scientific romances but also opportunistic Gothic tales (*The Island of Dr. Moreau*, for instance), social comedies about the cycling craze (*The Wheels of Chance*), whimsical fantasies about angelic visitation (*The Wonderful Visit*), and collections of light essays and journalism (*Certain Personal Matters*). It is important to emphasize the permeability between these different kinds of writing, the hybrid and 'impure' spaces from which the scientific romances appeared. Yet even so, it is from within this crucible of mixed elements that Wells was to forge a scientized framework for his fiction and political writings and

---

3. Frank D. McConnell, *The Science Fiction of H. G. Wells* (New York: Oxford Univ. Press, 1980), p. 88.
4. See Wells's preface to *The Scientific Romances of H. G. Wells* (1933; repr. in *H. G. Wells's Literary Criticism*, ed. Patrick Parrinder and Robert M. Philmus [Sussex: Harvester Press, and Totowa, N.J.: Barnes and Noble, 1980], pp. 240–41).
† From *Science Fiction* (Cambridge: Polity Press, 2005), pp. 31–32, 33–39. Reprinted by permission of Polity Press and the author. References to *The Time Machine* are to this Norton Critical Edition.

the evolutionary paradigm that dominated the English scientific romance before, and to some extent after, 1945.

The fusion of biological science and masculine romance, propounded by Andrew Lang and Rider Haggard, was directly borrowed by Wells from the writer Grant Allen. In late 1895, just after *The Time Machine* was published, Wells wrote to the seasoned Allen: 'I flatter myself that I have a certain affinity with you. I believe that this field of scientific romance with a philosophical element which I am trying to cultivate, belongs properly to you.'[1] Before we turn to Wells, then, Allen's short, prodigious career is worth examining because he offered a model of how to transpose a scientific training into popular literature, attempting to make diverse entertainments across many generic types cohere within a commitment to scientific naturalism.

In 1877 Grant Allen privately funded the publication of his first book, *Physiological Aesthetics*. Written whilst a professor involved in a failed university project educating the black population in Jamaica, it was dedicated to Herbert Spencer and promised to extend Spencerian thinking into a biological theory of aesthetics, displacing metaphysical speculation with a 'purely physical origin of the sense of beauty, and its relativity to our nervous organisation'.[2] Allen used the book as a calling card to announce his return to England and his willingness to serve in the advancement of Spencer's grand plan to synthesize all human knowledge into a developmental schema. Allen was unable to secure a scientific post: training for a scientific career might have been only in its nascent stages, but the book of an 'amateur' theorist was no longer a ticket to legitimacy either. Allen turned instead to daily journalism before a collapse in health pushed him into professional freelance writing from 1880. From then until his death in 1899, he produced a vast body of reviews, essays, scientific journalism, anthropological monographs, Spencerian speculations, short stories, Realist novels, detective fiction and Gothic shilling shockers.[3] . . .

* * *

What did Allen bequeath to H. G. Wells? In Nicholas Ruddick's view, 'Allen opened up the field for Wells's scientific romances'.[4] Even if the influence was that decisive, it was an ambiguous legacy. In the preface to *Strange Stories* in 1884, Allen apologized for the

1. Letter from Wells to Allen, late 1895, *The Correspondence of H. G. Wells*, 4 vols. ed. David C. Smith (London: Pickering and Chatto, 1998), I, pp. 245–6.
2. Grant Allen, *Physiological Aesthetics* (London: Henry S. King, 1877), p. 2.
3. For biographical information, see Peter Morton, 'Grant Allen: A Centenary Reassessment', *English Literature in Transition* 44, 4 (2001): 405–40. I have also relied on Edward Clodd, *Grant Allen: A Memoir* (London: Grant Richards, 1900).
4. Nicholas Ruddick, 'Grant Allen', in *Dictionary of Literary Biography*. Vol. 178: *British Fantasy and Science Fiction Writers before World War I*, ed. Darren Harris-Fain (Detroit: Gale Research, 1989), pp. 7–16: p. 16.

fact that a 'scientific journeyman' had 'been bold enough at times to stray surreptitiously and tentatively from my proper sphere into the flowery fields of pure fiction'.[5] When he died in 1899, the fusion of fiction and science was not unusual. Allen had produced a body of entertainments that were underwritten by a social Darwinian schema, and had been able to straddle the worlds of anthropological journals, the intellectual monthlies like *Fortnightly Review* and the *Tit-Bits* mass market. Yet Allen despised himself for having to do this. Edward Clodd reported in his memoir that Allen had been contemptuous of the fiction markets for which he wrote, and abandoned all pretence at serious art after the failure of his three-volume novel *Philistia* in 1884. Allen wrote to Clodd that 'I am trying with each new novel to go a step lower to catch the market', using devolutionary imagery for the very forms in which he dramatized these ideas.[6] Andrew Lang also reflected on Allen's peculiar career as 'a novelist against his will', a man longing only 'to write on deep scientific topics', appalled by the sensational trappings of his own hackwork.[7] Allen was caught between the aesthetic imperatives of high and low culture, but was also experiencing tension between the incompatible epistemologies of science and art. The critic David Hughes has examined the direct citation of Allen in Wells's work,[8] but one of the more important influences may be seen in Wells's curious mix of abject apology about the poor artistry of his writings combined with the intensely arrogant conviction that their evolutionary vision elevated them above the Realist novel. This contradiction would explode in Wells's dispute with Henry James, in which he dismissed his own work—'My art is abortion'—and yet parodied the contortions of James's aesthetic.[9] This is one origin of the conflicted assertions of lowly embarrassment yet transcendental messianism often associated with defences of SF as a genre.

At first H. G. Wells followed Allen's career trajectory. He began with science journalism and textbooks on physiology and biology, stuttering towards fiction with various early versions of *The Time Machine* that were published between 1888 and 1895.[1] Like Allen, he would gain notoriety as an author of fictions concerning sexual morality. Wells, however, first gained serious notice by changing

5. Allen, *Strange Stories* (London, 1884), p. iii.
6. Clodd, *Grant Allen*, p. 125.
7. Andrew Lang, 'At the Sign of the Ship', *Longman's Magazine* (December 1899): 189.
8. David Y. Hughes, 'A Queer Notion of Grant Allen's', *Science Fiction Studies* 25, 2 (1998): 271–83.
9. See Leon Edel and Gordon N. Ray (eds.), *Henry James and H. G. Wells: A Record of their Friendship* (Urbana: University of Illinois Press, 1959), p. 176.
1. 'The Cosmic Argonauts' was published in 1888 in *The Science Schools Journal*; 'The Time Traveller's Story' appeared in the *National Observer* in 1894. [See pp. 74–118 of this Norton Critical Edition.]

genre to non-fiction: *Anticipations* (1902), his book of forecasts on the condition of England in the year 2000, established him as a nationally important thinker and writer. His international reputation was confirmed with his controversial *Outline of History* (1919), which sold millions through the 1920s. Obituaries in 1946 regularly began by asserting Wells's world-historical significance (they completely failed to anticipate the rapid plummet of Wells's reputation in the post-war years). What I want to do here is establish how, in *The Time Machine*, Wells crystallized the possibilities of the scientific romance form inside an evolutionary paradigm.

* * *

Could one origin of science fiction be placed in the 'Further Vision' of the Time Traveller at the end of *The Time Machine*? The Traveller escapes death in the year 802,701 by pushing the machine further into the future. In an evocative sequence, the alternation of day and night slows to a 'steady twilight' as the planet ceases rotating around a huge and senile sun. London is replaced by a desolate beach, with signs of life reduced to scant lichen and the ponderous movement of a 'monstrous, crab-like creature', its antennae and 'vast ungainly claws' covered with 'algal slime' (p. 65). He pushes further forward to witness an eclipse, the beginning of the end perhaps, as the last sign of life—'a round thing, the size of a football perhaps'—induces nausea and 'terrible dread' in the Traveller (p. 67). Commonly regarded as one of Wells's most impressive literary passages, the perspective of cosmic time in this vision is expressed through sublime terror and awe: the 'sense of wonder' often pinpointed as the effect that is integral to SF. It is significant that any engagement with others falls away in this solitary encounter—time and again, the SF stories of Arthur Clarke or Isaac Asimov, for instance, will reach for this effect with a similar extrication from the social for the isolated cosmic perspective. Most importantly, though, this passage seems to be imagined through a rigorous projection of evolutionary biology. The Traveller initially advances 800,000 years, and tries to comprehend the transformed organization of human society through Darwinian ideas of adaptation and heredity. But the 'Further Vision' embraces genuine evolutionary time by conceiving of a post-human future. What use now for the precise discriminations of social behaviour in the Realist novel? Wells exploits the suggestive brevity of the romance form to evoke the radical difference of the future, yet does so from strict scientific premises.

In fact, the book is more riven and contradictory than this portrait suggests, and even this 'pure', asocial scientific Further Vision is conjured out of the flatly contradictory temporalities of Victorian biology and physics. William Thompson, the eminent physicist, had consistently refuted Darwin's theory of evolution from the early

1860s on the basis that the physics of combustion did not give enough time for natural selection to exert its gradual change on morphology. Indeed, Thompson rather alarmingly calculated that the sun would burn out only 10,000 years hence. Darwin could not counteract the entropic time of physics, since these calculations could not be refuted until theories of fission recalibrated the energy of the sun in the early twentieth century. No wonder the anonymous frame narrator can decide to resist the Traveller's interpretation of the future, then: it is a kind of 'solar mythology'.[2] The point is not that *The Time Machine* elevates the 'cognitive' perspective of science as a privileged locus of perception. Rather, what Wells helps inaugurate is the generation of fictions from the controversies of a messy experiential world where scientific assertions can be confounded by competing theories, recruited for ideological ends, or contested by other frameworks of explanation. Wells's success with the scientific romance in the 1890s signals that scientific ideas have become pervasive enough to begin to join this social conversation.

Reading *The Time Machine* is about constant readjustment, since the Traveller poses theories that often prove to be wrong. In this future London, he will theorize from above, sitting on hillsides offering lofty perspectives, but as soon as he descends and re-engages with the world he has to correct his view. In this sense, the story is told less by a detached cosmic evolutionist than by a confused and ill-prepared anthropologist in the field. The romance starts with his intimates considering him 'too clever to be believed', and the narrator undermining his scientific reputation (p. 12). He displaces his demonstration model of the machine in time for these sceptics, but the mysterious movements of objects on drawing-room tables only brings to mind Spiritualist trickery ('is this a trick', the Medical Man asks, 'like the ghost you showed us last Christmas?' [p. 12]). The Traveller's own narrative of his journey, told a week later, is replete with confessions of inadequacy, and the tale is advanced as a series of corrected mistakes. Readers who forget this heuristic mode of narration can risk failing to see the dissonance in the text, and thus over-fixing its allegorical meanings.

The Traveller, imbued with the theories of progress, anticipates that any human descendants in the far future will regard him as 'some old-world savage animal, only the more dreadful for our common likeness' (p. 20). His first encounter with the Eloi (probably derived by Wells from the Hebrew *elohim*, meaning 'gods') is therefore confusing. They are elegant and graceful, yet have the pallor

---

2. For background, see Gillian Beer, 'The Death of the Sun: Victorian Solar Physics and Solar Myth', *Open Fields: Science in Cultural Encounter* (Oxford: Clarendon Press, 1996), pp. 219–41.

and frailty of 'the more beautiful kind of consumptive' (p. 20). This weakness extends to their childish and 'indolent' inattention (p. 24), simplistic declarative language and passive relation to their decaying communal conditions. These are all markers of 'primitivism' to any Victorian anthropological observer. The Traveller's first theory is given as, alone on a hill, he watches the sunset from a rusting throne-seat.[3] This theory tries to sustain a sense of progress towards a utopia of communism, gender equality and sexual de-differentiation, and freedom from labour and disease. It manages this for all of three paragraphs, before arguing that such an achieved utopia is precisely what has resulted in evolutionary decline. The Traveller is committed to the Spencerian dogma of 'survival of the fittest': human striving and restless intellect is a biological imperative, and these have been reduced in utopia to 'purposeless energy' (p. 28). 'This has ever been the fate of energy in security', he moralistically concludes: 'it takes to art and to eroticism, and then come languor and decay' (p. 28).

The 'sunset of mankind' thesis clearly echoes Max Nordau's 'dusk of nations', elaborated in *Degeneration*, published in English earlier in 1895. As Nordau's target was the Decadent Movement, so the Traveller's first evocation of London is a satirical biologizing of both 1890s Aestheticism (all those beautiful, dying, effeminate consumptives) and the neo-medieval utopian futures of Edward Bellamy's *Looking Backward 2000–1887* (1887) and William Morris's *News from Nowhere* (1890). Bellamy's vision of the national syndication of all American corporations and the technological progress that would end labour strife and produce unalienated communality by the year 2000 produced Bellamy Clubs across America and even a Nationalist Party that had a significant role in US elections in the early 1890s.[4] Bellamy claimed the book had been written 'in accordance with the principles of evolution' and was thus a scientifically accurate forecast of 'the next stage in the industrial and social development of humanity'.[5] Morris had been prompted to compose *News from Nowhere* as a socialist riposte to the alienated 'machine-life' he saw depicted by the bourgeois Bellamy.[6] The Traveller's first theory is thus a sarcastic intervention into this utopianism. It shows a con-

---

3. Dethronement is a key thematic of the early Wells, as Patrick Parrinder notes in *Shadows of the Future: H. G. Wells, Science Fiction and Prophecy* (Liverpool: Liverpool University Press, 1995).
4. See John Hope Franklin, 'Edward Bellamy and the Nationalist Movement', *New England Quarterly* 2 (1938): 739–72.
5. Edward Bellamy, 'The Rate of the World's Progress', printed as Postscript to *Looking Backward 2000–1877* (New York: Signet Classic, 2000), p. 218.
6. Morris reviewed Bellamy in 1889: 'Looking Backward', in *Political Writings: Contributions to 'Justice' and 'Commonweal' 1883–90* (Bristol: Thoemmes Press, 1994), pp. 419–25. Citation from p. 423. Wells takes more explicit target at Bellamy and Morris in *When the Sleeper Wakes* (1899).

sistency with some of Wells's early scientific journalism that had set aim at the 'invincibly optimistic' public understanding of evolution as progress: 'On the contrary, there is almost always associated with the suggestion of advance in biological phenomena an opposite idea . . . —degradation.' His startling essays reinserted humanity (or more precisely the Anglo-Saxon claim to be the apex of human development) back into an evolutionary process that did not guarantee continued dominion at all. The fossil record spelt out displacement by younger, energetic species, subsequent decline and, in the end, 'the absolute certainty of death'.[7] From these earliest writings, Wells elides developmental biology with social moralizing. Such elisions seemed to make biology an over-mastering mode of knowledge, giving objective authority to ideological opinion. Yet inside the fictional frame, such assertions are constantly in play: the Traveller's views undergo constant revision.

The Traveller concedes that his view of 'decadent humanity did not long endure'—but in another sideswipe adds that unlike 'visions of Utopias and coming times', where societies are exhaustively explained by a convenient guide, these details 'are all together inaccessible to a real traveller amid such realities' (p. 34). Reversing the anthropological axis of power, the Traveller compares himself to a bewildered African: 'Conceive the tale of London which a Negro, fresh from Central Africa, would take back to his tribe!' (p. 34). This is a sign that moorings are being uprooted, and sure enough the Traveller finds that the savage energy apparently required for the evolutionary struggle to survive *has* been retained by human descendants—in the form of the subterranean Morlocks, the secret sharers of this idyll. Their addition does not simply negate the theory of decadence so much as extend it. Witnessing the pallid 'ape-like' creatures disappear down the wells to the machine shops below ground (they are also described as lemurs, spiders and anemones), the Traveller's second theory arrives fully formed, 'that man had not remained one species, but had differentiated into two distinct animals' (p. 38). It is now class politics that is subject to biologization: the divisive relation of Capitalist and Labourer originates this species divergence. Gentle decadent decline in the Eloi is joined by the figuration of simian or bestial descent down the evolutionary ladder in the Morlocks— a becoming-monstrous, a victory of the savage, plebeian Hyde over the civilized Jekyll, typical of the *fin de siècle* imagination.[8] This is

7. [H. G. Wells], 'The Rate of Change in Species', *Saturday Review* (15 December 1894): 655–6: p. 656. Many of Wells's early articles on this theme are collected in Robert M. Philmus and David Y. Hughes (eds.), *H. G. Wells: Early Writings in Science and Science Fiction* (Berkeley: University of California Press, 1985).
8. Of many recent studies, see for instance H. L. Malchow, *Gothic Images of Race in Nineteenth-Century Britain* (Stanford: Stanford University Press, 1996).

reinforced by the further readjustment the Traveller has to make to his theory, that the Eloi, once the political oppressors, are now the oppressed prey of their own servants. Marx had called capitalist accumulation vampiric; it will be avenged with a cannibalistic turn. High Victorian achievement is left stranded by this biological divergence. Scientific and technical knowledge is abandoned in the ruins of the Green Porcelain museum, its library a 'sombre wilderness of rotting paper' (p. 54). As he trudges back to the Sphinx, another hilltop view only restates his ideological commitment to degenerationism: 'It grieved me to think how brief the dream of the human intellect had been. It had committed suicide' (p. 61).

It is the incoherence of the Traveller's actions in relation to this theorizing that saves the book from didacticism (and that makes it a romance rather than a negative utopia). The Traveller is appalled by the Morlocks, a species described in the register of abjection, 'soft creatures' whose cloying touch produces 'quivering horror' (p. 60). Yet the Traveller is also consistently identified with them: he has the same mechanical bent, the same longing for meat, the same disordered nights, the same bloodlust to kill. Morlock vitality clearly marks them as suitable heirs, yet his sympathies reside with the Eloi, even after he tries out 'a Carlyle-like scorn of this wretched aristocracy in decay' (p. 50). 'The Eloi had kept', he explains, 'too much of the human form not to claim my sympathy' (p. 50). Yet almost immediately he casts away the death of Weena as a misplaced sentiment for something that 'always seemed to me . . . more human than she was' (p. 51). The escape from this confused set of identifications into the far future offers no better clarity, as I have suggested. The Traveller only sketches his moralistic degenerationism onto the cosmos, making the end of the world a rather local, late Victorian affair. It is a view the frame narrator encourages us to discard: 'live as though it were not so' (p. 71).

* * *

H. G. Wells: A Chronology

1866   Born 21 September in Bromley, Kent, the fourth and youngest child of Joseph Wells, a gardener and shopkeeper of modest means, and his wife Sarah, who before her marriage served as a lady's maid at Uppark, country home of the Fetherston-haugh family in Sussex.

1874   Begins attending Bromley Academy, a school for tradesmen's sons run by Thomas Morley.

1877   Joseph falls from a ladder and breaks his leg. The family finances, always precarious, collapse into disarray.

1880   Apprenticed to a draper in Windsor, who soon lets him go. Works equally briefly as pupil-teacher at a village school in Somerset. Sarah takes position as resident housekeeper at Uppark.

1881   Apprenticed to a pharmacist in Midhurst. Begins taking lessons at Midhurst Grammar School. Leaves the pharmacy to take an apprenticeship at a drapery in Southsea.

1883   Taken on as pupil-teacher at Midhurst Grammar School. Broadens program of self-education, reading widely in natural science and political economy. Prepares for national exams in science education.

1884   Wins government scholarship to the Normal School (later the Royal College) of Science, in Kensington, London. Attends lectures on biology and zoology by T. H. Huxley, dean of the Normal School.

1885   Receives first-class honors in summer exams, has his scholarship renewed.

1886   Interests widen to include literature and politics while commitment to his formal studies declines rapidly. Attends socialist meetings at the home of William Morris. Delivers paper on socialism to college debating society. Founds and (until April 1887) edits the *Science Schools Journal*. Meets his first cousin Isabel Mary Wells.

1887   Fails final examination in geology, loses scholarship, and leaves the Normal School without a degree. Takes teaching post at Holt Academy in northern Wales. Suffers crushed kidney and lung hemorrhages as a result of a collision in a school football match and is forced to resign from Holt. Convalesces at Uppark, devotes himself to writing.

1888   Takes teaching position at Henley House School, London. *The Chronic Argonauts* serialized in *Science Schools Journal*.

1890   Passes exams at London University for degree of B.Sc., with first class honors in biology and second class in geology. Elected Fellow of the Zoological Society. Hired by University Correspondence College to tutor students in biology.

1891   "The Rediscovery of the Unique," the first of his scientific essays to be accepted by a major periodical, appears in the *Fortnightly Review*. Marries Isabel in October.

1892   Meets Amy Catherine Robbins ("Jane").

1893   Lung hemorrhage recurs. Decides to give up teaching and focus exclusively on writing. Begins placing short stories, fiction and drama reviews, and essays on topics both serious and frivolous in a variety of London publications.

1894   Elopes with Jane. Seven episodes of what would become *The Time Machine* appear in *National Observer* (March–June). Moves to Sevenoaks.

1895   Divorces Isabel and marries Jane. Moves to Woking. *The Time Machine* serialized in *New Review* (January–May); first edition published by Heinemann in May. Also publishes two collections of short stories (*Select Conversations with an Uncle* and *The Stolen Bacillus and Other Incidents*) and a novel (*The Wonderful Visit*).

1896   Moves to Worcester Park, Surrey. Meets George Gissing. Hires J. B. Pinker as literary agent. Publishes *The Island of Dr. Moreau*, the second of his "scientific romances," as well as a domestic novel, *The Wheels of Chance*.

1897   Begins a lifelong correspondence with Arnold Bennett. Publications include *The Invisible Man*, *The Plattner Story and Others*, and *Certain Personal Matters*.

1898   Lung hemorrhage recurs. Convalesces on the south coast. Meets Henry James, Joseph Conrad, Ford Madox Hueffer (later Ford), and Stephen Crane. Travels to Italy with Gissing. Publishes *The War of the Worlds*.

1899   Publishes *When the Sleeper Wakes* and *Tales of Space and Time*.

1900   Publishes *Love and Mr. Lewisham*. Builds Spade House in Sandgate, Kent.

1901   First child, George Philip ("Gip"), born. Publishes *The First Men in the Moon* as well as the sociological study *Anticipations*.

1902   Invited to address the Royal Institution. Publishes a work of fiction, *The Sea Lady*, and of nonfiction, *The Discovery of the Future*.

1903   Second child, Frank Richard, born. Joins the socialist Fabian Society. Participates in the discussion group known as the Co-Efficients. Becomes friends with George Bernard Shaw, Sidney and Beatrice Webb, and Vernon Lee. Publishes *Twelve Stories and a Dream* and the nonfictional *Mankind in the Making*.

1904   Publishes *The Food of the Gods*, a scientific romance.

1905   Sarah Wells dies. Publishes two novels, *A Modern Utopia* and *Kipps*.

1906   A busy year includes a lecture tour in the United States; meetings with Theodore Roosevelt, Maxim Gorky, and Booker T. Washington; affairs with Dorothy Richardson, Rosamund Bland, and Amber Reeves; and the publication of a scientific romance, *In the Days of the Comet*, and two works of nonfiction, *The Future in America* and *Socialism and the Family*.

1908   Differences with Shaw and the Webbs lead to resignation from Fabian Society. Publishes a scientific romance, *The War in the Air*, and two works of nonfiction, *New Worlds for Old* and *First and Last Things*.

1909   Wells's daughter, Anna Jane Blanco-White, born to Amber Reeves. Moves with Jane to Hampstead, London. Publishes two novels, *Tono-Bungay* and *Ann Veronica*.

1910   Joseph Wells dies. Publishes *The History of Mr. Polly*. Begins affair with Elizabeth von Arnim.

1911   Publishes two collections of stories, *The Country of the Blind and Other Stories* and *The Door in the Wall and Other Stories*, a novel, *The New Machiavelli*, and a work of nonfiction, *Floor Games*.

1912   Publishes *Marriage*, a novel. Moves to Dunmow, Essex.

1913   Publishes *The Passionate Friends*, a novel, and *Little Wars*, a work of nonfiction. Begins affair with Rebecca West.

1914   Visits Russia in January. His son, Anthony West, born to Rebecca West. Publishes two novels, *The World Set Free* and *The Wife of Sir Isaac Harman*, and two works of nonfiction, *An Englishman Looks at the World* and *The War That Will End War*.

1915   Gradual falling out with Henry James made irreparable by Wells's satiric portrait of him in *Boon*. Publishes *Bealby*, *The Research Magnificent*, and *The Peace of the World*, the first two novels, the last a work of nonfiction.

1916   Tours battle fronts in France and Italy. The war is the main
        subject of the novel *Mr. Britling Sees It Through* and two
        nonfictional works, *What Is Coming?* and *The Elements of
        Reconstruction.*

1917   Brief religious phase results in *The Soul of a Bishop* (novel)
        and *God the Invisible King* (nonfiction).

1918   Recruited to produce war propaganda for the Ministry of
        Information. Joins committee charged with setting up the
        League of Nations. Publishes *In the Fourth Year: Anticipa-
        tions of World Peace* and *British Nationalism and the League
        of Nations.*

1919   Publishes *The Undying Fire*, a novel.

1920   Visits Russia, meets Lenin, Trotsky, Gorky, Moura Budberg.
        Publishes *Russia in the Shadows* and the immensely popular
        Outline of History.

1921   Visits the United States to cover the World Disarmament
        Conference in Washington, D.C. Affair with Margaret
        Sanger. Publishes *The New Teaching of History.*

1922   Publishes *A Short History of the World* and a revised *Outline
        of History*, as well as *Washington and the Hope of Peace* and
        the novel *The Secret Places of the Heart*. Joins the Labour
        Party and stands unsuccessfully for Parliament.

1923   A second unsuccessful run for Parliament. Begins habit of
        wintering in Grasse in Provence. Meets and begins affair
        with Odette Keun. Publications include the novels *Men
        Like Gods* and *The Dream*, the nonfictional *Socialism and
        the Scientific Motive* and *The Labour Ideal of Education*,
        and a biographical study, *The Story of a Great Schoolmaster.*

1924   The Atlantic Edition of *The Works of H. G. Wells* published.

1925   Publishes the fictional *Christina Alberta's Father* and the
        nonfictional *Forecast of the World's Affairs.*

1926   Controversy with the Catholic writer Hilaire Belloc over the
        Outline of History. Publishes the novel *The World of William
        Clissold.*

1927   Builds house with Odette Keun in Grasse. Publishes *The
        Short Stories of H. G. Wells* in addition to a new novel,
        Meanwhile, and a new work of nonfiction, *Democracy under
        Revision*. Jane Wells dies in October.

1928   Publishes his tribute to Jane, *The Book of Catherine Wells*.
        Other publications include *The Way the World Is Going* and
        The Open Conspiracy (both nonfiction) and the novel
        Mr. Blettworthy on Rampole Island.

1929   First BBC talk. Delivers speech in German Reichstag, pub-
        lished as *The Common-Sense of World Peace*. Publishes

a screenplay (*The King Who Was a King*) and a children's book (*The Adventures of Tommy*).

1930　With his son G. P. Wells and Julian Huxley, publishes the textbook *The Science of Life*. Moves to Chiltern Court, London. Publishes *The Autocracy of Mr. Parham* (novel) and *The Way to World Peace* (nonfiction).

1931　Diagnosed with diabetes. Breakup with Odette Keun. Death of Isabel Wells.

1932　Publications include a novel (*The Bulpington of Blup*), a textbook (*The Work, Wealth, and Happiness of Mankind*), and a work of nonfiction (*After Democracy*).

1933　Collects seven of his most popular works in the one-volume *Scientific Romances*. Also publishes the novel *The Shape of Things to Come*. Assumes presidency of PEN, the international writers' association. Begins affair with Moura Budberg.

1934　Visits Soviet Union and United States, meets with Joseph Stalin and Franklin Roosevelt. Publishes *Experiment in Autobiography*.

1935　Collaborates with director Alexander Korda on film version of *Shape of Things to Come* (released in 1936 as *Things to Come*). Moves to Regent's Park, London.

1936　PEN dinner in honor of his seventieth birthday. Nonfiction publications include *The Anatomy of Frustration* and *The Idea of a World Encyclopedia*. Fictional works include a novel, *The Croquet Player*, and a screenplay, *The Man Who Could Work Miracles*.

1937　Assumes chair of Section L of the British Association for the Advancement of Science. Publishes three works of fiction: *Star Begotten*, *Brynhild*, and *The Camford Visitation*.

1938　Publishes two works of fiction, *The Brothers* and *Apropos of Dolores*, and the nonfictional *World Brain*. Embarks on lecture tour of Australia.

1939　Publishes a novel, *The Holy Terror*, and three works of nonfiction: *Travels of a Republican Radical in Search of Hot Water*, *The Fate of Homo Sapiens*, and *The New World Order*.

1940　Remains in London during the Blitz. Autumn lecture tour in the United States. Publications include *The Rights of Man*, *The Common Sense of War and Peace*, and *Two Hemispheres or One World?* (all nonfiction) and the fictions *Babes in the Darkling Wood* and *All Aboard for Ararat*.

1941　Publishes what proves to be his final novel, *You Can't Be Too Careful*, as well as *Guide to the New World*.

1942　Publishes *Science and the World Mind*, *The Conquest of Time*, and *Phoenix* in addition to his D.Sc. thesis in zoology, titled *On the Quality of Illusion in the Continuity of Individual Life in the Higher Metazoa, with Particular Reference to the Species Homo Sapiens.*

1943   Awarded the D.Sc. degree. Publishes *Crux Ansata.*

1944   Publishes a collection of essays, *'42 to '44.*

1945   Publishes *Mind at the End of Its Tether.* Health slowly failing.

1946   Dies at home on August 13.

Selected Bibliography

Collections

(For titles of individual books, see Chronology, pp. 260–65)

The Atlantic Edition of the Works of H. G. Wells. 28 vols. London: T. Fisher, Unwin, 1924; New York: Charles Scribner's Sons, 1924.

H. G. Wells: Early Writings in Science and Science Fiction. Ed. Robert M. Philmus and David Y. Hughes. Berkeley and London: University of California Press, 1975.

H. G. Wells's Literary Criticism. Ed. Patrick Parrinder and Robert M. Philmus. Brighton: Harvester Press, 1980; Totowa: Barnes & Noble, 1980.

The Scientific Romances of H. G. Wells. London: Gollancz, 1933. Published in the United States as *Seven Famous Novels.* New York: Knopf, 1934.

The Short Stories of H. G. Wells. London: Ernest Benn, 1927.

Correspondence

Edel, Leon, and Gordon N. Ray, eds. *Henry James and H. G. Wells: A Record of Their Friendship, Their Debate on the Art of Fiction, and Their Quarrel.* London: Hart-Davis, 1958; Urbana: University of Illinois Press, 1958.

Gettmann, Royal A., ed. *George Gissing and H. G. Wells: Their Friendship and Correspondence.* Urbana: University of Illinois Press, 1961.

Smith, David C., ed. *The Correspondence of H. G. Wells.* 4 vols. London and Brookfield, VT: Pickering & Chatto, 1995.

Smith, J. Percy, ed. *Bernard Shaw and H. G. Wells.* Toronto and Buffalo: University of Toronto Press, 1995.

Wilson, Harris, ed. *Arnold Bennett and H. G. Wells: A Record of a Personal and a Literary Friendship.* London: Hart-Davis, 1960; Urbana: University of Illinois Press, 1960.

Biography and Autobiography

Hammond, J. R., ed. *H. G. Wells: Interviews and Recollections.* London: Macmillan, 1980; Totowa: Barnes & Noble, 1980.

Mackenzie, Norman, and Jeanne. *H. G. Wells: A Biography.* New York: Simon and Schuster, 1973.

Ray, Gordon N. *H. G. Wells and Rebecca West.* New Haven: Yale University Press, 1974; London: Macmillan, 1974.

Smith, David C. *H. G. Wells: Desperately Mortal. A Biography.* New Haven and London: Yale University Press, 1986.

Wells, G. P., ed. *H. G. Wells in Love: Postscript to* An Experiment in Autobiography. London: Faber and Faber, 1984; Boston: Little, Brown, 1984.

Wells, H. G. *Experiment in Autobiography: Discoveries and Conclusions of a Very Ordinary Brain (Since 1866).* London: Victor Gollancz, 1934; New York: Macmillan, 1934.

West, Geoffrey. *H. G. Wells: A Sketch for a Portrait.* London: Gerald Howe, 1930; New York: Norton, 1930.

Bibliographies

Hammond, J. R. *Herbert George Wells: An Annotated Bibliography of His Works.* New York and London: Garland, 1977.

H. G. Wells: A Comprehensive Bibliography. Rev. ed. London: H. G. Wells Society, 1985.

Scheick, William J., and J. Randolph Cox. *H. G. Wells: A Reference Guide*. Boston: G. K. Hall, 1988.
Smith, David C. *The Definitive Bibliography of Herbert George Wells*. Oss, Netherlands: Equilibris, 2007.

Criticism

• Indicates a work included or excerpted in this Norton Critical Edition.

Aldiss, Brian W. "The Great General in Dreamland: H. G. Wells." *Trillion Year Spree: The True History of Science Fiction*. London: Victor Gollancz, 1986. Pp. 117–33.
Batchelor, John. *H. G. Wells*. Cambridge: Cambridge University Press, 1985.
Begiebing, Robert J. "The Mythic Hero in H. G. Wells's *The Time Machine*." *Essays in Literature* 11.2 (Fall 1984): 201–10.
• Bergonzi, Bernard. *The Early H. G. Wells: A Study of the Scientific Romances*. Manchester: Manchester University Press, 1961.
———, ed. *H. G. Wells: A Collection of Critical Essays*. Englewood Cliffs, N. J.: Prentice-Hall, 1976.
———. "The Publication of *The Time Machine* 1894–5." *Review of English Studies* n.s. 11 (1960): 42–51.
• Cantor, Paul A., and Peter Hufnagel. "The Empire of the Future: Imperialism and Modernism in H. G. Wells." *Studies in the Novel* 38.1 (Spring 2006): 36–56.
Caudwell, Christopher. "H. G. Wells: A Study in Utopianism." *Studies in a Dying Culture*. London: Bodley Head, 1930.
Eisenstein, Alex. "Very Early Wells: Origins of Some Major Physical Motifs in *The Time Machine* and *The War of the Worlds*." *Extrapolation* 13 (1972): 119–26.
Farrell, Kirby. "H. G. Wells and Neoteny." *Cahiers Victoriens et Edouardiens de l'Universitié Paul Valéry, Montpellier* 46 (October 1997): 145–68.
Geldud, Harry, ed. *The Definitive Time Machine*. Bloomington and Indianapolis: Indiana University Press, 1987.
Gill, Stephen. *Scientific Romances of H. G. Wells: A Critical Study*. Cornwall, Ontario: Vesta Publications, 1977.
Hammond, J. R. *H. G. Wells and the Modern Novel*. London: Macmillan, 1988.
Hennelly, Mark M., Jr. "*The Time Machine*: A Romance of the Human Heart." *Extrapolation* 20:2 (Summer 1979): 154–67.
Hillegas, Mark R. "Cosmic Pessimism in H. G. Wells's Scientific Romances." *Papers of the Michigan Academy of Science, Arts, and Letters* 46 (1961): 655–63.
———. *The Future as Nightmare: H. G. Wells and the Anti-Utopians*. New York: Oxford University Press, 1967.
Hollinger, Veronica. "Deconstructing the Time Machine." *Science Fiction Studies* 14 (2). 42 (July 1987): 201–21.
Hughes, David Y. "A Queer Notion of Grant Allen's." *Science Fiction Studies* 25 (2). 74 (July 1998): 271–84.
• Hume, Kathryn. "Eat or Be Eaten: H. G. Wells's *The Time Machine*." *Philological Quarterly* 69.2 (Spring 1990): 233–51.
Huntington, John. *The Logic of Fantasy: H. G. Wells and Science Fiction*. New York: Columbia University Press, 1982.
Kemp, Peter. *H. G. Wells and the Culminating Ape*. New York: St. Martin's Press, 1982.
Lake, David J. "The White Sphinx and the Whitened Lemur: Images of Death in *The Time Machine*." *Science Fiction Studies* 6.1 (March 1979): 77–84.
• Luckhurst, Roger. *Science Fiction*. Cambridge: Polity Press, 2005.
• Manlove, Colin. "Charles Kingsley, H. G. Wells, and the Machine in Victorian Fiction." *Nineteenth-Century Literature* 48.2 (September 1993): 212–39.
McConnell, Frank D. *The Science Fiction of H. G. Wells*. Oxford: Oxford University Press, 1981.
Parrinder, Patrick, ed. *H. G. Wells: The Critical Heritage*. London and Boston: Routledge & Kegan Paul, 1972.
———. "*News from Nowhere, The Time Machine*, and the Break-Up of Classical Realism." *Science Fiction Studies* 3 (November 1976): 265–74.
———. *Shadows of the Future: H. G. Wells, Science Fiction, and Prophecy*. Liverpool: Liverpool University Press, 1995.
Partington, John S., ed. *The Wellsian: Selected Essays on H. G. Wells*. Oss, Netherlands: Equilibris, 2003.
Ruddick, Nicholas. "The Wellsian Island." *Ultimate Island: On the Nature of British Science Fiction*. Westport and London: Greenwood Press, 1993. Pp. 62–71.

Sargent, Lyman Tower. "*The Time Machine* in the Development of Wells's Social and Polit-
   ical Thought." *Wellsian* 19 (Winter 1996): 3–11.
Scafella, Frank. "The White Sphinx and *The Time Machine*." *Science Fiction Studies* 8 (3).
   25 (November 1981): 255–65.
Scholes, Robert E., and Eric Rabkin. *Science Fiction: History, Science, Vision*. Oxford:
   Oxford University Press, 1977.
• Showalter, Elaine. "The Apocalyptic Fables of H. G. Wells." *Fin de Siècle/Fin du Globe:
   Fears and Fantasies of the Late Nineteenth Century*. Ed. John Stokes. New York: St. Mar-
   tin's Press, 1992.
Slusser, George, Patrick Parrinder, and Danièle Chatelain, eds. *H. G. Wells's Perennial
   Time Machine*. Athens and London: University of Georgia Press, 2001.
Somerville, Bruce David. "*The Time Machine*: A Chronological and Scientific Revision."
   Wellsian 17 (Winter 1994): 11–29.
Stableford, Brian. "H. G. Wells." *Scientific Romance in Britain 1890–1950*. New York:
   St. Martin's Press, 1985. pp. 55–74.
Suvin, Darko, and Robert M. Philmus, eds. *H. G. Wells and Modern Science Fiction*. Lewis-
   burg: Bucknell University Press, 1977.
Suvin, Darko. *Metamorphoses of Science Fiction: On the Poetics and History of a Literary
   Genre*. New Haven: Yale University Press, 1979.
———. *Victorian Science Fiction in the UK: Discourses of Knowledge and Power*. Boston:
   G. K. Hall, 1983.
Wasson, Richard. "Myth and the Ex-Nomination of Class in *The Time Machine*." *Min-
   nesota Review* 15 (Fall 1980): 112–22.